The Fraudulent Footman

"James," she whispered softly.

He kissed her again, desire for her welling up inside him. He felt her lips pressing upon his with equal yearning as she responded to him. "There are certain . . . dissimilarities between our present situation and what I have envisioned," he whispered.

"And what have you envisioned?" she murmured.

Trent did not answer her immediately. If he quite frankly confessed that, in his thoughts, she had been wantonly naked and he likewise lying beside her, would she feel compelled to slap his face?

On the other hand, how could he tell her that, by rights, he should be the master of Haversham Hall? He should be able to pay her the lavish court which was her due, not the poor attention of a penniless footman.

Slowly, reluctantly, he pulled away from her. As James Trescott, the footman, he had very little to offer Lady Edwina. As Trent Haversham, wanted for the murder of his brother, he had even less.

"Sleep now, my lady. I shall be here if you need me," he said, tucking the covers in around her. She was already falling asleep. Her eyes were closed, the long dark lashes resting lightly on the soft translucent skin below her eyes. He watched her lips part slightly as she relaxed in sleep.

"Sweet dreams, my Edwina," he whispered, even though he knew she could not hear him.

A ROSE FOR Lady Edwina

MELINDA PRYCE

PINNACLE BOOKS
WINDSOR PUBLISHING CORP.

To Ted,
my Hero.

PINNACLE BOOKS

are published by

Windsor Publishing Corp.
475 Park Avenue South
New York, NY 10016

Copyright © 1990 by Linda K. Shertzer

First printing: June, 1990

Printed in the United States of America

Chapter One

Lady Edwina Danvers was no longer listening to the quite talented string quartet. Nor was she listening to the buzz of conversations which swarmed about her.

At last, her ears perceived that for which she had been eagerly awaiting. The melodious chimes of the large floor clock resounded through the Great Hall of Ashton Park. Lady Edwina tapped her small, cream-colored satin slipper in time to the clock's pealing of the hour.

'Only ten o'clock,' she thought, and sighed as the last echoes died away.

She had arrived at the ball a mere hour ago. Quite soon she had tired of the pointless conversations in which people had tried to involve her. She had made a few brief contributions to the various discussions for the sake of politeness, but felt no genuine interest in the topics. She cared very little about who had worn what ensemble at Almack's and who had lost what sum at White's.

She had managed to survive several awkward quadrilles with two or three young gentlemen. Worst of all, she had danced one decidedly distasteful waltz with the obnoxious Lord Scythe—and one was quite enough!

She had no intention of dancing with his lordship again. Therefore, she sought refuge in the small alcove beside the doorway which led to the Great Hall.

Away from the crush of the ballroom, she allowed herself to relax just a bit against one of the white marble pilasters which flanked the wide doorway.

Ordinarily, Lady Edwina avoided large social confrontations as she would the very pox. She had only agreed to attend this soiree because she did not wish to disappoint Lady Augusta Ashton, her nearest neighbor and one of the

5

few people she actually considered to be a friend.

' 'Twould be rude indeed to leave too soon,' Lady Edwina thought. 'Perhaps, in another half hour, I shall plead a headache and call for my carriage.'

The warm breezes of an evening in late June drifted through the long glass doors. The ballroom was close, but much less stifling than Lady Edwina remembered the rooms of Carlton House to have been on the few occasions when she had visited them. Nevertheless, for want of a better occupation with which to while away the next half hour, she lifted her fan of cream-colored Valenciennes lace, flipped it open, and slowly began to fan herself.

"Ah, there you are!" The masculine voice intruded, unwelcomed, upon her thoughts.

She quickly lifted her chin and drew herself up into the rigid carriage she always assumed when in the presence of others. This was the only outward sign she gave that she had been startled from her reverie.

She had been so intent upon her private thoughts that she had not noticed the approach of Lord Derwood Marchant, Viscount Scythe. With great reluctance, Lady Edwina slowly turned to face him.

'Why, oh, why must they always persist in sneaking up upon me?' Lady Edwina lamented. Then she grinned inside and answered herself, 'Because most of the gentlemen of your acquaintance are at least astute enough to know that when you see them approaching, you take great care to avoid them.'

Lord Scythe was standing so close to her now that she could clearly see every vein in his puffy-lidded, red-rimmed eyes and every pore in his sallow complexion. She could feel his fetid breath upon her cheek.

Having no wish to appear rude, regardless of who accosted her, Lady Edwina ever so slowly drew back several paces to distance herself from his unwanted proximity.

"I beg your pardon," she said with exceeding politeness. "I am afraid you caught me napping."

Lord Scythe adjusted his quizzing glass and peered down his long, aquiline nose, blinking several times as if trying to

6

focus upon her.

"Asleep while standing. How extraordinary!" he replied with genuine surprise.

"And I manage to accomplish it without falling over," Lady Edwina added, nodding modestly.

Mischievous thoughts played through her head. She could not resist remarking to him, "It would seem that I am not the only person capable of appearing awake while actually asleep."

"Indeed?" Lord Scythe drawled languidly. "In this very room?"

Lady Edwina nodded solemnly.

Lord Scythe insinuated himself even closer to her and whispered in her ear, "Could you point them out to me, my dear Edwina?"

Struggling to retain her serious demeanor, Lady Edwina shook her head. " 'Twould be pointless, sir," she answered, hiding a mocking grin, "as you would scarce believe me. Indeed, without the benefit of a practiced eye, these very persons appear in every way to be quite as normal as . . . well, as yourself, sir."

"How amazing!" he exclaimed. "And you say there are a great many of them?"

Lady Edwina nodded gravely.

"I had no idea that the talent was quite so universal," he declared in astonishment.

"More so than you would ever be aware, I'm sure," Lady Edwina concluded with a sigh of exasperation.

He was as oblivious to her jibes as he was to everything else that did not pertain directly to himself or to his possessions. Lord Scythe continued, "I wondered where you had taken yourself off to, my dear."

Lady Edwina truly had no desire to continue this, or any other, conversation with Lord Scythe. She was well aware, from previous experiences, that any interchange with him, no matter how it began, eventually deteriorated into a discussion of himself, his latest purchases, and the need of his six obnoxious children for the supervision of a new mother.

Lady Edwina allowed just the barest trace of a smile to

touch her lips as she had no wish to offer Lord Scythe what could be misconstrued as even the slightest encouragement for further social intercourse.

"Please excuse me," she said, nodding slightly. "I am exceedingly fatigued and—"

"But you still owe me a dance, my dear Edwina," Lord Scythe interjected before she could finish giving voice to her thought.

Having no intention of suffering through another dance with Lord Scythe, Lady Edwina informed him coolly, "Indeed, I have put paid to all my debts, sir. I do not even owe the greengrocer."

Lord Scythe waved his hand before him and wobbled unsteadily upon his spindly legs. "Fie upon the tradesmen!" he said scornfully. "I much prefer to spend my fortune where I shall obtain the most enjoyment from it."

Lady Edwina merely shook her head. 'It would be so nice,' she mused wistfully, 'to speak to someone with a brain which actually functioned!'

Lord Scythe was patting about the pockets of his obviously new jacket as if in fruitless search for something. Regardless of how well the purple velvet jacket was cut, it still failed to disguise the viscount's protruding paunch.

"Ah, the deuce," he mumbled to himself, yet certainly loud enough so that Lady Edwina should have no trouble at all in hearing him. "Weston has cut this jacket so perfectly for me that, at times, I can scarcely believe I have a thing in my pockets."

Lady Edwina refrained from making any reply.

Unmindful that she had made no response, his lordship continued his search.

"Of course, I am easily fit for my clothing, as I keep myself in excellent condition by boxing and riding," Lord Scythe said, making a conscious effort to tighten the muscles of his bulging little belly. "Capital exercises! I would wager myself the physical equal of any man half my age."

'And the mental equal of a child half again that age,' Lady Edwina thought, yet she said nothing for fear that opening her mouth should release not mere words, but a veritable flood of laughter.

His lordship continued to search through his pockets for a few seconds more.

"Ah, here it is!" With a great flourish that again set him to wobbling, Lord Scythe extracted from the pocket of his mustard-colored waistcoat a small, dark blue snuffbox, decorated with an exquisite miniature of a pastoral scene which was encircled by a row of tiny diamonds.

"I should heartily dislike to misplace this," he remarked. " 'Tis brand new. Devilishly expensive enough it was, too. It is quite exquisite, is it not? Quite worth every pound I paid for it," he said for her benefit, she felt quite certain.

Lord Scythe made a great display of opening his snuffbox with one deft movement of the hand so that Lady Edwina could not fail to notice it this time.

"Quite exquisite," Lady Edwina found she had to agree.

"I should offer you a bit, my dear," he said. "However, I am well aware that you are not inclined to the habit."

Lady Edwina merely shook her head.

His lordship extracted a pinch of snuff and applied it to his nostrils with a practiced hand.

"You see, I truly am mindful of you, Edwina, my dear," he reminded her. "I have been paying a great deal of attention to your preferences."

'You have neglected to note my preference for *solitude*,' she told him silently, but pressed her lips tightly shut.

He tucked the snuffbox back into his waistcoat pocket, withdrew a lace-edged, linen handkerchief from another pocket and blew his nose.

"I took great pains to see that the preferences of my dear, late wife were also well attended to," he stated. "And of course, I shall continue to deal with my next wife in like manner. Yes, I should consider my future wife very fortunate indeed, whoever she may be," he continued, throwing Lady Edwina a meaningful glance. "A townhouse in Mayfair. An estate in Northumberland. A fortune at her disposal. Very few worries. After all, I do have an heir already — as well as a few to spare."

'Indeed, I do believe we all could have been spared your

heirs,' Lady Edwina countered silently. She ruthlessly suppressed the small grin which threatened to play about her lips for fear that he should mistake her amusement at his pomposity for her consent to his plans.

"Young Derwood is already an accomplished sportsman, rather like his father in that respect," Lord Scythe said. "And a playful little chap, as well. Quite a droll sense of humor, actually. Why, just the other day, he shot the cap off my head gamekeeper. Nearly took the old fellow's ear off and gave him a new bald spot as well!" his lordship added with a hearty laugh.

"An inordinately playful child, I should say," Lady Edwina replied with just the barest lift of her delicate brows. "I quite plainly see the reason why you claim he is very like yourself."

"Of course, such spirited children are far beyond the abilities of the ordinary servant," Lord Scythe continued.

"Of course," Lady Edwina said with genuine conviction.

"Devilishly hard to retain a nanny or a tutor."

"No doubt," she replied sarcastically.

Lord Scythe turned to face her. "How good to know that you appreciate the necessity of the proper supervision of one's children, Edwina," he said.

Lady Edwina shrugged her shoulders in a gesture which indicated neither consent nor dissension.

Lord Scythe regarded her with minor alarm and repeated, "You *are* fond of children, Edwina, are you not?"

"I find most children to be as tolerable as any other small animals — puppies, kittens," she added, "weasels, rats . . ."

"I am sure you do, my dear," Lord Scythe interrupted again.

Lady Edwina seriously doubted that he had bothered to listen to a single word she had said.

"However, as you can plainly see," his lordship continued, "with so many charming children, I need place no demands upon my second wife to produce me an heir."

'Indeed not,' Lady Edwina thought with alarm. 'Your second wife should have the arduous task which none other has been able to accomplish — that of overseeing such odious progeny as you already possess.'

Suddenly, without so much as a by-your-leave, he seized her hand.

"Unless, of course, as my wife, she felt so inclined to endeavor to produce other offspring," he whispered hoarsely, leering down upon her.

Feigning a cough, Lady Edwina slipped her hand from his grasp and took yet another step backward.

Undaunted, he stepped closer still. "I am claiming the waltz you owe me, my dear. In the embrace of the dance, a lady might discover heretofore unknown inclinations toward a particular gentleman."

At last his persistence had brought Lady Edwina quite to the end of her vast supply of patience. This time she did not back away from him. Instead, she drew herself up to her full five foot two and set her soft lips in a thin, determined line.

"Lord Scythe," she pronounced, deliberately using his title so that he would know in no uncertain terms that she objected quite strongly to his profligate use of her given name. "You shall have to be content with the waltz which I already gave you. I am extremely fatigued and disinclined to engage in any further activities this evening."

Again, Lord Scythe seized her hand. "Perhaps at times, a lady might not be fully aware of her inclinations until a gentleman enlightens her. Allow me to teach you, Edwina."

She quickly extracted her hand from his grasp and said forcefully, "Lord Scythe, my days in the schoolroom are finished!"

"Then it is time to begin your nights in the bedroom," he replied, bestowing upon her a meaningful wink.

"Lord Scythe," Lady Edwina replied with an icy voice and glacial stare. "You are quite in your cups and therefore I shall ignore your blatantly indecent remarks. I bid you good evening."

As she turned and took two quick steps to flee his odious presence, she heard the sound of rending fabric.

She stopped and looked down to see the lace edge of her gold-colored silk gown trailing in a long, ragged strand from the hem of her dress to stop under Lord Scythe's evening shoe.

"How unfortunate!" Lord Scythe declared. "Please accept my apologies and allow me to purchase you a new gown."

"That is highly improper, Lord Scythe!"

He removed his offending foot from the damaged lace. With a strenuous grunt, he bent down to retrieve an edge of tattered lace. Offering it to Lady Edwina, he lifted it so high that a portion of her skirt also rose to reveal the petticoat beneath.

"I shall replace this gown and give you many others . . . an entire trousseau, as a wedding present, Edwina."

"That will not be necessary, Lord Scythe," she informed him coldly. She snatched the end of the trail of lace from his hand and smoothed her skirt back into place. With sharp, quick little movements, she began rolling the torn lace into a tight little ball. "I shall never have need of a trousseau as I have no intention of ever marrying."

"And why, pray tell, should a lady as lovely as yourself eschew the honorable state of marriage?"

"Speaking quite frankly, my lord—" Lady Edwina began.

"I have never known you to speak in a manner that was anything less than quite frank, Edwina," Lord Scythe interjected.

"Quite frankly, Lord Scythe," Lady Edwina continued, becoming greatly annoyed by his continual interruptions, "I have never met the man whom I would wish to marry."

Lord Scythe shook his head. "You are twenty-seven years old, Edwina. I should warn you not to continue to be too choosy. There cannot be many honorable men who would have a lady of your years."

Lady Edwina flipped her head haughtily. "I concern myself very little with who may or may not have me, sir. It is *I* who *will not* have any of them!"

She tucked the ball of lace into the crook of her arm.

"Good evening, my lord," she repeated as she turned from him.

With her head held high, her back as rigid as Sheffield steel, she departed, alone, to summon her carriage and to bid her hostess good evening.

* * *

"I vow, Edwina, your imperturbability never ceases to amaze me," Lady Ashton declared to her friend as they waited in the Great Hall for the Dynford carriage to be brought round. "Had that pompous ass done this to my gown, I should be suffering an extreme fit of apoplexy! And he should be nursing some good wounds himself!" she added with an emphatic nod of her head.

As if distracted by other thoughts, Lady Edwina rolled the little ball of lace round in her hand. "Oh, I suppose it was merely an unfortunate accident," she replied.

"Accident! The vicar's inexpressibles!" Lady Ashton declared.

"Augusta!" Lady Edwina exclaimed. Her friend's exuberance caused her to smile in spite of her distress over the events of the evening. "At any rate, I do not believe the damage is irreparable. And after all, he did offer to replace the gown . . ." She released a scornful little laugh. "On condition that I marry him!"

Lady Ashton snorted in disgust. "The man has been pursuing you since his first wife died almost a year ago. I vow," she declared as she lightly touched the ball of lace, "he would go to any lengths to relieve you of your pantaloons."

"I prefer to think it is because he would go to any lengths to find a mother to oversee those abominable offspring of his."

Lady Ashton snickered behind her elegantly gloved hand.

"You are too charitable, Edwina," her friend scolded. Then she pronounced with finality, "I assure you, this is absolutely the last time I shall allow that scoundrel to darken my doorway."

"Oh, you mustn't do that, Augusta," Lady Edwina cautioned. "Else how will the poor man ever find a new wife?"

" 'Twould serve him right if he never did," Lady Ashton asserted with an indignant lift of her head. "And 'twould be a great service to all the unmarried ladies everywhere in England."

Lady Edwina only smiled slightly, then returned to her customarily cool expression.

Noting her friend's renewed detachment, Lady Ashton ventured the observation, "But I have never known a length of lace to cause you to be so blue-deviled, Edwina. And you have been exceedingly blue-deviled all evening."

No response was forthcoming.

Lady Ashton lifted one fine brow in playful inquiry. "Could it be that you are pouting because fewer gentlemen than usual clamored to partner you about the dance floor?"

Lady Edwina raised her chin and looked haughtily down her nose at her friend, but there was a merry twinkle in her soft blue eyes. "In the first place, Augusta, *I* never pout."

The very thought of Lady Edwina's habitually imperturbable visage wrinkling up into a pathetic little moue was such a wretched impossibility that Lady Ashton laughed aloud at the prospect.

"You are quite correct, my dear," Lady Ashton owned.

Then Lady Edwina continued in a much less haughty tone of voice. "In the second place, while the company here this evening was, in general, extremely pleasant, I have yet to encounter anyone, anywhere, in particular," she concluded with an emphatic nod of her head.

Lady Edwina recalled her coming out ten years ago. As the eldest daughter of a wealthy earl she had been besieged by numerous suitors. Some had been rich, titled men and had seemed completely acceptable to her parents. Some had been mere fortune-hunters and had not been acceptable at all.

Regardless of their background or present financial circumstances, Lady Edwina had soon come to the unhappy conclusion that every one of them was a self-centered lackwit. *She* had not found them acceptable in the least—no, not one.

'Thank goodness,' she congratulated herself, 'after ten years, I have at last managed to discourage them all.'

"Perhaps you would have better success in finding an acceptable match if you would have given just one of those gentlemen even the slightest encouragement instead of frightening them all away with your cold dispassion," Lady Ashton advised her.

Lady Edwina showed some small degree of surprise at this remark. Had Lady Ashton suddenly developed the uncanny ability to read her mind?

"I take it that you have someone in particular in mind to whom I should offer such encouragement, Augusta?"

"Well, now that you mention it . . ." Lady Ashton began with a grin.

"Now, now, Augusta, you know well enough by now not to attempt to play my matchmaking mama," Lady Edwina warned, cocking her head at a censorious angle. "I am far too old for such nonsense."

"Too old," Lady Ashton chided her friend. "A mere babe in arms."

Lady Edwina pursed her lips and considered Lady Ashton's comment for just a moment.

"Very well," she agreed reluctantly. "I will concede that I may be closer to my youth than to my dotage, but I still insist upon retaining the right to chose the owner of those arms in which I shall repose."

"And none of the fine gentlemen of your acquaintance are possessed of such arms?" Lady Ashton whispered, bending her dark head closer to her friend's fair curls, the better to receive whatever confidences Lady Edwina chose to divulge.

But Lady Edwina remained erect and answered emphatically, "None."

Such surety silenced Lady Ashton for only a moment. "If it is neither the lace nor the company, what else could be troubling a lady of your generally placid nature?" she asked.

When Lady Edwina made no immediate reply, Lady Ashton ventured a logical assumption. "Ah, I know what it is that never fails to trouble you. Richard has been experimenting again."

At the mention of her brother's experiments, Lady Edwina emitted a weary little sigh.

"I shall take that as an affirmative reply," Lady Ashton said.

"He has succeeded in constructing another flying apparatus," Lady Edwina admitted reluctantly. "A rather flimsy looking contraption it is, too, to my way of thinking."

15

"I should not believe he would persist," Lady Ashton declared, placing her hand to her bosom in surprise.

"Especially after the first machine crashed and burned down the chicken house on the home farm," Lady Edwina said with a sigh of exasperation.

"At least you managed to save the chickens," Lady Ashton offered optimistically.

"And a great good fortune that was, too," Lady Edwina commented. "Else we would have grown exceedingly weary of roast chicken!"

"Whatever possessed him to tie that lantern to the front of his machine in the first place?" Lady Ashton asked.

Lady Edwina shook her head in bewilderment. "He was certain the night wind would be more efficacious in attaining flight. I tried to dissuade him, but I am only his elder sister," she said with a shrug of her shoulders. "Why should he pay heed to my worthless opinions?"

"Has he yet attempted to fly this current contraption?" Lady Ashton inquired, her soft hazel eyes wide with eagerness for any news of the eccentric young Earl of Dynford.

"Not yet," Lady Edwina replied, twisting the little ball of lace nervously. "However, early tomorrow morning, he plans to take his machine to the top of the hill upon which Grandpapa's old folly sits. He intends to fly from there."

Lady Ashton emitted a sound that was halfway between a gasp and a giggle. While the people of the neighborhood were concerned that the rather unconventional Earl of Dynford might do himself a serious damage during one of his attempts to fly, they also seemed to nourish a morbid curiosity regarding any news of any mishaps resulting from his strange excursions.

"I shall rise early tomorrow, too," Lady Edwina continued with a certain resignation. "I shall have to prepare bandages for whatever injuries he might sustain in the fall which will most certainly ensue."

"Given your brother's record, you will need your rest tonight," Lady Ashton remarked with a little giggle.

"And most probably those bandages tomorrow, too," Lady Edwina added, half to herself. Her heart wrenched within

16

her breast. While everyone else seemed to view her brother's unusual experiments with a mild amusement, she feared that each of her brother's mad attempts at flight would be his last.

She tapped her foot with impatience and demanded, "Where *is* that coachman?"

Realizing that Lady Edwina truly was in no disposition to jest, Lady Edwina ceased smiling and reached out to pat her friend's hand in consolation. "Richard has escaped serious harm thus far, Edwina. I'm sure he will this time, too."

"One can only hope," Lady Edwina replied with a nervous little smile. With great relief, she heard the footman announce her carriage.

Chapter Two

"Good night, Cobb," Lady Edwina said to the footman as he closed one of the heavy double doors of Dynford Manor behind her.

Her satin slippers made soft scraping sounds as she crossed the smooth gray-veined marble floor of the quiet, empty hall. She took a candle from the old oaken side table at the base of the stairs.

Juggling the lace ball and the candlestick between her two hands, and still attempting to hold on to the carved mahogany balustrade, she climbed the wide, curving staircase to the second floor. She then turned left to enter the wing which housed her own apartments.

Entering her bedchamber, she noted with dismay that the bedclothes had not been turned down again, nor had her night rail been laid out. Her lady's maid was nowhere to be seen.

"Stokes!" she called sharply.

There was no reply.

'Confound that girl!' Lady Edwina complained to herself, as there was no one else awake to whom she could complain. 'I am so deucedly vexed by servants who are too lazy or too incompetent to do their proper duties!"

Once again, Lady Edwina found herself wishing that the girl which her brother had insisted she hire from the parish workhouse had not turned out to be quite so scatter-brained. She herself would have preferred an experienced lady's maid from one of the agencies in London, someone with proper references attesting to a long and reputable service with a good family.

But her brother was quite adamant about helping the un-

18

fortunate inmates of the workhouse — and the scrawny young girl, with her limp brown curls and overly large brown eyes, *had* looked rather pathetically appealing.

"Stokes?" she called in a more questioning tone.

Still no reply was forthcoming. Surely nothing untoward had happened to the girl?

Lady Edwina opened the door to the small bedroom which adjoined hers.

The light of the single candle illuminated Rosalie Stokes, fast asleep upon her small bed. She was curled up like a child atop the coverlet, one arm hugging a crumpled pillow.

Stokes truly was barely larger and scarcely older than a child. No one could be sure of the girl's precise age, as she had been abandoned as an infant upon the parish workhouse steps, but Lady Edwina judged her to be no more than seventeen.

Lady Edwina placed the candle on the small table by the door, took the worn lap robe which lay folded at the foot of Stokes's narrow bed, and drew it up over the girl's arm and shoulder.

She quickly changed her expression to a sour grimace when she realized she had been smiling rather maternally down upon the sleeping maid. Retrieving her candle, she closed the door quietly behind her and returned to her own room.

Lady Edwina found it exceedingly difficult to admit that her greatest disappointment was the fact that, in the solitary life she had chosen for herself, she would never have children of her own.

Nevertheless, it was the life of her choice, and she determined to make the best of it. She knew she should be grateful that she had the opportunity for choice when so few others did.

She pushed any regrets from her mind.

As she placed her candle on the small rosewood table at her bedside, Lady Edwina noticed the morning's post still unopened on a small silver tray.

'Small wonder,' she mused silently. 'There was so much to do this morning, I scarcely had time for it. 'Twill serve well enough for a night's read,' she added with a disinterested shrug.

Given the erratic quality of the service provided by her lady's maid, Lady Edwina was quite adept at undressing herself without Stokes's assistance. She carefully laid her pale gold-colored silk gown and deeper gold-colored petticoat over the back of the large armchair by the fireplace. Her discarded chemise, pantaloons, silken hose, and lace-edged garters were neatly folded and placed on the seat of the chair.

She released her long, honey-colored curls from the tight chignon in which she customarily had it arranged, and brushed out the tangles.

After sponging off at the jasperware bowl and drying herself with a large Turkish towel, she pulled a soft silk night rail from one of the drawers of the large commode. She slipped the night rail over her head and crossed the room, eager to climb into her bed for a much needed night's sleep.

Lady Edwina picked up the waiting pile of correspondence and began to sort through the numerous invitations to balls, concerts, and soirees to which she would send her polite regrets.

She looked several times at the smudged writing on the crumpled letter at the bottom of the pile before she could be certain that it was indeed directed to her.

"Cecily," Lady Edwina said aloud, turning the letter from her younger sister over and over in her hands to examine it. "How could I fail to realize that this was from her? It looks as if she carried it with her all about London in the bottom of her reticule for at least a week before posting it."

'Just what I need after a day such as I have had!' she silently lamented. 'More witless chattering from Cecily.'

Nevertheless, Lady Edwina abandoned the rest of the correspondence in favor of news of her sister. She slit the wafer with her silver letter knife.

'Three weeks ago last Thursday.' Lady Edwina made a mental note of the date of Lady Cecily's correspondence. It had been nearly a month since her sister's last letter, and that one had been dated two weeks previous to its posting.

'Well, let us see what scrapes the girl has gotten herself

20

into, and hopefully out of by now,' she said to herself.

She plumped the feather pillows behind her and pulled the soft bedclothes up about her as she settled into the task of deciphering her sister's quite illegible handwriting.

My *dearest* sister,

At last I have the opportunity to write to you! You can have *absolutely* no idea how wretchedly *busy* we have been, Aunt Portia & I, what with all the balls & soirees & at-homes, not to mention the necessity of shopping for just the *perfect* ensembles to wear to such occasions, as one simply *cannot* be seen in the same gown too many times in a row or one will be considered *terribly unfashionable,* which would surely result in the *total ruin* of one's reputation among the *ton!*

'The girl writes exactly as she speaks,' Lady Edwina observed. 'It is indeed beyond my comprehension how she can string so many words together without pausing for breath yet not faint dead away.'

She drew a deep sigh and plunged again into her sister's letter.

London is positively *marvelous!* I wonder that you do not visit here more often, but then, I know you are as solitary as an oyster at heart & much *prefer* the isolation of the countryside, although for the life of me, I shall *never* fathom why!

Aunt Portia is well & sends you & Dickie both her *fondest* regards. I am so *exceedingly* fortunate to have her as a chaperone as she allows me to do whatever I wish without interference & her presence gives respectability to all my *exciting* adventures!

The house in Portman Square is as *enchanting* as ever. Please convey to Dickie my infinite *approval* of the recent refurnishing of the house, although I shan't be spending a great deal of time here, except perhaps to sleep, as the invitations to *all* the most *fashionable* parties are *deluging* us as if they had quite literally been floated on barges down the Thames!

Last night we attended the last subscription ball of the Season at Almack's & quite the most *extraordinary* thing transpired there . . .

"Lady Cecily, your eyes are like stars, your skin like the petals of a rose!" the Honorable Gervaise DeLauney declared as they executed the jaunty steps of the quadrille about the floor of the main ballroom at Almack's.

"La! Mr. DeLauney, you do say the strangest things!" Lady Cecily released a tinkling little laugh. "Stars are tiny and white and you know very well that my eyes are blue and of normal, human dimensions."

Lady Cecily quite deliberately turned those large, blue eyes up at the defenseless Mr. DeLauney and smiled engagingly.

"And as for my having skin like rose petals," she continued, turning her charming smile into an equally charming pout, "why, I shouldn't care for that at all as bright pink would be completely unsuitable with my new primrose-colored gown."

Mr. DeLauney laughed heartily and declared, "My dear Lady Cecily, you would be equally charming whether you were pink or blue or green or even quite, quite lily white."

Lady Cecily coyly turned her head to the side. Then, from under a deep fringe of dark lashes, she peeped provocatively up at her partner. "Why, Mr. DeLauney, how could you know that I am, indeed, quite, quite, lily white?"

The young Mr. DeLauney himself turned bright pink and stumbled over his own two feet as he attempted, unsuccessfully, to execute a final flawless fleuret as the quadrille ended. He returned Lady Cecily to the small group of chaperones seated to the right of the musician's balcony.

He bowed deeply to Lady Cecily and then turned and bowed to Lady Portia, who sat in a spindly chair, gossiping with another elderly lady seated upon an equally rickety-looking chair.

"Why, Mr. DeLauney, you've turned positively beet-red!" Lady Cecily exclaimed, giggling quite loudly.

"Yes, indeed, young man. You've gone quite beet red," Lady Portia echoed, staring up at him myopically.

"Lud! All that waltzing ain't healthful," declared the elderly lady who sat beside Lady Portia. " 'Twill bring about an attack of the apoplexy! Not to mention moral decay," she continued to grumble. " 'Tweren't a gaggle of waltzing fops what beat that demmed Corsican upstart. Mark my words, moral decay and ruin for the entire nation, *I* still maintain, although no one will listen to *me* any more."

Mr. DeLauney bowed to acknowledge the other lady, quite ignoring her tirade. "I am perfectly well, Lady Sheftley," he stuttered.

"I believe Mr. DeLauney may attribute his florid coloration to a number of reasons other than the dancing," Lady Cecily told Lady Sheftley, grinning mischievously at the young man.

"The dancing, the heat of the room. . ." he quickly suggested to the two elderly ladies who peered at him questioningly.

"La! You are quite correct, Mr. DeLauney," Lady Cecily declared, cooling herself languidly with her blue lace fan. "The room is quite stifling."

"Would you care for some refreshments?" he asked.

"Stale cakes or bread and butter?" Lady Cecily debated aloud to Mr. DeLauney. "Oh, la! I can get bread and butter at home. And freshly baked, at that, and no doubt more generously spread." At last, with a demure smile, she replied, "I do believe I shall just have a glass of lemonade."

"I do believe I shall just have a glass of lemonade as well," Lady Portia repeated to him.

Before he could offer Lady Cecily his arm with the bright hopes of escorting her to the tea room, Lady Portia added, "And a cake . . . or two. Perhaps a bit of buttered bread if it is cut nice and thin and if it is not too hard . . ."

"No, no! Lud, Portia!" interjected Lady Sheftley, slapping her on the arm with the tortoise shell sticks of her fan. "You'll entirely ruin your digestion with their abominable food. I've been coming here for years," she continued her tirade. "And that's all they've ever served. Lud! I'll be so overjoyed when

I've finally managed to marry off this last daughter as well as I've managed to marry off the other three."

Lady Sheftley jerked her purple turbaned head in the direction of the quiet, red-haired young lady who stood at her side. "Then I needn't come here any longer!"

"Why, Lady Sheftley," Lady Cecily exclaimed, wide-eyed with awe, "considering the fact that you have been coming here for *ever so long*, I marvel that you have never grown immune to the wretched refreshments."

"Yes, Louisa dear," Lady Portia, who had never expressed an original thought in her life, echoed. "With your iron constitution, you should be quite immune."

"At any rate," Lady Cecily continued, "I'm sure you shan't be coming here for much longer. Jane is such a dear girl. Surely, *someone* will offer for her!"

"Lud! I hope so," Lady Sheftley grumbled. She turned to Miss Jane Sheftley and poked her daughter in the side with her closed fan. "Go put some rice powder on your nose, gel. Try to cover those abominable freckles!"

While Lady Sheftley had been badgering her youngest daughter, Lady Cecily had been quite busily perusing the crowded room for something, anything, more exciting than the chaperones' conversation.

Lady Sheftley had to reach across Lady Portia in order to poke Lady Cecily several times with her fan in order to regain her attention.

"Heed my warning, gel," she told the inattentive young lady. "Never marry a red-haired man. No one wants speckled children!"

"Quite right," Lady Portia reiterated. "No one wants speckled children."

"Oh, I should not mind if my child were speckled . . ." Lady Cecily protested.

"Indeed, she would not mind," Lady Portia echoed.

". . . or blue, or green, or even quite lily white," Lady Cecily responded to Lady Sheftley, glancing pointedly at Mr. DeLauney.

The unfortunate gentleman's face turned quite crimson once again.

"Why, Mr. DeLauney, I do believe the heat of the room is beginning to bother you again," Lady Cecily remarked.

"Yes, yes," Mr. DeLauney stuttered. "I am exceedingly thirsty. Would you care to accompany me, Lady Cecily?"

"Thank you, no, Mr. DeLauney. I am quite comfortable. But by all means, *you* may be excused," Lady Cecily replied.

She watched with relief as he left for the tea room. His foolish adoration could be *so* tiresome, she decided. She had bigger fish to fry.

"At any rate, it does not signify, Lady Sheftley," Lady Cecily continued. "I much prefer a man of a dark countenance. For example, much like that gentleman over there." She indicated with a graceful nod of her head the pair of gentlemen standing between the gilt pilasters of the doorway and the statue which held aloft a candelabra. "I vow, the sandy-haired gentleman has been quizzing us for nigh on to a quarter hour. Surely, he must have some reason for doing so."

Lady Cecily thought it unnecessary to mention that, from her distant vantage point, she had been blatantly admiring the elegantly attired, dark-haired gentleman for an equal amount of time and had been driving herself to distraction trying to determine the best way to secure an introduction.

"I beg your pardon," the rather vague Miss Sheftley asked. "Which two gentlemen?"

"Those two," Lady Cecily declared. By extending her fan, she quite deliberately indicated, for all the room to see, the two gentlemen.

"Lud, gel! Don't draw their attention to us!" Lady Sheftley cried upon realizing what Lady Cecily had done. "Have you no subtlety?"

Lady Portia shook her head in dismay. "No subtlety at all."

"Demme, it's too late!"

"How marvelous!" Lady Cecily beamed. "They are coming toward us!'

Without appearing as if she were actually preening, Lady Cecily surreptitiously smoothed her soft white chiffon skirt over the bright primrose-colored sarcenet petticoat and adjusted her elbow-length silk gloves.

25

The two gentlemen stopped before Lady Sheftley and the shorter of the pair bowed low.

"So, Horace, did Boodle's burn to the ground?" Lady Sheftley demanded sourly before the sandy-haired gentleman could say anything by way of greeting. "That's the only thing that I know of that would pry you away from the green baize tables!"

"Beg your pardon, Aunt Louisa," Horace Sheftley replied. "Merely stopped by to inquire if you and Uncle are well, don't you know."

Lady Sheftley snorted and grimaced. "He's still alive and healthy, you'll be sorry to hear, since that's what you really came inquiring after."

"My dear aunt. . ." Mr. Sheftley began to protest.

"Oh, my!" Lady Portia exclaimed. "He's gone as red as that nice Mr. DeLauney!"

"And I'm sure you're still borrowing on your expectations, too, ain't you?" Lady Sheftley demanded.

"Dear Aunt Louisa," Mr. Sheftley said, holding a wide smile upon his lips as if his very life and fortune depended upon how many teeth he could manage to show her at one time. "Don't wish to spar with you, don't you know. Merely came to inquire politely after your and Uncle's well-being."

"Poppycock!" Lady Sheftley spit out. "You haven't gone to all the trouble of coming to Almack's just to bid me the time of day. If you can't inherit or gamble your way out of debt, you think to marry your way out. You've come in search of an heiress tonight, no doubt. I know *you* well enough, my boy!" she declared, shaking her fan in his face.

Lady Sheftley threw up her hands in surrender and muttered, "Ah, well, serves me right to be plagued by a shiftless nephew eager to inherit an entailed estate, when all I could manage to produce were four scatter-brained, speckled daughters."

She frowned and poked at Lady Cecily again. "Learn well, my gel, if you don't want to produce stupid children, don't marry a stupid man — although, Lud knows, any other kind are demmed hard to find!"

"They are so hard to find," Lady Portia repeated, shaking

her head sadly.

"Indeed, Lady Sheftley," Lady Cecily responded, "I shall surely heed your advice, for I am as fond of clever men as I am of dark-haired men."

The other as yet nameless, gentleman turned in her direction. He inclined his dark head as much as possible without doing damage to his perfect, snowy cravat. His green eyes sparkled under his dark brows as he regarded her with undisguised interest.

"But Lady Sheftley," Lady Cecily pouted. "You never told us that you were related to two such charming gentlemen."

"I'm not! And I thank my lucky stars I'm only related to this one by marriage," she said, waving her fan with disdain at Mr. Sheftley. Then she poked in the direction of the dark-haired stranger. "I have no idea who *this* one is! And if he's a friend of Horace's, I don't think I care to know him!"

Lady Sheftley poked at her nephew again. "So, Horace, who is this dandy you've brought with you?" she demanded, jabbing her fan in the direction of the unknown gentleman at Mr. Sheftley's side.

"Indeed," Lady Cecily demanded rather impatiently.

She continued to observe him with undisguised admiration. His skin was so fair that it appeared almost translucent. His hair was as black as the night sky. His eyes were green as the sea.

His immaculate cravat fell in perfect folds from his chiseled jawline. His bottle green superfine jacket conformed to his broad shoulders without a trace of buckram padding. His nankeen trousers molded quite provocatively to his muscular thighs.

In her life, she had never seen a man of such a handsome countenance, of such polished deportment, of such elegant — and expensive — attire.

"He's another wastrel, I suppose," Lady Sheftley grumbled loudly to her nephew. "Just like the others you have the bad judgment to associate with."

"Quite the contrary," Mr. Sheftley protested. "Aunt Louisa, allow me to present my friend, Nigel Haversham."

"Haversham? Haversham?" Lady Sheftley muttered, then

fixed him with a gimlet eye and demanded, "Any relation to that Baron, what's his name? Milton Haversham?"

Nigel Haversham inclined his head slightly and responded, "My cousin, Lady Sheftley."

"Humph!" she snorted. "Never did like him. Demmed hard man to deal with."

"I find that to be quite the contrary, Lady Sheftley," Mr. Haversham contradicted. "My cousin and I deal quite famously, provided that I am in London and he remains in Oxfordshire."

Lady Sheftley chuckled. "Not such a lackwit as Horace, are you?"

Indeed, he was not, Lady Cecily observed with growing approval.

"Nor are your pockets to let with as much frequency either, I'll wager," Lady Sheftley said, poking with her fan in that general area of the gentleman's jacket.

"Aunt Louisa!" Mr. Sheftley exclaimed in embarrassment.

But Mr. Haversham chuckled.

"Lady Sheftley," he replied, "my pockets are so deep that *if* they were to let, I believe I could house Prinnie and all his brothers — and perhaps a few of their by-blows as well!"

"Demme!" Lady Sheftley exclaimed with a whooping laugh that caused several of the people to either side of them to turn their heads with curiosity. "I've finally found a handsome man that ain't speckled nor stupid nor fleeing the duns, and I'm too old to do aught about it!"

A sly look came into Lady Cecily's blue eyes and a determined smile spread over her lovely face. 'Oh, but *I* am not too old to do something about it,' she decided.

Slowly opening her fan, Lady Cécily edged just a little farther away from her aunt and just a little closer to Mr. Haversham.

"My dear Lady Sheftley, since you know these gentlemen, perhaps it would not be amiss for Aunt Portia and myself to have the honor of making their acquaintance," Lady Cecily pleaded prettily.

Mr. Haversham proceeded to execute an elegant bow to Lady Portia, then turned to Lady Cecily.

"A pleasure," he replied, returning her admiring gaze. "If I am not mistaken, you are the younger sister of the Earl of Dynford."

"You know my brother?" Lady Cecily asked, turning her limpid blue eyes invitingly up to him.

"I made his acquaintance only once, several years ago before he had succeeded, and then but briefly, but I found him a most pleasant fellow," Mr. Haversham answered.

"And has my brother also had the pleasure of making the acquaintance of *Mrs.* Haversham?" she ventured.

"I greatly doubt it," he replied with a cool smile, "as my mother passed away quite some time ago."

"My condolences," Lady Cecily repeated, forcing a suitable expression of deepest sympathy onto her face. It was an extremely difficult task as, inside, she was rather jubilant in finding the appealing Mr. Haversham made even more appealing by his single state.

"I am sure my mother would have found his lordship's acquaintance delightful," Mr. Haversham said. "May I say that, since circumstances are such that my mother never had the pleasure of meeting your family, I feel it incumbent upon myself to foster the acquaintance."

Lady Cecily fluttered her long, dark lashes. "Oh," she exclaimed, "and I am quite certain that my brother's family should also derive great pleasure from becoming better acquainted with *you.*" She slowly opened her blue lace fan and moved it nonchalantly back and forth across her bosom.

"I trust you do not find the atmosphere of the room so stifling that you would not care to do me the honor of a dance," he suggested.

"Oh, dear, Mr. Haversham," Lady Cecily murmured quietly, as if she were quite taken by surprise that he should wish to continue their association. "I shall have to refer to my dance card."

She made a great pretense of opening the small card attached to her wrist by a silken cord, although she knew perfectly well that, whoever's name was penciled in, she should completely ignore it in Mr. Haversham's favor.

"Why, how fortunate!" she said, closing the little card

tightly and smiling charmingly up into his green eyes. "I am indeed unencumbered by any other partner for this dance."

"Then *I* am the fortunate one," Mr. Haversham replied, bowing low. He turned to Lady Portia and bowed again. "I shall see that she is escorted quite safely through the perils of the dance floor and returned quite unharmed to your tender care."

Lady Cecily extended her hand to Mr. Haversham, who allowed her to rest it gently atop his own as they made their way to the edge of the dance floor.

"Demme, Horace!" Lady Sheftley gave him a resounding whack on the elbow with her fan. "Jane is your very own *unmarried* cousin and you could not secure her a dance with that quite eligible young gentleman?"

Mr. Sheftley gave a helpless shrug.

"And as for you, gel!" With a swift backhand motion, Lady Sheftley whacked her hapless daughter, too. Miss Sheftley jumped to attention. "Lud! If you don't put yourself forward more, you'll end up sitting in this very place here." Lady Sheftley jabbed her fan downward into the chair cushion. "End up a maiden aunt, chaperoning all your sisters' daughters. And 'twould serve you right if they were each and every one of them just as lacking in wits as you are!"

Lady Cecily and Mr. Haversham waited at the edge of the crowd until the previous set had ended and the sets formed for the next dance.

"Why, Mr. Haversham," Lady Cecily said. "I do believe they have called a waltz."

"I shall be greatly distressed if you tell me that you have not yet obtained permission from our illustrious patronesses to waltz."

"Oh, la! Why, I was granted *that* upon my first visit here," she informed him with ill-disguised pride. "How could they refuse *me?*"

"How, indeed, could anyone?" he replied, smiling down upon her with his deep green eyes.

His right hand barely touched her back. Returning his smile, she lifted the side of her skirt at an angle which she knew would display her gown to its best advantage for all the rest of the room to admire.

Mr. Haversham gently lifted her right hand in his left and began the six little steps which brought them round in one full circle. They continued to circle in time to the music.

"You are quite an excellent partner, Mr. Haversham," Lady Cecily told him breathlessly. She knew the exertions of the dance heightened the delicate pink glow of her flawless cheeks. Likewise, she was well aware that the pink glow intensified the blue of her eyes.

"We have danced scarcely more than a minute, Lady Cecily. Pray tell, what criteria do you use to enable you to determine excellence so quickly?" Mr. Haversham inquired.

"You have not trod upon my toes, sir, no, not once," she replied.

He chuckled. "And you consider *that* excellence? You do not have very stringent requirements, Lady Cecily."

"Oh, not always, Mr. Haversham." Her blue eyes were wide with protest. "You see, my requirements vary, depending upon what I am judging."

Mr. Haversham nodded. "How interesting. I find I frequently use those very same criteria."

Peering coyly up at him from under her long, dark lashes, Lady Cecily remarked, "Based upon your varying criteria, Mr. Haversham, how do you judge *my* dancing?"

"Ah, Lady Cecily, you know quite well that I shall say that you dance divinely, as a gentleman should never comment unfavorably upon a lady's accomplishments, at least to the lady's face," he added with a grin.

"If you find my dancing inadequate, pray enlighten me, Mr. Haversham," Lady Cecily said, turning her big blue eyes up at him and pushing a pretty little pout onto her pink lips.

"I shan't tease you any longer, as I do anticipate your forming a favorable opinion of me," he answered. "You do indeed dance divinely. I should say that we complement each other upon the dance floor quite admirably."

Lady Cecily dimpled with pleasure.

"I am glad to hear you say that, Mr. Haversham. It allows me to retain my favorable opinion of you."

"I am so pleased to hear that you have already formed an

opinion in my favor," he countered with a wide smile. "Pray tell, did you use the same criteria as you used to judge my dancing abilities?"

"Oh, no, Mr. Haversham," she told him quite seriously. "For I could not form an opinion of your dancing until I had danced with you—"

"And you *could* form an opinion of my character before you met me?" he interjected. "How did you manage that?"

"Quite simple, actually. I determined you to be the most handsome, most well-disposed, and easily the most elegantly attired gentleman in the room," she stated quite bluntly. "And therefore, the gentleman who would most appreciate having the loveliest lady in the room as his dance partner."

"You have failed to mention my fortune, Lady Cecily," he reminded her.

She shrugged her creamy shoulders. "I see no need to seek after that with which I am already well supplied."

He chuckled again. "Ah, yes. I understand you are quite wealthy yourself, Lady Cecily."

She gave another little shrug to her smooth, ivory shoulders and laughed her tinkling little laugh. "I need not concern myself that the linendraper or the milliner will appear at my door with the constable to have me hauled away to debtor's prison."

"Your modesty is as engaging as your candor," Mr. Haversham told her with an amused smile on his lips. "Do you always speak so frankly?"

"Oh, indeed, I always speak my mind," she agreed. "I, personally, have always found it to be to my advantage to be quite frank, although I have encountered some people who, for some reason I fail to comprehend, have found it less advantageous."

"I believe honesty to be one of the most important traits of character to be sought in a companion," Mr. Haversham told her. "I find your beauty and candor to be a breath of fresh air in this stifling room. You would not credit how many ladies have professed undying love for me, when all the time I knew they were only interested in my fortune."

"Oh, I do so *detest* scheming people!" Lady Cecily exclaimed sympathetically. "You will find me quite forthright, Mr. Haversham."

"My dear Lady Cecily," Mr. Haversham told her with a laugh, "if you continue to be as delightfully candid as you are exquisitely beautiful, I am sure we shall deal extremely well together."

"If you continue to be as shamelessly flattering, I quite concur."

Mr. Haversham's husky laugh pealed through the room just as the music came to an end.

Lady Cecily found that they were not in front of Lady Portia's seat, but rather at the opposite side of the room.

"In our travels, we appear to have missed our posting station, Lady Cecily," Mr. Haversham remarked, still smiling.

"But I have so enjoyed our travels that I scarcely mind at all."

"I did promise your charming aunt that I would return you to her," he reminded her.

"Indeed, you did, Mr. Haversham."

"There can be nothing for it but that we must take another turn about the floor," he ventured the logical proposal.

Lady Cecily nodded her compliance. "Indeed, no other remedy comes immediately to mind."

She drew the corners of her soft, pink lips down into a playful little pout. "Unless, of course, you should care to relinquish me to the care of your companion, Mr. Sheftley," she suggested.

Mr. Haversham lifted his head arrogantly. "I never readily relinquish anything—much less the most exquisite creature in this room and, undoubtedly, in all of England. At any rate, I did promise your esteemed aunt that *I* should return you."

"So you did, Mr. Haversham," she replied with a sparkling smile. "So you did."

As the top couple was rather elderly, a sedate little quadrille was called for. Lady Cecily was just as glad. Although the waltz enabled her partner to hold her close and place his hand upon her narrow waist and slender back, she much preferred the dances where she did not dance so close to her partner and all the room could thus observe her fashionable attire.

She placed her hand in Mr. Haversham's and gracefully stepped through the quadrille with him.

"Do you come to Almack's frequently?" he asked.

"Oh, ever since I was granted my voucher, I have *never* missed an affair! And you?"

"I seldom attend."

"I thought as much," she said. "I know I should have remarked your presence here if you had."

"And had I known you would attend, I should have frequented this place with much greater regularity," he told her.

"And will you continue to do so now?" she asked. She smiled. How wonderful the world was when everything seemed to be working out precisely as she had planned!

"Alas, I depart tomorrow at first light for Haversham Hall," he told her with a great sigh.

Lady Cecily summoned every bit of what little willpower she possessed to refrain from crying out loud in protest against the inequities of the wretched life she led. Instead, she assumed her most wistful air and said, "I doubt that London will seem so pleasant after tomorrow."

"I must own that suddenly London holds for me, as well, a much greater attraction than formerly. However, my cousin is returning from the army tomorrow. I feel a certain familial obligation to be at Haversham Hall—in order to act as something of a buffer between the two brothers, actually," Mr. Haversham modestly admitted his diplomatic skills.

He bent slightly closer to her and confided, "You see, from the time they were children, the two have *never* gotten along. Every time they come together, there is such a fearful row. Why, I should not be surprised to see them someday come to blows, if not something worse!"

"How dreadful!" Lady Cecily exclaimed, although in reality she hardly cared a fig for the two unknown, battling cousins.

She was feeling quite disappointed to find that the music had ended and that she was once again standing before Lady

Portia.

"Alas! I am greatly distressed to relinquish you to the chaperonage of your most pleasant aunt," he said, releasing her hand.

"Indeed, sir?" she inquired lifting a slender brow in mock surprise. "I should never want you to feel distressed upon *my* account."

Mr. DeLauney stood beside her aunt, a look of reproach upon his face.

"I believe you missed our dance," he said petulantly.

"Our dance, Mr. DeLauney?" she asked, as if quite bewildered by his request.

"The waltz was *mine*, Lady Cecily," he insisted. "You promised!"

"Why, Mr. DeLauney, I *always* keep my promises. It was *you* who took yourself off to the tea room and left me here *quite alone* and without a partner," she pouted. "Mr. Haversham was kind enough to see that I was not neglected," she added, turning to this gentleman with a demure smile.

"Then I shall claim the *next* dance as mine!" Mr. DeLauney declared angrily, his curly eyebrows drawn down in indignation.

Lady Cecily shook her head. "Oh, no, Mr. DeLauney. You are very much mistaken," she said, referring to her dance card. "Yours was several dances ago."

"But you danced my dance with *him!*" Mr. DeLauney cried, gesturing angrily toward Mr. Haversham. "And I demand an exchange!"

The young man was protesting so loudly that those standing nearby were beginning to take notice of what transpired.

Mr. Haversham stared haughtily down at the young man and said very quietly, "Do you think this a fishmonger's that you can shout and barter here? Do you think this the bookseller's that you can demand an exchange of merchandise? Calm down, old sport, and go your way."

"Go my way?" he repeated, glaring at his opponent. "If I step outside, would you care to accompany me? And if not, shall we meet again at dawn on Hampstead Heath, with seconds? You have taken what is mine and I demand a fair

35

exchange!"

Mr. DeLauney stared at Mr. Haversham, clenching and unclenching his fists.

Lady Cecily watched Mr. Haversham return the young man's stare without flinching. Without being too terribly obvious, she glanced about her at the small groups of people who had now turned with avid interest to watch them. Oh, how exciting to be the center of attention! How delightful to have two such handsome gentlemen clamoring after her!

Mr. Haversham's voice lowered to a threatening whisper. "You dare to claim the lady as yours when your own eyes tell you that I am preferred? For once there is someone else who knows my true worth. I shan't even honor your challenge. You are far too paltry a sum for me to deal with. Go home, sir, and do not insult this lady—or me—further!" he ordered imperiously.

Mr. DeLauney unclenched his fists and dropped his gaze. The music for the next dance began and Mr. DeLauney faded away into the crowd.

Mr. Haversham turned to Lady Cecily.

"It appears that you have no partner for the next set," he remarked.

Lady Cecily pretended to look about, searching for her erstwhile partners. "It would seem that they have all quite vanished."

"I cannot bear to see a lady alone. And we do look so well together. Permit me?"

"Cecily, dear," Lady Portia offered timidly from her rickety perch.

Lady Cecily shot the elderly lady a withering glance, trying somehow to convey the message from her mind to her aunt's—'Do not *dare* forbid me this dance!'

Once at the edge of the dance floor, Lady Cecily said to him, "I have truly enjoyed our dances, Mr. Haversham. However, I wonder if you are aware that this will be our third dance this evening."

Mr. Haversham nodded and replied quite calmly, "I am."

"That is quite frowned upon here," she told him. Then she giggled conspiratorially. "Oh, Mr. Haversham, do we *dare?*"

He lifted his head proudly and bestowed upon her a reassuring smile. "My dear Lady Cecily, *we* are English! *We* dare anything!"

While she was quite absorbed in Mr. Haversham and in what she firmly believed was the favorable impression she had made upon him, Lady Cecily could not be oblivious to the raised eyebrows which followed them about the room.

'La!' she thought with a lift of her chin. 'They are all consumed with jealousy that the loveliest, most desirable lady in the room is dancing with possibly the most handsome, most elegant bachelor in the room.'

Lady Portia was not seated when Lady Cecily returned to her. Her wrinkled brow was pulled down over her watery gray eyes in a deep frown. Her thin lips were pursed tightly. She was tapping her foot quite rapidly.

Lady Cecily could not recall any other time when she had seen her aunt in such a pique of temper.

"It is time to depart," Lady Portia informed her niece.

"Indeed, it is not!" Lady Cecily protested.

"Indeed," Lady Portia whispered hoarsely to her niece, "I have been informed by Lady Jersey herself, and in no uncertain terms, I might add, that it *is!*"

Before she could even bid Mr. Haversham good evening and a safe journey, Lady Cecily found herself seized by the hand and all but dragged from the room.

'Why, I had no idea the old girl was so strong!' she marveled.

"Serves the saucy chit right," Lady Sheftley pronounced to her daughter as the figures of the two ladies were lost in the press of the crowd. However, she made quite certain that her voice was loud enough to carry to where Mr. Haversham was still standing, not so many feet away.

"Lud! I do hate the daughters of earls and dukes and whatnot, thinking they can defy convention." As she did not have Lady Cecily present before her, she began slapping the palm of her hand with her fan.

"And as for that Haversham fellow—Lud knows he's handsome enough and certainly rich enough, but if he thinks the daughter of an earl, especially *that* one, is going to stoop to marry a man with no title . . . well!"

Lady Sheftley laughed a scornful laugh and gave her hand a final slap with the closed fan.

"Ow! Demme, that hurts!" She gave her daughter one last whack with her fan. "Why didn't you tell me that hurts, you thoughtless gel?"

Lady Edwina folded the letter again along the erratic creases which Lady Cecily had made.

"It is just like Cecily to be asked to leave Almack's," she said with an exasperated shake of her head. "But she does not say if it was just for the evening or if it was a permanent expulsion."

She turned the sheet of paper over in her hand. "Just like Cecily, too, to be so concerned with informing me of what *she* did that she quite neglected to mention this extraordinary gentleman's name."

Lady Edwina shrugged. "It does not signify, at any rate, as, two days after his departure, most probably Cecily herself had entirely forgotten his name."

She laid the letter on the small silver tray, snuffed the candle, which had already burned quite low, and snuggled down into the coverlet to sleep.

'I vow, the girl certainly has more than her fair share of suitors,' she thought. 'And she delights in the attentions of each and every one.'

She watched the moonlight as it filtered through the leaves of the tall elms outside and played on the bedchamber walls. She sat up again to rearrange the pillows. Once they were positioned to her apparent satisfaction, she dropped her head into their softness.

'Although, I truly cannot see myself paired with any of the men she seems to find so appealing.'

Never had the pillows seemed quite so lumpy. Never before had the goosedown mattress seemed quite so prickly. Lady Edwina tossed back and forth.

'Of course, she was never excessively discerning in what she considered appealing in a gentleman. Perhaps I have been too particular—where has it gotten me? Alone here in the country,' she added with a rueful little snicker, 'hiding from desperate old widowers at boring country affairs.'

Lady Edwina punched her uncooperative pillow one last time and plunged her head into it, trying to give it one last chance to offer her some comfort for the night.

But comfort was not forthcoming.

"Surely, somewhere," she murmured, "somewhere, there is a man whom I can love and who will love me."

Chapter Three

"Home! How good to be home!" Major Trent Haversham called back over his shoulder to his companion as his long, muscular legs carried him down the swaying gangplank of the ship.

He bounded across the wooden planks and the stone quay of the London Dock and planted both feet firmly in a puddle of mud at the curbstone.

"Sir, your boots'll be all muddy!" Sergeant James Bosley protested. His limp forced him to follow more slowly.

"But, Bosley, it's *English* mud!"

Trent's broad chest expanded under his blue jacket as he drew in a great breath of air. His nostrils were filled with the acrid scents of saltwater, seaweed, bilge, and rotting fish, but after four long years of fighting on the Continent, everything in England smelled good to him.

"I suppose the first thing your lordship'll be wanting is a proper cup o' proper English tea," teased the wiry young soldier.

Trent shook his head. "You know perfectly well I'm not a lord, Bosley. I don't even bother to use my 'Honorable.'"

"I know that, sir," he replied, somewhat abashed. "When all us soldiers called you that, we was only joking, you know that. You were the only nob we knew what didn't take on such airs."

Bosley peered cockily at his superior officer with his one remaining eye. Lifting his right hand, with the small finger extended as if he were holding a delicate china cup, he asked, "Shall I be mother?"

Trent laughed. "No, Bosley. The first thing I want is some good English ale and a good Englishman with whom to share it."

Bosley laughed and Trent gestured for his companion to follow him.

"You're as good a soldier and as good a man as I could have wished to have serving under me," he told him, clapping his companion heartily on the shoulder. "I'd be pleased to down a pint or two with you."

"I'd be glad to, sir," Bosley replied, a wide smile and a profuse blush spreading across his scarred face. Major Haversham was not one to bestow his compliments lightly.

The two returning soldiers began to saunter down the cobbled streets of Wapping. They could barely contain their elation at being home safe at last. Like schoolboys home for a holiday, they skipped over the mud and fish offal puddled in the wagon ruts in the street. They laughingly dodged the burdens of the porters who were busily loading and unloading the newly arrived vessels. They returned the admiring glances of the prostitutes who walked the streets around the docks, but continued on their way.

"Excuse me, sir, but, well, won't you be wanting to be getting back to your family quick like, though?" Bosley asked, hesitating just a bit.

Even, white teeth showed through Trent's rueful smile.

"I have little enough reason to return home, Bosley," Trent reluctantly admitted. "My father passed away last year and, much to my regret, my brother and I never have dealt well together. However, after all the years that have passed, I still find myself foolishly hoping for any chance for a reconciliation."

"I still say 'tis a pity you weren't the elder," Bosley commented.

Trent shrugged his broad shoulders. "I think I shall be able to survive not being the Baron Haverslea. My father did leave me a sufficient income."

Trent turned quietly to watch the man limping at his side. He remembered well the first day James Bosley had come to serve under him, fresh, young and just a bit naive. An exploding shell had robbed him of the vision in one eye and had left him with a permanent limp.

Trent felt pangs of remorse and pity. He had had the

effrontery to bemoan a fate which left him able to live, if not extravagantly, at least comfortably, while good men like Bosley would be lucky if they could find the most menial employment now that the War with Napoleon was done.

Trent shook himself from his unpleasant reverie. 'No sense in depressing the fellow,' he reasoned and quickly changed the topic of conversation.

"But I'm sure, after all these years, that you are eager to see *your* family," he offered.

Bosley began to smile broadly. "My sister, Pamela, she wrote saying she married a fine man last April—a blacksmith in Little Oxlea. My mum went to live with them, as she's getting on in years. Pamela says there's room there for me, too, and her husband, Tom, he says he'll find work for me to do around the smithy."

Bosley's hand flew up to the patch that covered one eye. "Although what he could possibly find for the likes of half a man to be doing is beyond me."

"There's more to a man than eyes and limbs," Trent told him. "I'd sooner have you at my side, whether making merry or in the heat of battle, than any other man I know."

"You're just being kind, sir," Bosley said, casting Trent a skeptical glance with his remaining good eye. A bright flush rose up his cheeks.

"You, of all people, know I never say what I do not mean. At any rate, I'm certain you'll be happy with your family," Trent added. "But, just in case, if you ever need a situation, come to me at Haversham Hall. There will always be a place for you in my household."

Trent had survived the dangers of war and the final horrors of Waterloo, but he was not so certain that he would survive the coach ride from London to Haverton, the small village on the Thames in Oxfordshire about two miles from Haversham Hall.

Just after the coach left Oxford, three completely foxed young gentlemen had bribed the coachman into allowing them to try their hands at tooling the ribbons.

Therefore, although Trent had never enjoyed a close relationship with the son of his father's younger twin brother, it was with exceedingly great relief that he met his cousin, Nigel Haversham, at the posting inn in Haverton.

The only resemblance between the cousins was that Nigel, like Trent, also bore the hereditary Haversham coloring—jet black hair, the emerald green eyes, the clear, fair skin, although Trent's was turned a golden brown from years of campaigning in the sun.

Nigel's facial features closely resembled those of his mother's family. His forehead was high and wide, his nose straight and slim. All in all, Trent had to concede that his cousin, at twenty-five, was a particularly handsome young man.

Of course, Trent, in all modesty, still enjoyed recalling the words the admiring ladies had used to describe him. "Finely chiseled features," he owned, was rather accurate, but he did think that the lady who had described his eyes as "smoldering emeralds" had exaggerated just a bit.

"I must own, you appear no worse for the war," Nigel quipped, laughing heartily at his own pun. He followed Trent into the new maroon and gold carriage that Milton, fifth Baron Haverslea, had sent for him.

Trent laughed, too, settling himself comfortably against the plump maroon velvet squabs.

Nigel tugged at his perfectly fitting, cerulean blue jacket and brushed an invisible piece of lint from his knee.

"I am exceedingly glad to see you returned safely, Trent," he said. "Seeing you declared dead in the newspapers not once, but twice, and then having you miraculously resurrected when a proper count of the casualties was taken, has played the very deuce with my nerves."

"My deepest apologies." Trent bent forward in his best effort at making a bow while seated in a bouncing carriage. "The next time I am reported dead, I shall do my best to remain so."

"I am greatly reassured," Nigel replied. "To be quite honest, however, I feel I must warn you, not everyone at Haversham Hall shares my tender sentiments regarding your safe return."

Trent nodded, absent-mindedly twirling the gold-colored cord and tassel of one of the squabs.

"You need not remind me," Trent said, gazing unseeing at the vast stretch of rolling farmland which passed by them, colored gold and orange in the light of the setting sun. "I shan't readily forget my brother's animosity, but I thank you for your concern."

"Milton's hostility toward you had seemed to relent a bit when he first married Charlotte Pickering, oh, I don't know how many years ago," Nigel observed.

"Sixteen, Nigel. They were married sixteen years ago," Trent reminded his cousin.

Nigel laughed. He reached up and tapped his forehead with one long index finger. "I cannot credit that so much time has passed! What has happened to my memory?" he demanded.

"I, myself, remember it quite well," Trent replied, suppressing a sigh which held just the barest tinge of bitterness. "I was at Eton at the time. It was the first and only occasion upon which my brother ever wrote me a letter. While the greater part of the missive concerned itself with his hopes for an heir in nine months, the tone was pleasant—most unlike Milton."

"Milton? Pleasant? Milton is approximately as pleasant as . . . as a . . . chamberpot!" Nigel punctuated each word with a loud laugh. "But one must pity poor Milton. His prophecies of plentiful progeny to perpetuate the peerage have yet to prosper."

"Oh, prime, Nigel," Trent responded appreciatively. "Positively prime."

Trent was still chuckling to himself over his cousin's witticism, but Nigel's face began to take on a more serious appearance and his voice a more serious tone.

"One must face facts, however," his cousin continued. "Charlotte is becoming a bit long in the tooth to produce the desired heir. It looks as if that duty will fall to you, old boy. You need to marry, sire a strapping heir."

Trent chuckled. "Nigel, I am relieved to be done with

war. Why should I marry and continue the conflict on the home front?"

"But, Trent, you are the heir presumptive to the barony!" his cousin protested.

Trent merely shrugged his broad shoulders.

This gesture did not seem to satisfy Nigel. Trent could see his cousin's agitation growing.

"If Milton and Charlotte produce no heir — and at this point, I should seriously doubt that they will — and if you do not . . . Ye gads, old boy! Do you realize what that could mean?" Nigel demanded.

"Quite obviously," Trent responded with amused detachment. "*You* would eventually be the Baron Haverslea."

Was the little strangled sound which came from the back of Nigel's throat a laugh? Trent could not decide.

"A prospect which you view with the utmost dread, no doubt," Trent remarked sarcastically.

"I do indeed!" Nigel asserted, recovering himself. "I am an individual of a singularly indolent nature."

Trent swallowed the laughter which rose to his lips. It seemed that his cousin had a very realistic appraisal of his own character.

"Do you mean to tell me that the politics and intrigues in the House of Lords hold no interest for you?" Trent teased.

"I should say not!" Nigel responded almost immediately. "Neither does the breeding of cattle, the overseeing of crops, nor the disposition of drainage and manure on vast estates."

This time, Trent could not restrain his laughter.

"You are quite correct, Nigel," he said. "I truly cannot picture you striding through a cow pasture in your shining new Hessians."

"There is no trace of the country squire in me, I assure you," Nigel said, moving his head ever so slightly to either side so as not to destroy the fold of his cravat. "I am extremely partial to my London townhouse. If I ever do feel the desire to rusticate, I simply pay a visit to Cousin Milton for as long as I can bear his company and that of his insipid wife. I have no desire to make drastic changes in my life. They require too much effort."

"Do not become too complacent, Nigel," Trent warned him playfully. "Since Milton and Charlotte seem incapable of doing so, and I am extremely disinclined to do so, the responsibility of producing the next Haversham heir does, indeed, fall to you."

A wide smile spread across Nigel's thin lips. "Then you may be pleased to hear that I have lately begun to formulate plans regarding that eventuality."

"Nigel!" Trent exclaimed, leaning forward to congratulate him.

Nigel held up his hand quickly. "Mind you, I have made no formal proposal, but the lady is not unaware of my interest."

"And you tell me that you have no desire to make drastic changes in your life!" Trent jovially chided his cousin.

Nigel waved his hand before him in denial. "Oh, this change will not be drastic. The lady is quite amenable and will cause me no trouble, no trouble at all."

Trent raised his dark brows in an expression of mock surprise.

"The lady who causes a gentleman no trouble at all is, indeed, a rare find," he remarked with feigned sarcasm. "I insist you tell me all about this remarkable young miss."

"I met her at Almack's. She is a very lovely, accomplished young lady of good family and sufficient fortune," Nigel said.

Trent shrugged his shoulders and grinned mischievously. "Beauty, accomplishments, good family and a fortune. The lady sounds quite ordinary to me."

"Ordinary!" Nigel exclaimed in protest. "I shall convince you to the contrary."

The jiggling eased somewhat as the carriage began to slow.

"Alas," Nigel sighed. "I shall have to wait to regale you with an extensive inventory of the lady's numerous charms until a later time. I believe we have arrived."

"Welcome home, sir," the butler said as he opened the

46

wide front door of Haversham Hall and backed away, permitting Trent and Nigel to enter. "Mr. Haversham," he said, also acknowledging Nigel's presence with a nod of his gray head.

"Saunders, how good to see you still here," Trent exclaimed cheerfully. How gray the man had become in the mere four years he had been away!

"Your brother is awaiting you in the Rear Salon, sir," the butler informed him, closing the heavy door. "I shall escort you."

Before Saunders could turn to precede him through the Great Hall, a short, plump lady bustled up to Trent. She glanced nervously to every side, then clasped his hand firmly between both of hers. She quickly looked about her again, reached up and gave him a brief embrace, then rapidly backed away.

"Charlotte, how good to see you again," Trent told his sister-in-law after he had recovered from her rather unusual greeting.

Of course, she had wrinkled a bit about the outer corners of her deep-set brown eyes. There were a few extra strands of silver in her mousy brown hair. She had also added quite a few pounds to her already plump little figure since he had last seen her.

"You're looking quite well, Charlotte," he told her. While he was a man who customarily spoke the truth, Trent saw no need to speak the *entire* truth at all times.

"How you have changed," she said in a tiny, little voice that was barely above a whisper. "You left us just entering into manhood and have returned to us quite a gentleman of the world."

"I have seen too much of the world, Charlotte," he told her, smiling wearily. "I long to spend some quiet time in the country."

Charlotte nodded understandingly, but there was a strange, sad look behind her little, brown eyes. "I hope you attain what you so eagerly anticipate, Trent."

Saunders rumbled a throaty little cough, then interjected, "His lordship awaits, sir."

47

Charlotte faded away into the shadows of the Hall.

'How queer that he should greet me in the Rear Salon,' Trent pondered as he and Nigel followed Saunders down the dimly lit corridor to an insignificant room near the back of the house.

The Grand Salon had customarily been used for visitors. There had also been a smaller drawing room which had been used by the family alone in their times of privacy. Only insignificant callers, those whom some member of the family had particularly wished to set down, were ever shown into the Rear Salon.

Trent pursed his lips and decided to give Milton the benefit of the doubt. As the new Lord Haverslea, his brother certainly had the right to utilize the rooms and to dispose of callers in any way he wished.

The passage of time changes everyone, Trent knew. He realized that, at twenty-nine, he himself was no longer the same young man he had once been. He had thought that he was perfectly prepared for the changes in his brother, a man now past forty.

But Trent still found it necessary to exert all his self-control not to reveal his shock as he and Nigel followed the butler into the Rear Salon and Trent had his first sight of his brother in seven years.

Lord Haverslea's jaw, which had always looked in need of a shave no matter how recently his valet had been at him, had dissolved into a mass of pink flesh that ballooned out from above his immaculate cravat, imparting to him a remarkable resemblance to a bullfrog. His eyelids sagged over the bulging green eyes, enhancing the resemblance. The tip of his nose had acquired an immensity of proportion and a shade of crimson which only vast quantities of wine could produce.

Trent had not expected his brother to welcome him with a hearty embrace, but Lord Haverslea never even bothered to rise from the comfortable yellow damask-covered *bergère* in which he sat. He made a short gesture toward a maroon velvet side chair which Trent took as an invitation to be seated.

Trent settled himself into the uncomfortable little chair across from his brother, while Nigel crossed the room and settled himself quite languidly upon a large, green silk-upholstered sofa.

"It is good to see you again, Milton," Trent offered tentatively.

With a malicious chuckle, Lord Haverslea replied, "I never thought I *would* see you again, Trent. Especially after you were reported dead not once, but twice! You always were a deucedly lucky fellow."

"Do you begrudge me a bit of luck in merely staying alive, Milton?" Trent asked, the look on his face a mixture of surprise and hurt.

Lord Haverslea grunted with disdain. "Your luck will remain with you, no doubt, when I die without issue and *you* succeed."

"Milton!" Trent cried in protest. "Do not anticipate your own untimely demise. *I* surely do not."

"Surely none of us do!" Nigel interposed, rising from his seat. "Come now, Milton. You were gracious enough to send your carriage for us, but the drive has left me quite famished. I am eager to sample the talents of that superb French chef I understand you have hired."

But the soup was tepid and badly in need of seasoning. The fish had been dead at least a week before the chef had ever laid eyes upon it. The joint of beef was tough and overdone, and the roast potatoes were mealy. Trent could have sworn that the wine had been egregiously watered.

Trent felt certain however, when he regarded the rotund Milton and the plump, pink Charlotte, that very few meals at Haversham Hall were ever of such poor quality when they dined alone or with those whom they wished to impress. He was almost certain that, whenever his brother did entertain, he used the large formal dining room instead of the dimly lit, insignificant little dining room where they partook of this meal.

Trent could not help observing that, throughout the dinner, Lady Haverslea merely smiled insipidly. Each time she looked as if she were about to open her mouth to make some comment or response, she first darted a nervous glance out of the corner of her eye toward Lord Haverslea. Seeing the barest scowl come into his lordship's eyes, Lady Haverslea would quickly put a forkful of food into her mouth instead. Trent recalled that she had always been deucedly shy, but he could not remember her appearing positively cowed.

After dinner, Lady Haverslea rose and retired to whatever it was with which she occupied her time. Trent could not have pinpointed the precise moment of her departure, as the conversation progressed rather much the same whether she was present or not.

'I imagine one could be in a room with the lady and believe oneself alone,' Trent observed silently.

The wine was now being brought in by a pretty, red-haired scullery maid rather than by the butler or even a footman.

"Ripley!" Lord Haverslea bellowed her name. Annie Ripley curtsied and shook and almost dropped the decanter of wine.

"Where is Saunders?" Lord Haverslea demanded crossly.

Ripley blushed and stammered. Her eyes flickered nervously back and forth between Nigel and Lord Haverslea as she answered, "I . . . he . . . Mr. Saunders, he ain't well. The footmen neither. He . . . he said it'd be all right . . . I mean, that your lordship wouldn't mind if I . . ."

Lord Haverslea waved the jittery young girl away. "Make no mistakes, or both you and Saunders will be seeking new situations," he threatened.

"Oh, leave the girl be, Milton," Nigel interrupted. "She's a quiet enough little thing. Hardly know she's about. And when one does notice her, well, she's not so hard to look upon, is she?"

"She doesn't belong here," Lord Haverslea insisted, frowning irritably. "Gentlemen require the services of a footman, not a simpering, sniveling wench."

"Oh, I say, Milton, you must be in a foul mood, indeed, not to appreciate the girl's charms," Nigel scolded.

"Very well, then," Lord Haverslea conceded with bad

grace. Turning to Ripley, he ordered, "Leave us a few bottles, then be off to your kitchen duties." He ordered her away with a wave of his hand. "But mind you listen if we ring for more," he warned.

Nigel turned to Ripley and said in a softer tone of voice, "Why don't you bring us that excellent wine I brought, my dear, as a change from this rather inadequate vintage?"

Ripley's wide, brown eyes darted to Lord Haverslea to see if he would object. But Lord Haverslea was busily picking at his teeth with a slim, gold toothpick, and paid her no mind at all.

She quickly curtsied and disappeared to return with the desired bottles. She placed several bottles on the old, oaken sideboard. Then, with much careful deliberation, she placed an opened bottle before each gentleman. When she was finished with this task, she beat a hasty retreat to the kitchen.

As the evening wore on, Trent began to feel the relaxing effects of the wine. The tightness in his muscles from the arduous journey began to ease. He stretched his long, muscular legs out to their full length under the wide, oaken dining table.

"I must own, Milton, I believe I have never tasted a more . . . unusual meal," Trent said with more than a touch of sarcasm in his voice. "Now I am looking forward to a peaceful night's sleep in my old room. Unless, of course, you have other accommodations in mind more in keeping with the tone you have already set this evening, such as bedding me down in the stables with the horses?"

"Your brother would never treat you in such an out-of-hand manner!" Nigel protested vehemently. The way in which he slurred his words indicated that he was quite foxed. "I'm certain Milton has no wish to allow your abominable snoring to startle his excellent horses."

Trent and Nigel laughed, but Lord Haverslea only regarded them both with a sullen scowl.

"You will find your accommodations quite adequate — for one night's stay," Lord Haverslea informed his brother coldly.

"I beg your pardon," Trent said, blinking in surprise. "Did you say one night?"

"I believe my meaning was quite clear the first time," Lord Haverslea said, lifting his head haughtily, stretching out the numerous folds of flaccid skin beneath his chin. "There is no need for me to repeat myself."

Trent paused to sort his thoughts. "Milton," he said at last, "I realize that we have never dealt well together but . . . I assure you, I shan't incommode you in the least here . . ."

Lord Haverslea was firmly shaking his head, his jowls vibrating from side to side.

"Shall I remove myself to the Dower House?" Trent suggested. "I understand if you wish to put a bit more distance between us. I shan't even require the assistance of any of your servants to clean . . ."

Trent stopped in mid-sentence as he watched his brother continue to shake his head in refusal.

"Would you prefer I reside at Haversham House while you are here?" Trent offered. "And whenever you decide to visit London, I shall remove to the country . . ."

"You will have to make other arrangements, entirely separate from the Haversham holdings, for a permanent place of residence," Lord Haverslea replied icily.

Trent peered into the cold, green eyes that stared pitilessly at him from the length of the table.

"Very well, then . . ." Trent rose unsteadily to his feet. His balance drifted first to the left, then to the right.

'Curse it all,' he thought. 'I'm foxed! And at the very moment when I most need all my wits about me.'

"Very well, then." Trent found he had to repeat himself to maintain his train of thought. "I had hoped that, after all this time, we might become friends, Milton, but I realize now that can never be. I am sorry, Milton, heartily sorry. If you will be so kind as to write to our solicitor instructing him to relinquish my income to me instead of yourself now that I have returned, I shall burden you with my presence no longer."

After this exhausting speech, Trent unaccountably felt the need to seat himself again. With a great deal of effort, Trent

52

raised his aching head to look at his brother through the foggy haze of the candlelight.

Lord Haverslea toyed with the fruit knife, then extended it, stabbed an over-ripe peach from the silver basket situated on the table in front of him, and began to peel it very slowly.

"There is a small problem, Trent," he said at length. "Your money is gone."

Chapter Four

"Gone? How can it be gone?" Trent cried. He seized the edge of the table and leaned forward in his chair. "What have you done, Milton?" he demanded angrily.

"I needed some money to invest in the Brimhampton Canal, Ltd., a venture which they assured me would be a great success," Lord Haverslea made his quite matter-of-fact reply. With the silver-handled fruit knife, he lazily cut off a chunk of juicy peach, skewered it and popped it into his mouth.

"All of my own capital was already invested," he continued. "I took the liberty of using yours. If events had worked out properly, I would have made myself a tidy profit and your income would have remained intact."

Lord Haverslea sliced off another portion of peach and ate it. With the tip of the fruit knife, he pried the pit from the center of the peach and sent it rolling across the table to collide with the empty wine bottle, leaving a juicy trail in its wake.

His lordship looked up at his brother again and shrugged. "How could I have known that the Treasurer of that august body would abscond with all their assets?"

"You have no right!" Trent cried, his voice reverberating in his ears as if he were shouting in a great cave.

Lord Haverslea blinked and shook his head hard as if endeavoring to remain awake. "I had every right," he asserted. "You, of all people, are very much aware that you are not to receive control of the principal of your inheritance until next year when you attain the age of thirty."

"Confound that family tradition!" Trent mumbled under his breath.

He knew that what Milton said was true and that there was, indeed, no remedy for what his brother had done to him. Trent pressed his back against the chair and closed his eyes tightly to try to stop the spinning of the room.

Lord Haverslea spoke more slowly, pronouncing each word with increasing difficulty.

'So Milton is foxed, too,' Trent realized with foreboding. 'There'll be no reasoning with him this evening.'

"As the head of the family, and, therefore, the trustee of your income, I used your money as I saw fit, Trent."

"You mean misused," he answered through tightly compressed lips. His green eyes had narrowed to mere slits.

Lord Haverslea shrugged. "Fortunes are made and lost every day, Trent."

"Then I shall make my own fortune," Trent said with determination, slamming his fist decisively against the oaken table. "But you must advance me some capital with which to begin."

"I cannot do that, Trent," Lord Haverslea answered with an abrupt shake of his head.

Trent clenched the muscles of his jaw. The veins at his temples throbbed as his throat and cheeks burned crimson with rage.

"Cannot or will not? How can you be so callous?" he demanded.

He waited for some reply from his brother. When none came, he raised his head and glared at Lord Haverslea down the length of the table.

"You owe me at least that much, Milton."

With a great deal of difficulty, Lord Haverslea raised a shaky hand and clumsily polished the large pigeon's blood ruby set in a heavy gold ring against the lapel of his new superfine jacket.

"Every bit of the income of the estate is invested in its efficient running. Why, I have barely enough to satisfy my own modest needs."

Livid with rage, he sprang to his feet. "You thieving bastard!" he cried.

Nearly blind with rage, he began a great leap across the table with the firm intention of throttling his unscrupulous brother. The candlelight dimmed as a thousand tiny sparks

55

swirled before his eyes. Then all was blackness.

The wood of the table was cool against his face. Trent felt his right arm being pulled out from under him as his left shoulder was being raised and pushed until he rolled over onto his back. His head was pounding. He felt nauseated. He opened his eyes. Through the dim candlelight and his own blurry vision, he discerned the form of Nigel, knife in hand, poised above him.

Trent rolled quickly off the dining room table just as the point of the knife plunged deep into the polished, hardwood surface exactly where his heart would have been seconds before.

Grateful for his soldier's quick reflexes, Trent cautiously peeked over the edge of the table. Nigel was struggling to extricate the knife blade from the tabletop.

"What in the name of Hell are you trying to do?" Trent demanded. Grasping the edge of the table, he forced his wobbly legs to support him as he stood.

"Trent? Are you quite yourself again?" Nigel asked nervously, backing up but still warily brandishing the knife he had managed to extract.

"Why . . . why am I so groggy?" Trent asked himself aloud. He raised a shaking hand to his spinning head. "I . . . didn't consume that much wine."

"Whatever took possession of you?" Nigel demanded. He, himself, seemed to have recovered quite rapidly from his own overindulgence.

"What possessed *you?*" Trent countered. He gestured to the gouge the knife had made in the tabletop. "I awake to find myself your intended pincushion!"

"I had to protect myself," Nigel offered with a weak lift of his shoulders.

"Protect yourself?" Trent echoed. "From me?"

"Trent, have you honestly no memory of what you've done?" Nigel demanded.

"What do you mean? What have I done?"

Nigel pointed silently toward the grisly sight at the head of the table.

Lord Haverslea's head lolled down upon his breast. A bright red stain oozed down the wide front of his white brocade waistcoat where the fruit knife stuck out of his chest.

"My God! *I* did this?" Trent cried in horrified disbelief. "Impossible!"

Using the table for support, he staggered to his brother's side.

"You were arguing about the money of yours that Milton lost. Suddenly, you . . . you went mad! Positively insane!"

Nigel waved his hands at the sides of his temples to indicate Trent's befuddled state of mind. "Before I could prevent you, you stabbed Milton with the nearest weapon at hand. Then, for some unaccountable reason, you turned on me! Why me? Surely *I* am no threat to you."

Trent's eyes darted to the sharp knife which Nigel still brandished. "Are you not?"

"Oh, this." Nigel grinned sheepishly and tossed the knife onto the table top in front of him. The knife clattered across the wooden surface and skidded to a stop directly in front of the late Lord Haverslea.

"Milton! Forgive me!" Trent was exclaiming as he ran his fingers through his raven hair. He pressed the heels of his hands to his forehead as if that would help him to think more clearly.

"We may not yet be too late!" Trent said, hoping against hope. "It may be only a flesh wound. He may only be stunned. He *can't* be dead!"

He dropped his head to the still chest to listen for the sounds of a heartbeat. There was none. Trent lifted his head and peered into his brother's glazed eyes. His heart constricted with remorse as he realized there was, indeed, no hope.

As Trent straightened, he wavered unsteadily upon his feet. A searing pain tore through his right shoulder and down his arm. Clutching his wounded arm, he turned to see Nigel, bloodied knife in hand, standing behind him.

"Damn you, Trent!" Nigel cursed, squeezing the knife handle until his knuckles whitened. His eyes were bright, his nostrils flared with each heaving breath. "If you would only cooperate and hold still, we could be done with this."

"Nigel! You?" Trent exclaimed, his green eyes widening with the startling revelation. "But why? After all that you said in the carriage . . ."

Nigel arched a dark eyebrow and stared at Trent with disdain. "You would hardly expect me to say things which would make you suspicious of my intentions, would you now, old boy?"

If only Trent could shake the drowsiness from his head to think his way out of his present danger. He fought against his body's urge to sag wearily against the table. He had never been this dizzy before.

"You drugged me!" he exclaimed as his wits began to cut through the fog.

"Of course. And I did quite an excellent job of it, too, if it's taken you this long to reason it out," Nigel said with a scornful chuckle.

"And Milton, too?"

"Actually, that was quite kind of me, as the fellow felt no pain. How ironic that chubby old Milton should meet his doom at the business end of an eating utensil!" Nigel laughed aloud.

"And now you try to murder me?" Trent asked, wincing as he tried to move his injured arm.

"You have no one to blame but yourself if you are in pain," Nigel informed him petulantly. "If you were not possessed of such remarkable recuperative powers, I could easily have killed you as well, while you were unconscious, and then arranged the bodies so as to simulate a fight having occurred between the two of you."

Nigel's lower lip shot out. "I had planned it so well and you had to spoil it," he pouted. "Damn you, Trent!"

"A fight. But we only argued over money. No one will believe I killed him," Trent protested.

"But your hatred of each other is common knowledge."

"I *didn't* hate my brother! In spite of his blatant hostility toward me, I had always done my best to maintain a degree of civility between us."

58

Nigel pursed his lips and shook his head. "But, you've been away for four years, Trent. And in that time, I have had the opportunity to speak to various persons known for their remarkable inability to keep a confidence any longer than the moment required for them to turn and address the dinner partner seated at their other side. Each and every one of them was only too eager to listen sympathetically to my sad tale of the great animosity between the two Haversham brothers."

"I could never hate him enough to kill him!"

"Hatred is a strong motive, Trent. But you are quite correct, it is not enough," Nigel agreed. "Then consider this. You were a penniless younger brother. Now? Now you are the sixth Baron Haverslea. For just a little while longer, at least," he added. "Then *I* shall be where I belong—where I should have been all along, but for the caprice of fate which caused your father to be born before mine."

Then Nigel's lips pulled back to reveal all his teeth in a maniacal grimace. "Then *I* shall be the Baron Haverslea!"

The knot twisting in his stomach caused Trent to flinch. He realized that he was not merely dealing with an overly ambitious cousin, but with a veritable madman—and what was worse, a clever madman.

"I must own, Nigel, your logic is incontestable," Trent said, trying to distract his cousin. "You appear to have omitted nothing from your ruthless plan."

Nigel bowed politely in response. He then took several quick steps to circle the late Lord Haverslea's chair. Trent watched his cousin clenching and unclenching his fingers about the knife handle.

Trent shook his head, steeling himself against the pain in his arm. He was trying to concentrate all his senses on evaluating every aspect of his dangerous situation. His eyes traveled rapidly over the room, searching out his opportunities to seize a weapon.

He dismissed the delicate silver gilt candelabra. The knife protruding from the late Lord Haverslea's paunch was out of reach. He briefly considered one of the wine bottles, but Nigel's approach obstructed his access to the table.

'I'd take him if I had two good arms, though,' he consoled himself. Never had he felt so helpless—he detested the feeling.

As Nigel continued his approach, Trent began to back slowly, inch by inch, toward the doorway which led to the Main Hall. Every fiber in him bridled against running from a fight in cowardice. Nevertheless, he could not now deny the wisdom of a strategic retreat.

"It will never work, Nigel," Trent said. He gestured toward the doorway through which the maid had disappeared. He hoped to distract his cousin from his own movements toward the door and escape. "You have forgotten the servants."

"Oh, but I have not forgotten the servants," Nigel contradicted, shaking his head. "I am very aware of the fact that some servants enjoy making rather free with their employers' possessions, including their meals. And after the pathetic beverage Milton provided this evening, how could they resist sampling the excellent wine I brought? You will find the servants all asleep as well."

"Drugged."

Nigel nodded.

"But that scullery maid, Ripley . . ."

"Will swear to her dying day that she saw you stab your brother in a fit of murderous rage while he, in turn, stabbed you in self-defense," Nigel finished for him with a sly smile.

"Of course. The maid." Trent nodded slowly, recalling Ripley's nervousness and her careful placement of the wine bottles. "How did you manage to convince her to join in your nefarious scheme, Nigel?"

"Trent, I'm surprised that you need to ask," Nigel pouted. "You know a gentleman such as myself has certain . . . er, charms that are positively irresistible to women—even to scullery maids," he boasted.

"To be sure, you do," Trent replied acidly. "Exactly how much of your money did you have to offer her?"

Nigel's face flamed red with rage. "Enough!" he cried, lunging at Trent.

As Trent tried to sidestep, he landed a blow to Nigel's chin. The force of the blow would have felled another man, but Nigel's madness gave him uncanny strength. He again slashed through the shoulder of Trent's jacket into the muscles of his upper arm.

As Nigel raised the knife to strike again, Trent spun on his heels and darted through the dining room door, into the Main Hall, and out the two large front doors.

'I shall go to the constable and convince him of my innocence,' Trent decided as he broke into the cool night air.

Immediately he knew that was not the course to follow. Nigel would insist that Trent had murdered his brother, and Ripley, in his cousin's employ, would only agree. It was their word against his.

Trent slipped over the stone balcony into the bushes, then peeked through the branches at the doorway of the Hall. Nigel stood silhouetted in the pool of light which shone from the open door onto the wide front steps. The knife he still held in his fist glinted in the light.

Slipping from the protection of the bushes, Trent made a dash for the nearest tree, but he was unsteady upon his feet and stumbled as he fled. Nigel must have heard the noise, as Trent could hear his footsteps begin to follow him.

At last, Trent broke into the wooded area that bordered the park of the estate. Even as he fled, he could hear Nigel crashing through the trees in pursuit. He continued to run until the woods about him became quiet. Perhaps he had at last succeeded in eluding Nigel. He continued to make his way through the dark woods.

Trent was sick at heart as well as sick to his stomach, and weary to his very bones. Giddy from the drugged wine and weak from pain and loss of blood, he leaned his head against the rough bark of the tree just long enough to catch his breath. He turned from the tree to continue his flight and found himself at the rim of a small hill that sloped downward to the river Thames.

Believing that he was safe at last, Trent paused to watch the river flowing below him glowing back and silver in the moonlight.

The crack of a branch resounded through the quiet woods. The knife had been poised at his back, but Nigel tripped over an exposed root and stumbled forward. Pain burned through the flesh of Trent's thigh.

Trent brought his fist crashing backward over his assailant's face. Nigel tumbled backward, then lunged forward again. Trent caught the hand that held the upraised knife with his uninjured arm, fending off another blow.

But Trent was weak and tired. His injured leg gave out beneath him. He fell, but still retained his grip on Nigel so that the two tumbled over and over each other until they slammed against a small tree in a tangle of bushes at the hill's bottom.

The impact broke his grip and Trent continued to tumble into the river. He tried to regain the shore, but his strength was gone. He saw Nigel, on the riverbank, rise and put his hand to his chest as if trying to regain his breath. He knew Nigel saw him sinking, for the last thing he saw was his cousin smile as the waters closed over him.

Trent was not certain how he had managed to come ashore. He seemed to recall grasping at a large branch which had floated by and feeling the scrape of sand upon his knees as he crawled ashore, but his perceptions were distorted and unclear at best.

He did not know how far he had come or how many days he had been traveling. He could not rise, but only managed to stumble and crawl on all fours like a wounded animal. He could not tell whether he had slept or simply fainted from hunger and pain and exhaustion.

He knew only that it was daylight when he opened his burning eyes. He blinked twice and shook his head. He was in a fever. He must be delirious. That could be the only rational explanation for the strange object which was descending from the sky and crashing through the trees, headed directly toward him.

Chapter Five

"This way, men," the young Earl of Dynford called back to his entourage. He swung his brass-handled walking stick in a wide arc over his head and pointed it up the hill to his intended destination. "Ever onward!"

With rapid strides, he climbed the gentle slope to the top of the hill. Lord Dynford began beating the overgrown bushes back with his walking stick. He made his way to the other side of the weathered marble folly. The gently rolling hill dropped off abruptly on this side, giving way to a picturesque view of treetops and the River Thames beyond, glittering in the light of the early morning sun.

The heavily laden wagon lumbered behind Lord Dynford at a much slower rate of speed. Redding, the wagoner, pulled his vehicle to a stop before the folly. He firmly applied the brake and then leaped down from the wide seat. He tied the guidelines of the sturdy draft horses to a lean little aspen tree which had grown up along the neglected path.

"Perfect!" his lordship exclaimed as he reappeared from between the tall, thick Ionic columns. "Unload the wagon, men."

Nealy, the footman, looked uncertainly at Pringle, his lordship's valet. Pringle merely shrugged his shoulders.

"You heard his lordship," the valet said, jabbing a stubby thumb in the direction of the wagon. "Heave to."

From the back of the wagon they pulled a large, wooden and canvas contraption that bore a remarkable resemblance to the wings of some enormous bird.

"Gently, men, gently," Lord Dynford cautioned as his servants dragged the contraption through the brambles to the edge of the hill. "Those wings are fragile enough. I should

63

like to have the opportunity to fly with them *before* I do them damage."

"I just hope the wings are the only things what gets damaged," Pringle muttered to Nealy behind his lordship's back. "I bloody well don't relish the prospect of seeking a new situation if his lordship does himself in during one of these excursions of his."

Nealy, grunting and sweating under the load, merely nodded.

"He'll do it, too, one day, he'll kill himself," Pringle predicted sagely. "Mind what I've told you."

"Pity if he should," Nealy muttered. "On the other hand, then we wouldn't have to be doing this any longer, either."

"But think how bloody dull our lives would be then," Redding mumbled from behind.

The three men set the contraption at the edge of the hill.

"Nice job, men," his lordship said. He had divested himself of his cane, hat, and jacket and was walking about the apparatus for one final inspection.

Two wide oaken beams about six feet long were set approximately a foot and a half apart and securely nailed to a legless wooden chair. Another piece of wood was nailed in front of the chair to act as a footrest. Two small wheels pilfered from the home farm's wheelbarrows were attached to the bottom. Attached by heavy, iron hinges to the beams at either side of the chair were giant wood and canvas wings. The canvas was spread taut over six rows of wooden ribs. At the center of each wing, large leather straps provided his lordship with a handhold for operating the wings.

Lord Dynford settled himself into the chair and propped his feet up onto the footrest. He flapped the wings up and down to test them.

Yes, indeed, he smiled to himself as the wings responded. Everything was going splendidly!

"All right men!" Lord Dynford called back to Pringle, Redding, and Nealy. "Push!"

The wood creaked and groaned as the apparatus began to roll over the damp grass. It rolled with ease, faster and faster, until it reached the end of the precipice and sailed out over the treetops.

"Fly, m'lord! Fly!" Nealy and Redding cheered, waving their caps in the air over their heads.

Pringle cupped his hands to his mouth and cried, "M' lord, remember to flap your arms!"

"Flap, m'lord! Flap!" Nealy cried, still waving.

Redding poked him in the ribs. "No. You know his lordship's unflappable!" And Nealy and Redding whooped with glee.

Lord Dynford, jolted from the feeling of sheer ecstasy of at last being airborne, suddenly began to pump his arms up and down as hard as he could. The canvas wings flapped in response, but were not strong enough. The contraption paused in midair for several seconds, then plummeted abruptly into the branches below.

Lord Dynford's wailing whoop of terror mixed with the sharp snapping of the tree branches and the shredding of the canvas. The contraption slid over several treetops, leaving loose parts as it went, then dropped from sight.

"Cripes! Let's go get him!" Pringle cried, skidding down the hill in the direction he had seen his lordship crash. He ran through the woods, constantly searching the branches overhead for the torn and bloody remains of his lordship.

At last he saw him, dangling overhead.

Lord Dynford's apparatus was wedged into the branches of a large oak tree, about twenty-five feet above the ground. His lordship hung from the shredded canvas remains of one quite ruined wing, dangling about twenty feet above the ground.

"M'lord," Pringle called up to him. "Will you be needing any assistance in getting down?"

The canvas ripped a bit more, and his lordship now found himself hanging a mere fifteen feet above his valet. "At this point, I should not refuse any assistance offered," Lord Dynford called down.

The canvas ripped again.

"Not to put too fine a point on it, Pringle, but I should actively encourage such assistance right now, all things being considered."

Nealy and Redding had caught up to Pringle by now. Redding held out his large, beefy arms. "Jump, m'lord! 'Tis not far!"

Lord Dynford looked down. " 'Tis far enough."

Suddenly the woods echoed with a resounding crack. The branch which had been holding the wing in place snapped and Lord Dynford, canvas and all, landed in a most undignified mound on the leaf-strewn ground.

"Good show, m'lord," Pringle commented, reaching out his hand to assist the young earl to his feet.

"A very poor showing," Lord Dynford replied morosely. He brushed the leaves and dirt from the seat of his pants. "I could not manage to stay aloft even one minute. What am I doing wrong?" he demanded.

He flapped his arms up and down. "Could it be that I have not the strength?"

"Oh, no," Pringle said, shaking his head emphatically. "Not you, m'lord."

His anger and frustration getting the better of him, Lord Dynford kicked at a large pile of last autumn's leftover leaves.

A low moan rumbled from the pile of leaves.

"Pringle, I do seem to recall leaves as making a rustling sort of noise, rather than a groaning sort," his lordship said slowly. "Come assist me in examining this."

Pringle warily skirted the pile of leaves. "Indeed, sir." He prodded the pile with his toes. A similar moan emerged.

Lord Dynford and his valet bent quickly and brushed the leaves from the recumbent figure.

"Cripes! What a wretched mess!" Pringle exclaimed when he saw the dried blood which encrusted the tattered sleeve of the man's deep blue jacket and one leg of his filthy gray breeches.

"Poor fellow!" his lordship cried. "What could have happened to him to leave him in such a horrid state?"

"Highwaymen?" Nealy offered eagerly, a morbid leer on his young face.

"Aye, and they might still be lurking," Redding said, glancing about nervously. "I suggest we be getting along, m'lord."

Lord Dynford nodded in agreement. "Redding, Pringle, lift this man and carry him back to the wagon. I shall take him home."

Lady Edwina was seated in one of the rose-colored velvet chairs in the private sitting room which adjoined her bedchamber. The morning sun shone through the tall elms outside, providing illumination for her work.

She leaned intently over the ripped lace at the hem of the gold silk gown. Rosalie Stokes leaned over the back of her mistress's chair and peered down her little snub nose at her handiwork.

"Oh, m'lady, no one will ever be able to tell where the mending is," Stokes exclaimed.

"*Now* do you understand how it is done?" Lady Edwina asked with an exasperated sigh. "I certainly hope so. Then I shan't have to be doing this myself any longer."

"I try, m'lady," the young girl whined. "Honestly I do. I've just no hand with the needle. I truly wish I did, as a lady such as yourself shouldn't be doing her own mending."

Lady Edwina laid her work on the small rosewood table at her side and looked up at Stokes.

"Peculiar, is it not," she observed, "how needlework of a decorative nature *is* acceptable, and yet practical needlework is not considered an acceptable pastime for unmarried ladies of my age and station?"

"Oh, m'lady, you're not so awfully old," the young maid said with a nervous little laugh that clearly indicated that she thought otherwise.

Lady Edwina was not quite at her best at this early hour of the morning, and she still felt fatigued from the exceedingly wearisome ball at Ashton Park last night. There was the additional concern regarding the outlandish behavior of her sister in London and the unconventional behavior of her brother in the air.

Lady Edwina thought, 'Oh, but sometimes I *feel* so awfully old.'

Her thoughts were interrupted by the small cough which Haskell, the butler, always used to draw attention to himself. The stick of a man stood in the open doorway of her room, his silvery hair encircling his head like a nimbus. Lady Edwina could not remember a time when Haskell had not been the family's butler.

"M'lady," Haskell announced in stentorian tones which reverberated through the small room. "His lordship."

Lady Edwina blinked as the sound of Haskell's voice echoed away in her head. She leaned to one side, the better to see around Haskell for the approach of her brother. No one else was in the corridor.

Lady Edwina drew a deep breath before she asked, "Where is his lordship, Haskell?"

"M'lady," Haskell replied, not changing the volume of his address one whit. "The wagon accompanies his lordship."

Lady Edwina blinked again, trying to decipher the butler's cryptic message. She looked at him expectantly, but he failed to elaborate until she had pointedly asked him, "What is my brother doing with the wagon?"

"You don't think he talked Pringle into flying instead, do you?" Stokes mumbled from behind her ladyship's chair. Her fingertips dug into the soft, rose-colored velvet.

"Why, m'lady," Haskell answered in a voice which showed his obvious surprise that she should need to ask such a question. "He is doing what he always does."

Lady Edwina rose. Several things which her rather unusual brother could think of to do with a wagon came immediately to her mind. She was certain he was able to devise many more that she could never even begin to imagine.

He was attempting to fly again, that much was certain. But was he being brought home, unconscious in the wagon, or had he somehow managed to incorporate the wagon into his strange apparatus?

There was only one way to discover what her brother was up to now.

"Thank you, Haskell," she said. "I shall be down directly."

* * *

The large wagon lumbered over the stone bridge which traversed the small lake and between the two straight rows of ancient elms which towered above the long, cobbled front drive of Dynford Manor. The young earl, accompanied by Pringle and Nealy, hopped out even before the wagon pulled to a halt before the wide marble stairs which ascended to the double oaken doors.

"Almost!" Lord Dynford exclaimed when he saw his sister. "This time, I almost flew!"

"How very exciting, Richard," she responded without much enthusiasm. "No doubt, I shall be assailed with every detail." She glanced back at the wagon. Nealy and Pringle were removing a limp body from the wagon bed.

"Oh, Richard, not again." Lady Edwina looked up at her brother and sighed with dismay.

"Have him placed in the Green Bedchamber," Lord Dynford ordered Haskell.

Haskell opened the door wide to admit Pringle, Nealy and their burden. His face was an imperturbable mask of haughty disdain. He was quite accustomed to his master's unusual brand of house guest.

"Where did you find this one?" Lady Edwina asked.

"The poor fellow was lying unconscious in the woods below the folly," his lordship told her. "I found him when I fell through the trees practically directly on top of him."

Lady Edwina began to follow her brother into the house and up the long flight of stairs.

Lady Edwina shook her head. "Richard, you will never change," she chided her brother affectionately. "I remember, even as a young boy, you were always bringing home injured birds and stray puppies."

Lord Dynford grinned at his sister. "Can I help it if I have an exceptionally kind heart?"

Lady Edwina sighed. She could not scold her brother when what he said was entirely true.

"Nevertheless, Richard," she insisted. "As your elder sister . . ."

"Dear Winnie," he cajoled.

Lady Edwina wished he would not call her by that name.

It had been an acceptable nomenclature for an adoring older sister trailing solicitously through the nursery behind her toddling baby brother, but the name was now entirely unsuitable for persons of their age and station.

Nevertheless, her brother was all too aware that it still touched a soft spot in Lady Edwina's heart. He always used that name whenever he wished to convince her of the merits of one of his particularly harebrained schemes.

He reached out his hand and flipped one of her errant honey-colored curls back into place. "You are only three years older than I, yet you have always concerned yourself with Cecily's welfare and my own."

She looked up at him sternly, drawing her delicate brows closer together.

"Do not attempt to distract me, Richard," she warned, shaking a slim finger at him. "You know perfectly well that you and Cecily *need* looking after. Mama has been gone these past fifteen years and now that Papa is gone too, I feel it incumbent upon myself to advise my brother and sister in certain areas."

"For example . . . ?"

"These vagabonds you find wandering along the roadside," she told him, frowning all the harder. "Specifically, the last one. After you took the miserable fellow into our household and gave him a situation as a groom, he took himself off with not only one of our best horses, but with a good portion of the family silver as well!"

"No harm was done." Lord Dynford defended his actions. "The fellow was apprehended and the horse and silver returned."

Lady Edwina frowned even harder. "And your soft heart induced you to refuse to press charges. The blackguard went free to rob someone else!"

"But *this* poor fellow is different," Lord Dynford protested.

Lady Edwina shook her head. "I refuse to believe that any of these beggars would have the least scruple about burglarizing our home, or murdering us while we lay sleeping in our beds or . . . or who knows what else? I shudder to think! Richard, I really must insist, for our own safety, that you stop bringing in every vagrant you encounter!"

"But this poor fellow is truly injured!" Lord Dynford insisted. "I greatly fear for his life."

As they stopped before the door of the Green Bedchamber, he laid his hand on his sister's own delicate hand.

"As a member of the gentler sex, surely you can find it in your heart to assist this one poor, destitute human being. Can't you, Winnie?"

Lord Dynford bent his fair head closer to his sister's slim, oval face. When their identical blue eyes met, he grinned at her.

Lady Edwina tried hard to retain her censorious frown, but her brother detected a minute softening in her eyes.

"Very well," she conceded. "Let's see what pathetic scrap of humanity you have salvaged today."

Lady Edwina pursed her lips. She carefully regarded the mud-coated man sprawled across the fine linen sheets of the large bed. She raised a silent prayer of thanks that Pringle had at least had the good sense to pull back the priceless old bed coverings before depositing his untidy burden.

The stranger's face was so scratched and filthy that it was difficult to determine his age. Damp little strands of black hair clung to his high forehead. The nostrils of his slim, straight nose flared with each labored breath.

Lady Edwina turned to Pringle. "Would you be so good as to see that wretched uniform removed from him and searched for some sort of identification?"

"I had not noticed before, but these rags do still bear a vague resemblance to a uniform," Lord Dynford agreed.

"The briars did enough damage on the buttons and pipings," Lady Edwina said, gesturing disdainfully at the tattered cloth. "There appears to be a bit of red cuff that the water and sand has left."

"No indication of rank."

"You believe this fellow to have attained rank?" she asked scornfully.

" 'Tis difficult to tell much more about the man, though,

71

beyond the fact that he's one of ours."

Pringle's lip curled at the thought of giving the filthy clothing any more attention beyond a peremptory burning, but he knew he would obey Lady Edwina's instructions. Although he was his lordship's valet, Pringle, like all the other servants, was very much aware of who really ran the household.

"What sort of identification, m'lady?" Pringle asked, still intending to procrastinate as long as possible.

Lady Edwina raised her slim brows. "A letter, perhaps? Or a paper of discharge from the army, I suppose. What do such men carry? *Must* I think of everything?"

"Very good, m'lady," Pringle responded, with a clearly audible sigh. He hitched up his breeches as if he were hitching up his nerve at the same time. He bent over the unconscious figure and proceeded to his appointed task with the intention of getting it over with as quickly as possible.

"Pringle!" Lady Edwina stopped him. "Could you at least wait until I have left the room before undressing the fellow?"

"Oh!" Pringle quickly righted himself. "Very good, m'lady."

Lady Edwina turned to the footman. "Nealy, this person looks very much in need of a bath. Taking him to the stables and scrubbing him down seems out of the question in his condition. I suppose you will have to do it here."

Young Nealy's face had gone rather green but he, too, nodded his compliance.

Lady Edwina stopped by her own room.

Stokes was seated in the rose-colored chair, carefully examining the mending which Lady Edwina had so recently completed.

"Stokes," her ladyship began.

The young maid jumped to her feet, upsetting the sewing basket and sending spools of thread across the carpet. She immediately bent down and scrambled to gather them all together again.

"No need to startle so," Lady Edwina informed her. "I shall be needing the bandages we prepared earlier. Cotton wool dressing. My scissors."

Lady Edwina enumerated the articles which she wished

Stokes to prepare, although she harbored great doubts regarding the girl's ability to follow the instructions.

"I shall also be requiring your assistance in dressing the man's wounds."

An expression of mixed dismay and nausea spread over Stokes's face.

"I shall see to the poultice," Lady Edwina said as she turned to descend to the kitchen.

She found the housekeeper in the adjoining still room.

"Mrs. Haskell, I shall be needing the distillation of willow bark and several poultices to draw out infection," Lady Edwina instructed the housekeeper.

The thin, gray-haired little woman began rattling through the rows of small glass bottles lined up on the immaculate wooden shelves.

"Oh, dear. I can't seem to find it," Mrs. Haskell mumbled.

Lady Edwina herself began the search across the numerous bottles. "We would have no difficulty finding things if everyone returned objects to their proper position," she complained.

"Are you feeling poorly, m'lady?" Mrs. Haskell asked, stepping back to allow Lady Edwina to search unimpeded.

"No, not I . . ."

Mrs. Haskell's gray head nodded with understanding. "Another of his lordship's charity cases, I suppose."

"I'm afraid so, Mrs. Haskell," Lady Edwina answered. Then she added, "But this one does seem in a bit worse condition than the others. Ah, here it is!"

Lady Edwina lifted the small, pale green bottle and examined the meager contents. "We shall be needing more. Also, please request Cook to prepare a clear broth of chicken in the event that our patient regains consciousness. The fellow looks as if he hasn't eaten in days."

"Very good, m'lady," Mrs. Haskell responded.

When Lady Edwina reentered the bedchamber, the stranger had been stripped, washed, dressed in an old nightshirt of Lord Dynford's and tucked firmly under the covers.

His pale skin was stretched taut over his cheekbones, but it was easy now to see that he was a young man. His cheeks and forehead were scored with dozens of little red scratches, but Lady Edwina could easily discern that his features were much finer than those of the men her brother usually brought in from the roadside.

Lady Edwina reached out her hand and laid it gently upon the man's forehead.

"He's dreadfully feverish," she remarked. "I suspected as much from the flush to his cheeks. Yet there is a certain pallor . . . he must be in great pain as well."

"I don't doubt it, considering the nature of his wounds," Lord Dynford replied. "At first, I had thought him the victim of highwaymen."

"Desperate thieves they must have been, indeed, to attack this man," Lady Edwina told her brother. "To be sure, returning soldiers have no money."

Lord Dynford was about to continue when Pringle approached them. With only his thumb and forefinger, he gingerly held out the man's tattered jacket.

"Fine cloth and cut, m'lady," Pringle observed. "Could be an officer's coat."

Lady Edwina looked at the fellow in the bed and pursed her lips. "I highly doubt it is his by rights. Such articles of clothing can easily be obtained from the rag and bones man, can they not?"

"I suppose so, m'lady," Pringle answered, then quickly changed the subject. "I couldn't find no sort of identification, but there's money in the pockets."

Lady Edwina's brow creased into a deep frown.

"Money," she repeated.

"Four pounds six, and a few odd pence, m'lady."

Lady Edwina and Lord Dynford turned to each other.

"Rather odd, wouldn't you say?" she asked.

"Highwaymen would hardly go to all the trouble of assaulting a man and then not take his money," Lord Dynford replied.

"Not very likely," she agreed.

"While the men were seeing to him, I could not help but noticing—mind you, I'm no physician—but it seemed to me as if the man had been stabbed thrice!"

Controlling her initial alarm, Lady Edwina turned to Lord Dynford with only a slim eyebrow lifted in surprise.

"Devilishly lucky for him that his assailants were so inept that they only inflicted flesh wounds," Lord Dynford said.

"Indeed," Lady Edwina commented without emotion.

"I had begun to suspect as much, but now I am convinced that robbery was *not* the motive for the attack on this man. I believe someone was truly trying to kill him and was interrupted in the act."

"Nonsense!" Lady Edwina declared forcefully. "More than likely, he's a highwayman himself, injured when they had a falling out among themselves regarding the division of their booty."

"Four pounds six. Pathetic small booty," Lord Dynford said. "And what if he is a highwayman? Perhaps the nearly fatal results of this falling out with his cohorts will induce him to mend his dastardly ways."

Lady Edwina shook her head with exasperation. "Richard, you would hold out hopes for the redemption of Old Scratch himself."

Lord Dynford began to reply in his own defense, but when he realized that she was only being facetious, he threw his hands up in a gesture of mock surrender.

"I shan't argue with you further as I know from previous experience that it would be futile," he said, his blue eyes twinkling with mischief. "You were a headstrong young girl and you are becoming increasingly so as you approach middle age."

"Middle age! The very idea!" Lady Edwina drew herself up to her haughtiest five foot two. "Well, it is nearly time for dinner and you still need to tidy yourself up from your excursion."

"Yes, and it was splendid, Winnie. Absolutely splendid!"

Seeing that her brother was about to launch into one of his exceptionally long monologues regarding his favorite subject, Lady Edwina gently took his arm and began to lead him toward the door. Nealy and Pringle took this as their cue to be gone as well.

"Now, now. I shall be more than pleased to listen to every

word you have to say at dinner. Why don't you dress now?" she suggested. "It's very nearly time and you know what a snit Cook can work himself into when we're late. He is one of the few truly competent servants we have left from Father's staff. I surely would not want to lose him."

"You always say that about Cook, Winnie, but somehow, I have the impression that it is *you* who dislikes having her schedule disturbed," Lord Dynford accused.

"I?" she inquired, placing her hand over her bosom as if terribly affronted. "How can you say that when you know perfectly well that I never allow anything to disturb me?"

Lady Edwina continued to guide her brother toward the door with gentle pressure on his back.

"The man is fortunate that the bleeding has stopped by itself. Stokes and I will bandage him and dose him well with Mrs. Haskell's brew. Then I shall change and join you for dinner. *I* shall not be late."

Lady Edwina closed the door behind her brother's retreating figure. She frowned suspiciously at the man in the bed.

"You *shall* recuperate," she ordered the unconscious man. "I have no intention of having you die in *my* house. And when you have recuperated, I intend to see you on your way and good riddance! I'll not allow you to take advantage of my brother's generosity the way that other wretched fellow did."

Chapter Six

Lady Edwina dried her hands on the small Turkish towel which hung at the side of the Sheraton stand in the corner of the Green Bedchamber. She very carefully smoothed the wrinkles from the rumpled towel.

"Where *is* that girl?" she demanded, anxiously awaiting the appearance of Stokes. "If she moves any more slowly, she will begin to move backward!"

Mrs. Haskell had delivered the hot poultices a few minutes ago and Lady Edwina was concerned lest they should cool and lose all their efficacy before the maid should arrive with the bandages.

Lady Edwina paced impatiently up and down the bedchamber. Several insistent tugs at the bellpull had not served to effect the materialization of Stokes. At last she stepped resolutely to the bedchamber door and pulled it open.

The lady's maid was engaged in a leisurely conversation with Pringle, who was holding the tray which Stokes had been ordered to bring.

"Stokes!" Lady Edwina felt that one word should be sufficient.

The lady's maid and the valet turned to her ladyship, both faces flushing bright crimson. Pringle leaned closer to Stokes as he handed the tray to her and whispered something which Lady Edwina could not discern.

"Pringle, his lordship is dressing for dinner. I believe that he will have sufficient duties for you to attend to without your needing to come to Stokes for work," she said as dismissal.

Pringle turned and sauntered off down the hall in the direction of his lordship's rooms.

To Stokes, she said icily, "How long did you intend to keep

me waiting?"

"I'm sorry, m'lady," Stokes whined. "I didn't know. I mean, you never really were too specific regarding how long you wanted to wait."

Lady Edwina pursed her lips and returned to the bedchamber. Stokes followed immediately upon her heels and placed the tray she carried upon the small table at the bedside.

"Did you wash your hands?" she asked sternly.

"Of course, m'lady," Stokes declared. "I did everything just as you told me."

Lady Edwina was doubtful but, upon examining the tray which Stokes had brought in, she was surprised to find everything prepared precisely to her instructions.

"You didn't say, m'lady, whether you wanted me to send Nealy to town for the apothecary," Stokes said.

"The apothecary?" Lady Edwina repeated with a frown. "We shan't be needing him."

"But won't this one be wanting bleeding, m'lady?" She nodded toward the figure in the bed.

"Barbarous practice!" Lady Edwina exclaimed. "This man has lost enough blood. I certainly shan't allow any more to be taken from him."

"No, m'lady," Stokes replied, then mumbled, "They won't be getting past you, m'lady."

Lady Edwina reached out and gently pulled back the sheets to expose their patient. The nightshirt reached only to the man's knees, revealing two muscular, hairy calves and sinewy feet. Pringle had not bothered to fasten the neck opening of the nightshirt, leaving exposed a broad expanse of chest covered with curling wisps of dark hair which rose to the base of his throat.

"Oh, m'lady, should you be doing this?" Stokes asked, her thin little cheeks flushed deep crimson.

"I shan't tolerate missishness now, Stokes," Lady Edwina warned her maid sternly.

However, she, herself, felt a strangely unaccustomed warmth rising in her throat at the sight of the firmly corded muscles and the mat of dark hair that curled softly over the

78

man's chest. She swallowed hard.

"We must do what must be done," Lady Edwina pronounced bravely. "Duty first, you know, Stokes."

"Yes, m'lady," Stokes answered, then grumbled under her breath, "I've noticed that quite a bit about your ladyship."

If Lady Edwina overheard her maid, she gave no sign of it. She picked up the small pair of scissors from the tray which also held the bandages. With one deft movement, she slit the sleeve of the nightshirt up to the shoulder.

"When I have applied the poultice, be ready immediately with the cotton wool, then the linen strips," she told Stokes. "And for goodness sake, do not drop any of them. They *must* be clean."

Lady Edwina slid her slim fingers under his arm, enjoying, in spite of herself, the sensation of the warmth of his solid flesh in her hand.

"Now hold his arm up and do not jiggle it," Lady Edwina ordered. "This will undoubtedly cause him pain. And we must take great care not to reopen his wounds."

Lady Edwina was satisfied with the competence with which Stokes carried out her instructions. Yet despite the care they both took, the man began to moan as they wrapped the last of the linen strips about his upper arm.

"I . . . I suppose we must bandage his leg now, m'lady?" Stokes asked, displaying even more trepidation than she had upon beholding the injured arm.

Lady Edwina straightened herself after making a few final adjustments to the linen fastenings. She reached out her hand to lay it lightly on his forehead.

"He does not feel any warmer now than when we began," she said. "I believe we can safely proceed."

Using only her thumb and forefinger, Lady Edwina grasped the hem of her brother's old nightshirt and slowly slid it up the man's smooth thigh just enough to uncover the wound directly below his hip. Little curling strands of dark hair which escaped from under the edge of the garment began to tickle her fingertips. She quickly dropped the fabric and, trying to keep her hand from shaking, reached for the poultice which Stokes held out to her.

By the time Lady Edwina and Stokes had finished bandaging the leg wound, the man was deeply flushed and breathing heavily.

"He don't look none too well, m'lady," Stokes commented.

"Nevertheless, we must dose him before we can allow him to rest," Lady Edwina said, reaching for the small bottle and the silver teaspoon on the tray.

"Yes, m'lady," Stokes mumbled under her breath. "It's our duty to dose him, even if it kills him."

"Hold his mouth open, Stokes," Lady Edwina ordered.

"Oh, m'lady!" Stokes cried, horrified. "Must I actually *touch this* . . . ," she bestowed upon him a look of deepest revulsion, "this person?"

"Stokes, you bandaged this person," Lady Edwina reminded her.

"No, m'lady. *You* bandaged him. I only handed you the things."

"Come, Stokes. No faint hearts now."

"I don't want to touch him," Stokes began to whine. "A body don't know where he's been!"

Lady Edwina clucked her tongue. "Don't be such a ninny, Stokes. Do you think he will give you warts? He is merely a man, not a toad."

Stokes sighed, leaned over the bed and, with a look of resignation, pried his mouth open.

"I don't see what you've got against toads," Stokes mumbled. "Seems to me your ladyship would have figured out by now that toads, in general, are a good deal more trustworthy than some of the men Lord Dynford's brought in from the roadside."

Lady Edwina administered the required dosage. The man swallowed involuntarily and began to mumble.

"What is he saying, Stokes?"

"Can't rightly tell, m'lady," she answered, backing away from the bed. If Lady Edwina decided that she wanted to know what the man was saying, she might order Stokes to interpret the mumblings, and that might require her to get close to him again.

Suddenly, he cried out, "After them, men!"

Stokes, recovering from her startle that a man who looked so ill should be able to command such volume, asked, "Was he a soldier, m'lady? An officer?"

Lady Edwina pursed her lips and frowned. "I supposed him to be a soldier, but an officer? I highly doubt it. Such men seldom have the fiber of an officer. More than likely, the only men he commanded were his band of cutthroats."

He did not cry out again, but continued to moan softly. "Oh, Charlotte. Poor Charlotte. I am so sorry."

"Who's Charlotte?" Stokes asked.

"I am sure I do not know," Lady Edwina replied sharply. The question that intrigued her more was what he had done to the luckless Charlotte. For what misdeed did he beg her forgiveness?

Lady Edwina frowned at the man who had settled again into a fitful sleep. She was surprised to realize that, in her concentration upon the injured man's ravings, she had not put down the bottle of distillation of willow. Vexed that any man should have the ability to distract her from her intended course of action, she jammed the stopper into the mouth of the bottle and set it firmly on the small table beside the bed.

'Oh, you present a truly pathetic figure, whoever you may be,' she silently berated the unconscious man. 'But still I fear that you are no better than any of the other reprobates my foolish brother has tried so hard, and with so little success, to reform.'

Glancing at Stokes, Lady Edwina said firmly, "Stay with him until I return. I must dine with his lordship."

Stokes grimaced but made no reply. She regarded the unconscious man nervously. "Shouldn't I be helping you change for dinner, m' lady?" she suggested.

"No need, Stokes. I am quite accustomed to doing for myself," Lady Edwina said. "But this man is still in a fever and does need you. You must bathe his forehead with cool water occasionally."

"Oh, m'lady . . ." Stokes began to whine.

"None of that again," Lady Edwina said sternly. She pointed to the stand in the corner. "There is water in the pitcher and you may dampen an edge of the towel. When I return, you may retire for the night and I shall stay with him."

As Lady Edwina closed the door behind her, Stokes settled into a chair by the fireside, as far from the man in the bed as possible.

Lady Edwina changed quickly into a pale peach-colored silk gown with matching satin slippers. She loosened the tight knot in which she customarily arranged her hair and brushed her waist-length curls until they glistened in the light of the setting sun which shone through her bedchamber windows. She twisted her hair back into a thick chignon and tucked it in with two ivory combs.

As there was no one in the corridors, she allowed herself to dash down the wide staircase and through the Great Hall. She pulled up sharply before the doors of the drawing room and sedately entered.

Lord Dynford was standing alone before one of the long windows which opened onto a view of a vast expanse of velvety green lawn sloping gently past tall elms and down to a small lake. When he saw Lady Edwina, he quickly left the window to rush to her side, taking her arm.

"B'gads! What a triumph, Winnie!" he exclaimed. "I cannot begin to express . . . one can never fully comprehend . . . unless one actually experiences flight . . . and this time I came so close!" He shook his head again and sighed wistfully, "Almost."

"I know, my dear," she said wearily. "Just like you almost flew last week and the week before that, too. And you've hurt yourself again as well."

She reached up and gently dabbed her silk handkerchief at the small scratch on her brother's cheek, even though it had stopped bleeding long ago.

How she wished he would abandon these foolish dreams of flying! Deep within her breast, her heart wrenched each time she knew he was making another futile attempt. She had the horrible premonition that he would one day kill himself.

But he was twenty-three years of age. He was an earl. She was only his sister. There was very little she could do to stop him.

"I crashed through the trees," he admitted, somewhat abashed. Brushing his hand across the small scratch, he quickly added, "But it's just a flesh wound."

"You'll have a scar, no doubt," she warned sternly, hiding her regret that anything should mar her beloved brother's handsome face.

Lord Dynford flipped his chin to a rakish angle. "Ah, but think of the aura of devil-may-care panache that scar will impart to me in the eyes of the ladies."

Lady Edwina cast him a censorious look from under lowered brows and tried her best to hide a smile for her irrepressible brother.

"When the ladies discover that you are determined to fly, I am sure they will, quite wisely, have nothing to do with you," Lady Edwina replied tartly.

"And Pringle informed me that you've torn yet another shirt," she continued to scold. "I hope I shall be able to mend it. I just wish you weren't so careless. Heaven knows, clothing costs enough."

"Have we had a sudden reversal of fortune, that you are so frugal?" Lord Dynford asked, alarmed.

"There is no lack of funds," Lady Edwina reassured him. "Nevertheless, there is no reason to waste . . ."

Greatly relieved, Lord Dynford waved his arm out in a grandiose gesture, declaring, "No price is too high, no sacrifice is too great to achieve one of man's oldest dreams!"

"Honestly, Richard!" Lady Edwina scolded. "Between you with your head full of flight and Cecily with her head full of nothing, the responsibility for the welfare of this family falls entirely upon me."

"You really must stop worrying so, Winnie. At twenty-seven, you are already considered a spinster. If you continue to worry, you will develop gray hair and wrinkles and a huge, hairy wart on the end of your nose."

Lord Dynford reached out and playfully tapped her on the end of her nose.

83

"Then you will be an *ugly* spinster. We can't have that now, can we? B'gads! Then we shan't ever manage to get anyone to offer for you."

"I have not noted any great assets in those who *have* offered for me," she replied acidly.

"The men who have offered for you were all quite honorable men."

"Perhaps, by the calendar, they were men. But in their words and actions, they were all boys," she corrected. "Handsome, wealthy, and stupidly irresponsible boys!"

"You can hardly consider the Earl of Crompting a boy," Lord Dynford contradicted. "Surely, he would have made you an acceptable match. He is wealthy enough. And think of the position you might have held at Court," Lord Dynford reminded her, the mischievous twinkle returning to his blue eyes.

"You know perfectly well that his lordship is over seventy and no longer attends Court functions," Lady Edwina replied flatly.

"Then for the life of me, I shan't ever fathom why you continue to reject Lord Scythe. At least he is reasonably young."

"Forty, if a day," she proclaimed. "Lord Scythe also dotes upon half a dozen exceptionally disagreeable, extremely spoiled, not to mention extraordinarily unattractive children. His first wife presented them to him in rapid succession. The lady then had the good sense to depart this life. I have not yet decided whether the poor thing expired of exhaustion or due to sheer horror at what she and the viscount had perpetrated upon the world."

"I get the distinct impression that you don't like children, Winnie," Lord Dynford said in mock horror.

"Children are perfectly charming in their proper place, which, I might add, is as far from me as possible," she answered.

But she *did* like children, Lady Edwina admitted to herself—and to herself alone. Often she found herself daydreaming of a home of her own filled with handsome, lively children and a husband who truly loved her. How could she

84

admit to her brother that, with the responsibility for two siblings who had never bothered to grow up, she had no desire whatsoever to attach herself to another man who needed looking after like a child?

When she married, *if* she married, it would be to a man who was not only capable of taking care of himself, but who was strong enough to accept the responsibility of caring for her as well.

After a moment's reflection, Lady Edwina looked up and added, "I'm not so certain there's a man alive who I feel would truly suit me."

Lord Dynford laughed. "So say you."

"I have never yet met such a man."

"Mark my words, my girl," he predicted sagely, holding one finger aloft for dramatic emphasis. "One day you shall meet the man that does suit you, and then — B'gads! — Heaven help you both!"

Lady Edwina grimaced, but was prevented from replying by the entrance of Haskell to announce dinner.

They entered the Great Hall and continued past the main dining room, which was still in darkness. They entered the small private dining room which was used only by the family.

The furniture was older in this room, but still well-upholstered and highly polished. Lady Edwina saw to that. Just because a room was small, there was no reason that it should be neglected.

Lord Dynford took his seat at the head of the table. "I am so glad we are dining alone this evening," he told her as Haskell assisted her to be seated at the table. "After a day such as today, I don't think myself capable of remaining in a conscious state while Cecily and Aunt Portia dominate the conversation, chattering endlessly about absolutely nothing. And indeed, what a day it was! Marvelous, Winnie! Absolutely marvelous!" Lord Dynford exclaimed, throwing out his arms.

The enthusiastic gesture upset the bowl of clear chicken broth garnished with quenelles which Haskell had just ladled out from the Sevres tureen on the sideboard and was about to serve to his lordship. One quenelle went rolling across the carpet.

"So sorry, Haskell," Lord Dynford commented, watching it roll under the sideboard.

"I shall retrieve it later, m'lord," Haskell said. "The hounds shall feast tonight."

Lord Dynford returned to Lady Edwina to continue his account.

"Upon reassessing my information, I shall be able to improve the design of my apparatus. The chair is too heavy by half. A mesh of strong leather straps, affixed to the structure with brass instead of the heavier iron rings will give me more room to maneuver and will cushion any instability. I have also calculated, according to my own theory, which I consider far superior to any other I have ever encountered . . . at any rate, I have calculated that the angle of the wing in inverse proportion to the width of the wingspan, when multiplied by the velocity of the wind divided by the elevation of the trajectory angle, will enable me to achieve flight from . . ."

Lord Dynford stopped abruptly when he saw the look of blatant self-justification on his sister's face.

"I beg your pardon," she said haughtily. "Pray continue. I believe we were just discussing how we should enjoy an evening free from endless chattering."

Lord Dynford mimicked his sister by raising one eyebrow to the same angle. He peered down his nose at his sister. "A gentleman *never* chatters, my dear."

"Of course not, Richard," she replied. She did not look up from her soup for fear that her brother would see her laughing.

Somewhat abashed, Lord Dynford abandoned his account for another subject. "What news from London?" he asked as he dipped his silver spoon into the broth and fished about to capture the last quenelle.

"As usual, I am still trying to decipher Cecily's abominable handwriting."

"Then what does Aunt Portia report?"

"Aunt Portia's script is no better."

Lord Dynford laughed. "If ever there were two of one mind . . ."

"That is precisely the problem," Lady Edwina complained. "From all I have observed, one mind is all they have functioning between the two of them."

"Now, now. Aunt Portia was an excellent chaperone when you made your coming out. I heard her say so herself before they left."

"If by excellent you mean sitting with the rest of the chaperones at Almack's and eating as many of their wretched refreshments as possible while I was forced to endure the attentions of one tedious partner after the other, then Aunt Portia was truly excellent."

"Why, Winnie! I shudder to think what Father would say if he could hear you speak so of his little sister!"

Haskell replaced the empty soup plate with a steak of very pink salmon which his lordship attacked with a hearty appetite.

"I don't mean to be hard on her," Lady Edwina said. "She is a dear old lady. She is just not capable of restraining Cecily from committing the acts of pure mindlessness to which she is prone." She shook her head. "We should never have allowed the two of them to go off to London alone."

"*I* surely could not go!" Lord Dynford exclaimed, looking up from his salmon. "You know I am at a critical point in my experiments."

"Falling through the trees," Lady Edwina scoffed. "You are at the point of being critically injured."

"And you know I find the *ton* so boring, Winnie," Lord Dynford added. "I see no sense in wasting time drinking and gambling when I can be about my experiments, which would be of benefit to all mankind."

"Benefit mankind?" she asked skeptically. "I truly fail to see how sailing through the air will benefit all mankind."

"But *you* could have gone to London, Winnie. Aunt Portia and Cecily wanted you to go with them."

"You know very well, I have as little use for the *ton* as you. I have even less use for Cecily's and Aunt Portia's interminable shopping and gossiping. At any rate," she asked, looking up at him from over her half-eaten salmon, "if I had gone, who would be here to look after you?"

Lord Dynford smiled affectionately at his sister from across the table. Lady Edwina allowed herself the luxury of returning a small smile.

"Have you yet been able to decipher when they will be returning?" Lord Dynford asked, after which he finished off his salmon.

"As soon as Cecily has captured the heart of every eligible bachelor in London. At least, I believe that is the translation of the mysterious ink scratches she sent me today. Or perhaps the correct translation is 'When she has bought enough to enable each shop owner in Pall Mall to retire to Stratford.' "

Lord Dynford laughed heartily, then attacked the wafer-thin slices of rare roast beef with which Haskell presented him. With a sigh of relief, he said, "Then we can anticipate quite a few more weeks of peace and quiet."

"How delightful," Lady Edwina remarked sarcastically. "I know I shall certainly find quiet while you go crashing about through the treetops. And I shall certainly find peace while a total stranger recuperates upstairs."

Chapter Seven

Lady Edwina carefully laid her peach-colored silk gown on her bed and changed into a gown of plain, yellow muslin. She released her long hair from the neat twist and tied it back with a yellow, satin ribbon at the nape of her neck.

She knew that, although it was early summer, the night air in the country could turn extremely chill. Anticipating a long night's vigil, she took with her a warm cashmere shawl.

She returned to the Green Bedchamber, prepared to spend the night looking after the latest recipient of her brother's well-intentioned, albeit misplaced, charity.

Stokes still sat in a chair drawn up to the fireplace. Her head lay supported in her hand. She was fast asleep.

Standing close beside her, so as not to make any noise that would disturb the injured man's restless sleep, Lady Edwina whispered, "Stokes. Go to bed. I shall sit with him now."

Stokes awoke with a start. "Oh, I'm sorry, m'lady," the young girl exclaimed loudly. "I didn't mean to drop off like that . . ."

"Hush, Stokes," Lady Edwina ordered, holding a single finger before her lips. Glancing back over her shoulder at the man in the bed, she reassured her maid, "He is still sleeping. There is no harm done."

Stokes stood and stretched her long, thin arms and reached behind her to rub her aching neck and back.

"Oh, m'lady," she whined. "Sleeping in a chair is wretchedness itself. 'Tis nothing for a lady such as yourself to be doing."

"Then I suppose I shall just have to suffer, as I certainly have no intention of climbing into bed with our house guest," Lady Edwina stated.

"Oh, no, m'lady! Of course not," Stokes protested. She shot Lady Edwina a sly glance. "Never meant to imply such like, neither, m'lady."

"I am sure you didn't, Stokes. Now, off to bed with you." Lady Edwina chased her away with a wave of her hand.

Turning to go, Stokes pursed her lips and muttered to herself, "Can't imagine such a cold fish as your ladyship climbing into bed with anybody, anyways."

"Oh, Stokes, just a moment," Lady Edwina called to the girl as she reached the doorway.

Stokes, her face a bright pink, turned with a start. "Before you retire for the evening, would you be so good as to ask Mrs. Haskell if she thinks she will be needing me again or if she can continue to prepare the distillation of willow bark by herself. Also, ask her how much longer she believes the process will take."

"Yes, m'lady," Stokes answered slowly.

From the expression on her face, it was easy enough for Lady Edwina to see that the girl dreaded having to tackle the long dark corridors and steep flights of dark stairs at this late hour.

"Come now, Stokes," Lady Edwina chided her maid. "After stiffening in that chair, the exercise will be beneficial."

Lady Edwina instructed Cobb to build up the fire in the bedchamber and to move the large, comfortable chair which Stokes had occupied closer to the bed.

As Cobb closed the door behind him, Lady Edwina sighed wearily and her shoulders drooped. Alone for the first time this day, she could at last allow her stern veneer to drop just a bit.

Then she remembered the man in the bed. She raised her chin to its customarily haughty angle, which she believed made her appear taller and more imposing than she actually was.

She moved the sheet back only enough to uncover the man's arm and upper leg. She examined the bandages. They were still clean and dry.

She spoke aloud to herself. "There is no further bleeding and I see no evidence, as yet, of putrefaction."

She looked at the man in the bed and said to him, "My brother was right. You *are* a deucedly lucky fellow."

She covered him again with the sheet and heavy blanket. She reached up to feel his forehead. She frowned and pursed her lips.

"You are still feverish. Did Stokes not . . . ?"

She quickly crossed from the bed to the corner of the room. Her frown deepened as she felt the small Turkish towel. It was still dry.

"Blast that girl!" Lady Edwina swore under her breath. "I am surrounded by fools and incompetents!"

She draped the towel over her arm and picked up the bowl and pitcher.

"My brother is foolish enough to think that he can hire proper servants from inmates of workhouses and vagabonds he finds along the roadside," she murmured testily. "He *will* fly before he finds anyone competent that way."

Pushing the tray of bandages further back, she placed the bowl on the table beside the bed and poured a bit of cool water into it.

She used to be able to rely on Haskell, she thought with a weary sigh, but she believed that he now was rapidly approaching his dotage. Very soon, she feared, he would be of as much use to her as the others.

She dipped one corner of the towel into the cool water, wrung out the excess, and began to wipe it soothingly over the man's burning forehead.

"And everything is left for me to do," she sighed.

As she traced the contours of his face with the soft cloth, she felt her anger with Stokes ebbing, replaced by a feeling of tenderness within her breast.

"If we cannot get the fever to break, you may not be such a deucedly lucky follow after all," she told him.

Lady Edwina suddenly realized that she was talking aloud to an unconscious man. She released a little chuckle of amusement at the ridiculousness of her monologue.

"I should be greatly surprised to hear you reply," she told him. "I don't even know if you are able to hear me, but somehow, it makes it easier for me to give you proper care when I can talk to you. And I don't really suppose it much matters what I say to you, as I know you are in no position to repeat gossip."

She silently looked down at the man lying helpless in the bed. Beneath the skin, translucent with pain, his cheeks

91

flushed a deep crimson and his brow was hot with fever and dry as parchment.

Lady Edwina glanced from the little green bottle to the clock on the mantle and back again. She decided that it was time for another dosage. She held the bottle up before his fast-closed eyes.

"Now I must get some of this into you," she told him. "I expect your full cooperation."

She carefully leaned over the edge of the bed.

"Open wide," she ordered.

With one delicate finger, she touched his lips and opened his mouth. His lips felt hot and dry and cracked from the fever. His breath was warm as he exhaled on her hand. She released her hold on him to measure a small dose onto a silver teaspoon. As she began to administer the medication, he closed his mouth and the liquid dribbled down his chin.

She scowled at the unconscious man. "If we are going to get this medicine into you, you really must cooperate," she scolded.

With her silk handkerchief, she wiped the spilled liquid from his chin, brushing against the thick black stubble that covered his firm jaw. She could not explain why she gave in to the urge to stroke his rough chin once again with her bare fingers.

She had expected it to be coarse and prickly, yet it was surprisingly soft to her touch and the skin beneath was warm and smooth.

"Now . . ." She shook herself back to the task at hand and repeated, "Now, you really must take your medicine."

Leaning over him once again, she opened his mouth and began to pour in another dose. Her slippered feet slid across the thick carpet. She felt herself losing her balance as she tipped farther and farther over the bed. Hands full of spoon and medicine bottle, she was incapable of halting her rapid descent.

She landed, face first, on his chest. He exhaled sharply and moaned. The curly black hairs of his chest tickled her cheek and neck. She felt his chest rise and fall with each breath. She could even feel his heart beating.

Lady Edwina righted herself as quickly as she could manage, trying with only one hand to get a grip on the soft feather ticking of the mattress.

"Oh, I am so sorry," she apologized. "You do not need to be hurt any more."

But, much to her relief, the man lay still and breathed quietly and evenly. Then she noticed with dismay the splash of more wasted medication on the sheet.

Why, oh, why had she sent Stokes away? she asked herself with an exasperated sigh. No matter how inept the girl was, she could certainly have used her assistance now. And where was the girl, anyway? It should not be taking her this long to inquire of Mrs. Haskell.

'If I find she has been dillydallying when I needed her . . .' she thought angrily.

Lady Edwina found she was too concerned with the injured man to continue being angry with Stokes and she dismissed her lady's maid from her mind altogether.

She held the bottle up to the firelight, mentally dividing the remaining quantity into approximate dosages.

"You need this. It will do a great deal to relieve that fever." She frowned and told him sternly. "So we must stop this foolishness!"

After several moments of deliberation, Lady Edwina decided that there was only one logical course to follow. Lifting her skirt, she climbed into bed beside him.

She cradled his feverish head in her lap. Through her thin muslin skirt, she could feel his warm head pressing heavily against her leg.

She filled the teaspoon, then leaned over and placed the bottle on the table. She opened his mouth and poured in the required dosage with no trouble at all. He swallowed it again automatically. Lady Edwina was grateful that it did not provoke him into another outburst of feverish ravings.

She sat quietly with him, his head still in her lap. She gently brushed the strands of black hair one by one across his forehead.

He did not stir and she was glad of it.

"You truly do not look like the usual type which Richard is in the habit of bringing home," she mused aloud. "You are . . .

well, to own the truth, you are far too handsome."

Suddenly he moaned and opened his eyes. Lady Edwina was confronted by a pair of the most extraordinarily green eyes she had ever seen. They were glazed with fever and she felt sure that he did not see her.

"Oh, indeed, you *are* handsome," she whispered to him.

Gently, she began to stroke his brow. He closed his eyes again and breathed a deep, contented sigh.

"What could you have done," she asked him, "to make someone want to hurt you so badly?"

Lady Edwina looked down at the handsome face in her lap. She continued to stroke his forehead, gently pushing from side to side the dark strands of hair. As if compelled by a force beyond her control, Lady Edwina found her fingertips wandering from his forehead to stroke again the soft, black stubble on his cheek.

Merely inches from her hand, the broad chest with its softly curling hair lay exposed. How tempting to reach out and run her fingers across his chest . . .

"Oh, Edwina!" she chided herself. "What thoughts you have, you wicked, wicked woman!"

She felt her heart pounding in her throat as she gave in to the immediate temptation. She reached out timidly to his bare chest and gently twisted a small strand of dark hair about her finger.

It was soft, and the skin was warm beneath her touch. She flattened the palm of her hand to the firm muscles across his chest. His skin burned like fire, her own cheeks began to burn as well.

"Mrs. Haskell said . . . Oh!" Stokes cried as she pulled up short in her headlong entrance into the room. "Excuse *me*, m'lady," she said saucily.

Lady Edwina's hand quickly retreated. She scrambled to disentangle herself from her skirts, to rise from the comfort of the feather bed, and to replace her patient's head gently upon the pillow.

"Stokes!" Lady Edwina peered witheringly down her nose at her lady's maid. "How many times must I tell you — *always* knock *before* you enter *any* room!"

94

"Sorry, m'lady," Stokes replied, blushing profusely, but with an impertinent little twist to her lips. "I had no idea your ladyship would be . . . quite so *involved* with your work."

"Well, what have you to tell me regarding Mrs. Haskell and her brew?" Lady Edwina demanded, brusquely, brushing the wrinkles from her crumpled skirts.

"Mrs. Haskell said she'd have it by the morrow towards noon. She said she figured there should be enough left in the bottle to last the night."

Lady Edwina tightened her lips as she recalled the wasted spillage.

"Thank you. And good night, Stokes," she said quickly.

"You're certain you'll be all right here . . . alone . . . all night?" Stokes asked, pursing her lips.

"I shall be perfectly safe," Lady Edwina affirmed tartly.

Stokes's brown eyes were overly wide with innocence as she nodded her head in the direction of the bed and asked, "And him?"

"He will be . . ." Lady Edwina began, then stopped suddenly when she saw the impertinent little grin that twisted her maid's lips.

"Good night, Stokes," Lady Edwina said sternly.

"And you have a good night, too, m'lady," Stokes replied.

Chapter Eight

Drops of cool water fell on his face. At first Trent thought that it was raining again. Vague recollections of sodden days without shelter swam through his head. He dreaded having to endure yet another storm that would leave his limbs chilled and quaking, while the core of his body burned as much as before.

He tried to raise a hand to brush away the raindrops, but his arms were as heavy as lead and the movement made him wince in pain.

It was not rain, he realized as awareness gradually returned to him. It was a cool, damp cloth, drawn gently across his burning forehead by soft fingertips.

Trent gradually became aware that the ground beneath him was not rough and hard any longer, but was so soft that he seemed to be sinking into it. No, it was not earth, as he had at first supposed, but a fluffy pillow and a downy mattress.

He was no longer wearing his uniform either. And where were his boots?

Softness about him? No footwear? He was dead and laid out in his coffin and they had all simply forgotten to inform him of the event!

His eyes flew open with a start.

The sinister black shadows and the glowing red of some preternatural fire flickered before his eyes. For just a brief moment, he feared he had indeed died and had ended up in the nether world.

He forced his eyes to focus. With a feeling of great relief, he saw that he was in a bed with a canopy spread above him and that the quite ordinary flames were contained within a quite normal fireplace.

Bits and pieces of the memories of his escape from Haversham Hall and the murderous Nigel came quickly back to him, but there remained stretches of time of which he had absolutely no recall.

'A bed. Inside a house.' The thought crept up upon him, then seized him with alarm. 'Oh, no! Has Nigel succeeded in capturing me? Is he holding me captive, part of some diabolical plot known only to his deranged mind?'

As soon as he had formed the fearful thought, he realized that this could not be so. Had Nigel found him he would have wasted no time in dispatching his bothersome cousin and Trent would be dead indeed.

'If I am not at Haversham Hall, then where am I?' Trent asked himself.

Perhaps if he could manage a view of the room, or a glimpse of the person attached to the gentle fingers that had soothed his brow, he could determine where he was.

He rolled his head to one side against the soft pillow. Even this slight effort caused his head to throb with pain. His right arm and right leg ached, too. He closed his eyes and abandoned, for the present, any thought of discovering more about his surroundings.

In spite of his injuries, he was thankful that he was still whole and, best of all, that he was still alive!

He drifted into sleep again, the first restful sleep he had known in countless days.

Trent opened his eyes to bright daylight. His head no longer ached and he found he was better able to assess his immediate surroundings. The intricately embroidered bed curtains hanging about him were obviously very old but were kept in such good repair that they still appeared almost new.

He leaned his head to one side and looked about him. The rest of the furnishings of the room were also in excellent taste and obviously expensive. But they were not like any room he could ever recall having visited, and they were certainly unlike any of the rooms at Haversham Hall.

Trent was still wondering where he was when he saw the lady. She was standing beside his bed, pouring clear water from a small jasperware pitcher into the matching bowl. She poured very slowly, so as not to spill a drop, and when some of the water did splash out of the bowl onto the tray beneath, she wiped up the spill with the edge of a large Turkish towel just as soon as she had set the pitcher down.

'No doubt, the lady is exceptionally neat,' Trent thought with amusement.

She must be a lady, Trent told himself, for no serving maid ever looked like that! He watched as she raised her arms to pat back into place the soft, honey-colored wisps of hair that had escaped from the ribbon which held them in their appointed place. Then she smoothed her hands over the pale yellow skirt to straighten it.

Trent watched her as she turned about in the course of her activities. The thin muslin swirled against the curves and hollows of her body. She was as delicately boned as a young girl, but the softness of her flesh and the delightful roundness of her breasts and her bottom told Trent that she was definitely a woman.

She dipped another edge of the towel into the water and wrung out the excess. She turned to him just as he quickly pressed his eyes tightly shut again.

Her hand was soft and the damp towel was cool on his forehead. He raised his eyelids just enough so that he could covertly watch her through the fringes of his lashes.

"How are you feeling this morning?" she asked him gently in a soft, low voice.

He tensed. How could she have deduced that he was awake — and observing her?

But as she continued speaking to him without waiting for an answer, he realized that she was not aware that he had regained consciousness.

"Your fever has abated. Your wounds are healing," she stated quite emotionlessly. Then she shook her head and sighed. "There is no logical reason why you should remain unconscious."

She drew the damp cloth once again over his forehead and continued down his beard-roughened cheek. The water stung the hundreds of little scratches that he had not realized were there until now. But her touch was gentle, almost a caress.

98

Her finely drawn brows knit into a heavy frown. Trent thought that her vivid blue eyes appeared more tired and more worried than the eyes of any lady so lovely should ever look.

She exhaled a deep sigh. Trent felt his blood surge as he watched the twin mounds of her breasts move up and then down beneath the fabric of her bodice.

He struggled to suppress the smile which fought to expose itself so shamelessly upon his lips. With her as his nurse, he knew he would either recuperate rapidly or die trying.

She sighed again and said wistfully, "I wish you would recover."

The lady removed the cloth from his forehead. He continued to watch her from under lowered lids as she folded the towel into a neat little square and placed it precisely in the corner of the tray on the table beside his bed.

Once again, she turned to him. She reached out her empty hand this time. Her bare fingertips gently stroked his cheek down to his jawline. Then she disappeared from his line of vision.

'Who is she?' he cried in his thoughts. 'I am certain I do not know. If I had ever met *her*, I would surely remember!'

Trent was tired, but not so ill that he did not want to remedy immediately this woeful lack of knowledge.

He closed his eyes tightly and tossed his head from side to side, groaning softly. Peeking through his lashes, he noted with satisfaction that the lady was again approaching the bed. He opened his eyes wide.

While she had been frowning, he had not noticed the small dimple just above the left corner of her mouth. The dimple deepened as her soft, pink lips spread into a smile.

"Where am I?" he asked, but the words caught in his dry throat. "Where am I?" he tried to repeat, again with as little success.

Just as suddenly as the dimple had appeared, it disappeared. The lady's lips pressed into a firm, straight line.

"So, you have decided to return to the land of the living?" the lady asked sarcastically. She tilted her head slightly to the left, arching one eyebrow.

'It could hardly have been something he had said. Was it

something he had done?' Trent wondered, bewildered by this drastic change in his ministering angel. He shifted his aching arm. 'I do not feel as if I have been in a condition to do much of anything, let alone something obnoxious enough to deserve the lady's censure.'

At last, he managed to say, "Where am I?" He was surprised that his voice sounded so rasping and hoarse.

Without replying, she turned to the bedside table and poured a small amount of cool water from a Waterford decanter into a glass.

"Drink this," she ordered.

She reached out and slipped her arm under the back of his neck, helping him to rise just enough to sip the cool liquid.

Trent began to drink greedily, but she firmly pulled the glass from his lips.

"Enough. Enough," she said. Her voice was stern, but her touch was gentle as she eased him back down onto the soft pillow. "You've only taken a little water since yesterday. I would wager it had been several days since you've eaten anything solid."

Trent could not remember how long ago that fateful meal at Haversham Hall had been.

"Do you feel capable of taking some nourishment?"

He nodded eagerly.

"I shall have some warm broth brought to you," she informed him as she replaced the glass on the tray.

"Thank you," Trent answered in a more normal tone of voice. "I feel much improved already."

The lady only nodded as if it was quite natural that he should immediately comply with her plans.

"Can you please tell me where I am and whom I may thank for such gracious hospitality?" he asked her.

"You are at Dynford Manor, ancestral home of the Earl of Dynford," she answered.

Dynford Manor? Dynford Manor was down-river, and indeed, on the other side of the Thames, if memory served him correctly.

"How? How came I to this place?" he asked.

"His lordship found you on our property and brought you to our home."

"I have no recall . . ."

"You were wounded and delirious with fever," she informed him. Trent could not detect the barest trace of sympathy in her voice.

He nodded, yet it still seemed incredible that he had, apparently, managed to travel so far in his weakened condition.

He had never met the Earl of Dynford, but he seemed to recall hearing others speak of his lordship as an elderly man.

"The Earl is most kind," he answered. "Have I the honor of addressing his lordship's daughter?"

The lady gave a delicate little snort which, with a bit of imagination, could have passed for a laugh. "Hardly," she answered.

With a grin, Trent mused, 'If she is not his daughter, then his lordship is deucedly lucky to have such a lovely young wife to comfort him in his old age.'

The lady began to pull and pat at the heavy bedclothes, forcing them into order after the apparently restless night her patient had spent beneath them. Trent smiled to himself as he watched her. No bedcovering would dare remain unruly when confronted with this lady's strength of will!

Trent pictured her ladyship bullying a doddering old lord in much the same imperious manner as that with which she handled the bedclothes. Perhaps his lordship deserved Trent's pity more than his envy after all.

"Permit me to express my thanks to you as well, Lady Dynford," he ventured politely.

The lady straightened her back and lifted her chin, giving herself the illusion of greater height.

"I am *not* the Countess of Dynford," she corrected him. "I am his lordship's elder sister, Lady Edwina Danvers."

Trent pursed his lips to prevent himself from smiling. He was not certain if he wanted to smile because he had discovered that the lady was not someone's wife, or because she made such an effort to give the illusion of being hard as a loaf of day-old French bread. But he had eaten enough stale food during the War to know that even crusty, day-old bread can have a tender interior. There must be some tenderness somewhere inside the lady, else she would not have cared for him so well.

"Excuse me, my lady. I was under the impression that the Earl was rather advanced in years. Forgive me for saying so," he added, a playful smile spreading across his lips, "but you appear *remarkably* well-preserved to be his lordship's *elder* sister."

Lady Edwina turned away from him to adjust the bed curtains hanging at his feet. She replied in her customary, emotionless fashion, "You are obviously confusing the present earl with my father, who passed away two years ago."

"Oh, then I do beg your pardon," Trent answered, completely abandoning all jest. "May I extend my condolences, my lady, even at this late date?"

She nodded her head ever so slightly and answered, "Thank you." Her brows drew together thoughtfully as she was apparently considering him. "Were you acquainted with my father?"

"I, my lady?" Trent answered with surprise in his voice. He raised his left hand to point to himself and shook his head. "No. Not I."

Her ladyship nodded, then continued her line of inquiry. "May I ask, sir, to whom my brother and I are extending our hospitality?"

"Tre . . ." The sound had barely begun to escape from his lips when Trent realized that, considering the circumstances under which he had left Haversham Hall, it might be prudent to hide his true identity, at least until he could assess more fully his situation here.

He coughed to hide his hesitation.

"Would you care for another drink?" she asked.

Trent remembered the feel of the soft crook of her arm under his head. The corners of his mouth twitched upward. "Yes. Thank you, my lady," he answered, coughing again.

Trent found her ladyship's arms of much more comfort than the small sip of water he took.

She drew the glass from his lips as she had once before, but continued to cradle his head in the crook of her arm. Was he just being vain, or did she appear to be enjoying his closeness as much as he was enjoying hers?

How sweet her scent! Not the cloying, heavy smell of the perfume that certain "ladies" on the Continent employed, but the fragrance of a thousand newly opened blossoms in an English country meadow on a spring morning. Her very scent made him glad to be returned to England, and he drew in a great breath of her.

How comforting her soft arms! Trent nestled his head deeper into the shelter of her breasts.

She drew back quickly, letting Trent's head fall to the pillow with a thump. She raised her chin and looked down her nose at him haughtily.

"I will lay your impertinence to the fact that you are ill, sir, and thus are not fully aware of your actions," she said coldly, but he thought he detected a slight tremor in her icy voice.

"Do not judge me too harshly, my lady," Trent protested with a weak little grin. "No man is ever so ill that he cannot appreciate what comfort a woman can offer."

She turned from him quickly, but not before he had noted the blush that rose rampant up her smooth cheeks. Did he imagine it, or did her hand tremble slightly as she replaced on the tray the glass of water that she had still been holding?

Lady Edwina cleared her throat with a delicate little cough and prompted, "Pray, continue, sir."

Trent raised his eyebrows questioningly.

"You were about to tell me your name."

He gave another small cough. It still rankled that he must lie, so he answered slowly, "Trescott, my lady. James Trescott, at your service."

Lady Edwina responded with a slight inclination of her head. "Where are you from, Mr. Trescott?" she asked.

Greatly relieved that her ladyship had seemed to accept his false identity as the truth, Trent continued, "London, my lady." At least he could ease his conscience with the fact that, technically, this answer was not a lie.

"You do not speak like a Londoner, Mr. Trescott," Lady Edwina observed.

"I have traveled extensively, my lady," Trent said. "Perhaps that has affected my speech."

"Perhaps," she agreed grudgingly. "What brought you to Oxfordshire all the way from London?"

"I was paying a visit to friends, my lady." It was true that he was paying a visit, he conceded, although, considering what had transpired at Haversham Hall, he could hardly call them "friends."

"And what is your occupation, Mr. Trescott?"

"I am a soldier, my lady," Trent answered with complete honesty.

"What did you do before you were soldiering, Mr. Trescott?"

Trent tossed out his left hand in a noncommittal gesture. "Oh, a little of this, a bit of that," he replied with a smile.

"I supposed as much," she replied with a sour little twist to her lips. "And now that you are done soldiering—do you plan to continue doing a little of this, a bit of that?"

"Oh, no, my lady," Trent replied as solemnly as he possibly could. "Now that I have done with waging war, I intend to be doing a great deal of this—and quite a lot of that, as well," he added with a mischievous grin and a lift of one eyebrow.

He thought he briefly glimpsed a responsive smile. "And you know very well that you supposed that much, too, my lady," he added with a sly grin.

Instead of the complete smile that he had expected his clever quip to evoke from her ladyship, Lady Edwina's pretty little lips pressed firmly together and she quickly changed the topic of conversation.

"What misfortune befell you, to put you in such desperate straits?" she asked, ever so slightly moving her hand out to indicate his quite helpless position.

Trent attempted to think of something, besides coughing, which would delay her ladyship's inquisition, but his still befuddled brain refused to conjure up anything plausible.

Lady Edwina began tapping her foot impatiently against the carpet. She crossed her arms under her breasts, pushing closer together the cleavage which showed above the fashionably low-cut bodice.

Her ladyship could not possibly have any idea of how dashedly difficult she was making it for him to concoct a believable tale!

He placed his hand on his forehead. "Forgive me," he said. "Perhaps it is due to my injuries, but I sometimes have difficulty in remembering . . ."

"How convenient," she remarked, cocking her head and tapping her foot harder. By now, Trent knew for a certainty that this lady would not be content until she had received an answer which she considered satisfactory.

Trent closed his eyes and slipped his left hand down to cover them. "It is so difficult to concentrate with the pain . . ."

"I am sure a soldier such as yourself can rise above such difficulties," she said. Trent detected not an ounce of pity in her voice.

Trent's answers to all the other questions had been simple enough—a mixture of truth and slight exaggeration.

'How can I tell this little icicle even a small portion of my true predicament?' he pondered. 'This quite proper lady will feel it her bounden duty to notify the authorities immediately, will she not? And I shall be returned to my original dilemma—my word against Nigel's.'

"Mr. Trescott?" she asked, reminding him that he still owed her an answer.

Trent found himself remembering from somewhere in the back of his soldier's mind that the best defensive maneuver is often to attack.

"My lady, excuse me, I had thought you English," he exclaimed.

Taken by surprise, the demanding look left her face, to be replaced by a look of bewilderment.

"I . . . I *am* English," she stammered.

"Impossible," he protested. "For I see by your Inquisition of me that you cannot but be a Spaniard. Again, a thousand pardons."

He had hoped for a smile at his bit of playful teasing, but instead, a look of sarcasm came over the lady's lovely face.

"I am indeed English," she reassured him. "And while, *unfortunately,* we English gave up torture long ago, I think you will find us every bit as obstinate as any Spaniard."

Trent saw his hopes for distracting her disappearing like smoke up a chimney. He was sure the lady could be obstinate, indeed.

"Would you care to tell us of your mishap? Or shall I revive a quaint old custom and send a footman for the thumbscrews?" she asked. A tiny gleam of whimsy in her blue eyes gave Trent some hope after all.

"It was highwaymen, my lady," Trent ventured the most plausible explanation.

Lady Edwina showed no sign at all of either agreement or disagreement. She only replied, "And yet, when we found you, you had more than four pounds upon your person."

"Indeed," Trent inquired with a lift of his brows. "And were *you* the one who searched my person to find this money?"

Lady Edwina pressed her lips together. Her cheeks began to flush. She raised her chin and continued, "Your possession of such money would cause me to believe it unlikely that you were beset by highwaymen."

Trent recalled keeping a few pounds in a purse in his waistcoat pocket. He had believed that he would not immediately need greater quantities and had left the balance of his military pay safely within his trunk. With any luck, his trunk was still in his room at Haversham Hall. Unfortunately, his money was doing him precious little good there.

"My lady! Are you calling me a liar?" With a theatrical gesture, he placed his left hand to his breast. "Why, you cut me to the quick!" he declared.

"Not at all, sir," she answered him coolly. "I am simply cautioning you to tell your tale and tell it well. Do not make a liar of yourself."

The lady was clever. He wouldn't be able to deceive her with just any tale, Trent was forced to acknowledge with growing admiration.

"Well, I was indeed beset by highwaymen, but only by a few," he continued, deciding to retain the simplicity of his original story. "And I succeeded in driving them off."

"How courageous," she replied with a skeptical little twist of her lips.

With his left hand, Trent gestured at his injured arm and thigh. "My lady, you can see, my adventure entailed considerable damage to my own person."

"Could you identify the men who attacked you?" she asked.

"Unfortunately, I could not give you any details, my lady," Trent replied with a shake of his head. "Afterward, I wandered about, unknowing, delirious with fever . . ."

"Well, if you wish, I shall notify your family and friends of your mishap. Would you be so good as to give me their name and direction?"

Trent's green eyes flickered wide with alarm and his heart jerked within him. 'Undone at last!' he feared. But he quickly recovered his calm demeanor.

"That won't be necessary, my lady," he protested, trying to keep his tone of voice as normal as possible. "You have already been exceedingly kind to me. I would not want to inconvenience you further."

"I assure you, I would find it a small inconvenience."

"To own the truth, my lady, I have no remaining family, in London or elsewhere," Trent admitted sadly.

It was true. His mother had passed away years ago, his father only last year, and now Milton was also deceased. Trent refused to consider the traitorous Nigel a part of his family, regardless of what the family records might indicate.

"I am sorry to hear that," she answered with a more sympathetic tone of voice. "But, surely, your friends . . ."

"We were not what one could call truly close friends, my lady. And I am sure that my friends will not be expecting to hear from me again."

If there was one thing about which Trent was most emphatically certain, it was that Nigel would be exceedingly surprised to hear from him again.

"Nonsense, Mr. Trescott," her ladyship insisted. "If they are truly your friends, they will certainly wish to know of your misfortune and your residence with us, however temporary it may be. And I, personally, should be most relieved to know that you will be assured of accommodations upon your departure from Dynford Manor. Their names, please?"

Her persistence reminded him of a feisty little spaniel worrying a bone.

"My lady, I would gladly answer all your questions but . . ." He closed his eyes and breathed a heavy sigh. "I am still unwell, and weak from fever and hunger. Might I rest again for a while?"

Trent's eyes were still puffy and heavy-lidded. There remained a certain pallor to his skin.

"Very well," her ladyship conceded. "You may rest while I see to that plate of broth which I had promised to you."

107

Trent was not certain how long it had been since he had eaten, but now that he was no longer in a fever, he found that he was ravenous.

He heard Lady Edwina open and close the bedchamber door. When he looked again, her ladyship was gone.

Trent snuggled down into the soft feather pillows and contemplated his predicament.

'Wounded. A fugitive. Possessed of a fraudulent identity. Sheltered in a house of strangers,' he enumerated his woes. 'And what of Nigel? Does he think me dead or is he still seeking to kill me? And how am I to find him out and expose his treachery in my present condition?'

Trent stretched out his left hand and gingerly tapped at the bandage on his right leg. He winced and quickly left off his tapping.

'At the moment, I am in no condition to confront Nigel. Surely these people would not turn me out until I am recovered,' Trent reassured himself. A rueful little grin appeared on his lips as he thought, 'Then again, I am not so certain I can predict what the unfathomable Lady Edwina would do.'

If she discovered who he was and that he was sought for his brother's murder, surely she would summon the constable without hesitation. She was rather like a diamond, he thought. Beautiful, desirable, and cold and hard as rock.

She was his lordship's elder sister, he recalled her mentioning. A lady of her age and beauty should be wed. It must be her sharp little tongue and her snappish wit that warded off whatever suitors may have come. Trent had a great deal of difficulty in imagining any man refusing Lady Edwina otherwise. Her lips appeared so soft, her body so embraceable . . .

He summoned his thoughts back to his problems with Nigel. Perhaps at some later time, he would be able to contemplate her ladyship. At the moment, he had more pressing considerations.

'As I recall, there was a gamekeeper's cottage which overlooked Haversham Hall,' Trent carefully began to formulate a plan. 'My father had a new one built at a more convenient location and simply abandoned the old one. I am sure that Milton preferred other activities to ordering an old gamekeeper's cottage be demolished. I doubt that Nigel is even aware of the building's continued existence.'

As these thoughts ran through his head, Trent was so intent as to be hardly aware that he was gesturing with his left hand. He clenched his fist and pounded upon the mattress with decisiveness.

'I shall hide in the old cottage! I shall watch that wretched Nigel from a distance, night and day! I shall find a way in which to expose his guilt . . .'

Trent stopped his pounding.

"And prove my own innocence," he said aloud with a touch of wistfulness in his deep voice.

Chapter Nine

A plain little brown-haired maid carried in a small, short-legged tray. She warily placed the tray on Trent's lap, then quickly backed away.

"Her ladyship said you was to have this," the girl told him.

Trent peered down at the meager quantity of clear broth in the lone soup plate on the tray. It appeared as if an equal amount had been splashed out of the plate onto the tray.

"Are you quite certain that this is all that her ladyship requested for me?" he asked.

"Oh, I'm sure her ladyship'll give *you* more," the maid told him with a sly grin, then rapidly departed.

Trent shrugged his shoulders. He truly wished he could fill in those gaps in his memory. What had he done in his delirium that would make the maid so sure that Lady Edwina would give him preferential treatment? On the other hand, what had he done that would cause her ladyship to be so cold?

Trent shrugged again and automatically began to lift his right arm to reach for the silver spoon beside the soup plate. A sharp pain seared its way to his shoulder. He held his aching arm limply at his side and, after the pain had subsided, lifted the spoon awkwardly in his left hand.

He was clumsy and weak from lack of nourishment. It took considerable maneuvering to settle the spoon properly between his trembling fingers and to dip it into the broth.

It was difficult to bend his wrist to this unaccustomed angle in order to raise the spoon to his waiting lips. His clumsy fingers fumbled, the spoon flipped, and the contents dribbled down the open front of the nightshirt, trickling between the hairs of his chest.

"Blast! What a mess!" he exclaimed in exasperation as he dropped the spoon that had taken so much effort to raise. He scanned the tray for a serviette, but found none. He dabbed at the chicken broth droplets with his bare fingers.

The realization of the ridiculousness of his appearance made Trent chuckle, and his annoyance began to ebb. Resigned to his fate, Trent renewed his struggle with the recalcitrant spoon.

He had heard of people who were able to use both hands equally well. What a pity, he thought, that he was not one of them.

Trent's subsequent attempts to feed himself were no more successful than the first. When there was no more broth remaining in the soup plate, he found himself just as hungry as when he had begun, as well as a great deal messier.

The maid had never returned. Without the use of one arm and one leg, Trent was unable to push himself to a more erect position and was unable to reach the bellpull at the side of the bed. He would just have to wait until Lady Edwina returned — *if* she bothered to return to him.

The slight rattle of the porcelain doorknob woke Trent. The room filled with the spring-flowered scent of her perfume as she entered. He welcomed Lady Edwina with a broad smile.

She had changed into a blue gown which echoed the color of her eyes. She appeared less tired and less worried, but Trent would have preferred to see some emotion on that lovely face instead of the impassive mask she seemed habitually to wear.

She had rearranged her long, loose hair into a neat chignon at the back of her head.

'I'll wager she believes that coiffure makes her look exceedingly sensible,' Trent thought, grinning in spite of himself.

The image flashed into his mind: he was reaching up to unpin those unjustly imprisoned tresses. They tumbled shamelessly down in luxurious waves over her soft, smooth, and definitely bare shoulders. Reluctantly, Trent shook the picture from his brain.

Lady Edwina blinked when she saw the soupy mess which had spread down his chest. She tilted her head and the elusive dimple made a brief appearance. Trent could have sworn that she almost laughed aloud.

"Mr. Trescott! First you tell me you were beset by highwaymen," she exclaimed. "Now your meal has apparently attacked you!"

"Was ever a man so bedeviled by Fate, my lady?" Trent returned with a theatrical heavy sigh.

He had hoped to see her smile again, but she only asked, "Did something go amiss?"

"Why, of course not, my lady!" he exclaimed in forceful denial. "I have not enjoyed a meal in this fashion since I was, oh, perhaps two or three years old."

This time, Trent was gratified to watch her ladyship struggle to keep that lovely smile from her lips. But still he could not help but wonder what it could be that made her wish to hide her smile. He could readily see the lady was not missing any teeth. Whatever else could it be?

"I find that I cannot use my injured right arm and, while my left hand is adept at lifting solid food, I am finding it rather difficult to manage soup," Trent explained.

"You have fed yourself?" she demanded in surprise.

"I have since I was slightly more than one year old, my lady," Trent boasted with exaggerated pride. "I was an exceedingly precocious child."

"But Stokes was supposed to have fed you," she exclaimed. "Oh, that girl!" she began, frowning darkly. Then she pressed her lips tightly together as if to prevent herself from saying more.

She snatched the tray from his lap and, with rapid little steps, carried it to the door. She placed the tray outside in the hall. She grasped the knob and was about to close the door with a forceful slam, but suddenly checked herself. She closed it quietly and returned sedately to the man in the bed.

Trent was somehow not surprised to find that his ice maiden had quite an anomalously fiery temper. Nor did it surprise him to see that she kept her temper, as well as everything else about her, tightly under control.

She picked up the Turkish towel from its place on the tray and dipped it into the bowl of water. She began to dab at the yellow stains of chicken broth which spread down the front of the nightshirt.

She rinsed the edge of the towel in the water and turned to him again. After hesitating briefly, she began to dab at the exposed part of Trent's chest.

Trent had felt the warm broth trickle all the way down to his navel. He wondered if the intrepid Lady Edwina would dare to pursue the renegade chicken broth that far.

"I fear I am wearing more of the meal than I consumed," Trent grimaced as he lifted a portion of the soggy nightshirt which clung to his chest.

"Indeed, Mr. Trescott," she said, and her voice cracked. "It appears you have suffered more damage from your battle with your breakfast than I had at first supposed."

She rose and replaced the towel upon the tray in the same neat fashion.

"I shall send a footman in to bathe you," she told him, not daring to look at him.

"Thank you, my lady," Trent replied.

"I realize that you might not be accustomed to having this service performed for you," Lady Edwina continued, "but as you are incapacitated, perhaps you would not mind if he shaved you, as well."

Trent rubbed his bristly chin with his left hand. "I shall do my best to restrain my screams of terror when the fellow approaches my throat with a sharpened razor, my lady," Trent reassured her.

"When you have finished bathing, I shall have more broth brought to you," she told him.

"Not by this Stokes, I hope." He raised his index finger aloft and made the pronouncement, "Fine cuisine must always be eaten, never worn."

"Have no fear, Mr. Trescott," she reassured him. Her voice was cool, but he could see the laughter dancing in her blue eyes. "Regardless of who brings you your meal, this time, you shall be filled."

Trent patiently suffered through the clumsy ministrations of the young footman, whose name, he discovered, was Nealy. Exhausted, he was dozing again when Lady Edwina returned, followed reluctantly by the same maid.

Stokes wore a look of abject penitence. Trent chuckled to himself. He could just picture Lady Edwina's eyes flashing with blue fire as she scolded the impertinent Stokes.

The maid carried what appeared to be the same tray, laden with a portion identical to that before, except this time, all of it was in the soup plate. As Stokes gingerly placed the tray before Trent, he noted that the tray also held not one but two serviettes.

Stokes, cautiously eyeing her mistress, tugged at the large chair by the fireside until it was directly beside the bed.

Lady Edwina smoothed the back of her skirt before seating herself in the chair. She lifted one serviette from the tray, snapped it open with a quick flick of her wrist, then tucked it neatly under Trent's chin.

Trent watched the amusement dancing in the maid's brown eyes as she watched her mistress. She had pursed her lips as if to keep from saying something which was obviously on the very tip of her tongue.

Trent chuckled again. He estimated that the drastic change in Stokes's behavior from insubordination to subservience would be of a rather short duration.

"Is there anything else your ladyship'll be needing?" Stokes asked.

"That will be all for now, thank you," Lady Edwina replied, clipping her words.

Stokes exited hastily.

Lady Edwina leaned over and lifted the silver spoon from its place beside the soup plate.

"*You* are going to feed me, my lady?" Trent asked with a grin.

"That does not suit you?" she asked. Then she shrugged her slim shoulders. "You have your choice, of course, Mr. Trescott. Myself, Stokes, or Nealy. Or perhaps you feel so much improved that you would care to attempt to feed yourself again?"

She tilted her head to one side. It seemed to Trent that Lady Edwina always made that gesture whenever she asked a question to which she expected a whimsical reply.

'The lady is indeed possessed of a sense of humor,' Trent noted with satisfaction. 'But why would a lady this lovely ever attempt to hide it?'

Trent answered aloud, "I am quite satisfied with your exertions on my behalf, my lady. Quite satisfied," he stressed. He looked at her intently, attempting to fathom the blue depths of her eyes.

Lady Edwina sat absolutely still, returning his gaze, the silver spoon still poised in midair over the soup plate. It was as if some strange phenomenon had caused time to cease its never-ending onward rush.

Lady Edwina was the first to break their locked gaze. The silver spoon which she held tinkled gently against the edge of the plate as she dipped it in.

He watched the slender fingers as they wrapped gracefully about the silver spoon handle. He followed the curve of the honey-colored tendrils of hair as they curled about her tiny, pink ears. He watched the blue eyes, fringed with darkest brown, that solicitously watched his every mouthful, but not again did she dare to look directly into his eyes.

Trent was hungry, and he ate as quickly as Lady Edwina could refill the spoon. But he was as unused to being fed by someone as she was to feeding another. The broth trickled from the corner of his mouth down his chin.

Lady Edwina quickly picked up the second serviette and dabbed at the runaway broth with a soft and gentle touch.

Trent felt the brief urge to eat a bit less neatly just so that she would touch him again. He decided against doing so. After all, he certainly did not want this lovely lady to think he was some sort of half-wit, incapable of performing a task as simple as eating. Indeed—the thought rose unbidden into his consciousness—he would like to cause the beautiful, enigmatic lady to know that he was quite capable of performing a wide variety of activities.

"Might I have some more, please, my lady?" he asked when the soup plate was empty.

Lady Edwina looked at him and nodded. "A hearty appetite is a good sign that you are rapidly recovering."

Once again she lifted the soft, white serviette and dabbed at the corners of his mouth.

"I suggest you try to nap again while I see that more is brought to you," she said as she rose.

"More broth?"

"Did you not find it to your liking, sir?" she asked, her slender brows raised in injured pride. "I should think you would find even our modest fare an improvement over Army victuals."

"Your cook is excellent and the service, in particular, is superb," he told her, smiling into her eyes. "But I believe that I could use something a bit more substantial."

"Very well," she agreed, almost pleasantly. "While I attend to this matter, I suggest you avail yourself of the opportunity for an afternoon nap."

"Porridge," Trent pronounced flatly when Lady Edwina lifted the lid from the silver porringer on the tray which Stokes had just placed upon his lap. He was trying very hard not to allow his upper lip to curl in distaste.

"Porridge," Lady Edwina repeated emphatically.

"It's not precisely what I had in mind for dinner, my lady."

"You have been seriously ill, Mr. Trescott. We cannot allow you to eat anything which will result in dyspepsia."

He sighed heavily. Unfortunately, he was in no position to order his own meals and would simply have to be content with what was offered him.

"But porridge?"

She nodded condescendingly and replied, "I guarantee, it will be unlike any meal you have ever had since you were, oh, two or three years old."

Trent looked up at her. He could see it! The dimple just above the left corner of her mouth. And there was a warm, merry little gleam behind her icy blue eyes. He held her eyes with his and smiled.

Inexplicably, she closed herself off from him again. More puzzled than ever, Trent was determined to draw out this mysterious lady.

"Porridge," he said with finality, and cursed himself for not being able to devise a more clever phrasing to maintain the lady's interest.

"You did ask for something a bit more substantial," she reminded him.

"Yes. It is substantial, if nothing else, my lady," he conceded. "Perhaps not as substantial as eggs, or chops, or toast with marmalade, or . . ."

116

"Patience, Mr. Trescott," Lady Edwina admonished, reaching out to pat his shoulder consolingly. "All good things come to him who waits."

Trent looked up into her ladyship's expressionless blue eyes. "Do you know that for a certainty, my lady?" he asked. "What do you await? And are you managing to do so with patience?"

Her blue eyes seemed to cloud over and she hesitated.

Trent sadly watched her eyes grow sharp and hard again.

"What I await is my own concern, Mr. Trescott," she answered coldly. "And I do so with more patience than you would ever credit."

"Alas, my lady, if *I* could but have your certainty . . ."

Lady Edwina closed the door behind her and leaned against it with mixed feelings of exhaustion and relief.

She had nursed ill and injured people before. It was, indeed, demanding work seeing to the renewed health of another. But never had she recalled it being so positively draining! And not merely physically, but emotionally, as well.

Mr. James Trescott was a handsome man, she was forced to own.

'He is also a devilishly clever man,' she thought with a nagging suspicion. 'And who knows what he is? A highwayman? A murderer? Or just an unfortunate soldier, fallen upon hard times?'

Lady Edwina straightened herself.

'It does not signify, at any rate,' she told herself, shaking her head. 'I have quite enough to worry about without this man adding to my problems. And in a few days, he will be gone from here and my life restored to its normal order.'

She began to walk down the corridor toward her own rooms to prepare for dinner with her brother. She would have preferred to take a cold collation in the peace and quiet of her small sitting room, then spend the rest of the evening reading. Instead she would be forced to listen to Richard prattle about the latest developments in the rebuilding of his infernal air machine.

The reading material she found waiting for her after dinner

117

was not the sort she would have chosen if she had been able. Another letter from Lady Cecily had been delivered with the morning post, which Lady Edwina had not had the opportunity all day to read.

'Quite unlike Cecily to write again so soon,' Lady Edwina thought, then realized that her sister's previous letter was over three weeks old when she had received it.

'Cecily's posting habits are as erratic as her mental processes,' Lady Edwina observed as she broke the rather haphazardly applied wafer.

She squinted and drew the candle closer to the edge of the table. The increased illumination did nothing in the least toward rendering Lady Cecily's handwriting more legible.

My *dearest* sister,

To think I should have feared that being asked to leave stodgy old Almack's that evening could have interfered with *my* popularity — as if *anything* could — for I am quite universally liked, if I do say so myself! At any rate, the very next day, I apologized so *prettily* to each & every patroness — yes, even that *horridly* rude Sally Jersey, if one could call her a lady — that they could scarcely find it in their hearts *not* to forgive such an *abjectly penitent* sinner such as I!

And the following day, Aunt Portia & I were to Mrs. Williamson's musicale, which was *quite* stylish as she has recently redecorated her music room, & I was asked to sing a bit for them, which I was well pleased to do as I do consider myself a quite *excellent* singer, if I do say so myself, *much* better by far than the weak-throated ladies one *usually* encounters at such affairs, & absolutely *everyone* complimented me quite shamelessly after the performance.

The next evening, Aunt Portia & I attended the Countess of Thinnes's at-home, which was *ever so* entertaining, & the Dowager Duchess of Montevain, who is such an *old dear* & was there as well, invited us to a little soiree she has planned for Tuesday next, which I understand is to be a *dreadfully* smart affair which it is rumored even Prinnie may attend! How *marvelous!* I cannot tell you how *eagerly* I anticipate this soiree! . . .

The driver drew the elegant Dynford carriage to a stop directly in front of the Grosvenor Square townhouse of the Dowager Duchess of Montevain.

A delicate ivory kid glove extended itself from the door which the footman had hastened to open. With the footman's assistance, Lady Cecily gracefully emerged from the carriage, all ivory kid and pale blue silk. Lady Portia, a little shadow of gray brocade, succeeded her out of the carriage.

"Oh, do wait, Cecily," Lady Portia cried after her niece as the girl fairly flew up the short flight of marble steps to the front door.

"Oh, do *hurry,* Aunt Portia! We are late enough as it is." Lady Cecily heaved an exasperated sigh and bounced up and down impatiently from one foot to the other. She fidgeted with her fan, and then her shawl, and then her reticule while she waited for her elderly aunt to alight from the carriage, smooth her skirt and wrap, and catch up to her on the sidewalk.

"*I* was ready hours ago, my dear," Lady Portia reminded her niece with an injured little sniff.

"Well, I should have been ready, too, if I could have but found my blue reticule."

"You are forever misplacing your reticules," her aunt told her.

"It was quite understandable tonight, Aunt Portia," Lady Cecily pouted, twisting the string handle of her reticule until the little silken pouch circled round and round, then back again. "I vow, I have been in *such* a dither anticipating tonight! Suppose Prinnie should arrive? Why, 'twould just *make* Lady Montevain's evening!"

"Indeed, it would," Lady Portia agreed. "Not to mention *yours.*"

They ascended the short flight of steps and the haughty butler condescended to allow them to enter.

The foyer was quite a crush. Lady Cecily found she had to seize Lady Portia's hand, tuck it into the crook of her arm to keep her close, and pull her along behind her in order not to lose her in the mob.

"Oh, I do wish I did not have to drag you to these things!"

Lady Cecily mumbled, half concerned for her aging aunt's welfare, yet equally aggravated by her own inconvenience.

"So do I," Lady Portia whined pitifully. "How I hate these crushes."

Lady Cecily patted her aunt's hand comfortingly, all the while relentlessly dragging the old lady on behind her.

The crowd seemed to thin out just a bit at the door to the salon.

"I shall find you a comfortable chair near the window and a large plate of something delicious," Lady Cecily promised as she dragged her aunt onward.

"Wasn't that an empty chair?" Lady Portia asked as she was drawn rapidly past such.

"Your eyesight is going, poor old dear. It only appeared to be an empty chair," Lady Cecily responded. She was heading with fixed intent upon the far end of the salon, where a large group of people were congregated.

'It must indeed be Prinnie,' Lady Cecily supposed. 'I can think of no one else invited who would be capable of drawing such a crowd.'

There was one lone vacant chair near a window. Lady Cecily propelled her aunt quickly toward it. With grateful exhaustion, Lady Portia collapsed into the green cotton-velvet *bergère*.

"I shall return in an instant," Lady Cecily promised again, with as little intention of keeping this promise as any other one she had ever made.

She headed toward the edges of the congregation of people. Being of rather short stature, she found it exceedingly difficult to look over the tall, wide shoulders of the gentlemen and some of the matrons, who were every bit as wide.

"Jane! Oh, Jane, my dear!" Lady Cecily hallooed, raising her hand high and waving with her handkerchief when she spied her friend at the opposite end of the encircling crowd.

Heedless of whose instep she decimated, Lady Cecily made her way to where Miss Sheftley was standing.

"I cannot see through this crush," Lady Cecily complained to her friend. "Who is drawing such a crowd? Is it Prinnie himself?"

Miss Sheftley gave Lady Cecily a smug little grin. "Ah, yes. You have missed all the excitement. Serves you quite right for being so tardy."

"Oh, Jane, don't be cross," Lady Cecily coaxed beguilingly. "I truly did not mean to spill the claret punch on your white gown last night while you were conversing with that charming Lord Upshire. Truly I didn't!"

Miss Sheftley only replied with a withering glance.

Receiving no reply from her highly piqued friend, Lady Cecily merely shrugged her shoulders. "La! If you will not satisfy my curiosity, Jane, then I shall go elsewhere."

Miss Sheftley heaved a petulant sigh. "Oh, very well, then. No, it is not Prinnie. Even better."

"What could be better?" Lady Cecily demanded skeptically.

"Lord Haverslea!" Miss Sheftley gushed. Her beady little brown eyes had grown quite wide, her speckled skin quite pink with excitement.

"Oh, pooh!" Lady Cecily pouted. "I hear he's a rather unpleasant old fellow who is ever at odds with his wife, his tenants, even his very own brother."

"Then I am sure you would not wish to make his acquaintance," Miss Sheftley said, her eyes gleaming maliciously.

Lady Cecily flicked her fan open and looked haughtily over the top of it. "I should say not!" she pronounced emphatically.

"A pity," her friend replied with a snickering little laugh. "As his lordship has been asking for you."

Lady Cecily's fan halted, poised in midair. Her eyebrows flew upward and her blue eyes widened in surprise.

Just as quickly, she regained her composure and languidly began to fan herself again.

Well, certainly his lordship would want to make her acquaintance! After all, she was known to be a beauty, an heiress, and exceptionally well-connected. Mr. Haversham was quite taken with her and, doubtless, had informed his cousin. Why, she should not be surprised in the least if, as head of the family, his lordship had come to assess her suitability as a match for Mr. Haversham.

Lady Cecily patted her blonde tresses to assure their proper arrangement and smoothed her silken skirt. Well, she certainly would not disappoint him!

"Asking for *me?*" Lady Cecily demanded with wide-eyed innocence. "Why should he be asking for *me?*"

Miss Sheftley snickered. "Why, indeed?"

"Well, it would be exceedingly impolite to keep his lordship waiting any longer. Oh, do be a dear and get a little something for Aunt Portia over there," Lady Cecily finished as she abandoned Miss Sheftley.

She threaded her way through the crowd, again heedless of the crushed toes and elbowed ribs of others, yet all the while uttering, "Oh, pray, excuse me!" so prettily that she was quite certain that they would all forgive her just as readily as Miss Jane Sheftley had.

She searched ahead of her.

'Why, oh, why *does* the Baron have to be a man of mere average height so that I cannot see him above the crowd?' she lamented.

As she slowly made her way closer through the crowd, she noted that his hair was every bit as black as Mr. Haversham's. 'Indeed, I would have thought a man of the Baron's years to be much more gray-haired. There must be a strong family resemblance there,' she decided. 'I fancy I shall have a dozen little black-haired, green-eyed babies.'

At last she could see him clearly.

'Oh, that wretched Jane has got even with me!' she pouted silently and stamped her foot. 'It is only Mr. Haversham and not the Baron at all!' Then her face brightened as she reconsidered, 'Oh, well I *am* pleased to see him, too.' And she edged further forward so that he should see her.

"Leaping across the table, he plunged the jeweled dagger deep into his helpless brother's breast!" Nigel exclaimed, his fist stabbing the empty air.

The ladies waved their fans. The young lady to her right swooned against the gentleman at her side.

"Suddenly he turned upon me, knife in hand!" Nigel cried, whirling in the opposite direction and raising his own empty hand high above his head as if brandishing a deadly weapon. "In the flickering candlelight, his visage was contorted into a grotesque mask of rage! His eyes gleamed blood red, lit from within by the fires of madness and fueled with the kindling of hatred!"

The ladies fluttered their fans. "Why, it is every bit as exciting as a gothic!" gushed the plump little lady at Lady Cecily's side.

She placed her hand upon her ample bosom and swooned quite deliberately into the arms of the gentleman accompanying her.

"Valiantly, I deflected his blows! He drove me from the dining room!" Nigel, arms crossed before him protectively, backed up a step to indicate his retreat. The crowd murmured, "Ooooh!"

"He drove me from the Hall!" Nigel took yet another step back. The crowd repeated, "Oooh!"

"Out onto the wild moors, his madness propelled him, driving me before it like chaff in the whirlwind!" Nigel continued, stretching his arm, palm out, to indicate the expansive wasteland. "His madness imparted unto him an unholy power that rendered even my strength as nothing."

Nigel's voice dropped to a husky whisper that, nevertheless, could be heard to the edges of the crowd.

"But in his madness were the seeds of his own undoing, for he saw not the craggy precipice before him," Nigel recounted, raising his hand to indicate the heights. "And he knew not even the very moment of his own, hideous death as he plunged into the water far below!" His raised hand plunged dramatically to point to the floor.

Nigel finished his account by dropping his chin upon his chest, as if exhausted by the very recounting of the lurid tale.

Just when Lady Cecily thought his tale was done, Nigel began to shake his head slowly from side to side and raised his hand to his heart.

"I can bear him no ill will, as his madness rendered him truly incapable of comprehending his own foul deeds. My deepest regret is that I was unable to retrieve his body from the river to bring him home for Christian burial."

The crowd murmured, "Aaah!" and stood perfectly transfixed.

Nigel's head remained bowed. Sensing that his tale was told and that no more was to be got from him, the crowd began to filter away to other sources of amusement. Only Lady Cecily remained.

Nigel raised his head.

"My dear Lady Cecily!" he exclaimed, stretching out his hand to her. "How wonderful to see you again! I have been inquiring after you all evening. Lady Montevain told me you were invited,

123

but you were so late that I feared that some untoward occurrence had prevented you from attending."

She gazed up at him with adoring, blue eyes. "I should *never* have been so late if I had known *you* were returned to London. And I have missed your stirring performance! Pray, where did you learn such a lurid tale and how to perform it to perfection? I marvel that you do not go on the stage, sir."

Nigel tucked Lady Cecily's hand into the crook of his arm. "Come stroll with me in the garden, my dear Lady Cecily."

Lady Cecily smiled her most charmingly. "How pleasant," she replied.

He observed a new crowd gathering, threatening to engulf him.

"I find that I am greatly in need of some fresh air at this moment," he informed his would-be audience, and began to lead Lady Cecily away.

Once in the cool shadows of the Montevain garden, Nigel said, " 'Twas no tale, Lady Cecily. Do you recall my telling you that my cousin and his brother were exceedingly antagonistic toward each other?"

Lady Cecily nodded, wide-eyed and silent.

"The very day of his return safe to us from the war, my cousin Trent ran mad and murdered his brother."

Lady Cecily gasped and fluttered her fan. "How *horrid* for your family!" she cried sympathetically.

"He attempted to murder me, too, but I managed to elude him," Nigel continued.

"By your superior wit, no doubt," she pronounced, smiling up at him with undisguised admiration.

Nigel returned her smile.

"Oh, I am *ever* so glad you are safe!"

"Not only am I safe, Lady Cecily," he informed her. "I am also now Lord Haverslea."

"No!" she breathed, opening her eyes wide with surprise. Then her pretty pink lips spread in a very pleased smile. "You have no idea how exceedingly happy I am for you."

"Oh, I think I have *some* idea."

Chapter Ten

"He most surely can tuck into a plate of victuals, m'lady," Stokes muttered as she passed Lady Edwina in the doorway of the Green Bedchamber. This was the third plate of creamed kidneys on toast points which Stokes had served to Trent this morning. He had also devoured two peaches from the conservatory and an entire pot of tea.

"While Mr. Trescott is recovering, he may have as much as he pleases," Lady Edwina told her maid. As she intended to turn the fellow out as soon as he recovered, she saw no need not to treat him well while he remained.

"Very good, m'lady," Stokes mumbled as she exited.

Lady Edwina smiled with satisfaction. This morning her patient was much improved. It would not be long before he was out of that bed, out of this house, and out of her life altogether.

The image of the back of James Trescott receding into the distance away from Dynford Manor brought a sudden shiver to Lady Edwina's shoulders.

Why should the fact that she would never again see those strong shoulders or those emerald eyes, never again hear his contagious laughter, cause such a wrenching within her breast? Oh, to be sure, he was a witty and clever conversationalist and a delight to look upon, but those characteristics were no reason to have such strong feelings regarding the man's imminent departure.

Lady Edwina busied herself with rearranging the items on the table beside his bed and pushed the unwelcomed regrets far from her mind.

"More tea, Mr. Trescott?" she inquired, lifting the silver teapot by its teakwood handle.

"Thank you, but no, my lady," Trent replied, sighing with

125

deep contentment and patting his stomach. "At last I am able to eat something more substantial than broth and porridge. Alas! The excellent fare of Dynford Manor has been my undoing."

He leisurely stretched out his left arm and shrugged his shoulder muscles.

"I am longing to get out of bed and out of doors for some badly needed exercise," Trent said.

"Have no fear, Mr. Trescott," Lady Edwina told him. "Very soon, you shall be up—and out."

In spite of herself, she felt admiration and a strange sense of longing at the sight of Trent's muscles rippling beneath the fine lawn of the nightshirt as he flexed his broad shoulders.

'Yes,' Lady Edwina decided as she turned deliberately away from the man in the bed, 'the sooner James Trescott is gone from here, the better.'

"Good morning!" Lady Edwina allowed herself a small smile of greeting as she heard her brother's cheery voice as he crossed the threshold.

His lordship's face brightened even more when he saw Trent propped upright against several pillows in the large bed.

"Ah, Mr. Trescott, at last we meet face to face!"

"Forgive me for not rising, my lord," Trent said.

Trent swept his left arm out in a wide circle in an effort to make a fine leg while still sitting in bed. Lady Edwina gasped and held her breath as she watched her fine silver and delicate china in imminent peril of being dashed to the floor.

Yet he completed the elegant gesture quite skillfully. Slowly she allowed herself to breathe again.

Then the thought occurred to her: how could a mere vagabond execute the bow with such competence? And why would he choose to bow? Would he not merely tug his forelock for the earl? Indeed, there was more to James Trescott than met the eye.

"We shan't compel you to stand at Dynford Manor, Mr. Trescott, not even on formality," his lordship replied with a jovial laugh. "Please accept my apologies for not welcoming you sooner to our home, but each time I came to inquire as to your welfare, you were napping. I trust that my sister has made you comfortable."

"Her ladyship has been hospitality itself," Trent said. "I am

126

truly grateful, my lord. Hedgerows make abysmal sleeping quarters."

His lordship indicated the empty plate on the tray. "My sister informs me that you are eating quite heartily. I am glad. I much prefer feeding you to burying you."

"We are in complete agreement on that point, my lord."

Lord Dynford seated himself in the chair beside the bed. He leaned back and crossed his legs in front of him.

"My sister also tells me that you were here from London to visit friends and were set upon by highwaymen after leaving their home. She also tells me that, among other occupations, you have been a soldier."

Trent chuckled. "Did her ladyship also inform you that all of my activities have been legal, my lord?" Although he spoke to her brother, Trent was smiling up at her, a mischievous grin lighting up his green eyes.

Lady Edwina turned from Trent. She could not allow herself to return that smile. In a few more days, he would be gone. And in those few remaining days, she must be certain to maintain between them a distance commensurate with their respective stations in life.

"To be sure, sir!" Lord Dynford responded with a laugh.

"I have no doubt that we should have won the war much more quickly if her ladyship had been set to gathering secret information for us about those Frenchies."

"And what secrets might one gather about *you*, Mr. Trescott?" Lady Edwina inquired.

"I?" Trent returned. "Why, I have no secrets from my friends, my lady."

"Well, you may certainly consider yourself among friends now, Mr. Trescott," Lord Dynford assured him.

Her brother had reassured the man too quickly, Lady Edwina thought. She, herself, would have liked to pursue the matter by asking Mr. Trescott what secrets he had to keep from those whom he did not consider his friends. She also wondered what criteria he used to discern his friends from his enemies.

Lord Dynford paused only a moment, then said, "So, Mr. Trescott, have you any immediate plans?"

Lady Edwina's ears prickled and she had a sudden sinking

feeling in the pit of her stomach. It was a feeling she had experienced before, presaging that no good could come from the turn her brother had abruptly given to this conversation.

"I am intensely interested in leaving this bed, my lord," Trent replied.

"And that you shall, Mr. Trescott!" the young lord assured him enthusiastically. "And when you have succeeded in accomplishing that, will you be returning to London?"

Trent shook his head. "I have no plans to do so, my lord."

Lord Dynford firmly planted both hands on his knees and leaned forward. "Well, Mr. Trescott, I am not a man to mince words. If you have no better prospects, and to be quite candid, I sincerely doubt that you do, we would be pleased to have you join our household staff."

Lady Edwina could feel her eyes widening with indignation and an angry flush rising up her cheeks. How could her brother be so foolishly trusting? It required every bit of self-control which she possessed to refrain from firmly boxing her younger brother's ears.

She moved her hand to rest on her brother's shoulder instead. The fine cloth of Lord Dynford's jacket wrinkled as her fingers tightened on his shoulder.

"We are ever in need of a competent footman," Lord Dynford continued, oblivious to her silent rebuke.

"A footman, eh?" Trent repeated.

"My lord, perhaps Mr. Trescott is not suited to a footman's work," Lady Edwina told her brother through tightening lips. "Perhaps he would be more comfortable working as a groom — out of doors — out of the house," she stressed.

Trent rubbed his roughened chin. "I thought I had sustained sufficient damages in my struggle against my attackers. However, after having suffered through Nealy's attentions, I certainly believe that what you say regarding your footmen is so. I believe I shall be most pleased to serve as one of your footmen, my lord."

"Have you ever held such a position before, Mr. Trescott?" Lady Edwina demanded.

"No, my lady," Trent answered. "I cannot say that I have."

"How strange," she commented. "In your life of 'a little of this and a bit of that,' you have never been a footman."

"No one has ever requested that service of me, my lady," he replied. "Until now."

"Your situation in service here as yet remains to be seen."

"Are you objecting, my lady?" Trent asked. "I should have thought that his lordship was the authority here."

Lady Edwina's eyes widened at the man's impertinence. "Are you in any way familiar with what a footman's duties might entail, Mr. Trescott?" she demanded.

After a brief moment of hesitation, Trent slowly answered, "Vaguely, my lady."

"I feel certain that a man of your obvious intelligence should be able to learn your duties quickly and properly," Lord Dynford told him. "And we shall make every effort to assist you in doing so."

Her brother had obviously mistaken Mr. Trescott's hesitation regarding disclosure of his previous situations as concern over his abilities to handle the position. Lady Edwina, however, would make no such error. Regardless of how attractive or charming this stranger might be, she had no evidence that he was any more trustworthy than that other rascal who had attempted to make off with the family silver.

"I shall endeavor to surprise you both by the quickness with which I learn my duties," Trent replied. "I might even be able to perform them well enough to please her ladyship's discerning tastes."

She tilted her head slightly and replied coolly, "I am a woman neither easily surprised nor easily pleased, Mr. Trescott."

"She isn't," Lord Dynford confirmed.

"Not easily pleased, eh?" Trent repeated to Lord Dynford.

"Not a bit," his lordship replied.

Trent lifted his gaze to meet hers. She deliberately turned from Trent. She was determined not to encourage him in his unseemly behavior.

"Is this the reason she remains unmarried even at her age?" Trent asked his lordship.

"She is exceptionally fastidious regarding her choice of suitors," Lord Dynford responded. "You would not believe the perfectly acceptable offers she had refused."

"As the head of the family, could you not have insisted she accept one of them?"

Lady Edwina gave an audible little snort of disgust.

Lord Dynford shook his head. "No one forces Lady Edwina into anything," he pronounced with finality.

"Stubborn then, as well?"

"Positively pigheaded!"

"Bad tempered?"

"A veritable harridan!"

Lady Edwina fairly bristled. How dare her very own brother speak of her in such disparaging terms and with this impertinent stranger. How dare this rogue make such an exceedingly personal inquiry regarding her! If she were not a lady, she should derive great pleasure from boxing the ears of the pair of them!

"Oh!" Lady Edwina found, much to her dismay, that she could restrain her little scream of agitation no longer.

The two men stared at her briefly. Then Trent turned back to Lord Dynford and commented, "I believe you have assessed her character aright, my lord."

After her initial outburst, Lady Edwina managed to regain her customary composure.

She smiled tightly and said to her brother with exaggerated politeness, "My lord, how very unlike you to be discussing your own sister in this fashion." She shot Trent a withering glare. "And with one of the footmen, as well."

"Does that comment indicate that you give your approval to my taking the situation, my lady?" Trent asked her brightly.

She lifted her chin and peered haughtily down her nose at the two men. "You both seem to be enjoying yourselves immensely. I, however, am not. Good day to you both."

"Come, come. It was only in harmless jest, Winnie . . ." Lord Dynford began.

"Winnie?" Trent repeated, turning questioning green eyes up to Lady Edwina.

She raised her chin to its customary angle. Somehow, she still did not quite feel as if she were achieving the appearance of hauteur for which she continually strove.

"If you will excuse me, I have more pressing duties to attend to," she said, raising her chin even higher. With deliberate steps,

130

she strode from the room.

Nigel gave his head just the barest nod. "You will do." He waved a gesture of dismissal to the tall, strapping, dark-haired young man who stood before him nervously twisting his cap. "I expect you to arrive at Haversham Hall within the week."

"Thankee, m'lor'. Thankee." The newly hired footman bobbed his head up and down as he backed from the room.

Nigel looked up from the neatly penned recommendation which the agency had sent. The butler of Haversham House in Berkeley Square stood in the doorway of his office, awaiting his lordship's next instructions.

"Did the agency send any others, Allenby?" Nigel asked.

"No, m'lord," he answered. "That was the last. Did your lordship find any of them satisfactory?"

"Only that last one, and the one other fellow," he complained. "At this rate, I shall *never* be able to complete my household staff."

"If I may be so bold, m'lord, I am wondering if it is truly necessary for your lordship to put yourself through all the bother of hiring a completely new household staff for Haversham Hall," the butler observed. "You know, of course, m'lord, that we here at Haversham House are ever at your lordship's disposal."

"Yes, yes," Nigel replied sharply. Of course they were ever at his disposal. He was the Baron now!

"But you must stay here," Nigel insisted. "Having so recently come into the title, I cannot yet be certain when I shall be in London and when I may retire to my country estates."

"There are your own servants from your former residence, m'lord," Allenby reminded him.

Nigel sent the butler a chilling glare. "The estates of a *baron* surely require more servants than I have been maintaining in my modest little house."

"Surely, m'lord," Allenby replied, bowing low. "I had no idea that the situation at Haversham Hall had deteriorated to such an extent."

"My cousin cared little for the running of the estate except for what profit he could milk from it," Nigel answered. "And his wife is such a timid, poor-spirited little creature that the insubordination of the servants was quite appalling."

"A pity, m'lord. A pity."

"The true pity is that I can find so few servants who meet my requirements," Nigel grumbled.

"Might I venture to say, m'lord, that there may be few applicants for the position who meet your rather stringent requirements," Allenby said hesitantly.

"Nonsense! I am not an unreasonable man," Nigel pointed out to the apparently forgetful butler. "Is it my fault if I merely wish to have my household ordered precisely to my liking?"

"Of course not, m'lord," Allenby agreed.

Of course not! Nigel knew.

It was not his fault that he had had to dismiss the entire staff of Haversham Hall. Why, any one of them might not have been entirely drugged upon that fateful night. Any one of them might take it into his head to inform the constable, or to try to blackmail him!

He brushed invisible pieces of lint from the leg of his new nankeen trousers.

It was not his fault, either, if he wished to create a certain picturesqueness to suit his livery by having all dark-haired servants of a certain similarity in size and height. He *did* have a certain reputation to establish with the *ton*.

He polished the ring of pigeon's blood ruby set in heavy gold against the lapel of his new maroon superfine jacket. Of course it must be maroon. Maroon and gold were his colors. Of course he must always wear them.

And it *most certainly* was not his fault if he required large, strong footmen to protect him from those who wished to harm him. Who knew what dastardly villains might be lurking in the shadows of the park, prepared to murder and rob him at the slightest opportunity? Who knew which distant relative might suddenly take it into his head to do away with him just as he had so easily disposed of Milton and Trent?

He snorted. Milton had been such a fool! He was so trusting, so gullible. He had been so easy to dispose of that it had almost been a shame to do it.

Trent was another matter entirely, Nigel thought angrily. Trent had insisted upon trying to make this difficult for him!

132

Trent had refused to succumb to the drug. Trent had refused to stand still long enough to be stabbed properly.

But he had succeeded in spite of all Trent's efforts to the contrary — and he always would! His cousin was no match for his superior mind. And he would make very certain that anyone who contemplated *his* murder would not have such an easy time.

Ha! He was so clever, he could easily foil them all. He would surround himself with the largest, the strongest, perhaps even the most ill-tempered footmen . . .

Suddenly Nigel slammed his fist down on the top of the elegant ebony desk, crumpling the pile of references, and jolting the complacent old butler.

"It is all the fault of that damned agency, you know, Allenby! I am under the firm belief that they are sending the best servants to the Marquis of Carlough. And why?" he demanded, slamming his fist against the desk again. "Why? Simply because he is a marquis! That is why!"

"Exceptionally unsportsmanlike of them," Allenby remarked.

Nigel clenched his jaw until his cheek muscles bulged. "Indeed. But I shall show them all," he added with a low chuckle.

"Will there be anything else, m'lord?"

"I think not, Allenby."

"Very good, sir. Luncheon will be ready for your lordship in half an hour."

"Thank you," Nigel mumbled.

He was no longer thinking of the problems entailed in finding just the perfect servants to create the overall effect he desired in his household. He was contemplating the final touch, the pièce de résistance, as it were, which would crown his accession to the barony — his wife!

He had known Lady Cecily Danvers would be perfect for him from the first moment she had laid her adoring eyes upon him that evening at Almack's. Her quite blatant admiration of his own excellent qualities was a delight to him when so many people never really understood what a marvelous person he truly was.

Her creamy complexion, fair hair, and sparkling blue eyes were the perfect foil for his own dark handsomeness. Her delicate figure would exactly match the exquisite proportions of the

133

rooms of Haversham Hall.

The lady's fortune was also the perfect complement to his own wealth. And as the sister of the Earl of Dynford, an old and much respected title, she gave him an entrée to the best of the peerage.

He was fabulously wealthy, as he always had been from birth. He was possessed of a title, as he always should have been. And soon, he would be possessed of the most beautiful wife in London, indeed, in all of England.

He was Lord Haverslea! Who would dare scorn him now?

"Trescott! What are you doing?" Lady Edwina demanded, half in surprise and half in apprehension, as she entered his bedchamber.

Trent was clinging to the small table beside the bed. His legs wobbled. His trembling hand was outstretched as he prepared to grasp the windowsill in his efforts to circumambulate the room.

Unable to move his feet quickly, Trent turned only his head toward her, a most serious expression upon his face.

"Both of my feet are touching the floor," he observed. "My legs are straight. My knees are rigid. My torso is erect. Why, my lady! I appear to be standing," Trent replied, as if he were quite surprised to find himself in such a ridiculous position. "However, please feel free to correct me if I am wrong," he added with a merry twinkle in his eyes.

Lady Edwina pressed her lips tightly together and bustled over to him.

"You are quite correct in your observations, Trescott," she said, taking his uninjured arm and draping it over her shoulder in order to prevent him from falling. "You are a rather intelligent fellow to have discerned this entirely by yourself."

"I did give fair warning that I would surprise you my lady," Trent answered. Resting his weight upon his uninjured leg, he shifted his arm about her ladyship's shoulder, drawing her closer to him.

"Do not surprise me by allowing me to find you lying unconscious upon the floor, bleeding again," she warned Trent as she placed her hand gingerly about his waist and assisted him to take a few more halting steps past the window.

He wore only a thin, lawn nightshirt. Through the fine fabric, she could feel his ribs and the firmly tensed muscles along his side.

She wanted to concentrate upon supporting him in his efforts to walk. She tried to push from her mind the sensation of the warm, taut flesh beneath her fingers as he moved at her side. She tried not to think about how snugly she fit into the warm crook of his arm.

"My wounds are healing quite nicely, my lady," he reminded her. "You, yourself, have told me so."

"That is true, Trescott," she agreed, pushing all thoughts of how comfortable he felt against her far into the back of her mind. "However, I should not want you to be so hasty in your efforts to recover that you do yourself another damage. Bloodstains are so difficult to remove from the carpet."

"What experience has your ladyship with bloodstains?" Trent asked in mock horror. Without waiting for a reply, he continued, "What an image that conjures in my mind! Your ladyship kneeling upon the carpet, bucket and water nearby, soap and brush in hand. 'Out! Out! Damned spot!' " he cried dramatically.

"Are you an admirer of William Shakespeare?" she inquired, tilting her head to the side to look up at him. Perhaps if she could not ascertain more about Trescott's past by direct questioning, she could discover something through mere casual conversation.

"Who in England has not heard of the Bard, my lady?" he answered with a little shrug of his shoulders.

"Few common soldiers, I would venture to say."

"But, my lady, I have always flattered myself by thinking that I was rather *uncommon*," Trent said, smiling down at her.

They had passed the windows and were approaching the wide fireplace. Lady Edwina kept him close to the wall so that he would have more than just herself upon which to lean.

"You have told me that you were not always a soldier either, Trescott." She saw no reason not to continue questioning him while they walked.

"I was once a little boy, my lady," he offered.

"Where did you live as a child, Trescott?"

135

"I lived with my mummy and my da," he replied with a chuckle.

Lady Edwina pressed her lips firmly together to avoid laughing. "And where did they live?"

"I have told you before. I come from London, my lady."

"Do your parents still reside in London?" she asked pointedly.

"Again, as I have told you before, my parents are both deceased."

"Had you any brothers or sisters?"

Trent lowered his head and stumbled slightly on his injured leg. "Just one, also deceased."

Lady Edwina bent her head to look at the floor so that the man would not see her grimace. She had cautioned him once to tell his tale well. The man had certainly heeded her advice, as thus far she had not been able to detect any discrepancies in his story. Of course, she conceded, it was exceedingly easy to maintain the continuity of one's story when most of the characters were dead.

She wished to stay with him—to question him further, she told herself, unwilling to own that she enjoyed his proximity. But she had felt him stumble and did not wish to overtax him. Besides, as he leaned his weight against her, the man was becoming deucedly heavy!

She turned to direct him toward the bed.

"Trescott, you are a man of singular misfortune," she observed with a lift of her eyebrow.

"Quite the contrary, my lady. I consider myself extremely fortunate to have been found by Lord Dynford and to have received such tender care from yourself."

Lady Edwina felt his fingers begin to stroke softly the side of her neck. 'How dare he!' she bristled.

'Well, perhaps he would not dare,' she decided upon further reflection. The man's entire body was quivering with the exertion of walking this much so soon after his illness. She would attribute this gesture to his weakness and her overactive imagination.

She had to own, she did find the warmth of his body and the gentle pressure of his arm on her shoulder strangely soothing and yet strangely exciting.

'No! I am allowing my fancies to get the best of me,' she told

136

herself. Lady Edwina shook her head and quickly brought him to his bed.

"Well, Trescott," she said with a little crack in her voice. "I think you have done quite enough walking for the moment."

Still, it was with an unaccountable reluctance that Lady Edwina released her grasp about Trent's waist. As he lowered himself onto the edge of the bed, his arm slipped from about her shoulders. Her heart thudded to a stop in her throat when Trent did not completely withdraw his arm, but let it come to rest about her waist.

"Thank you for the lovely stroll, my lady," he said, smiling up into her eyes. "I eagerly anticipate the next one."

His eyes were so green shining up into her own that she felt drawn into them as if into a whirlpool. She drew back quickly from the edge of the dangerous precipice to which she had unwittingly wandered.

"Trescott," she told him coolly while moving slowly away from him. "The next time you feel inclined to stroll in your invalid condition, I suggest you ring for Nealy, who is better able, physically, to support you."

"But he is, by far, inferior company, my lady," Trent remarked.

She turned from him quickly so that he should not see the flush which continued to rise up her cheeks regardless of how hard she tried to will it away.

Lady Edwina slowly backed toward the door. "As you are feeling so much improved, Trescott, you shall be assuming your duties as footman very soon. For now, I suggest that you rest while you yet have the opportunity."

She closed the door tightly behind her. She lifted one hand to touch her burning cheek.

'You addle-brained goose!' she scolded herself. 'You have not blushed since your first . . . well, perhaps second season. 'Tis no time to renew the silly habit!'

Chapter Eleven

Lady Edwina paced rapidly back and forth, slicing through the long rays of late evening sunlight which dappled the rose, red, and gold flowers scattered across the drawing room carpet. At last Lord Dynford appeared at the doorway.

Lady Edwina immediately stopped her furious pacing and whirled to face him. She lifted her chin and pressed her lips tightly together.

"How kind of you to join me for dinner, Richard," she remarked sarcastically. "You have only kept me waiting for twenty minutes."

"Now, now," Lord Dynford began, holding his palms out, as if to protect himself from her biting sarcasm. "Don't scold, Winnie."

But she did scold. "This is the fifth time in as many days that you have been late for dinner," she said, placing a hand on each hip. "I have spoken to you several times regarding this lapse, yet you continue to ignore me. This is most unlike you, Richard."

"On the contrary, Winnie," Lord Dynford replied. "You know very well that with my experiments, it has always been extremely difficult for me to come to regular meals at regular times. It is *you* who has always insisted upon adhering to a strict schedule."

"Do not attempt to lay the blame at my feet, Richard," she ordered imperiously, lifting her chin even higher.

"Dear Winnie." His lordship smiled and laid his hand upon her arm. "If I were left to my own devices, I should have starved to death by now. Whatever would I do without you and your rules to see that I was properly fed and cared for?"

Lady Edwina sighed with exasperation. Was she more dismayed by her brother's careless disregard of his own health and welfare? Or was she more dismayed by her own inability never to remain angry with her carefree brother for any length of time?

"Come with me now, Richard," she said, taking his arm. "Do you think you can find your way to the dining room alone? We truly must hurry, as you do appear to be upon the very brink of starvation."

He allowed her to escort him into the small family dining room.

"What detained you this evening?" she inquired as she sat in her usual chair, which Haskell held out for her.

"James Trescott," Lord Dynford answered readily, seating himself.

Haskell set a steaming dish of sautéed prawns before each of them. Lord Dynford immediately set to peeling off his prawns.

Lady Edwina picked up her fork but made no movement to take anything to eat. She made a little grimace at her brother. "James Trescott. I suspected as much. I hope you two have not been enjoying yourselves at my expense again."

Lord Dynford lowered his fork and regarded Lady Edwina with pleading eyes. "Will you *never* allow me to forget that small indiscretion? Trescott is rather witty, and well, I simply got caught up in the spirit of the jest." He made a helpless little gesture with his shoulders. "But it was not really malicious. And it truly was not my fault, Winnie."

"Of course not, Richard," she answered patiently. "It so rarely is."

"Neither is Trescott to blame," the young earl protested. "B'gads! He's a prime fellow!"

"I'm sure that *you* think he is," she answered flatly. "You have spent the past five evenings in his company while I have been relegated to my room like some aged and useless governess to spend my declining years reading lurid gothic romances."

"But you are forever telling me how much you enjoy reading alone," he protested. Suddenly he laughed aloud and exclaimed, "Winnie! Can it be that you are *jealous* of the time I spend with our patient?"

Lady Edwina flipped her head as if to toss away the very idea. "Quite the contrary," she replied. "I am much gratified to be relieved of the arduous duties of playing nursemaid to a grown man."

"Is that why you seem to have been avoiding Trescott lately?" Lord Dynford asked. He popped a prawn into his mouth, then chewed, all the while watching Lady Edwina and waiting for an answer.

"I have no need to avoid Trescott," Lady Edwina answered, peering disdainfully down her slim nose. "*My* duties entail seeing that the man is bandaged and fed. It is *not* my duty to entertain him."

"B'gads, Winnie! Must everything be duty to you? Can you not do something once just because it amuses you?"

"There are quite enough people here doing what amuses them," she replied. "Someone must do what must be done."

"You really should join us sometime, Winnie," his lordship tried to coax her. Then he exclaimed with boyish enthusiasm, "He and I always have such a capital time together!"

"Oh, I am certain that you do," Lady Edwina remarked with a humorless little chuckle. "And that was all well and good when he was still confined to bed recuperating as your somewhat dubious guest."

Lord Dynford began to protest, but she shook her head and continued. "But the man is now up and about and a footman in our employ. He should be attending to his duties in order to earn his keep, not wiling away the time chatting with you," she complained. "And in our best bedchamber, still!"

"Well, as the Earl of Dynford, I have decided that one of his duties is to chat with me," her brother informed her. "Trescott shows a great interest in my experiments with flight."

"I am sure he would show an equal interest in garden slugs if it would enable him to postpone performing any actual physical labor," Lady Edwina replied tartly.

Ignoring his sister's sour comment, his lordship continued, "Were you aware that the fellow saw me in my apparatus, crashing through the trees the day that I found him? Oh, I do wish you could have seen the expression of absolute relief on Trescott's face the first time I told him that I was actually attempting to fly! The poor fellow confessed to me that, all this time, he has been worrying that he had gone mad in his delirium . . ." Lord Dynford began laughing heartily.

"How delightful," Lady Edwina remarked with a still, little

smile. "Now I am living with not one but *two* madmen."

"When I told him of my design problems, he suggested that I consult a certain Sir George Cayley of Brompton Hall in Yorkshire. I understand the gentleman has also conducted experiments with flight, as well as experiments to increase the distance which cannon shot might be projected." Lord Dynford pressed his palm against his forehead. "I understand the gentleman is rather shy, and has published very little of his work. Small wonder I had not noted his work before."

"I daresay, there are a great many things which you have not noted, Richard," Lady Edwina replied.

"Yes, you are quite correct. I am usually so busy thinking only of my experiments. Why, only the other day . . ."

Lady Edwina was not paying full attention to her brother as he began to ramble on again about his plans and theories. Certain insidious little suspicions which she continued to harbor about this Trescott fellow had begun again to gnaw at her.

"When Trescott first regained consciousness, he thought that our father was still the earl," Lady Edwina said, half to her brother and half to herself. "Even though he was mistaken regarding father, how could he have known any particulars about the Dynfords at all if he were just an ordinary soldier? And how could this Trescott fellow be acquainted with Sir George Cayley and his experiments?"

But Lord Dynford was too preoccupied with his own thought to answer Lady Edwina's questions. "I, personally, am delighted that he suggested Sir George to me. I shall begin an extensive correspondence with the gentleman immediately!"

"Richard! Are you not concerned over this problem?" Lady Edwina inquired sharply.

Suddenly drawn back to the present by her reprimand, his lordship slowly laid down his fork and looked up at his sister with a puzzled expression. "Problem?" he repeated her question. "I was not aware that a problem existed, Winnie."

"Of course not, Richard," she replied sarcastically. She shook her head and murmured, "You so rarely are."

Lady Edwina looked her brother directly in the eye in order to retain his complete attention. "The time has come for you to face facts, Richard," she pronounced sternly. "I realize that James

141

Trescott seems perfectly harmless to you, but there is just something about him which does not ring true to my way of thinking."

"Then what dreadful secrets do you think Trescott is concealing? No, do not tell me!" his lordship declared, holding up his hand dramatically yet all the while chucking to himself. "He is the disinherited son of some nobleman. He was disgraced and sent into exile from his father's castle. He then stabbed himself thrice and spent countless days in the woods, hungry, thirsty, and feverish, in order to insinuate himself into our home with the sole intention of pinching the silver!"

Lady Edwina opened her mouth to answer, but her reply stopped midway in her throat. To answer yes would be patently absurd. On the other hand, to answer no would mean that James Trescott's story might indeed contain more than a grain of truth.

"Come now, Winnie," his lordship continued. "What reason have you to believe that Trescott is anything other than what he tells us?"

Lady Edwina took the time to order her thoughts into the most logical sequence for convincing her brother that she was correct.

"Consider the speed with which he assumed his duties as footman," she offered. "Yet he maintains that he has never before served in such a capacity."

Lord Dynford shrugged his shoulders. "That does not signify. One can deduce simply by speaking with him that Trescott is an intelligent man. And quite honestly, Winnie, the duties which our footmen perform are not so rigorous that they require any mental acrobatics. Even Nealy performs his duties satisfactorily."

Lady Edwina decided that the subject of Nealy's adequacy was still open for debate. However, Nealy's abilities were not the issue at hand, so she said nothing whatsoever to distract her brother from her intended course of discussion.

"I find this James Trescott far more mannerly and well-spoken than the usual vagrant which you have brought into our house from the roadside," she continued. "He has even quoted Shakespeare to me, Richard."

"Not his love sonnets, Winnie!" Lord Dynford cried, clutch-

142

ing his hand to his breast in a gesture of fraternal outrage. "Shall I call the fellow out for compromising your virtue?"

"That remark does not even warrant a reply," she told him, fixing him with an icy stare.

Lord Dynford shrugged again. "What does it signify, Winnie? An intelligent man gathers knowledge in whatever situation he may find himself," he answered more sensibly.

"But the man has been here for almost two weeks and we know very little more about him now than we did when he first arrived," she protested. "And even then, the only information which we have about him is that with which he himself has supplied us. And how much of that can we be certain is the truth?"

"Why ever should the fellow lie to us when we have treated him so well?" Lord Dynford asked, an expression of genuine perplexity upon his face.

"He is extremely reticent regarding any aspect of his past," she offered as final, damning evidence. "Surely there is something suspicious about a man who will not discuss his past."

"Perhaps," answered his lordship very quietly, "there are many painful memories in his past that the man does not wish to recall by recounting them to us."

Lady Edwina was silently considering the man's wounds. He could hardly have done himself the injury. Someone had indeed meant to hurt him. But why? If robbery were the only motive, why had he still been possessed of money when they found him? And if murder were the true motive, what had the man done and who had hated him enough to deem him deserving of such a grisly end?

Then her eyes narrowed and her lips pursed. "I would still feel safer in my bed at night if I knew more about the man."

"And if I know you, Winnie, you are determined to ferret out precisely what lies behind our Trescott."

"*Our* Trescott?" Lady Edwina repeated. She shook her head. "He is not *my* Trescott. And I assure you, I have no intention of spending my days quizzing a . . . well, a mere footman regarding his personal affairs. Why, the man may go to blazes for all I care. I have not the slightest interest in any of these vagabonds which you habitually bring in from the roadside, let alone a specific interest in James Trescott."

Lord Dynford grinned broadly at his sister and remarked, "For one who is not interested in this Trescott fellow, you certainly have a great deal to say regarding him."

Lady Edwina snatched up her silver fork. The prawns had grown cold in the dish. Nevertheless, she focused all her concentration upon spearing one so that her brother would not notice the bright flush coursing rapidly up her cheeks.

Lady Cecily brushed the damp tendrils from her neck and sniffed conspicuously the small nosegay of posies.

The only relief to be had in all of fashionable London was a leisurely drive about Hyde Park in the comparative cool of the late afternoon. Today, Lady Sheftley and Miss Jane Sheftley had been invited to accompany them in the Dynford's elegant blue and gold landau.

"Lud! Why do we stay in the city in this demmed heat?" Lady Sheftley demanded. She slapped her fan open and began beating it rapidly about her profusely perspiring face.

"Why do we, indeed?" Lady Portia echoed.

Observing her from the corner of her eye, Lady Cecily thought that Lady Sheftley looked as if she would like to give the brightly shining sun a whack with that fan just like she struck everything else which did not comply with her own peculiar standard of behavior.

"Indeed, why do we stay?" Lady Cecily repeated, opening her fan and waving it before her in perfect imitation of Lady Sheftley.

"You know perfectly well why *you* stay," Lady Sheftley told Lady Cecily, smacking her knee with her fan. "So don't play stupid."

"Don't play stupid, Cecily dear," Lady Portia warned her niece.

Lady Cecily pulled another wispy strand from her neck and feigned profound interest in her nosegay. "La! I haven't the faintest idea what you two—"

"And don't pretend *we're* stupid, either," Lady Sheftley continued to scold. "I know your game, my gel."

"Game, Cecily?" Lady Portia repeated. "What game is that, my dear? You know you are abominable at piquet and at whist."

"You'd remain in London until your ears fried in this heat as long as Lord Haverslea remained here as well," Lady Sheftley told her. "You're not the only female in London hanging out for a husband. And with his looks, and fortune, and now a title, Lord Haverslea will take his time to pick and choose. I shouldn't set my hopes too firmly on his lordship, if I were you."

Lady Cecily sniffed languidly at her posies. Let that spiteful old harridan mock her if she wished! She knew her own game far better than *any* of them could have told it to her.

"His lordship and I have found each other to be *exceedingly* companionable and reason enough to stay in town beyond the season," Lady Cecily admitted coyly. "But that does not explain why you and Jane have not departed for your country estates in Sussex."

"Oh, I'm not prepared to leave London just yet," Lady Sheftley told her. "I've a particular reason for staying."

"I should have thought you would have a particular reason for *leaving,* as all the eligible bachelors would be in Brighton by now," Lady Cecily said.

"Oh, no, my gel. I shall stay in town just long enough to watch you make a complete fool of yourself."

Although she should have dearly loved to give Lady Sheftley a kick in the shin with her neatly booted little foot, Lady Cecily merely smiled sweetly and said, "What a most extraordinary reason for staying! Of course, I suppose someone who has exhausted all one's prospects in town must look to other people's activities to amuse them. For myself, I am quite occupied with my own affairs—all the shops and balls and at-homes. That is why I do prefer the city."

"We do prefer the city," Lady Portia affirmed, nodding her head vigorously.

"As do I," the new Lord Haverslea's voice interjected. "Ladies," he greeted them as he reined in his coal black stallion to keep pace with the sedate speed of the landau.

His maroon superfine jacket and buff nankeen trousers contrasted with the gleaming ebony of the horse and the man's own black hair like garnets and topazes set against black velvet.

Lady Cecily patted her new straw bonnet and perked up the little silk flowers just above the pink satin bow tied jauntily at the side of her face.

"Why, Lord Haverslea, what a pleasant surprise!" she declared, opening her blue eyes quite wide and smiling alluringly up at him over the top of her nosegay.

He raised his dark brows. "Are you surprised to find me here or are you surprised that I enjoy life in the city?"

"Oh, la! It is your presence which took me quite by surprise, Lord Haverslea," she told him with a delightful little laugh. "I have become quite well aware that life in London was among your preferences."

"Quite so," he replied. "I find the company of an exceptional lady greatly enhances my enjoyment of London."

Lady Sheftley pointed her fan at the rump of the black horse prancing beside her. "I see you've found some new preferences, too, Lord Haverslea," she said.

"Lady Sheftley, I have always been partial to black horses."

"I daresay, now that you've succeeded to a title, you'll find preferences that you never even dreamed you had!" Lady Sheftley declared.

"You are quite correct in that respect," he replied with a smile. "Now that I have the responsibility of the fortune and the barony, I find I have quite an absorbing interest in perpetuating the title." He turned and smiled at Lady Cecily. "And a marked preference in regards to accomplishing that end as well."

Lady Sheftley made a sound that seemed halfway between a snort and a laugh. " 'Tis nothing new there. Never met the man yet who didn't have a marked preference for *that!*"

Miss Jane Sheftley at last opened her mouth to speak. "Well, Mama, there was that one rather odd cousin of Papa's . . ."

Lady Sheftley rapped her fan sharply across her daughter's knuckles.

Lord Haverslea was having some small difficulties in keeping his spirited black in pace with the slow-moving landau.

"Alas, ladies, I must not keep my horse waiting," he announced with regret. He patted the prancing black's glistening withers.

"Before you depart, Lord Haverslea," Lady Cecily called to

him, "I should so like to express my gratitude for the flowers. How kind of you to send them this morning!"

His lordship bowed from his seat atop the spirited horse. "My lady, they wither to insignificance beside your radiant beauty."

Lady Cecily blushed prettily and smiled coyly up at him from behind her nosegay. "Why, Lord Haverslea, what a charmer you are!"

The black stallion began to start and fidget. Lord Haverslea pulled the reins in sharply. "Alas, I must bid you adieu, then, and I look forward to your next at-home."

Lady Portia blinked her watery blue eyes, looking very much like a little gray owl which has suddenly been awakened at noon. "Why, we are always at home, sir, unless of course we are out."

"I am *quite* certain my aunt will always be pleased to receive you, Lord Haverslea," Lady Cecily answered, adding demurely, "As would I. Until next Thursday afternoon?"

"Splendid." And Lord Haverslea galloped away.

Lady Cecily turned an exceedingly smug smile upon Lady Sheftley from behind her very conspicuously displayed nosegay.

So the old girl was expecting her to make a fool of herself. Well, Lady Sheftley could wait until she turned quite blue in the face! Small chance of her appearing foolish. Things were progressing quite to her satisfaction.

"That's quite a frisky young stallion there," Lady Sheftley remarked to Lady Portia, nodding after the retreating horse and rider.

"Yes, indeed," Lady Portia agreed pleasantly. "And the horse is not so bad either."

Chapter Twelve

Trent winced. Even though he no longer had difficulty in moving and walking, his right arm and leg still ached in the early morning damp. Once again, the wagon jolted over the green tussocks of grass on the way up the hill to the old folly.

"You're in for a rare treat, Trescott," Redding warned him with a chuckle.

"It will be nice to watch his lordship flying from the top of the hill for a change," Trent replied.

Pringle, riding in the rear of the wagon with Nealy and the apparatus, laughed and said, "It'd be nice to watch his lordship fly at all."

Redding made some sort of unintelligible grumble, then said, "If God had meant for man to fly, He would've given him feathers and made him lay eggs."

Trent turned to the wagoner. "You don't think his lordship will succeed?" he asked.

Redding shrugged.

"Sure he will," Nealy asserted brightly. "Especially with those new improvements his lordship's made to this . . . this thing." He patted the wooden structure between him and Pringle.

Lord Dynford, who had galloped his roan mare on ahead, awaited them at the folly.

"Come, come, you laggards!" he called, motioning them forward with his riding crop. "The day is dawning and I shall miss the rising of the morning breeze and then I shall have to wait until tomorrow. I am most anxious to test these modifications."

Redding reined the team of heavy draft horses to a halt in front of the folly. The footmen sprang down from the back.

Trent eased himself down a bit more carefully. He knew he was not going to be of much help, but when his lordship had invited him along, Trent could not refuse.

He grabbed the tip of one wing with his left hand and began to help the others to haul Lord Dynford's new apparatus from the back.

"Gently, fellows, gently," Lord Dynford cautioned them. "I've made certain adjustments to my design which, while rendering it a bit more fragile, will certainly render it a great deal more airworthy."

This new apparatus was indeed much easier to remove from the back of the wagon than the last one. The two large beams of oak had been replaced by two lighter beams of birch. The legless chair in which his lordship had sat had been replaced with a mesh of leather affixed to the beams with hooks of brass instead of iron.

The ribs of the wings were composed of thinner strips of a lighter weight wood. They also were affixed to the center beams with rings of brass. Instead of canvas, the wings were covered with fine, white silk.

Lord Dynford circled his latest contraption, inspecting it before his flight. It was absolutely perfect, he decided as he finished his perusal.

How could he have been so foolish before? he demanded of himself. To try to sit while flying! How ridiculous! Anyone who observed a bird in flight would notice that it appeared that the creature was lying upon its belly on the wind as it moved its wings up and down.

And that is precisely what he would attempt to do. This time, he would succeed!

Lord Dynford eagerly stripped off his jacket and tossed it carelessly behind him. Pringle caught it before it hit the damp ground. He creased it neatly and laid it upon the wagon seat.

"Are you quite certain you should be doing this, my lord?" Trent asked.

"Quite certain, Trescott!" his lordship replied. "As much as I should wish for each of you to know the absolute elation of soaring above the treetops, I am just selfish enough to desire

149

for myself that *first* golden moment."

"Quite so, m'lord," Pringle agreed, nodding for confirmation to the footmen circled about him. "I don't think none of us here would be wishing to rob your lordship of your golden moment, as it were."

"No, indeed, m'lord," Redding echoed. Young Nealy, hiding behind the large shoulders of the wagoner, snickered behind his hand.

"How generous of you all," Lord Dynford responded. "But enough of the niceties. To work, men!"

Once again, the apparatus was dragged to the edge of the precipice. Redding held the contraption steady while his lordship, assisted on either side by Pringle and Nealy, gingerly lowered himself into the rope mesh. Pringle lifted the two leather straps, looped them across Lord Dynford's back to keep him from falling out of his mesh, and buckled the straps to the harness. Lord Dynford grasped the two leather handles which would work the motion of the wings.

"Good luck, m'lord," Redding told him.

"You'll fly this time, m'lord," Nealy cried enthusiastically.

"Do be careful, my lord," Trent said. He tried to keep the worry he felt from showing in his voice. He tried not to frown with concern for the young earl's safety.

"And don't forget to flap *immediately,* m'lord," Pringle reminded him, beating his own arms up and down in imitation.

"I shan't! I shan't!" Lord Dynford said. He pulled on the straps and the wood and silk wings slowly beat the air. Then he exclaimed, "But let us be off!"

The new, lighter apparatus was also much easier to push. The rising wind of dawn whipped past the earl's ears, pushing back into his own face his cry of delight as he poised in midair above the trees.

His delight turned rapidly in to a scream of fear as, much sooner than any of them had anticipated, the front of the apparatus dove downward and his lordship found himself dropping from the sky upside down.

Trent and Pringle ran to the edge of the hill and peered down. Immediately below their feet, tangled in the treetops, the tattered silk still billowed in the breeze.

"Ah, well," Pringle sighed. "At least his lordship won't be so hard to find this time."

The footmen slid down the narrow path which led to the base of the hill.

The apparatus had wedged itself, nose down, between two tall oaks which grew so close together as to almost share a single trunk between them at the base. Lord Dynford, still securely belted into his mesh harness, was dangling upside down from his precious contraption. His lordship groaned.

Pringle looked up and called, "M'lord, will you be needing our assistance in coming down?"

Lord Dynford drew a great shuddering breath before speaking. "Why, Pringle, you know how I do so hate to bother you all."

Pringle stood watching him silently.

"Pringle!" Lord Dynford ordered sharply. "Get me down from here!"

Something must indeed be wrong if his lordship spoke in such imperative tones. Pringle called up to him, "We'll get you down, m'lord. Just hold tight!"

"No need for me to hold the apparatus. It has quite a grip on me." Lord Dynford gasped again. "Pringle, I suggest you make all possible haste to get me down from here!"

"Has your lordship done yourself a damage?" Pringle asked.

"Damage? Damage?" Lord Dynford repeated through tightly clenched teeth. "Of course not. I merely don't wish to be late for luncheon."

Trent, brow furrowed, lips pursed, perused the situation. Usually a person hanging upside down for any length of time turns quite crimson, but his lordship's face was dead white. Trent did not know the extent of his lordship's injuries, but he did know that his lordship must be removed from that tree — now.

Trent turned to Redding and said, "Stay here. And be prepared to catch his lordship should he fall."

Redding merely cast him a skeptical glance and mumbled, "I hardly think his lordship'll enjoy being treated like a

151

cricket ball."

"Nealy, run back to the manor," Trent added. "His lordship may be seriously injured and in need of attention."

The young footman looked exceptionally regretful to be away from the site of possible blood and gore. He scrambled rapidly up the hill.

"Come, Pringle," Trent continued. "You climb this trunk. I shall climb the other. Between us, I believe we can extricate his lordship."

"Cripes, it's been years since I've climbed a tree, Trescott!" Pringle said with a nervous laugh. " 'Course, if it's the only way . . ."

"We certainly cannot take him back the way he came," Trent answered.

"Quite so," Pringle agreed. He grabbed the lowest branch of the tree, placed his foot against the trunk, and began to haul himself up into the branches.

On the parallel trunk, Trent followed him up a bit more slowly. His leg was aching abominably, but he proceeded on the hopeful assumption that he could rescue his lordship from his upside-down peril before the strength in his leg gave out. Pringle certainly could not do it alone.

The upside-down smile with which Lord Dynford greeted them looked strange indeed.

"Fancy encountering you both here!" his lordship tried to exclaim cheerily through his gritted teeth. "Why, I had no idea you also frequented this place!"

"It's good to see your lordship in one piece, too," Trent replied. It was quite clear to him, however, that Lord Dynford was in intense pain. "What hurts, my lord?"

"Oh, my pride . . ." Lord Dynford groaned again and admitted, "My leg."

"Patience, my lord. We shall have you down straightaway," Trent assured him. "Seize hold of Pringle, my lord. I shall attempt to unbuckle your harness and release you."

The buckles were on Trent's side. Wedging his boot in a crotch of the branch, he tried to unfasten the leather from the brass. But the brass had scraped against the bark of the tree and burrowed into the wood so deeply that Trent could not manage the task.

Trent attempted to wiggle the apparatus just enough to loosen the buckles from the wood. His lordship's contraption creaked and the top, which was actually the tail, began to tip forward, threatening to send his lordship flipping out of the tree.

Trent and Pringle grabbed either side of the apparatus until it was steady once again.

"Obviously not the way to proceed. Pringle, can you reach these buckles from where you are?" Trent asked.

"Let me go, m'lord," Pringle told Lord Dynford.

With some difficulty, the valet managed to pry open his lordship's grip from about his waist. Lord Dynford immediately shifted his iron clasp to Trent's waist.

Pringle leaned forward over his lordship's suspended body. The branch cracked and Pringle drew back quickly, embracing the trunk of the tree for security.

"Can't reach it, Trescott," Pringle told him, shaking his head. "Not without sending the whole thing crashing down."

Lord Dynford was holding Trent so tightly that he was beginning to restrict the motion of his rib cage to allow the free passage of air.

"My lord, please! I shall need to breathe occasionally," Trent reminded him with a grunt. "Just to keep up my strength, you understand."

"Yes, yes," his lordship agreed, releasing his frantic grasp. "I suppose it helps with the thinking, too."

"Among other things," Trent agreed. "Well, what to do now, Pringle?"

"Nothing else for it, I suppose," Pringle answered cryptically. He delved into the pocket of his breeches and extracted a foot-long folder. He flicked the knife open and proceeded to slice through the leather straps as if they were butter.

"Here's the last," Pringle warned. "Hold to him tight-like."

Trent had no trouble complying with Pringle's advice, as his lordship had such a grip about his waist that Trent could not have loosed him if he had wanted to.

The blade of the folding knife sliced through the last strap. Trent caught the weight of his lordship's shoulder on his injured leg. Lord Dynford's knee jabbed into Trent's injured arm. Pringle reached out quickly to steady the pair.

Trent fought down the pain which spread throughout his body. He blinked away the stars which spun about his head and threatened to blot out his vision.

"Let his lordship's feet drop, Trescott," the valet said. "I've got his lordship quite secure."

Trent slowly released one of Lord Dynford's legs, then the other while Pringle kept a fierce grasp upon his lordship's torso.

"Nicely done, men," Lord Dynford, once again right-side-up, gasped.

"Are you quite well, m'lord?" Pringle asked. Lord Dynford nodded, but his face was every bit as white as the tattered silk of the ruined wings which flapped in the breeze about them.

"We'll get you home, m'lord," Pringle reassured him. "You're quite safe now."

Redding stood at the base of the tree, his long arms stretched up to receive his lordship. Pringle slowly lowered Lord Dynford into Redding's waiting arms.

"With your permission, m'lord," Redding mumbled. Without even letting his lordship's feet touch the ground, Redding flipped the man over his broad shoulders and began to climb up the hill.

Pringle called up to Trent, "Will you be wanting me to come up again to help you down, Trescott? You don't look so well yourself."

Trent shook his head. "Merely a momentary twinge of an old wound, Pringle," he replied with an insouciance he did not truly feel. "I shall be fine. Just get his lordship home."

Lady Edwina entered the drawing room through one of the large double doors which opened out upon the garden. Midsummer and the flowers in the garden were exceptionally lovely, she acknowledged with a bit of surprise. The two men which Lord Dynford had hired as gardeners when he saw them sitting by the roadside, apparently with nothing better to do, were not nearly so incompetent as she had at first feared they would be.

Even James Trescott had adjusted nicely to her schedule after those first few difficult days when he had the erroneous impression that his sole duty was to sit and converse with his lordship — an impression which her brother *would* persist in encouraging!

For the past few days, however, Lord Dynford had set Trescott to working in the stable. Lady Edwina was relieved to see him performing some useful tasks, and to know that the tasks kept him out of the house and away from her.

In fact, the house was exceedingly quiet this morning, devoid of even the usual noises of her brother's frantic activities preparing his precious experiments. Perhaps he was sleeping late this morning. Perhaps this mad infatuation with flight had at last left him just as quickly as it had seized him. Perhaps, in the future, she would not be leading quite so beleaguered an existence after all.

She removed her straw gypsy hat and laid it upon the green and white striped settee situated between the two sets of double doors. She placed her wicker basket beside a porcelain vase upon a rosewood table and began sorting the fresh-cut flowers.

"M'lady!" Haskell's voice boomed like thunder behind her. She jumped, upsetting the vase of fading flowers. The water spread across the tabletop and trickled down onto the carpet.

"Oh, Haskell! Do not creep up upon me that way," she scolded, placing her hand over her thumping heart. Then she frowned, puzzled. "Haskell, you usually cough before announcing."

"Why, yes, m'lady. I do," he replied with surprise. "I have apparently forgotten to do so." He proceeded to emit his customary cough and then to announce at his customary volume, "M'lady, you have spilled the contents of the vase upon the carpet."

Lady Edwina glanced back and forth between her butler and the water that she had been watching drip upon the carpet for over a minute now. She looked up one last time at Haskell and replied coolly, "So I have. How careless of me."

"M'lady, shall I have the housemaid mop it up?"

Lady Edwina sighed. "That would be most kind of you, Haskell."

"I shall attend to it at once, m'lady." Haskell turned toward the door, paused, then turned again toward her. "Am I to understand, then, that your ladyship is dismissing me and does not wish to hear what I've come to say?"

"What have you to tell me, Haskell?" she asked with another little sigh. She supposed that, in the future, she would simply have to accomodate herself to Haskell's increasing peculiarities.

"M'lady, his lordship requires the brandy."

So that was the reason for the peace and quiet this morning, Lady Edwina realized with dismay and a touch of foreboding. Her brother had slipped out early without telling her in order to conduct another of his mad experiments. She pursed her lips and pressed her eyes tightly closed. She knew quite well that there was only one circumstance under which her brother required the brandy.

"Where is his lordship, Haskell?" she asked as she made her way to the sideboard.

"I'm not certain, m'lady."

"Why don't you hazard a guess, Haskell," Lady Edwina ventured with forced patience.

"His lordship is still dangling from the tree, m'lady, unless of course, Trescott and Pringle have succeeded in extricating him."

"Of course," Lady Edwina replied. She began to sigh again, then stopped. It was useless to sigh. It was equally useless to try to make any sense whatsoever out of the inmates of Dynford Manor.

"Instruct Pringle to bring his lordship to his bedchamber when they have succeeded in extricating him," Lady Edwina said. "I shall be awaiting them there with whatever medication and bandages might be necessary."

She lifted the decanter of brandy and a snifter and headed for the stairs.

"Almost, Winnie! Almost!" She could hear her brother's

loud lament ringing through the Hall.

Trent and Pringle supported a limping Lord Dynford between them as they entered the Hall and ascended the wide mahogany stairs. They deposited his lordship on the daybed in his bedchamber. Pringle began to assist Lord Dynford in removing the tattered remnants of his shirts, while his lordship brushed the leaves and twigs from his hair.

"I vow, Richard," Lady Edwina remarked. "If you are plucked from a tree one more time, you will turn into an apple."

Lord Dynford ripped off his rumpled cravat and flung it down beside him in disgust. "I have come so close so many times. What am I doing wrong, Winnie?" he wailed. "Why can I not fly?"

"I hope this comes as no shock to you, Richard, but, quite frankly, you are not a bird," Lady Edwina informed him.

"B'gads, Winnie! Could this be true?" he demanded, wide-eyed. "You would not lie to me, would you?"

Lady Edwina twisted her lips into a wry little grimace. "Have another brandy, Richard." She poured the amber fluid into the snifter and offered it to her brother.

"I cannot understand why my apparatus will not fly!" he grumbled as Pringle assisted him into another shirt. "I thought my design infallible. And Trescott has worked so hard to build such a sturdy model."

"So, Trescott," Lady Edwina said. She glanced over to Trent with one eyebrow raised inquisitively. "That is what has kept you so occupied in the stable. You have joined his lordship in his mad quest?"

"Surely, your ladyship can have no objections to the company which I keep," he replied.

Pringle bent over and began to tug at Lord Dynford's top boots.

"Ouch! Blast! Pringle, stop!"

Large beads of perspiration had sprung out on his lordship's forehead. With a shaking hand, he seized the brandy snifter and downed the contents in a single swallow. He shuddered visibly as the burning liquid coursed down his throat.

"I do believe I have injured myself far more seriously than I had at first supposed," Lord Dynford remarked, holding out the snifter to be refilled once again. Lady Edwina complied and Lord Dynford downed this brandy as rapidly as he had the others.

"You cannot say that I have not warned you," she told his lordship with a sanctimonious nod of her head. "I have feared an occurrence of this nature all along. Personally, I think that you may consider yourself very fortunate not to be dead!"

"Now, now, Winnie," Lord Dynford pleaded. "I am discouraged enough. I do not need your reprimands at this moment."

He did look exceedingly dejected, she thought. Perhaps he had suffered enough. She turned to Pringle, who was still standing before his lordship, awaiting further instructions.

"You must be more careful," Lady Edwina told the valet. "You cannot just go ripping the boot from his leg. Such things must be done slowly, carefully."

She handed Pringle the decanter, then waved him away from her brother. She bent over to attempt to remove the boot herself, just as she had described.

"Damn! Winnie, stop!" Lord Dynford cried. His skin had gone ashen but his eyes were red and misted over.

"I dislike having to do this as much as you do . . . " Lady Edwina began.

"Oh, I sincerely doubt that, Winnie," his lordship replied with a shaky voice.

He vigorously motioned for Pringle to relinquish the decanter into his possession. He grasped the bottle, poured another snifterful, then quickly drank it. A bright spot of red had begun to diffuse across each pallid cheek.

"Excuse me, my lady, but you are going about this in a most incompetent manner," Trent offered from his observation post in the corner. He was leaning against the China paper-covered wall, his arms crossed over his broad chest, his long legs crossed one over the other.

"Incompetent?" Lady Edwina turned to him and raised one eyebrow. "Doubtless, Trescott, you have been a valet for many years and are well acquainted with the proper manner

158

in which one removes a gentleman's boots."

"More so than your ladyship," he remarked. "If you'll forgive me for saying so," he added, although Lady Edwina had the distinct impression that there was not one regretful bone in the man's body.

Trent untangled his long legs and pushed off from the wall. He left the corner and came to stand directly beside Lady Edwina.

He smelled of oak and leather. There was still a bit of scraped-off bark dusted through his black hair. Lady Edwina wanted to reach up and brush it from his ebony waves just like she had wanted to reach down and twirl the soft hairs of his chest about her fingers. Except this time the man was totally conscious, and there were others in the room. Thus, she maintained her ladylike demeanor.

"You are quite correct, my lady," Trent told her. "I have never been a valet, but I have been a soldier, and I have removed the boots of quite a number of injured men."

"It does not surprise me to hear you say that, Trescott," she told him. "Nor would I be at all astonished to hear that you had also been a footpad and had removed the boots of a number of unfortunate victims as well."

"Winnie!" Lord Dynford mumbled from the daybed. "Have you changed your mind? You no longer think Trescott is here to pinch the silver, but that he is after our footwear?"

Lady Edwina flushed with embarrassment, then pursed her lips tightly together. Why should she care a fig if Trescott knew that she had serious doubts regarding his honesty?

Trent laughed aloud. "I assure you, my lady, neither your family silver nor your dainty slippers are my preoccupying interest."

He held out his hand toward Lord Dynford. "But, my lord, if you will allow me?"

Lord Dynford had been throwing down glass after glass of the brandy, although the pace of his imbibition had begun to slow somewhat. The decrease of his speed owned not so much to the fact that it was becoming increasingly difficult for his lordship to empty the decanter as to the fact that it was becoming increasingly difficult for his lordship to fill the snifter.

"Trescott, you may feel free to do whatever you see fit to stop this damnable pain," his lordship mumbled, waving his hand somewhere in the general direction of his foot and sloshing the brandy over the leg of his torn and filthy duck breeches.

"Very good, my lord," Trent replied. He turned to Pringle. "Have you your knife?"

Pringle hesitated a moment, then reached into the pocket of his jacket. Much to Lady Edwina's horror, Pringle withdrew his folder and handed it to Trent.

"Pringle! Where did you obtain such a knife?" Lady Edwina demanded.

Pringle shrugged. "I need it for his lordship's protection."

"But, Pringle," she protested, "his lordship never goes anywhere that he would encounter such danger as to warrant such . . . such *large* protection!"

Pringle shrugged again. "Well, m'lady, it's also rather handy for cutting his lordship down from the trees from time to time."

Trent had dropped to one knee before his lordship. Lady Edwina watched, eyes widened in surprise, as Trent deftly slit the expensive new boot from heel to top. The boot slipped easily from Lord Dynford's swollen ankle. His lordship sighed with relief.

Trent tossed the ruined boot aside and returned the knife to Pringle. After peeling off his lordship's cotton hose, Trent gingerly examined the puffy, blue and purple mass of flesh.

"Your ankle appears to be badly wrenched, my lord," Trent told him, rising again. "Fortunately, that and a few scratches are the extent of your injuries, as far as I can determine. A bandage and a few days of disuse should have your lordship back in prime style."

Lady Edwina was relieved to hear that Lord Dynford's injuries were not more extensive. However, she was still rather taken aback by Trent's cavalier treatment of his lordship's footwear.

"Trescott, you have ruthlessly butchered a helpless boot," Lady Edwina observed, gesturing at the hapless victim.

160

Trent nudged the boot gingerly with his toe. "Ah, but the boot was not sacrificed in vain. His lordship's ankle should heal completely within a few weeks. Had Pringle or yourself continued, you would surely have damaged his lordship's ankle to the extent that he might always have walked with a limp and a cane. Or perhaps he might never have walked upon it again at all."

"And where did you read Medicine, Trescott?" Lady Edwina asked sarcastically.

"I have only my previous experience, my lady. The ankle had swollen and become entrapped in the narrow boot. To force it would have been to damage the delicate tissues of the joint."

Lady Edwina silently regarded Trent, considering his words. She clenched her jaws tightly together when she realized the harm she might have inadvertently done to her beloved brother.

"Perhaps you are right," she conceded reluctantly. Perhaps this Trescott fellow might prove worthy of his hire after all, she decided. So much the better, as a great deal of time and effort had gone into effecting his recuperation. It was about time the man began to repay them.

Trent still stood beside her, rocking back and forth on his heels in a most insolent manner instead of continuing with his assigned tasks. What was the man waiting for? Did he suppose she should be thanking him effusively for merely performing his rightful duties?

"Have you anything more to say to me, my lady?" Trent asked, lifting one dark brow.

She hesitated a moment. At last, she replied, "No, I do not."

She turned abruptly from Trent to Pringle.

"See that his lordship is made as comfortable as possible while I bandage his ankle," she ordered.

Lady Edwina turned again to see to her brother. Lord Dynford's head lolled against the back of the daybed.

The empty decanter of brandy lay cradled in his arms. He was fast asleep and snoring loudly.

"Ah, his lordship has already seen to his own comfort,"

Trent remarked with a chuckle.

Lady Edwina placed her finger against her lips, and shooed Trent and Pringle from the room.

She eased the empty decanter from his arms and the glass from his limp grasp. She placed them on a side table.

Taking a rolled-up strip of linen from the tray which Stokes had brought into his lordship's bedchamber before his arrival, Lady Edwina knelt at the foot of the daybed. Propping her brother's foot upon the soft cushion, she firmly wrapped the bandage about his injured ankle.

She needed another bandage, and as she rose to retrieve it, she kicked his lordship's ruined and discarded boot.

'Oh, that Trescott! How can he be so smug?' she fumed silently. Who did the man think he was, talking to her as if her were an equal, and taking such liberties with his lordship's property?

Of course, if he had not spoken up when he did, her brother surely would be in a bad way. The man was possessed of a variety of experiences, and was quite intelligent, too. Why must he persist in not only offering encouragement, but in actually, physically *helping* her brother in his strange, futile, and obviously dangerous experiments?

Of course! She felt truly enlightened as the thought struck her. This was the first of her brother's experiments which Trescott had actually witnessed while in a condition to be truly aware of what was transpiring. Perhaps he had never before realized how dangerous trying to fly could be. Certainly, his lordship's latest mishap had revealed to him the full import of ceasing these senseless excursions!

Trescott was an intelligent man. Perhaps he could be prevailed upon to persuade her brother that he truly was in great peril.

Anything was certainly worth a try when her brother's health and well-being were at stake.

With these thoughts firmly in mind, she decided to enlist Trescott's aid immediately. She rose and headed toward the door, fully intending to find James Trescott.

But at the doorway, she paused. She had no idea where Trescott was. She certainly had no intention of condescending to seek him out. The man was impertinent enough.

She could not send another footman to summon him. Suppose her brother should then discover that Trescott's sudden discouragement had all been her idea? His lordship never listened to her advice as it was, but at least she had been able to maintain the dignity of a concerned older sister. If he ever discovered that she had sunk so low as to use such subterfuge to obtain her desired ends . . .

Well, she would not do it that way! And she had time. It was a certainty that her brother would not be doing any more experiments, at least not until his ankle healed.

Chapter Thirteen

Her face clouded with exasperation, Lady Edwina grumbled to herself as she headed for the library, book in hand. 'Richard has never been able to interest himself in Shakespeare or Pepys or even Scott. I can accept that,' she thought philosophically.

For the first three days following his injury, she had tried to interest her brother in some other reading matter, all to no avail.

'If he wishes to spend his days recuperating reading books on birds, well, I suppose there are worse pastimes—but now this!'

Three days ago, her brother had received a letter from Sir George Cayley. He had expressed delight that someone else should be interested in 'aerial navigation.' The baronet had even gone so far as to send Lord Dynford a six-year-old copy of volumes XIV and XV of *Nicholson's Journal of Natural Philosophy, Chemistry and The Arts,* which contained parts one and two of an article written by himself.

Lord Dynford had read and reread the article to her until she thought she should toss the whole of the correspondence out the attic window. Ha! Then he should truly see it fly!

Her brother now spent every waking moment perusing the articles, discussing his revised theories with Trescott, and making new drawings for designs of his own.

'I sometimes find myself wondering who is more bird-witted, Richard or Cecily,' she continued to grumble as she entered the library and set the unwanted book on the large oaken table in the center of the room, 'or the people who encourage them in their unconventional behavior.'

An insistent tapping at the far end of the library attracted her attention. Lord Dynford was recuperating in his bedchamber upstairs. The servants were all about their duties. Who else was there? She made her way toward the end of the rear of the library.

"Trescott," she sighed with relief when she espied his agile figure perched high atop the ladder which permitted access to the uppermost shelves of the library.

Raising her voice to be heard over the incessant tapping, she called up to him, "Has his lordship given you permission to be here? I certainly do not recall doing so."

"Ah, good morning, my lady," he called his cheerful greeting down to her without leaving off his endeavors. A small hammer in one hand, a chisel in the other, he was systematically attacking the iron rollers at the top of the ladder which fit into the runners that ran the length of the wall across the shelves.

"Was his lordship's boot not sufficient prey?" she asked. "Must you now damage the library?"

Trent laughed and continued his efforts.

"I believe that in his enforced physical inactivity, his lordship's mind conjures all manner of necessary repairs which had heretofore escaped his notice," Trent said. "Three days ago his lordship gave me an extensive list."

"Unfortunately, few of our servants have been handy with tools as of late," Lady Edwina explained.

"Yesterday, I repaired the broken sashes of an attic window. The day before, it was the loose hinges and squeaking drawers of his lordship's wardrobe and dressing table," Trent enumerated his tasks to her ladyship. "Today I shall attempt to mend the runners of this ladder."

Lady Edwina gave a delicate little snort of derision. "I certainly wish you luck with your present task, Trescott. Many have tried, but no one has been able to make that ladder work properly for as long as I can remember."

"A man can only do his best, my lady." Trent shrugged and continued working.

"There is another matter at which I should like you to try your best."

When he continued his tapping, she called again. "Trescott! This is a matter of the utmost urgency."

"Very well, my lady," Trent responded without slowing the pace of his industry. "I am listening."

"I would prefer not to speak to your feet," she said. She did not want to tell him how disconcerting if was to look at those legs enswathed in cotton hose and powder blue breeches and to remember how those same legs had looked bare, under a thin, lawn nightshirt. She really would rather not be reminded right now of the feelings that his scantily clad body had aroused in her.

Trent looked down upon her. "Begging your pardon, my lady, you may be as light as the proverbial feather, but I rather doubt that this old ladder will support the both of us."

"I have no intention of climbing up a ladder," she informed him haughtily. "Please be so kind as to descend."

He turned back to the rollers and began tapping again. "When I have finished, I shall be most pleased to converse with your ladyship, but his lordship's explicit instructions were to repair this ladder. I must attend to this first, if you please."

"It does not please me!" she said sharply. "If you do not listen to me immediately, there may not be a lordship to give you instructions in the future!"

"I shall be down straightaway, my lady," Trent said.

He made another tap or two on the runners, then pushed the tools into one of the large pockets of the leathern apron which he wore over his blue and gold Dynford livery. He sat upon one rung of the ladder and rested his feet upon a lower rung. He leaned forward and propped his elbows upon his knees.

"What problem with his lordship do you find so urgent, my lady?" he asked, frowning with concern. "And why should your ladyship think to come to me with this problem?"

"Trescott!" she told him sharply. "I realize you are unaccustomed to service, but neither am I in the habit of conversing with sitting servants while I stand."

"I do beg your pardon, my lady." Trent unfolded his long legs from under him and stretched them out to the floor. He rose to stand at the base of the ladder, quite close to where Lady Edwina was standing.

She drew in a deep breath at his proximity. He smelled of dusty old books and the leathern apron. His clear green eyes gazed down at her, waiting.

She swallowed hard, berating herself for what she believed was her own cowardice regarding broaching this matter. Summoning her usual dignity, she returned Trent's intense scrutiny.

"Trescott, for some reason which I fail to understand, my brother seems to think very highly of you," Lady Edwina began.

"I am flattered," Trent responded, then added with a lift of his eyebrow, "At least by his lordship's opinion of me. I find Lord Dynford a most pleasant young man."

"I should like to see that his lordship eventually becomes a most pleasant *old* man."

"I am sure he would agree with your aspirations for him, my lady," Trent said with a little smirk at the side of his lips.

"Then these mad attempts at flight must stop," she ordered.

"But Lord Dynford is most interested in flight, my lady."

"He is *obsessed* with flight," she corrected, "to the exclusion of everything else. All these years, I have done all I can to dissuade him, but to no avail."

"If your ladyship has had no success, why should you think that I . . . ?"

"My brother thinks that you are quite a 'capital fellow' — those were his words. And as my brother regards you so highly, Trescott, I thought perhaps a few well-chosen words from you might persuade him to abandon these foolish and dangerous excursions."

"Your brother is no fool, my lady," Trent told her. He was no longer grinning, but speaking in earnest. "He is a most imaginative, inventive, and tenacious man. And as you may see from his correspondence with Sir George Cayley, his is not the only great mind preoccupied with achieving flight."

Lady Edwina made no reply.

"As for danger, well, no great endeavor was ever accomplished without some risk. And while his lordship may have sustained various abrasions and contusions, there is nothing serious . . ."

"Nothing serious!" she interrupted. "I would venture to say that most people would consider falling out of a tree to be rather serious."

"My lady, any *ordinary* human being may fall *out* of a tree," Trent said. "I would wager that your brother is the only person who has fallen *into* a tree."

But Lady Edwina was not to be cajoled. Her blue eyes glared up at him, flashing a warning.

"At any rate, my lady," Trent said, a bit more conciliatorily, "a

167

wrenched ankle hardly places his lordship's life in imminent peril."

"Must I wait until they carry him home on a gate?" she cried. "These attempts at flight must stop!"

Trent was still shaking his head. Why must this infernal man continue to refuse to comply with her one, simple request?

Her life had been proceeding so smoothly, in spite of the occasional burst of excitement generated by her brother's experiments. But in the few months in which this man had been with them, she found herself becoming quite easily agitated. This was most unlike her. Most disconcerting of all was the fact that her agitation was usually due to this man.

"I understand your ladyship's quite natural concern for your brother, but I still fail to see any convincing reason why—"

"Why?" she fairly screamed. "Have you no eyes? Can you not see that one day he will surely kill himself?"

"Or one day he will surely fly," Trent countered calmly.

At first, Lady Edwina was too awestruck by his calm acceptance of the possibility for success to reply. At last, she managed a hoarse whisper. "You are as mad as my brother!"

"Lord Dynford is not the only man who ever dreamed of attaining the impossible, but he may be one of the few who ever came so near to success."

Lady Edwina was silent. Until this moment, she had only considered her brother as a foolish, overgrown child, pursuing some lunatic delusion. Could it be that his ideas were not so mad after all?

"Have you been so concerned about his failures that you never stopped to consider the possibility of his success, my lady?" Trent asked her.

Her anger was slowly ebbing. She looked up into his eyes. He had taken a few steps and now stood very close to her.

"No, Trescott," she answered quietly. "In truth, I had not."

"Lord Dynford is so near success, he must not stop now. Please believe me, then, when I tell you, my lady, that while I am here, I shall do all within my power to ensure his lordship's safety when he conducts his experiments."

"No doubt, in the same, efficient manner in which you cared for him the other day." she remarked with a mocking little twist to her lips. "Why, Trescott, I cannot begin to tell you what comfort that affords my spirit!"

"It was a most unfortunate occurrence, my lady," Trent explained, smiling apologetically. "His lordship is still attempting to determine why the wing structure failed to support his weight and collapsed, sending him crashing into the trees."

Lady Edwina waved her hand before him. "Please, Trescott. It is difficult enough just to think of what happened. I truly do not need to hear a vivid description."

"His lordship and I are already discussing extensively what modifications might be made to ensure a safe and successful flight in the future."

"So, Trescott, you have read the principles of Architecture in addition to Medicine," she asked, tilting her head slightly to peer intently into his eyes.

"Do you think we cannot improve the apparatus? Oh, ye of little faith," he chided her with a mischievous grin.

"*And* Divinity?" she added, allowing herself another small grin. "I am indeed impressed."

Trent smiled, swept his arm out and made a deep bow. "My lady, I have only just begun to astound you with my diverse and sundry skills."

He grasped the ladder and gave it a small pull toward himself. It creaked, then slid easily along the runners. He nudged the ladder in the opposite direction. It glided smoothly down the rows of books. He bestowed upon her a waggish grin.

"If I had not witnessed it with my own eyes, I should not have believed it!" Lady Edwina exclaimed. "I was so weary of grappling with that ladder that I was upon the verge of tackling the task myself, either with a hammer or a hatchet! And I was not so particular about which I used."

Trent laughed aloud.

"Do you think me incapable of handling such implements?" she demanded.

"I must own, your ladyship brandishing hammer and hatchet does indeed present quite a picture!" he replied with a wide grin.

"And why should it surprise you, Trescott, if I should undertake a few repairs?"

Trent's hand slowly moved up to cradle Lady Edwina's cheek.

"You are very like your brother in that respect. Nothing you could undertake would surprise me. I believe you to be quite capable of accomplishing whatever you have set your mind to."

His hand felt cool against her burning cheek. She had come to seek his aid. Now she feared that she had indeed found much more than what she had been seeking!

Lady Edwina pulled away at the same moment that Trent dropped his hand. He quickly climbed the ladder and began tapping away again at the runners which they both knew to be completely repaired.

She said nothing, but turned on her heels and rapidly retreated from the library. She raised her hand to her face. In her mind, she still felt his smooth palm caressing her cheek.

She could not credit her own strange reaction to this man. He was undeniably handsome, but so many of the men she had encountered since her coming out were handsome as well. He was intelligent and clever — indeed, that was a drastic change from most of the men she had met!

His very presence summoned from the depths of her being both a chill and a fever that enveloped her totally — a feeling she had never known could exist within her. And, for pity's sake, — he was her footman!

No! It was inconceivable that she should have any feeling for this man beyond a lady's customary concern for the well-being of her staff! She was the daughter of an earl — a lady in her own right. And who was this fellow, this James Trescott? She still harbored a nagging doubt that James Trescott was not even his true name.

The very idea of her forming any emotional attachment whatsoever for a mere footman was ludicrous — and completely unacceptable!

The wheels of the maroon and gold carriage jiggled over the well-worn cobbles as it turned off Oxford Street onto Orchard Street and made the wide turn around Portman Square to stop before the Dynfords' home. The strapping, black-haired footman bounded down from his perch to lower the steps and open the carriage door.

170

Lord Haverslea emerged from the carriage, then imperiously waved the footman out of the way while he himself held out his hand to assist the ladies to alight.

He most solicitously handed Lady Portia out first. She stood, shaking out the pale gray silk skirt of her gown and adjusting her white cashmere shawl.

Lady Cecily extended her hand to Lord Haverslea. He did not release her hand after she had set foot upon the ground, and she made no effort whatsoever to draw it back. He tucked her hand into the crook of his elbow, then offered Lady Portia his other arm.

"I vow, I never realized the theater could be so entertaining!" Lady Cecily exclaimed. "Indeed, it is so much more enjoyable when there is not such a crush."

"Yes, indeed," Lady Portia said. "Without such a crowd of people, one can see the performance all the better."

"Oh, la! Who gives a fig for the performance, Aunt Portia?" Lady Cecily demanded. "Without such a crush, people could see *me* all the better!"

With her free hand, she smoothed the skirt of her new turquoise gown with little pink rosebuds affixed to the center of the quite low-cut bodice, to the points of the scalloped hem, and to the cuffs of the little puffed sleeves. She adjusted her elbow-length gloves, which were of a shade of pink exactly matching the decorative rosebuds, while she transferred from hand to hand the nosegay of pink rosebuds which Lord Haverslea had sent to her. Her pink kid slippers peeked out from under the hem of her skirt.

"They could not help but watch a lady as lovely as you," he told her. "Indeed, my dear, you were quite the most fashionable lady there this evening."

"Oh, la! If they were watching me, then they could not help but notice that I was accompanied by clearly the most handsome lord in London!" she exclaimed, gazing adoringly into his green eyes.

"Indeed, we do make an incomparable pair!" he answered.

"Quite a pair," Lady Portia echoed.

Lord Haverslea turned quickly and nodded, smiling, at Lady Portia. "Quite a trio," he corrected. "We must not forget this charming lady."

Lady Portia's wrinkles deepened as she returned Lord Haverslea's engaging smile. "Oh, dear, such a flatterer!" she exclaimed. She turned to her niece and sighed wistfully, "You *are* quite lovely, Cecily, my dear. If only I could wear such dazzling colors . . . "

"Oh, la! Do not fret, Aunt Portia," she comforted the elderly lady as they entered the townhouse. "How many times must I tell you that, with your pale complexion and silvery-white hair, you would look a positive fright in anything but that lovely soft shade of dove gray? And anyway, if you and I were both to wear bright colors, why, we should make an absolutely *horrid* clash! How unfashionable we should appear!"

"Quite so, my dear, quite so," Lady Portia agreed. "We should not wish to appear unfashionable."

Lady Cecily carelessly discarded her lace shawl over her shoulder. The footman caught it by the tips of his fingers just before it reached the floor.

"Lord Haverslea," she said, never once releasing his hand, "would you care for something? Tea, lemonade, brandy . . . ?"

"Indeed, thank you," he answered. "A brandy would be perfect."

"Yes, I think I should like to have —" Lady Portia began.

"Oh, la! How can you think of drinking anything at this hour and at your age, Aunt Portia?" Lady Cecily exclaimed in horror. "Why, you should be up the remainder of the night with acute dyspepsia!"

"Ah, yes," Lady Portia agreed. "I do suffer from dyspepsia from time to time."

"Precisely my point! And it always seems to occur on those evenings when you have been eating late." Lady Cecily bent forward to scrutinize her aunt very closely. Her eyes narrowed as she demanded, "Are you quite certain that you are feeling well this very evening, Aunt Portia? I do believe our outing has overtaxed you."

"I am indeed exhausted from following you about," Lady Portia admitted.

"I know just the thing for you, my dear," Lady Cecily said, reluctantly releasing his lordship's hand and placing her arm about her aunt's shoulder to guide her toward the stairs. "You want a good night's sleep!"

"Yes," Lady Portia answered, stifling a yawn. "I should love to have some sleep. Good evening, Lord Haverslea. Good night, Cecily dear."

Without looking behind her, Lady Portia slowly climbed the steep staircase, her withered hand gripping the wrought-iron banister for support.

Without glancing back at her aunt, Lady Cecily took Lord Haverslea's arm and led him into the drawing room. She turned to the footman. "Well, don't just stand there," she ordered. "Attend to his lordship's requirements. And I think I should enjoy some ratafia biscuits."

Still carrying Lady Cecily's lace shawl, the footman opened the liquor cabinet, withdrew a decanter of brandy and placed it on the sideboard beside the snifters, then scampered off toward the kitchen.

"Oh dear, Lord Haverslea," Lady Cecily said, turning to him suddenly with wide, blue eyes, her hand gently placed against her bosom. "In my concern for my dear elderly aunt's welfare and my haste to supply you with refreshment, I fear I have unwittingly placed myself in a *most* compromising position. We are, I fear, quite alone."

She continued to gaze at him, her eyes wide and expectant. 'It is now or never,' she told herself, holding her breath with anticipation.

Lord Haverslea bowed with extreme politeness. "My lady, you have nothing to fear from me."

Suddenly the innocent expression changed to a teasing little pout. "Oh, what a pity! Surely you are not such a tame cat that I have *nothing* to fear from you!"

Lady Cecily thought she should scream in frustration if this did not induce him to declare himself!

After what seemed an interminable span of time, he took a step closer to her.

Ah, she felt she could breathe again.

"I repeat, my dearest Cecily, you have nothing to fear from me," he said, taking her hand. "My intentions are most honorable."

He had called her Cecily! She found it most difficult not to bounce up and down with glee. 'Dare I call him Nigel?' she debated.

Of course she dared!

"I always did think you were quite an honorable gentleman, Nigel," she replied, gazing into his eyes with as much sincerity as she could summon.

He reached out and took both of her hands in his.

"Then, since your dear aunt has retired for the evening and I should not wish to disturb her rest, and since your brother, as head of the family, is absent, then I shall be so bold as to speak my intentions directly to you."

'Oh, speak to me, Nigel! Speak to me!' she cried inwardly.

With a quite innocent expression upon her lovely face, she said aloud, "Why, Nigel, you have always spoken directly to me. Whatever could my aunt or my brother have to do with your intentions?"

He assumed a quite serious demeanor. "Cecily, I do think we deal rather well together," he announced.

"Oh, indeed." She would agree with him if he said the moon were a custard tart topped with Devonshire cream.

"Our fortunes are quite well matched," he continued in a most sensible tone. "No one could accuse either of us of marrying for money."

"Oh, indeed." She would agree with him if he said that the Thames were claret punch.

"And no one could deny that you and I are an exceedingly handsome couple both in fashion and in figure."

"Oh, indeed." Well, of course, she would be exceedingly fashionable all by herself, but with this handsome man beside her, she would *really* cut quite a dash through the *ton!*

"I realize I am a baron and you the daughter of an earl. There will be some who will maintain that you might have aimed a bit higher on the marriage mart . . ."

"Oh, Nigel, I hardly think *that* an insurmountable barrier," she replied with a tinkling little laugh.

"Then might I suggest that you and I could do no better than to join these exceptional attributes of ours in the bonds of matrimony?"

Success! Lady Cecily's eyes grew even wider and her hand flew to cover her mouth. She was grinning in a *most* triumphant and unladylike fashion. With her hand over her mouth, he would merely assume she was taken completely by surprise.

"Why, I suppose I should have some time to consider your offer," she said coyly. 'Consider! My auntie's pantaloons!' she thought. But she must not let him think her too easily won!

"Consider?" he echoed. "Cecily, I am rather disappointed. I had always judged you to be a most impetuous lady."

"Oh, Nigel! I should *never* want to disappoint *you!*" she exclaimed. 'I shall be delighted to marry you!

The Ultimate Success! the new Lord Haverslea exulted, riding homeward in the dark interior of the carriage.

He had been born to his superb good looks and vast fortune. He had carefully cultivated his wit, his intellect and his impeccable good taste. By his own machinations, he had righted the wrongs of Fate and attained the barony and the vast estates which should have been his by birth.

And now he had found a wife quite equal in every way to his station and requirements.

Of course, he would have to abide by the archaic dictates of propriety and wait a year until he was out of mourning for his two cousins before he could marry the lady. Damn Milton and Trent! Even from the grave they would try to spoil his plans.

But everything else was coming up to his expectations quite nicely. He could afford to wait.

Dynford Manor was quiet—too quiet, again. Lady Edwina had already knocked upon her brother's bedchamber door. When she had received no answer, she made so bold as to enter anyway. He was not there.

Where could he be? she wondered. With his injured ankle, he had barely managed to hop about with the aid of his walking stick.

She glanced about for Pringle, thinking he might be able to inform her of the whereabouts of her brother. Neither could she locate the valet.

"Stokes," she demanded as she entered her own bedchamber. She broke off in midsentence as she saw that her bedchamber was empty as well.

Have they all deserted me? she wondered. She left her suite in search of Haskell.

The silvery-haired butler was standing by the door in the Hall.

"Haskell, what are you doing just standing about?" she asked.

"M'lady," his voice reverberated through the Great Hall. "I await his lordship."

"Then you know where his lordship is?" she asked.

"His lordship is out, m'lady," Haskell answered.

The thought came to her that getting information from Haskell was approximately as easy as getting peaches from an apple tree.

"Haskell," Lady Edwina demanded, "is his lordship experimenting with his flying contraption again?"

Haskell nodded. "As I recall, Pringle and that Trescott fellow were discussing his lordship's latest machine at breakfast. And I did hear his lordship mentioning something about the barn as he was leaving."

'The barn?' she repeated to herself as she spun about and walked up the stairs as quickly as she could without sacrificing her ladylike dignity before the butler.

Scarcely two weeks had passed since her brother had injured his ankle in his last attempt. He should barely be walking about the drawing room, much less all the way to the stables.

Her brother should not even be walking to the stables at all! She had asked Trescott to try to dissuade him from these mad excursions. "Damn his eyes!" she cursed, and felt quite certain that he deserved every malediction. The man had entirely disregarded her one simple request and was, even now, assisting her brother with the instrument of his certain doom!

She made her way through the manor to the conservatory and out the door into the garden. She walked with rapid little steps past the gardens to the edge of the park. The tall elms, oaks and beeches shaded the path through the coppice to the stables.

Even before she reached the large building, she could hear the

176

rasping sounds of the saws and the incessant rappings of the hammers. She reached out her hand and pushed the stable door open.

"Richard!" Much to her dismay, she noted that his lordship was seated upon one of the dining room chairs. Well, whoever had brought such a fine piece of furniture out to the stable should surely get the sack, she reminded herself. On second thought, her kindhearted brother would never permit it.

"Winnie!" Lord Dynford exclaimed. He quickly rose, throwing the two journals he had been perusing onto the vacated seat.

All sounds of construction ceased as Pringle and Trent looked up.

"Trescott!" was all she said to him. She opened her mouth to say more, but no words would come. She would have shouted her anger at him for disobeying her. She would even have expressed her disappointment that he had not met her expectations of him as an honorable and intelligent man. But there were no words to express the hurt that she was feeling.

"But you have never come here before, Winnie," Lord Dynford exclaimed. "To what do we owe this singular honor?"

Lady Edwina laughed a rueful little laugh as she went to stand beside her brother. "I certainly meant to convey no honor. I came because I was concerned for your well-being, as no one else seems to be," she added with a sharp look at Trent.

"But come see my lovely new apparatus, Winnie!" he invited, ignoring her censure. He extended his arm to indicate the strange-looking machine in the center of the stable. He grabbed the cane that had been hanging on the arm of the chair and began to lead her ladyship toward his precious machine.

"Ouch!" his lordship exclaimed and collapsed again into the chair. " 'Tis deucedly frustrating to be so incapacitated with this ankle!"

Lady Edwina wanted to scold her younger brother for his stubborn insistence upon trying to walk. When she saw the expression of pain on his face, she decided to remain silent.

"Trescott, old fellow," Lord Dynford called.

Trent laid aside his hammer and came to the side of his lordship's chair.

"Since I can't get about properly, you'll show her ladyship

about the apparatus, won't you?" his lordship asked.

Trent made a slight bow. "Very good, m'lord." He turned to Lady Edwina, bowed again, and gestured toward the strange apparatus standing in the center of the stable. "If you would, my lady."

She left his lordship's side and began to circle the apparatus.

"Have a care, my lady," Trent said, taking her elbow to assist her in making her way about a large pile of white silk which lay beside the apparatus.

She accepted his aid only for as long as it took her to skirt the pile of silk. Then she inconspicuously pulled her arm away from him, tucking her elbow in closely to her side.

"I must own, it is the most unusual thing that I have ever seen," she said.

The other machines which his lordship had ordered constructed, with their ribbed and movable wings, had all borne a striking resemblance to plucked birds. This apparatus bore a stronger resemblance to a boat with two large, rigid appendages at either side. As yet, the appendages were bare of any fabric.

"How do you expect to fly this thing without real wings?" she asked, her curiosity aroused. She reached up to touch the large appendage closest to her. She began to chuckle softly. "Indeed, you needn't have gone to the trouble of constructing an entirely new apparatus. From the looks of this thing, you would have done just as well to go up to the attics and bring down one of Grandmama's old panniers!"

"But I ain't done with it yet, m'lady," Stokes offered. She peered at her mistress from over the top of the large pile of white silk which she was busily stitching.

"Stokes!" she exclaimed. "Have you deserted me, too?"

Stokes grinned sheepishly, shrugged her shoulders, and continued to stitch.

"If you are sewing the wings together, I am quite sure this thing will not remain aloft!" Lady Edwina sniffed sarcastically.

"Oh, no, m'lady!" Stokes protested. "I've been watching you. Pringle says I'm getting to be quite a dab hand at it . . ."

She threw a quick look over to Pringle. Her thin little face flushed and she dropped her gaze to concentrate on her work again.

From his seat at the other side of the stable, Lord Dynford began to laugh. "The linendraper has declared that I spend more money on bolts of silk than you do, Winnie."

Lady Edwina regarded the expanse of white and silently agreed.

"Allow me to continue the Grand Tour, my lady," Trent said, offering his arm again to afford her balance over the litter-strewn floor.

Lady Edwina pointedly ignored him.

"It was no small wonder that his lordship had not managed to remain aloft with the movable winds," he explained as he followed her about. "As Sir George Cayley had pointed out in his articles, man's pectoral muscles are not constructed to function in the same manner as do a bird's."

He tapped at his chest, denting the white cotton of his shirt. Lady Edwina recalled the firm smooth chest muscles under that shirt and the softly curling dark hairs which covered his chest.

'A fine time to think of *that!*' she chided herself. 'Oh, Edwina, you do need to find another pastime with which to occupy your wanton thoughts!'

"Instead of mere physical strength, man must reply upon his mental strengths," Trent continued, tapping the side of his head with his forefinger.

She thought they were all quite weak in the head to be attempting to realize this wild fantasy.

Trent was continuing enthusiastically, "While a strong man may lift himself with the proper apparatus, if air transportation is to be anything beyond a mere diversion, there must be some other way of transporting several persons and their goods."

"Quite an interesting theory," she agreed. "And that is the purpose of the immovable wings?"

"Precisely." Trent passed his hand in a slight bump over the top of the bare wing structure.

Lady Edwina tried to concentrate on the theories of flight which he was explaining to her and not on the sight of the gentle curve of the palm of his hand. To watch the curve of his hand brought back to her mind the feel of that hand upon her cheek.

"This wing will be concave, to catch the air, to make use of the resistance the air exerts upon an object passing through it," he

179

explained.

Then he passed his hand under the structure. She found herself wondering what it would be like to have that hand gently caressing not only her cheek, but other parts of her anatomy as well. She pinched herself to stop such lascivious thoughts. After all, she was supposed to be angry with the man!

"Impressive, Trescott," she admitted. "Still, if it does not work . . ."

"It *will* work, my lady," he insisted.

"Splendid, is it not? And I owe it all to Trescott for suggesting that I contact Sir George," Lord Dynford declared, patting the journals on his lap. "Between the two of them, I know I shall fly in this, Winnie! I know I truly shall!"

Chapter Fourteen

Stokes burst into the drawing room crying excitedly, "M'lady! Oh, m'lady! Come watch his lordship go!"

The book which Lady Edwina had been reading tumbled to the floor as she jumped up with alarm. But she stood there, awestruck and bewildered.

"He cannot possibly attempt to fly today!" she cried in protest. "They cannot have finished such a complicated piece of work in so few days. And his lordship's ankle has still not completely mended."

Stokes hopped up and down impatiently and whined, "Oh, hurry, m'lady, hurry — before he sets off and we miss it all!" She grabbed Lady Edwina's hand and pulled her to the front doorway of Dynford Manor and out of doors.

Lady Edwina stopped at the top of the marble steps. It was exceptionally windy today, and the breeze was already unusually chill for late summer. Her muslin skirts beat against her legs and little wisps of hair pulled loose from her chignon and whipped about her face. She shivered and drew her arms closer against her.

"Where is his lordship, Stokes?" she asked, looking about the wide cobbled circle at the front of the Manor, down the tree-lined drive, then across the green lawn spread before them.

"No, no, m'lady. There he is!" Stokes spun her ladyship to face the gray stone facade of the large, old building. She pointed straight up.

Lady Edwina shaded her eyes with her hand and scanned the sky.

"My gracious, has he finally succeeded?" she asked. But as she searched, she saw nothing but empty blue above.

"Not yet, m'lady," Stokes said. "His lordship's still on the roof. Oh, thank goodness, we ain't missed it!"

Lady Edwina's hand and jaw dropped simultaneously. "The roof," she repeated blankly. Her heart twisted inside her and the bones of her spine tingled with a chill which owed nothing to the stiff breeze which now beat about them.

It was bad enough when Lord Dynford had first insisted upon climbing up into trees wearing his wings. He had never managed to climb high enough in the heavy apparatus to pose a severe threat to his life. Even sailing off the hilltop had only resulted in a sprained ankle. But the roof was four stories up, and it was a long way down.

"His lordship is still on the roof?" Lady Edwina repeated, hoping that perhaps she had not heard aright the first time.

Stokes was nodding vigorously. "Pringle told me that his lordship said that according to his calculations, today's the perfect day, what with the wind and all."

Lady Edwina paced nervously back and forth. If he had already flown, she would have been truly excited to celebrate his momentous success. But he was still upon the rooftop of Dynford Manor, still waiting, still in danger of killing himself when the wing structure collapsed again as it had so many times before and he hurtled to the marble steps and the cobbled drive below. And she would be here to witness it.

She wanted to turn back inside, to run up the stairs until she was safe within her own apartments. She wanted to lock the door and hide her head under a pillow until her brother's entire maniacal scheme was finished. She had no desire to witness this, his last futile attempt at flight.

But she stayed, transfixed to the spot. It was not out of any morbid curiosity that she remained, but because he was her brother whom she loved. If she could do nothing now to stop him, at least she could be with him at the end.

"Look there, m'lady!" Stokes was still bouncing about, pointing to the wide expanse of lawn that sloped from the house, past the ancient elms, down toward the lake. "There's Pringle and Trescott down there waiting for his lordship to land. Do you really think his lordship'll go that far?"

"I certainly hope so, Stokes," Lady Edwina murmured quietly, never taking her eyes from her brother. "I certainly hope so."

"M'lady!" Haskell declared as he came up beside Lady Edwina. In spite of the sound of the wind whipping past her ears, she could hear the butler quite clearly. "His lordship is upon the roof."

"Haskell," Lady Edwina said with sudden inspiration. "You must call his lordship down immediately. And tell him to be sure to use the stairs."

Haskell looked upward, then looked again to her ladyship.

"M'lady, I have grave doubts that he will hear me," he protested.

"Oh, he will hear you, Haskell," Lady Edwina assured him. "I have faith in you."

"Why, thank you, m'lady," he replied with a deep bow. Then his long stick figure bent backward and he emitted a bellowing cry upward. "M'lord! Her ladyship requests your immediate presence at the front of the Manor!"

Lord Dynford's face peered over the edge of the roof. He was encased in a new harness of rope mesh. This was attached by new leather straps and brass rings to the wooden supports of the large, silken fabric-covered wings outspread to each side of the apparatus which rose above him.

"M'lord!" Haskell called. "Will you require my assistance to negotiate your contraption down the stairs?"

Lord Dynford shook his head. Then he stuck his finger into his mouth and withdrew it, holding it up to determine the direction of the wind.

With a sickening feeling in the pit of her stomach, Lady Edwina watched him nod. He was satisfied with the wind. He was indeed about to attempt to fly one more time.

With a great effort, Lord Dynford pushed himself out from the highest peak of the roof.

"M'lady!" Haskell declared. "His lordship is aloft."

Lady Edwina dared not move. She dared not breathe. She could only stand staring upward as her brother leaped from the roof.

She screamed, expecting to see him plummet to the marble steps below. But the silken wings caught the wind and held him suspended above them.

He floated, dipping slightly up and down as the wind carried him farther and farther out, along the cobbled drive, past the lawn, over the towering elms.

"He did it, m'lady! His lordship's flying!" Stokes shouted. In her excitement, she had grasped Lady Edwina's arm and was still holding it as she bounced up and down from one foot to the other.

Lady Edwina ignored her maid as she followed her brother's path through the sky with incredulous wonder. He *had* done it! He *was* flying!

Suddenly his apparatus wobbled. The tip of one wing dipped and caught against the topmost twig of the tallest tree. His lordship dropped from sight.

"M'lady," Haskell announced. "His lordship has alighted."

Lady Edwina managed to detach herself from the ecstatic Stokes. She snatched up her skirts and ran down the lawn. Stokes had soon recovered and began to follow.

"M'lady!" Haskell called after Lady Edwina. "Where are you going? Would you not prefer to use the carriage?"

Trent had barely finished assisting a dripping wet Pringle to sit on the grassy bank when he turned abruptly and dove into the lake again. With long strokes, he quickly made his way to the broken apparatus floating in the middle of the lake.

Lady Edwina pulled up sharply at the shore of the lake and glanced frantically about.

"Pringle! Where is his lordship?" she demanded as she ran up to him.

Pringle was clutching his left leg. His face was red and contorted in pain. He managed to point one shaky finger out to the middle of the lake.

"Pringle! what happened to you?" Stokes demanded, falling to her knees beside him.

"Rosie! I tried my best to catch his lordship before he went into the lake," Pringle explained between gasps. "But he ran into me and I fell in." He moaned loudly, clutching his leg and rocking back and forth in his pain. "My foot got caught in the mud and my leg twisted as I fell. I think it's broken!"

"Don't worry, Pringle," Stokes said, holding him in her

184

arms. "We'll have it set properly. You'll be all right. I'll take care of you."

Lady Edwina looked out over the lake. Trent had reached his lordship's wings. Parts which had broken loose from the apparatus were already sinking below the surface. She waited interminable seconds before his head reappeared, only to sink again.

Nealy and Cobb were making a great deal of noise with their clumsy attempts to launch a small rowboat onto the lake. Redding, accompanied by Haskell, pulled the wagon to a halt behind her. Redding jumped down and began to assist Pringle up into the wagon. Stokes wrapped the blanket which Haskell handed her about the dripping valet.

Lady Edwina tried to block all of these distractions from her mind. She held her breath, waiting for her brother's fair head to break the surface of the water. Her eyes searched for Trent, too.

'I do not think I could bear to lose them both!' It was not so much a thought as a feeling from the heart.

She blinked at the realization of what she had been thinking, but it was not important. The only thing that really mattered now was that two heads should emerge from the surface of the lake.

At last Trent lifted Lord Dynford's fair head above the surface. Haskell, Stokes and Redding sent up a loud cheer from the shore. Lady Edwina, her knees turned to pudding, merely breathed a deep, thankful sigh of relief.

Nealy and Cobb had reached Trent and Lord Dynford. while Trent clung to the side of the boat with one hand and lifted, the other two pulled his lordship's limp body into the boat.

Trent had climbed into the boat. Lady Edwina watched as he bent over her brother, his broad shoulders pumping up and down as he worked to press breath again into his lordship's body.

As they reached the shore, Lord Dynford began to cough up water and to choke and wheeze.

"I did it! B'gads, I did it!" his lordship managed to mumble between fits of coughing.

185

"Thank God, he's breathing again," Lady Edwina heard Trent remark to Nealy and Cobb as they lifted his lordship up into the wagon.

'Thank God, they are both safe!' Lady Edwina sent up her silent prayer of gratitude.

Lady Edwina watched the remnants of Lord Dynford's wings sink irretrievably into the bottom of the lake. She shuddered.

'If Trescott had been delayed only a few seconds more, my brother would be accompanying that damnable contraption to its watery grave.' Suddenly, she frowned. 'If Trescott had not encouraged and even assisted him, there would have been no such damnable contraption.'

"M'lady, his lordship is wet!" Haskell observed. "Will your ladyship be requiring the use of a blanket?"

Trent extended his hand to her. "My lady, if you please." He grasped her gently about the waist and lifted her quite easily into the back of the wagon with her brother.

"You, too, Stokes." The maid giggled and blushed as Trent assisted her up onto the wagon seat beside Pringle.

"Hold tight to him, now," he instructed her. "We don't want that leg to move, do we?"

Stokes shook her head furiously and clasped Pringle tightly about the waist.

Trent helped Lady Edwina wrap the large, red and black horse blanket about his lordship. He then wrapped a second blanket about himself.

"Return Lord Dynford to the Manor quickly," Trent ordered Redding. "We must be certain that his lordship does not take a chill."

"I am perfectly well," Lord Dynford protested between bouts with his racking cough. He pulled the horse blanket closer about him to ward off the chill that shook him to his very bones.

"I am determined to see that you remain so," Lady Edwina informed him, hovering over him as Trent and Nealy lowered him onto the edge of his bed.

"B'gads, Winnie! It was wonderful!" Lord Dynford exclaimed.

"Do not try to talk now, Richard," she told him.

"But, Winnie, it was wonderful!" he repeated more loudly. He was again seized by a fit of coughing.

"Yes, yes. I am sure it was quite splendid. But come now," she coaxed. "We must get you out of these wet clothes. Nealy," she summoned the young footman.

"Where is Pringle?" Lord Dynford asked.

"Pringle was injured, but he will recover," Lady Edwina told him as simply as possible so as not to cause her brother any additional concern. "Cobb took him to his room and we have sent for the apothecary."

Lord Dynford nodded, but could say nothing because of the persistent cough which continued to shake his battered body.

"Nealy, I leave it to you to see that his lordship is removed from these wet clothes and properly dressed in a flannel nightshirt," Lady Edwina ordered.

She pulled open his lordship's wardrobe and searched several drawers until she encountered the nightshirt which she sought.

"Oh, I could've found it, m'lady," Nealy protested weakly.

She handed the nightshirt to Nealy, then wagged her finger at him. "Do not disappoint me," she warned.

Nealy gulped and replied, "I'll do my best, m'lady."

"Haskell, close those windows," she ordered, following him to the windows to be certain they were properly shut.

"I also believe his lordship should have a fire, Haskell," she said, following him to the hearth to watch as he laid and kindled a satisfactory blaze. "We cannot have his lordship taking a chill now, can we?"

She turned to her brother and informed him, "I must see to Pringle now. I shall return as soon as possible."

As she turned and walked toward the door, she was already busily planning for whatever might be necessary to effect his lordship's rapid recovery. She would have to oversee Mrs. Haskell's preparation of a large batch of distillation of willow bark. She would need to instruct Cook to prepare not only some rich chicken broth but several possets as well.

"Is there anything you wish me to do, your ladyship?" Trent asked.

She was startled from her cogitations. She was not aware that he had followed her out of the room. As a matter of fact, she had tried quite pointedly to ignore him.

She spun about angrily to confront him. "Trescott, you may go—" She abruptly closed her mouth, resisting the temptation to tell this horrid man to go to perdition. She regained her usual composure and instead said quite coldly, "I think you have done quite enough damage."

"Damage?" Trent demanded incredulously. "Not to put too fine a point on it, my lady, but I just saved his lordship's life!"

"His life would not have been in danger if he had not still been pursuing his mad quest for flight!" she cried.

"You surely do not blame me for this unfortunate accident, my lady," Trent asked incredulously.

"I do indeed," she replied with a continued coolness which she truly did not feel. She felt more like throwing something at this dangerous intruder who had so drastically disrupted her quiet family life.

"My lady, you cannot possibly hold me responsible for the caprices of the wind and the vagaries of arboreal growth," Trent protested.

"You did not try to discourage him from his experiments, as I asked. No. You actually had to go so far as to *encourage* him to further attempts! My brother would *never* have continued with his mad dreams without your encouragement," she insisted angrily.

"Do you truly believe that?" Trent asked. "Then you do not know your brother as well as you think you do, my lady. His lordship is a determined man. He would have continued his efforts with or without me."

Lady Edwina shook her head. "If you had complied with my original request, Trescott, this would never have occurred."

"I promised you that I would make certain that your brother did nothing foolish. I have kept my word, my lady," Trent said. "I prevented him from launching himself from the rooftop until he had designed and overseen the building of the new model. Because of that, your brother achieved his dream to-

188

day. If he had used his old model, he surely would have met his end smashed upon the cobblestones of the drive below."

"No, Trescott! Not another word!" she said forcefully as she began to move quickly down the corridor. "We knew nothing about you. We still know nothing about you. Yet we took you into our home and cared for you. And this is how you repay us? You are worse than the others!" she accused.

"Others?" Trent repeated.

But Lady Edwina was too distraught to allow him to interrupt her train of thought.

"The others may have stolen a few worthless trinkets." She threw out her hand in an angry gesture. "In your thoughtless disregard for my wishes and for his lordship's safety, you may have robbed me of one of the people I cherish most in this world. I not only do not particularly wish to speak to you, Trescott, but at the present time, I do not even want to look upon you!"

She turned her back upon him and began to walk away. Suddenly she spun about to face him again. She gestured disdainfully at his clothing.

"And get yourself out of those wet things!" she ordered. "You are dripping upon the good carpet!"

Chapter Fifteen

"Good morning, Stokes," Trent greeted her cheerfully. He was leaning casually against the wall at the top of the stairs. He had been waiting for her appearance.

" 'Morning, Trescott," she answered with a little nod of acknowledgment. Warily, she tried to maneuver herself and the large tray she carried about him and up the steps.

"How is Pringle?" he asked her, undaunted by the maid's continued reluctance to remain in his presence.

Stokes giggled and blushed, then looked up at him petulantly. "Lady Edwina tells me that his fever's gone and that his leg was set properly. He'll be able to walk just fine again, in time."

"Lady Edwina *tells* you?" Trent repeated. "Do you mean to say that you've not been assisting her ladyship in caring for Pringle?"

He tried to sound surprised when, in fact, he was not surprised in the least. He had been watching her ladyship's activities for several days now.

"Her ladyship's been up and down, up and down, between Pringle and his lordship," Stokes replied. As she had to use both hands to steady the heavy tray, she bobbed her head in imitation of Lady Edwina's erratic movements.

Then Stokes shook her head. "You know her ladyship—always insisting upon doing it all by herself." She began to whine, "Even though there's others what would be all too willing to help her with . . ."

She stopped in midsentence and grimaced down at the tray. "Instead, I'm supposed to be bringing breakfast to her ladyship—although Heaven knows she don't eat none of it. And I'm supposed to ask if his lordship's in need of anything, too."

"Allow me to assist you with that tray, Stokes," Trent offered. "It appears to be exceedingly heavy."

"That it is, Trescott," she agreed.

He reached out and took the heavily laden tray from her.

She relinquished it without the least fuss, adding shyly, "Thank you."

"On the contrary, perhaps I should be thanking you." Then Trent assumed an air of surprise and said, "Why, Stokes, as you are empty-handed, I would venture to say that you have apparently completed your duties. If I were you, I should consider myself free to pursue other activities."

At first, Stokes looked puzzled. Then she offered him a cautious smile as she began to slip down the stairs. Pausing and turning halfway around, she said, "You know, Trescott, you're not bad by half, regardless of what her ladyship may say about you."

The first time Trent had attempted to inquire after his lordship's well-being, Lady Edwina had imperiously ordered him from the room.

For the past three days, each time he had tried to approach her, not only had she refused to listen to him, she had pointedly refused even to see him. Perhaps this time her ladyship would be so angered by his persistence that she would expel him from Dynford Manor most peremptorily, and without even a reference!

Trent frowned. He had no wish to be exiled from Dynford Manor. When he had first found himself here, he had been grateful merely for the temporary refuge.

It came as no surprise to him that he had been immediately attracted by the Lady Edwina's beauty. The chilling distance she habitually maintained between herself and others had piqued his curiosity. Her sharp mind and the little spark of humor which peeked out from beneath that cold veneer were what kept that interest alive. He would feel extremely reluctant to leave the Lady Edwina when the time came to go.

But he knew that he must leave her — and soon. His wounds were completely healed. It was well past time for him to return to the gamekeeper's cottage at Haversham Hall. Even if his brother had acted the part of the thief, Trent felt it his familial duty to avenge the unfortunate Milton upon the treacherous Nigel. And Trent could not rest until he had exonerated his own name as well.

First, however, he needed to convince Lady Edwina that he had never meant to do Lord Dynford any harm.

Trent balanced the tray in one hand and knocked quietly upon his lordship's bedchamber door. At the soft response from the other side, he slowly pushed the door open and stepped inside.

The warm, stifling air from the bedchamber hit him like the blast from an open oven. Trent had heard Nealy complaining in the servants' dining hall that her ladyship continually badgered him to supply her with fuel to maintain the fire at this constant blaze during his lordship's illness.

Trent looked toward the bed. Lord Dynford lay bundled in thick coverlets drawn up to his chin. His face was flushed and he was breathing with a heavy, rasping noise, but Trent felt a great relief upon seeing that his lordship was still breathing at all.

The chair beside his lordship's bed was empty. Trent glanced about the room for Lady Edwina.

She was bent down before the hearth. With the poker, she pushed another log onto the already blazing fire. As she rose, Trent watched her grasp the mantel to assist herself in standing upright upon her unsteady legs.

Still hesitating by the door, Trent whispered to her, "May I serve you breakfast now, my lady?"

Noticing his presence for the first time, Lady Edwina slowly turned tired eyes upon him. Limned with red from lack of sleep, her eyes appeared even more blue than Trent had remembered them when he conjured her face before him each night as he fell asleep.

Her lips tightened when she saw him and her tired eyes darkened. At first, Trent believed that her ladyship would again order him to be gone. Then she lowered her gaze and shook her head.

"I am far too exhausted to perpetuate whatever hostilities I may feel toward you, Trescott," she said wearily. She turned away from him and replaced the poker in its stand.

She was speaking to him again, and with some degree of civility, however small. Trent felt a brief surge of hope. Perhaps in her hours of solitude while caring for her brother, Lady Edwina had at last come to realize that she had mistaken his intentions.

Trent brought the tray the rest of the way into the bedchamber and set it upon the low table before the fireplace.

"How is his lordship today, my lady?" Trent asked cautiously.

"Not very well, I fear," she replied quietly, shaking her head.

She raised her hand to brush from her forehead the few bedraggled strands which had escaped from their customary, tight chignon. She left a slight smudge of soot across her brow.

"He is tired, yet he has difficulty in resting because of his incessant coughing," she continued. "Honey and whiskey do little good."

"I am very sorry to hear that. What did the apothecary recommend?" Trent asked.

Lady Edwina flipped her hand in the air and expelled a little sound of disgust. "He has given us certain medications. I shall see that his lordship is dosed as indicated, but I have little faith in the efficacy of his concoctions."

She threw her hands up in resignation. "Of course, there is always the apothecary's favorite recourse to treat fever."

"Surely you would not . . ."

She shook her head. "I would not willingly allow my brother to be bled." She hesitated and sighed. "But sometimes, I think I would be willing to try almost anything to see him recovered."

Her footsteps dragged as her ladyship made her way from the mantel to the bedpost and at last to the chair beside his lordship's bed at the other end of the room. She held her chin high, yet Trent thought that her shoulders drooped as if she were carrying a great burden.

'She should not have to carry such a burden alone,' Trent thought. 'If only she would allow me to help her.'

Trent watched as she lowered herself into the chair. Her very body seemed to sink wearily into the soft upholstery.

'How much longer can she force herself to attend to Lord Dynford and Pringle without having a care for her own well-being?" Trent wondered.

He knew that her ladyship would consider such a personal question a gross impertinence on his part. At this juncture, he had no desire to upset her further, so he merely asked politely, "And how is your ladyship faring?"

She raised her chin, just as she had so many times before, but Trent did not think she had managed to lift it quite so high this time.

"I shall fare quite well, Trescott," she replied coolly. "I always have."

"I would wager that your ladyship has not slept in many a night," Trent ventured quietly.

"Why, Trescott, my staff is so competent and reliable that I have slept each night like a babe in arms," she assured him with a little twist of her lips.

"Have you any confidence in *my* abilities, my lady?" Trent asked tentatively.

"There have been infrequent occasions," she answered noncommittally.

"Then allow me to offer you further evidence of my dependability, my lady," Trent said. He pushed a small chair up to the table.

"M'lady, your breakfast is served," he said in his best, albeit somewhat quieter, imitation of Haskell.

With a weary little smile on her face, Lady Edwina gave a quick shake of her head. Then she turned from Trent back to Lord Dynford and placed her hand upon his lordship's forehead.

"He is experiencing increasing difficulty in breathing and his fever continues to rise," she said, frowning with concern. Trent heard her voice crack as she added, "I fear we are approaching the crisis."

"Then you will need all your strength to nurse him through it. You must take some nourishment, my lady," Trent insisted.

"I shall eat later, Trescott," she told him flatly.

"I suggest that you breakfast now, my lady. The food will not stay warm for long," Trent cautioned her. "Even in this room."

"Then I shall dine upon a cold collation — at a later time!" she repeated with greater emphasis.

"I believe that is the same reply you made to Stokes at dinner yesterday evening, and at luncheon and breakfast as well."

"I do not recall your presence at those particular conversations, Trescott," she remarked with surprise. "Have you some extraordinary mental powers of which we are unaware?"

"Only the powers of observation, my lady. I deduced as much by the large amounts remaining upon the plates which your ladyship ordered returned to the kitchen," Trent admitted.

She turned to him, one eyebrow raised to an inquisitive angle. "Are you in the habit of perusing refuse, Trescott?"

"Most assuredly," he told her in as serious a tone as he could summon while his eyes retained their merry twinkle. "One can learn a great deal about a person by observing those things which that person considers not worth keeping."

He bowed deeply again, sweeping his arm toward the low table in a gesture of invitation. "Shall we see what her ladyship is discarding today?"

With a great flourish, Trent lifted the lid from the first serving dish. *"Voilà, madame! Une omelette aux champignons!"* he announced in impeccable French.

Lady Edwina regarded him with increasing surprise. "Trescott, where did you learn to speak French—and so well?"

"Even in a foreign land, a soldier must eat," Trent answered, smiling. Then he peered with great seriousness into her blue eyes and added, "As must you, my lady."

Lady Edwina merely stared at the omelette smothered in creamed mushroom sauce and shook her head.

"Ah, well. *Au revoir, omelette,"* Trent sighed as he replaced the lid with finality.

He lifted the next lid. *"Des côtelettes d'agneau,"* he announced, tilting his head to smile up into Lady Edwina's tired eyes.

"No, thank you," she replied, evidencing very little interest in the lovely grilled chops.

Trent shrugged. *"Au revoir, côtelettes."* He replaced the lid and moved his hand to the next dish.

"Des croissants, madame," Trent announced.

The sudden, brief appearance of Lady Edwina's small dimple brought a great feeling of gratification to Trent. Perhaps his

195

efforts to induce her ladyship to eat were not for naught after all.

"Those are scones, Trescott," Lady Edwina corrected.

Trent shrugged. "Alas, that does not translate very well, my lady. Those Frenchies never could prepare a proper scone. In my humble opinion, their culinary expertise is vastly over-esteemed."

Lady Edwina shook her head. "No, thank you, Trescott. I truly could not eat a bite."

"Not even if we place upon this delicious scone some of my lady's favorite Seville marmalade?" he coaxed Lady Edwina.

"How did you know my favorite . . . ?" she exclaimed with surprise.

"Aha!" Trent cried in quiet triumph, holding a single finger aloft. "Now your ladyship witnesses the personal advantages which may be derived from the worthwhile pastime of perusing refuse!"

Lady Edwina threw both hands up in surrender and gave a quiet little laugh. "Very well, Trescott. You have convinced me. I shall have a *croissant*."

"I regret to inform your ladyship that our supply of *croissants* seems to be exhausted," he told her with exaggerated formality. "Could I interest you in some fine scones?"

"Only if they are covered with marmalade," she bargained.

"All shall be as you wish, my lady," Trent assured her. "Then I must see what I can do to convince you to avail yourself of a bit of rest as well."

Trent stepped toward the chair in which her ladyship was seated. He offered his arm to assist Lady Edwina to rise.

She had barely risen and taken a step toward the table when she suddenly collapsed at Trent's feet.

"Edwina!" he cried in alarm.

In one swift movement, he knelt beside her and cradled her in his arms. He rose, lifting her easily. He crossed the room and placed her gently upon the daybed.

Several impatient jerks at the bellpull summoned Nealy, who was immediately sent to fetch Stokes.

"Stokes, prepare her ladyship's bedchamber," Trent ordered. "Please take this tray with you, too, just in case we can induce her ladyship to eat something."

Stokes snatched up the tray and immediately departed.

Trent turned to Nealy. "I trust you to see to his lordship until I return."

Nealy nodded vigorously and proceeded to toss another log onto the fire.

Trent gently enveloped Lady Edwina in his arms and lifted her effortlessly. He began to carry her to her bedchamber.

"Come, Edwina," he whispered softly in her ear. "Your scones and marmalade await you."

"I am perfectly capable of self-locomotion," she protested sleepily.

"Indulge me just this once," Trent replied.

Lady Edwina sighed and leaned her head against his shoulder. Trent pressed her more closely to him. He rested his cheek against her soft hair, savoring the sweet floral scent of her.

Stokes had already drawn back the bedclothes. Trent lowered Lady Edwina gently into the bed.

"Thank you, Stokes," Trent said to her. "When her ladyship awakens, you must see to it that she eats something. You must not allow her to leave the bed until she has eaten."

Stokes emitted a tiny little laugh of derision. "*Nobody* forces her ladyship to do anything, Trescott. You should know that by now."

"I realize that her ladyship is obstinacy itself," Trent said. "If she protests, summon me."

Stokes regarded Trent with a sly grin. "Wouldn't her ladyship be surprised to know that when she and his lordship were ill, *you* were taking charge?"

Trent made no reply, but only returned her look with an enigmatic smile. At length, he said, "Her ladyship is in my capable hands, Stokes. I believe Pringle needs your kind ministrations now far more than her ladyship, don't you?"

Stokes's sly grin broadened into a complete smile. "Oh, yes, sir. I do indeed," she said as she made her way out the door.

Trent bent over and unfastened the slippers from Lady Edwina's feet. Deciding that it was a wise move to leave her ladyship otherwise completely dressed, he pulled the coverlet about her, then sat beside her on the edge of the bed.

He reached behind her head and pulled the two ivory combs from her hair to release the tight chignon. The long, honey-colored curls cascaded over the pillow. Trent brushed the disheveled curls from her face. With his thumb, he rubbed gently to remove the small smudge of soot remaining on her forehead.

She had worked herself to exhaustion these past three days. She tried so hard to present such a stern veneer to the world, but he had seen a softer part of her character, a part that cared deeply for others. Was it any wonder that she hid all her emotions? The slightest slip would expose to the world how truly vulnerable she was. He wondered what could have happened to cause her to act so aloof.

A lady so gently bred should not have to carry such responsibilities as she did, Trent thought sadly. How desperately she needed someone who would take care of her for the rest of her life.

He sat watching her, his eyes caressing the soft curves of her cheek. He would gladly care for her while he was able to remain at Dynford Manor. God knew, even after he had gone, he would continue to care about her for the rest of his life. But he could not help her when he could not even help himself. He must prove his innocence.

Lady Edwina blinked and finally opened her eyes.

"James?" she said with surprise despite her drowsiness. "You have brought me here?"

His heart swelled to hear her consciously call him by his given name. Then he felt his heart give a sharp twist. "James" was the name he had given himself. Would he ever be able to hear her call him by his true name? How could he even begin to explain to her . . . ?

"There was not much room upon the daybed in his lordship's bedchamber." A little grin spread across his lips as he suggested, "The next time you decide to faint, might I suggest that you use your bed rather than the floor?"

"What? And waste this expensive carpet?" she mumbled with a sleepy little smile.

Trent smiled as he reached out to smooth the tired lines from the corners of her eyes.

"You must sleep now," he told her. "You have eaten very little and you have not slept in two days."

She shook her head. "I must attend to my brother," she insisted, attempting to rise.

"Please be sensible," he said, placing his hand firmly upon her shoulder, easing her back onto the pillows. His hand slid from her shoulder down her arm and lifted her limp hand in his. When the lady made no protest, he continued to hold her soft hand. "You must perceive that, at the moment, you are in no condition to attend to anyone."

"But who will care for my brother?" she demanded.

"Nealy and I."

She twisted her lips into a wry little smile and remarked, "No doubt Nealy read Medicine at the same University as yourself."

"Did I neglect to tell you? Nealy was a don while I was at Oxford."

Lady Edwina cast him a skeptical smile.

"And Pringle . . . ?"

Trent frowned with exaggerated seriousness. "I do not believe Pringle ever attended university."

She looked intently into Trent's eyes and said slowly and with greatly exaggerated clarity, "I meant, who will care for Pringle?"

Trent grinned mischievously at her. Then he told her firmly, "Just trust me when I tell you, Pringle will be cared for. You are not to trouble yourself regarding anyone's recuperation but your own."

"The distillation of willow," Lady Edwina continued, attempting to rise again. "Mrs. Haskell becomes increasingly forgetful . . ." Her mind jumped from one problem to the other. "Cook must be instructed regarding which dishes . . ."

Trent, still holding her hand, shook his head and scolded her gently, "This is a large house with many servants. When will you learn that there is no need for you to do everything yourself?"

She considered his words for a moment, then began shaking her head. "No," she decided. "I cannot, in good conscience, demand anyone's time and care lying about in this bed while there are truly ill people who need attention."

"I shall care for you, Edwina," Trent said softly.

Lady Edwina regarded him silently for a long time. For just a moment, Trent fully expected her to begin to upbraid him for his impertinence.

"You called me Edwina," she said. Her eyes were soft and searching.

Trent shrugged. "You called me James — and you said it first."

When she made no protest, Trent grew bolder. He moved his hand again to her shoulder.

"No, I distinctly recall you calling me Edwina as you carried me to my room," she insisted.

"I should never dream of being so impertinent, my lady," he said as he began to stroke her cheek gently with his forefinger. He brushed the corner of her mouth at the precise spot where the elusive dimple should appear if her ladyship ever deigned to smile again.

Oh, he knew very well where the dimple would appear. He studied the lines and planes of her face very carefully every opportunity he had.

She leaned her head slightly to the side in response to his caress, cradling his hand between her shoulder and her cheek in the soft, warm hollow of her neck.

He grew bolder still. He slid his hand down from her cheek to wrap about her chin. He cradled her soft chin in his hand. He leaned forward and gently kissed her.

"James," she whispered softly.

He kissed her again, desire for her welling up inside him. He felt her lips pressing upon his with equal yearning as she responded to him.

"I have thought of this moment often, Edwina," Trent said.

To his infinite delight, she responded, "As have I."

"There are certain . . . dissimilarities between our present situation and what I have envisioned," he whispered.

"And what have you envisioned?" she murmured.

Trent did not answer her immediately. If he quite frankly confessed that, in his thoughts, she had been wantonly naked and he likewise lying beside her, would she feel compelled to slap his face?

On the other hand, how could he tell her that, by rights, he should be the master of Haversham Hall? He should be able to pay her the lavish court which was her due, not the poor attentions of a penniless footman.

Slowly, reluctantly, he pulled away from her. As James Trescott, the footman, he had very little to offer Lady Edwina. As Trent Haversham, wanted for the murder of his brother, he had even less.

"Sleep now, my lady. I shall be here if you need me," he said, tucking the covers in around her. She was already falling asleep. Her eyes were closed, the long dark lashes resting lightly on the soft translucent skin below her eyes. He watched her lips part slightly as she relaxed in sleep.

"Sweet dreams, my Edwina," he whispered, even though he knew she could not hear him.

He pressed his jaws together in anger and frustration at the sheer futility of the emotions he was feeling. Being near her fueled a fire which, of necessity, must only consume itself. In fairness to them both, he must not allow what had transpired ever to happen again.

He looked at her one more time, then turned reluctantly away.

Trent returned to Lord Dynford's bedchamber, leaving the door open as he entered.

"Trescott, leave the door closed tight," Nealy warned. "Her ladyship's orders."

"Extinguish that fire," Trent ordered, ignoring Nealy's objections. "It only consumes more of the oxygen in the air."

If Edwina could see him now, would she accuse him of also having read Chemistry? Trent wondered with amusement.

He strode to the windows and threw them open. The crisp summer breeze puffed out the heavy brocade draperies, blowing away the stifling dry heat of the fire.

"But her ladyship . . . !" Nealy continued to protest.

"Her ladyship is occupied elsewhere for the moment. Come, come, my good man! Surely you can carry out such simple instructions without Lady Edwina's constant supervision, can you not?" Trent asked, appealing to the young man's pride.

"Well . . . ," Nealy hesitated "I . . . I suppose so."

Trent nodded. "Are there any large potted plants in the conservatory which might be removed to his lordship's bedchamber?"

"I don't know," Nealy answered slowly. Then, as if with a sudden inspiration, he announced, "But I'll find out!"

"Capital!" Trent replied, clapping him on the shoulder. "If there are, will you and Cobb bring as many into the bedchamber as you can? The air in here is stifling and must be refreshed."

"We'll try our best, sir."

"I'm sure you'll succeed," Trescott reassured him. "You would not want her ladyship to be disappointed, would you, Nealy?"

"Wouldn't be the first time, Trescott," Nealy remarked with a wry grin as he departed for the conservatory.

Chapter Sixteen

Lady Edwina awoke with a start. She could tell by the rosy pink glow which suffused her bedchamber that it was just after dawn.

'My gracious! What o'clock is it?' was the first thought which passed through her head. Glancing to the clock on the mantle, she read half after five.

'I have slept the entire day and through the night as well!' she lamented. Feeling exceedingly guilty, she exclaimed aloud, "Richard! How could I have neglected him for so long?"

She flipped back the coverlet and swung her feet from the bed. Blackness sprinkled with stars spun about the edges of her vision. As her feet touched the floor, her legs buckled beneath her. She clutched at the edge of the mattress.

"Oh, m'lady, you're awake!" Stokes cried. Jumping from her chair by the fireside, she assisted her ladyship to sit upon the bed.

"What happened?" Lady Edwina murmured.

"Don't you remember, m'lady? Why, you fainted dead away from not eating nor sleeping! Trescott carried you here. Oh, m'lady," Stokes wailed. "Don't you remember nothing?"

"Yes, Stokes. Yes, I do," Lady Edwina answered quietly as she rested lightly upon the edge of the bed.

Every detail of yesterday morning came flooding back to her. James's strong arms about her. James's thoughtful care for her. James's warm and tender kisses. And her own willing response to those kisses!

'What must he think of me?' she wondered. 'A shameless wanton with no regard for propriety?'

She could not suppress the little smile that began to play about her lips. 'But, oh, how truly wonderful those kisses were,' she dared to admit to herself.

She gave herself a hard mental shake as she thought, 'And I am a fool for surrendering to such feelings when there are so many other, more important things to attend to.'

"How is Lord Dynford?" Lady Edwina demanded.

Stokes shrugged. "I suppose he's all right, m'lady. I mean, I haven't heard that he's dead yet."

"How comforting to hear you say that," Lady Edwina remarked sarcastically.

"I'm sure you'd be the first to be told," Stokes whined, offering her ladyship small consolation.

"As much as I trust your word, Stokes, I believe I shall see to his lordship's condition myself."

Lady Edwina bent down to retrieve her slippers. This time, the spangled darkness washed up over her like a wave. If it had not been for Stokes's quick movement, she would have gone tumbling over upon the carpet.

"I'm sorry, m'lady, but you must remain in bed. Trescott's orders," Stokes informed her as she helped Lady Edwina back into the bed. She fluffed the pillows and helped her ladyship ease back against them.

"Trescott's orders! So, James Trescott is a vile usurper of the rightful authority at Dynford Manor?" Lady Edwina demanded, raising one eyebrow.

Stokes only blinked in bewilderment and Lady Edwina decided that wit was indeed wasted on her lady's maid.

"What has this Trescott fellow been doing during my brief infirmity?" Lady Edwina asked.

Stokes shrugged. "Oh, lots of things, m'lady. Taking care of you and Lord Dynford, mainly. Why don't you eat now, m'lady?" Stokes suggested. "I'll go down and bring you up a nice pot o' tea and some lovely scones and marmalade."

"I shan't be able to eat a bite until I see to my brother's condition," Lady Edwina insisted.

"But Trescott told me that you must eat before you be allowed to go back to tending his lordship."

"Allowed? I do as I please! A mere footman such as James Trescott certainly has no authority over *me*," Lady Edwina declared with a haughty laugh and a proud flip of her head.

"Do I detect signs of a mutiny here?" Trent growled menacingly from the doorway, but Lady Edwina caught the merry twinkle in his green eyes.

"I am seriously contemplating one unless someone can tell me how my brother is," she warned him.

"Are you quite decent, then, my lady?" he asked from the doorway.

"I am always decent, Trescott," she answered. "I am also fully clothed. You may enter."

Trent nodded to Stokes, who went scurrying from the room. From the doorway, Trent's long legs carried him to Lady Edwina's bedside.

"Are you feeling improved this morning, my lady?" Trent asked.

She was with him alone again in her bedchamber, and she in her bed! Her cheeks began to flush as she recalled his kiss and her own eager acceptance of it.

It seemed that his wit was as ready as ever to amuse her, yet Trent looked exceptionally sad. She could almost feel the hurt he must be experiencing inside to have such sadness in his eyes, but she could not fathom from where such hurt could come.

It surely would not be because she had rejected his advances. Indeed, she had most shamelessly let the man know that his advances were exceedingly welcome. Yet he appeared withdrawn and reluctant to renew the possibilities which yesterday might have engendered.

It was just as well, she supposed. After all, the man was her footman! Such an association would never do! She had a great many responsibilities that must take precedence. But oh, how she wished that she were not so encumbered!

"Trescott," she said in a commanding voice. "I insist that you inform me of his lordship's condition."

"His lordship is doing as well as can be expected," he answered with the utmost formality.

"What sort of reply is that?" she demanded testily. She frowned and pointed an accusatory finger at him. "Trescott, something is amiss and you are not telling me! How is my brother?"

205

"There is no cause for alarm, my lady. I have come to tell you that your brother is alive and very well," Trent comforted her. "He passed the crisis a bit after the midnight hour. His fever is gone and he is resting quietly now."

"Passed the crisis! How could he have passed the crisis without me?" she demanded incredulously.

"I daresay, a great many things come to pass without your presence, my lady."

"You failed to awaken me, Trescott!" she scolded.

"You can cast no blame upon me on that account, my lady," Trent defended himself. "I stood beside your bed for countless hours, beating upon a tray with a wooden spoon. Despite my best efforts, you insisted upon lolling about in a most indolent manner."

She eyed him with amusement. "It was not your 'Sonata for Tray and Spoon,' but everyone's detestable tiptoeing about which woke me."

"Ah, I understand now why your ladyship so appreciates the services of Haskell," he replied, smiling.

Suddenly she cried impatiently, "I really have no time to be wasting in idle chatter, Trescott. I am quite certain that Mrs. Haskell has ruined the distillation of willow in my absence."

"The good housekeeper was astounded when her dormant abilities of recall were again actualized."

"By a few rather flattering comments from yourself, doubtless?"

Trent bowed modestly. "I am sure you will find this batch quite equal to your exacting standards, my lady."

Lady Edwina stared at him for a moment, stunned. Then she said, "Cook! I must discuss the proper foods for my brother . . ."

"Cook has prepared those foods which he knew were his lordship's favorites," Trent told her. "And a few of yours, as well, my lady, if you would only deign to eat them."

"At your suggestion, again?" she asked, tilting her head slightly.

"Cook is a man of great talent. He needs no suggestions from a humble footman such as myself."

Lady Edwina was surprised and just a bit hurt to find that

her world did indeed go on quite well without her constant supervision, and admittedly, with just a little help from this man who called himself James Trescott.

"Indeed, Trescott, you *have* quite commandeered Dynford Manor."

"At your command, my lady," Trent said with an exaggerated bow, "I would storm the very gates of hell."

"I do believe you would," she replied.

She looked at Trent, feeling as if she were actually seeing him for first time. How could she have been so wrong? How could she ever have held him responsible for the unpredictable little gust of wind which had sent her brother's marvelous flying machine crashing through the trees and into the lake?

She realized now that Trent was a man who could be replied upon to be responsible for not only her home and family, but for her as well.

Nevertheless, that insidious little voice in the back of her mind returned to spoil the moment. How could a mere vagabond and footman such as James Trescott have come by this talent for organizing and supervising a household?

Stokes returned with a steaming teapot, a china cup, and a plate of scones and marmalade upon a tray.

"Come and eat, now, m'lady," Stokes said. "A hot cup o' tea. And just one of these nice little scones here Cook made just for you."

Trent lifted a scone from the plate and covered it generously with marmalade. He held it before Lady Edwina's mouth.

"I believe you missed your favorite yesterday morning," he told her.

"Why, Trescott," she remarked, "you are so well informed about me, one would think that you had spent several days watching every move I make."

Trent drew back as if terribly offended. "Not *every* move, my lady!"

Trent brought the scone close to her mouth. "At the moment, my lady, I should like to watch you eat."

"Very well," she agreed grudgingly. "But just one."

"That will be an adequate beginning," Trent said.

Lady Edwina opened her mouth and bit off a bite of scone.

Upon hearing a muffled little giggling sound, Lady Edwina glanced over to Stokes. Her lady's maid stood watching them with lips pursed tightly. She looked as if she were afraid that if she opened her mouth, she would burst from the laughter which she was trying so hard to keep bottled up inside.

"Stokes, have you no other duties to attend to?" Trent asked her.

"Yes, sir," she replied, quickly placing the tray on a side table. She clapped her hands over her mouth and made a hurried exit from the bedchamber.

" 'Sir'?" Lady Edwina repeated.

"Stokes is exceedingly polite," Trent answered.

"What duties could Stokes have that she should be so anxious to attend to?" Lady Edwina asked. "I have not seen her move that quickly since last July when she disturbed a nest of hornets while picking blackberries."

"I believe that Stokes has found nursing Pringle back to health to be an extremely gratifying experience. And if I am not mistaken, Pringle has been eagerly anticipating her daily attentions."

Lady Edwina gave a soft little chuckle. "Stokes and Pringle. I would not have thought it. I never even noticed . . ."

Yet obviously Trescott had, she thought with a grin. The man was competent not only in managing affairs of the household, but affairs of the heart, as well. The grin slipped from her lips as she wondered how well this man could resolve their own dilemma of the heart.

"Doubtless, Stokes will be anxious to spread throughout the servants' quarters her tale of how her ladyship was fed," Trent observed with a chuckle. "Servants do enjoy a good gossip."

Lady Edwina regarded him from under lowered lids. "Have you been with us for so long that you have become an expert on the habits of servants, Trescott?"

"I told you before, I am a man of varied experiences," Trent admitted.

"I also seem to recall you telling me that you had never been in service before," she pursued.

"I am also a man of varied acquaintances," Trent replied.

"And all your acquaintances like to gossip?"

Trent nodded. "To be sure."

"Then, although you yourself have never been in service before, you have friends who are?" she asked, tilting her head to look up at him.

"My lady barrister, you sound as if you are quite prepared to take your place before the bar," Trent said, laughing. Then he countered, "Have you found servants to be the only people who gossip?"

"Unfortunately, no," she admitted.

She grimaced. Oh, the man was silent as an oyster! As she finished another scone and took several sips of tea, she determined more than ever to discover as much as she could about this mysteriously reticent man with whom she felt herself falling in . . .

No! She refused to allow herself even to *think* of such a possibility! Oh, why did she feel all at sixes and sevens about this man?

"There!" she said, finishing the last of the scone. "Are you satisfied now that I have made a perfect glutton of myself?"

Trent nodded. "Now you must rest."

She began to protest, but he was already drawing the draperies closed again. She swallowed her protest and settled down into the soft mattress and pillows.

Snuggled into the downy covers, she allowed herself the luxury of watching Trent stretch his long arms up to draw each rose velvet drapery shut. She watched the black hair as it waved down the back of his head. With great reluctance at his leaving, she could not help but admire his broad back and narrow waist and hips as he left the room.

It was extremely comforting to know that he was here to take care of her.

Stokes bustled into Lady Edwina's bedchamber, scuffling her shoes, coughing, humming, and making as much noise

209

as she possibly could.

"Oh, good, you're awake, m'lady," Stokes said.

"The room was darkened. My eyes were closed. I was lying quite still. Whatever could have made you think that I was asleep?" Lady Edwina asked, raising herself up on her elbow. "What is it now, Stokes?"

"Oh, m'lady," she began to whine. "That wretched Lord Scythe has come calling for you."

Lord Scythe! Lady Edwina grimaced with disgust. Whatever in the world could the man be thinking to come uninvited?

"Haskell denied him," Stokes continued. "But the little toad's so puffed up with his own importance, he entered anyways and planted himself in the drawing room to await your ladyship." Stokes paused and grimaced. "I'm so sorry, m'lady, but none of us can seem to get rid of him!"

Exactly like that overbearing little cockscomb to place his own desire to call upon them above their own wishes—no, their very necessity at this time—for privacy, Lady Edwina thought with increasing disgust. At any rate, what did his lordship consider so important that he should betake himself all the way out to Dynford Manor in the first place?

"Trescott said we shouldn't wake you just on Lord Scythe's account and that we must allow his lordship just to sit and wait 'til he tires or gets hungry and then he'll leave," Stokes explained. "But it's been an hour now, m'lady," she wailed, "and honestly, he don't show no signs of ever taking our meaning!"

Stokes grinned wickedly and leaned closer to Lady Edwina's ear. In a conspiratorial whisper, she offered, "I'd be happy to summon Redding to toss the little poppinjay out on his . . ."

"No, no! Calm yourself, Stokes," Lady Edwina told her with alarm. " 'Twould never do to treat his lordship so." With an equally scheming grin, her ladyship added, "No matter how much we should like to do just that."

Stokes giggled.

Lady Edwina sighed and stretched her weary muscles.

'Ah, it was so good to sleep untroubled,' she thought. 'But

now, reality intrudes upon my idylls. There is Lord Scythe to deal with.'

With extreme reluctance, she swung her legs out of bed and slid her feet into her slippers. Stokes quickly bent to tie the ribbons which held the small kid slippers in place. With another sigh, Lady Edwina rose from the bed and walked to the washstand.

She splashed water over her face and dried herself with the towel which hung at the side. She turned to peruse her reflection in the glass which hung above her dressing table. With the flat palm of her hands, she attempted to smooth the wrinkles from the lavender muslin gown in which she had slept.

"Oh, m'lady, let me fetch you a fresh gown," Stokes exclaimed. "You can't go seeing that old dandy without looking presentable!"

"No, Stokes," she said stepping closer to the dressing table and taking her brush in hand. "His lordship has been told I am unwell. If I greet him looking too fashionable, he will not believe me, and then I shall be quite saddled with his unwanted company."

Lady Edwina brushed the tangles from her long hair, then twisted it into her usual tight chignon. Giving herself one last look in the glass, she asked, "Well, Stokes. Do I meet your rigid standards for presentability?"

Stokes shrugged. With a helpless look on her face, she answered, "Well, you look your usual, m'lady."

Lady Edwina smiled with satisfaction. If she looked her usual, that meant that she radiated her same stern, forbidding appearance. Precisely as she wanted!

Lord Scythe leaned languidly against the mantel, pinching his snuff from his little enamel box. He did not move when he saw her enter.

"Ah, Edwina, my dear," he drawled. "I knew you would not deny me." From the way in which he slurred his words, Lady Edwina surmised that, even this early in the day, his lordship had already attained his customary level of intoxication.

"You make it extremely difficult to do so, sir," she replied coolly.

211

At her words, Lord Scythe pushed himself off from the mantel and sauntered over to the center of the room where Lady Edwina was standing. He did not stop until he was quite near her. Before she could back away, he reached out his hands to grasp both of hers, then drew them close to his own chest.

"My dear Edwina, I have to come to offer you my unfailing support in your time of trouble," his lordship declared.

"How kind of you, sir," she replied politely, hiding her surprise at his outburst. "If I ever encounter a time of trouble, I shall consider your most gracious offer—but not until then, thank you."

She tried to slip her hands from his, but his grasp was too strong. He pressed closer against her.

"Come, come, my dear," he said. With one hand, he held both of hers firmly against his chest while his other arm coiled about her shoulders like a snake. "No need to dissemble with me. I have come to offer you my assistance and my condolences."

"Your condolences," she repeated in a derisive tone of voice. "I have no need of your condolences—nor of your assistance!"

His arm about her, he continued to press her toward the sofa. Clumsily, he dropped to the seat, pulling her down beside him.

"Perhaps not now." He held her tightly and whispered in her ear. His acrid breath smothered her. "However, it is common knowledge throughout the county that your brother has contracted a most horrid case of pneumonia and will soon surely die."

"You have been most severely misinformed!" she pronounced coldly, all the while struggling against his embrace.

But his lordship, intent upon his course of action, continued speaking without allowing Lady Edwina further opportunity to protest or to explain. "What will become of you, my dear Edwina? Everyone knows that your brother's heir is a distant cousin who neither knows you nor cares aught for your welfare."

He continued to press closer to her, bending her over onto

the sofa. "What will you do when that distant cousin displaces you? Where will you go? Who will take care of you?"

She struggled to push Lord Scythe from her as he continued to press her ever lower onto the sofa.

Without waiting for her reply, he declared, "Marry me now, so that we shall not have to wait a year after your brother is dead. I shall take care of you as you shall take care of my home and children."

"I have always taken care of *myself*," she asserted with a lift of her chin and a great shove against him to push him away. "And have done so quite well!"

"Ah, you always have been a proud beauty!" he exclaimed, pouncing upon her.

"And you sound like the villain in a gothic novel!" she countered. A sharp poke to his ribs caused his lordship to grunt and release his grasp of her. As she sprang from the sofa, Lord Scythe tumbled to the floor.

"You are a fool to reject my offer, Edwina," Lord Scythe warned her from his position on the floor. He rubbed his insulted bottom. "You have no other suitors even now. Once your brother is dead, you will *never* find another better than I!"

Raising her chin, she declared furiously, "Ah, but there you are wrong, sir! Very wrong!"

"No one else has paid you court for years, Edwina," he answered quite bluntly. "I should have to see this man before I would believe you."

Before Lady Edwina could answer, a loud cough resounded through the drawing room.

'Thank heavens for Haskell!' Lady Edwina breathed a sigh of relief.

But when she turned, it was not Haskell but Trent who stood in the doorway. There was, indeed, a great deal more than simple gratitude in the glance she threw his way. She could not hide her smile at the sight of him. In truth, she did not want to hide it. Her heart thumped against her breastbone when he returned her smile.

She knew it now, and had no desire to hide it, even from herself. She had fallen quite hopelessly in love with James

Trescott, her footman.

"So sorry to intrude, my lady, but his lordship is awake and requests your presence," he announced.

"A timely interruption. Thank you, Trescott," she replied. "I shall go to him immediately, while you see to his lordship's departure."

Trent bowed and answered, "With pleasure, my lady."

He turned to Lord Scythe, still seated upon the floor, and asked him with exaggerated gravity, "Will your lordship be requiring my assistance?"

Lord Scythe sniffed indignantly and rose under his own power. He held himself up, looking in every way like the little puffed toad Stokes purported him to be. Lady Edwina almost laughed aloud.

"As you can plainly see, sir, my brother is well on the way to recovery. I shall have no need of your condolences for many years to come. And I shall never have need of your proposal of marriage. Good day, sir."

Lord Scythe gathered up his beaver hat and ivory-handled walking stick. "Have my carriage brought round," he ordered imperiously.

Once Trent had departed, Lord Scythe turned to Lady Edwina. "Needn't tell me," he declared indignantly. "Got eyes in my head. It's you and that footman, ain't it?"

"And what if it is?" she demanded, glaring at him defiantly.

Lord Scythe sputtered and stuttered and at last recovered from his shock just enough to say, "Well, you've made your own bed, so to speak, and now you shall have to lie in it. If I were you, I shouldn't be too concerned with having to decline any more invitations from the *ton*. They'll all cut you dead once this news gets about."

"Indeed? I have never really concerned myself with what the *ton* thinks," Lady Edwina said in a tone of voice so pleasant as to totally obscure the anger she felt. "Of course, I may rely upon *you* to be sure they tell the tale correctly."

Lord Scythe made no reply, but staggered from the drawing room to the hall and out to his carriage.

Quite exhausted, Lady Edwina sank down into the soft

cushions of the sofa. She almost laughed, to see such a little cockscomb finally receive the set down of which he was so badly in need.

But she could not allow herself to laugh. Indeed, once the *ton* received the word that she nourished a *tendre* for her footman, she would indeed be laughed out of every fashionable drawing room in London.

It was bad enough that they considered her brother quite eccentric, her sister quite scatter-brained, and her maiden aunt quite bird-witted. But she had always prided herself upon being the sensible one in the family. She should greatly dislike to have it said that *she* had done anything to tarnish the family name.

What was worse, there had been nothing between her and her footman to warrant such censure. A single kiss was all that had occurred. And if things continued as they were, nothing further ever would, to her infinite regret.

She leaned forward, resting her elbows upon her knees, as she contemplated the repercussions of the insufferable Lord Scythe's visit. At last, she allowed herself a light little chuckle which progressed to outright laughter.

Not even under pain of execution would such a conceited little fop as Lord Scythe admit to the world that he had been bested in an *affaire de coeur* by a mere footman!

Lady Edwina sank back in relief upon the soft cushions of the sofa and allowed herself to laugh again.

Chapter Seventeen

"Ah, good. You are still here, my lady," Trent said as he returned to the drawing room.

Lady Edwina quickly resumed her rigid posture and did her very best to erase the smile from her lips.

"Has his lordship departed, Trescott?" she asked.

"Indeed, my lady," he answered. There was a twinkle in his green eyes. "Apparently, after all the time his lordship spent waiting here, he suddenly recalled a pressing engagement elsewhere."

She gave him a weary smile of gratitude.

He crossed the room to stand before her. "Begging your pardon, my lady, put you still look rather overtaxed. Shall I escort you to your brother's bedchamber or would you prefer to retire again to your own?"

"Oh no, Trescott," she replied, shaking her head. "I want to see my brother."

He bowed deeply and held out both hands to assist her to rise. He drew her gently to her feet and wrapped one arm about her.

"With your permission," he added quickly, "in the event that you have any additional trouble in maintaining your balance."

"How kind of you, Trescott," she answered quite formally. It would have been hardly fitting to express to him the true excitement she felt at having his arm fold gently about her, offering her his comfort and support.

She could walk perfectly well and she knew it. But the warmth of his arm about her and the motion of his body as he walked by her side was too wonderful to give up. She said nothing and continued to lean on him for support.

She felt a twinge of sadness thinking that perhaps this would be the only occasion upon which she could enjoy being in his arms once again. He had proved to be a dutiful footman. He was not so presumptuous as to attempt any further advances. And she was not so lacking in propriety that she would pursue him. Things would ever remain as they were at this moment.

The door to Lord Dynford's bedchamber was open. The fire in the hearth had died down to embers. The room had cooled. It appeared as if every potted plant in the conservatory had been brought into his lordship's bedchamber and arranged about him.

In his fever, his lordship had tossed and turned upon his bed and picked at the bed clothing. Now he lay quite still. His face, which had once been burning crimson, was now quite pale. Only yesterday, his breathing had been loud and labored. Now his breathing was undetectable beneath the layers of thick coverlets.

"My brother is dead!" her ladyship cried, halting in midstep as she entered the room. "You have lied to me! You lied to me simply to induce me to eat! That is inexcusable!"

She swept her arm out to indicate the unusual appearance of her brother's bedchamber. "And you have transformed his bedchamber into a veritable jungle! That is incomprehensible!"

At her outburst, Lord Dynford opened his eyes.

In a hoarse voice that was barely above a whisper, he informed her, "I am quite alive, Winnie, I assure you."

Lady Edwina recovered from her shock and rushed to his ride. "Oh, Richard, I am so glad to see you well!"

"I am improving," he acknowledged modestly. "And I find that I've grown rather partial to this jungle, as you call it. I fear I have neglected our marvelous conservatory far too long."

Lady Edwina's eyes widened with hope. For the first time in many years, her brother had expressed an interest in something besides flying. Could it be that he had at last satisfied his craving for flight and would now turn toward another all-consuming passion?

She breathed a small sigh of relief. Plants were infinitely safer than flying machines, were they not? However, she decided to keep a watchful eye upon her brother just in case he began cultivating foxglove and belladona.

"But what has happened to you, Winnie?" Lord Dynford demanded weakly from his sick bed. "One rarely finds you in such a state of agitation."

"I? Agitated?" she asked, raising a haughty eyebrow. She smoothed the skirt of the dress she had slept in and patted at her hair. "How could I ever become agitated? Nothing in the least bit disconcerting ever transpires in our quiet country home."

"Halloo! Winnie! Dickie!" came the piercing cry through the hallway, echoing up the stairs with glass-shattering shrillness. "I am home at last!"

Lady Edwina sighed. "I do believe that Cecily is home," she pronounced with a marked lack of enthusiasm.

She looked at her brother's still pale face and dark-ringed eyes. At the moment, he truly was in no condition to face their younger sister's incessant, nonsensical chattering.

"That can mean but one thing," Lord Dynford predicted from his bed.

Lady Edwina nodded. "She has run through this quarter's allowance once again."

Lord Dynford shook his head. "How she is able to do that is beyond my comprehension. Father left you each enough to live quite comfortably for the rest of your lives."

"She has the additional income from the considerable capital which her godmother bequeathed her as well," Lady Edwina added.

"A pity Mama's great-aunt did not take to you as well, Winnie," Lord Dynford remarked. "She always maintained that you were too headstrong and independent a girl to her way of thinking."

"I function quite well *without* Auntie McGowan's bequests," Lady Edwina said with a proud lift of her chin.

Lord Dynford gave a weak little chuckle. "After all these

218

years, I am beginning to believe Auntie McGowan was correct in her assessment of you."

Lady Edwina shook her head and clucked her tongue. "It has taken you this long to determine that? Yes, it is just as I have suspected all along. You and Cecily are truly blood-related and *I* was found abandoned upon the doorstep of Dynford Manor and kindly adopted."

Before Lord Dynford could open his mouth to reply, Lady Edwina continued, "I must go, unless you want Cecily and Aunt Portia to invade your domain."

He waved his hand at her in a most insistent manner. "Go! Go!" he declared forcefully, despite his weakened condition. "Immediately!"

She turned toward Trent. "Trescott," she said, "I trust you to attend to my brother's comfort while I shall be otherwise occupied."

"Yes, my lady," Trent nodded his compliance.

She left the room, feeling confident that her brother would continue to recover in Trent's capable hands. She wished she could feel as confident of her own continued sanity as she approached her scatter-brained sister and their dear, dotty old Aunt Portia.

Lady Edwina stopped at the top of the flight of stairs to watch her sister swirling about the Hall in an elegant lavender and white merino traveling suit. Lord Dynford might find it difficult to understand how their sister could run through her funds so quickly. Lady Edwina had no such puzzlements.

"Halloo! Winnie! Dickie!" Lady Cecily continued to call as she paced about the Hall. She pulled off one pink kid glove and tossed it at the nearest chair. The glove slid to the floor and lay there, unheeded.

Two of her own footmen were hauling a small trunk into the Hall. They set it beside two much larger trunks.

"No, no!" Lady Cecily scolded. "That does not belong with my things. That is Lady Portia's."

Immediately behind the footmen entered two lady's maids. The plump, little one was dressed in a mousy brown bombazine gown which exactly matched the color of her mousy

219

brown hair. She carried two hatboxes by their strings.

Lady Cecily addressed her. "Oh, Mason, you know where my things belong. Lady Portia's maid will see to her things, won't you . . . ?"

She stopped in midsentence, turned to her aunt and whispered, "What *is* her name?"

Lady Portia opened her mouth to reply. No answer emerged, and she glanced to the side, as if the answer were to be found in the corner of her eyeball.

"Yeckley, m'lady," the thin, elderly lady's maid reminded them both.

"La! What a name! 'Tis no wonder I can never recall it," Lady Cecily exclaimed, tossing her parasol at Mason, who miraculously caught it in spite of her hands being full of hatbox strings. "Now wherever can they be? Winnie! Dickie!"

Lady Cecily's little pink morocco boots pitter-pattered across the gray-veined marble floor of the Hall as she peeked into the vacant drawing room to one side, then into a smaller drawing room to the other side, then back into the center of the Hall to call again. "Halloo!"

She turned to the little gray shadow trailing behind her. "I am quite certain they are at home, Aunt Portia."

"Yes, of course, they are at home," Lady Portia replied.

"They never, positively *never*, go anywhere!" she complained. She pulled off another glove and tossed it just as carelessly onto another chair.

"Indeed, never," Lady Portia repeated.

"And wherever could Haskell be?" Lady Cecily demanded. A look of exasperation crossed her face and she tapped her foot impatiently.

"Haskell has always answered the door," Lady Portia observed.

"He was very old. Oh, horrors!" She clasped her hand to her heart and cried, "Do you suppose he has died?"

"Why, Haskell would never do such a thing. Then who would announce us?"

"I did write to them informing them of our arrival, did I not?" Lady Cecily asked, a tiny little frown creasing her perfect brow.

Lady Portia frowned as well. *"Did* you?"

"Well, if you cannot recall, how do you expect me to?" Lady Cecily asked peevishly.

"I cannot recall, Cecily dear."

Lady Edwina watched her sister flit from doorway to doorway with Lady Portia constantly at her shoulder, repeating everything Lady Cecily said. Lady Edwina had heard that the Hindus in far-off India believed that, upon death, the soul of a human might transmigrate, to be born again in the body of an animal, and that after spending a lifetime as an animal, the soul might transmigrate to a human form again, for good behavior, as it were. She began to ponder the possibility that, at some point in time, her aunt had been a parrot.

Lady Cecily raised her limpid blue eyes to her sister, who was still standing on the stairs watching all the commotion below.

"Ah! There you are!" she cried, tearing off her fashionable traveling bonnet and tossing it carelessly onto a side chair. She missed the target and the expensive bonnet went tumbling to the floor.

As she descended the stairs, Lady Edwina noted with only the slightest degree of envy that not one curl of her sister's elegant coiffure was misplaced. Recalling her own rumpled curls whenever she wore her bonnet, Lady Edwina truly marveled at how Lady Cecily always managed to look so neat when all about her, she created chaos.

Lady Cecily lightly embraced her sister, barely touching cheek to cheek.

"I am so relieved to be home before dark!" Lady Cecily declared.

"It is such a relief," Lady Portia said as she, too, embraced Lady Edwina.

"How good to see you again, Aunt Portia. This is quite a surprise, Cecily," Lady Edwina said.

"La! You cannot be surprised to see me, Winnie," Lady Cecily said with a little giggle. "I live here."

"We live here," Lady Portia agreed.

Lady Edwina sighed. "You gave us no intimation of your

imminent return in your last letter."

"But of course I did, silly Winnie," Lady Cecily insisted.

"She did, Edwina," Lady Portia repeated, nodding her gray head vigorously.

When Lady Edwina shook her head, Lady Cecily turned to Lady Portia. "Oh dear, I suppose I did indeed forget to write." She turned quickly again to Lady Edwina. "I do hope this is not an inconvenience, Winnie, dear."

"We truly would not want to inconvenience you, my dear," Lady Portia echoed.

"You live here," Lady Edwina reminded them with an exasperated sigh. "You know your rooms are always kept in readiness for you."

"M'lady!" Haskell announced with surprise as he suddenly entered the Hall. His booming voice reverberated even above Lady Cecily's high-pitched chatter. "Lady Cecily Dynford and Lady Portia Dynford have arrived."

Lady Cecily released a delicate little gasp of delight. "How marvelous! More company! Now we truly *are* a party."

"I love a party," Lady Portia echoed. Then she said the first truly original thing she had said all afternoon. "Why, Haskell, you are not dead after all."

"Indeed not, m'lady," Haskell replied gravely. "Then who would announce you?"

Lady Cecily was busily searching about her again. "Now where are those footmen to see to my trunks?"

"We have a great many trunks," Lady Portia informed Lady Edwina.

"They have taken your things to your bedchambers," she told them. Then she frowned and began to scold, "Cecily, have you left London because you have run through your allowance again?"

Lady Cecily flipped her blonde curls with an air of insouciance. "Hardly, Winnie," she replied. "I have been exceedingly sensible this time. I daresay, you would be quite proud of how sensible I have been."

"Quite a sensible girl," Lady Portia concurred.

"Then to what do we owe this unexpected visit?"

"It is not an unexpected visit, silly goose," Lady Cecily

protested. "True, I may have forgotten to inform *you* that I was coming, but *I* fully expected to be here."

Lady Edwina refrained from making the observation that, while Lady Cecily may have brought her body to Dynford Manor, she had left her mind in London—if she had ever been possessed of one to begin with!

Lady Cecily began to ascend the stairs, followed by Lady Portia.

"I am home to talk to Dickie," she announced. "Wherever is he? Oh, Winnie, I have the most stupendous news!"

"Quite stupendous," Lady Portia echoed.

"By the bye, Winnie," Lady Cecily called back to Lady Edwina. "What in the world have you been doing? Your hair is a horrid mess! Is that truly the style out here in the country? And you look as if you quite literally have slept in your clothing!"

Lady Edwina regarded her sister coolly. "Cecily, what possible reason could I have to sleep in my clothing?"

"Dickie, my dear, wherever are you?" Lady Cecily called in quite musical tones as she proceeded down the halls. Lady Portia and Lady Edwina followed as if quite swept along in her wake. She marched boldly into his lordship's bedchamber.

"Why, Dickie!" she exclaimed. "Whatever are you doing retiring this early in the evening?"

Lord Dynford was still rather groggy from having been awakened from his nap so suddenly. He did not answer immediately.

"Richard has been ill," Lady Edwina said, insinuating herself protectively between Lady Cecily and Lord Dynford.

"Poor dear," Lady Cecily remarked automatically.

"Poor dear," Lady Portia repeated, reaching out past Lady Edwina to pat Lord Dynford's hand.

"I do hope it was nothing contagious!" Lady Cecily suddenly realized, backing up a pace or two.

Trent had arranged two more chairs near the bed. Lady Edwina seated herself in the chair closest to Lord Dynford. Lady Cecily, still fearing contagion, ever so gracefully nudged Lady Portia out of the seat farthest from his lordship.

She brushed from her face a frond of the potted palm situated near the foot of Lord Dynford's bed.

"You've redecorated since I was last home, Dickie," she commented, looking about. "I vow, it is a most unusual arrangement."

She brushed the palm frond away again.

"But I have a *marvelous* piece of news!" Lady Cecily continued her chatter. "Just the thing to set you to rights again. I vow, I am fairly bursting to tell you. I could not entrust it to a letter. I simply had to make the drive all the way from London just to tell you myself. Oh, it was an *abysmal* drive. I vow, the roads are in ever so dreadful a condition and I was fearful every moment that we should be set upon by highwaymen. But my news is quite worthy of the effort—"

"Cecily!" Lady Edwina interrupted her sister. "Will you get on with your tale?"

"I shall be pleased to do so just as soon as you stop interrupting me," she pouted. "Oh, I vow, all these interruptions when one is attempting to tell one's story are *so* annoying!"

"Then, pray, tell us this marvelous news and alleviate our suspense!" Lord Dynford demanded.

"I am to be married!" she cried, reaching out and squeezing Lady Edwina's hand.

"How wonderful for you, Cecily," Lady Edwina replied.

She *was* pleased to hear this news, genuinely pleased. She had always known her lovely, flirtatious sister would have no difficulties in securing a brilliant match. And at last, Cecily would be someone else's problem!

"Of course, you have all my best wishes for happiness." Lady Edwina gave her sister's hand an affectionate pat.

"Oh, Dickie, as you are the head of the family, I suppose I shall have to have your permission." Lady Cecily turned her most engaging smile upon him. "But I don't suppose that will be a problem when you hear what I have to say."

From his sickbed, Lord Dynford frowned with bantering sternness. "Firstly, I insist upon knowing who this quite presumptuous fellow is."

"He is *marvelous!*" Lady Cecily enthused. "So handsome! So witty! So rich!"

Lady Edwina made a small nod toward her brother. "If the decision were mine to make, Richard, I should give my approval in a trice. From all she has told us, we need know no more about him to be certain that he is the perfect husband for our Cecily."

"Oh, indeed, he is!" Lady Cecily replied.

"Indeed," Lady Portia voiced her considered opinion.

"However, he is not a gentleman," Lady Cecily corrected.

"Cecily! What have you got yourself involved in?" Lord Dynford demanded.

"No, no, silly Dickie," Lady Cecily scolded her brother. *"Honi soit qui mal y pense."*

Lady Edwina cringed at the sound of her sister's cold-blooded murder of the French tongue and of the noble sentiments of the Order of the Garter.

"I mean, he's not *just* a gentleman," Lady Cecily amended her description. Preening herself, Lady Cecily announced proudly, "I am betrothed to Nigel, Lord Haverslea!"

The bowl and pitcher crashed to the floor, shattering into hundreds of little pieces.

"Trescott!" Lady Edwina cried.

Trent stood staring past his hands, which were outstretched before him as if he still held the bowl and pitcher, out to the shards scattered over the carpet, but his eyes appeared to be turned in upon his own thoughts.

"Trescott," Lady Edwina repeated loudly, trying to gain his attention. She rose from her chair to stand by his side. "What is the matter?"

"A clumsy slip of the hands, my lady," Trent replied, shaking himself back to a realization of what he had just done. "I was not aware that the bowl was still wet. Please accept my apologies. The cost will be deducted from my wages."

"I was not aware that a footman made that much in a year," Lady Cecily observed. "Dickie, I believed myself to be generous, but you are becoming an outright profligate regarding the wages of your staff."

"Trescott." Lady Edwina reached out her hand and laid it upon his arm. "Do not become so anguished over a mere pitcher and bowl. They were neither so expensive nor so rare that they cannot be replaced, at no penalty to yourself," she tried to console him.

She was extremely concerned about this drastic change in Trescott. He was usually so composed. Yet now his face was flushed and he appeared distracted, as if he were concentrating more upon his own thoughts than upon anything she could say to him.

"I shall clear away the wreckage immediately, my lady," Trent said. He seemed to have fully recovered his senses, yet at the same time, appeared not to have heard a word Lady Edwina had said.

He dropped to his knee and immediately began to gather the shards of broken pottery.

Lady Edwina returned to her seat beside her brother. But she could not shake her concern over what could be troubling him so.

"Cecily, now I know you are confused," Lord Dynford was telling his younger sister. "Although I do not recall ever making his acquaintance, I do recall people describing the Baron as a rather pudgy, unpleasant fellow named Milton, and I do believe he was already married."

"No, no! *He's* dead. Nigel is the new baron," Lady Cecily corrected.

"Nigel Haversham," Lord Dynford said, frowning thoughtfully. "Yes, I do seem to recall making his acquaintance once several years ago. However, I do think I should meet him again in his new station before giving my consent to this marriage."

"Nigel felt quite the same," Lady Cecily said, opening her pink silk reticule and digging about inside. "That is why he has sent you this most gracious invitation to Haversham Hall." She extracted the letter and waved it in Lord Dynford's direction.

"Allow me," Lady Edwina said, taking the letter. She slit the wafer and began to read:

My *dearest* Winnie,

I have such momentous news! Aunt Portia & I shall be returning home with the fortnight . . .

"Cecily!"

"There!" Lady Cecily exclaimed in triumph. "I am not so forgetful as you would make me out to be. I *did* write to you regarding my return!"

"I knew you had," Lady Portia affirmed her faith in her niece. She reached over and patted the girl's arm. "You simply neglected to place it upon the butler's tray."

Lady Cecily shrugged. "La! It does not signify now, at any rate. They have the letter after all."

She began to poke through her small, densely packed reticule once again.

"Ah! Here it is!" She produced another crumpled piece of stationery and handed it to Lady Edwina. However, she left her sister no time to read it, as she began to recount the contents herself.

"He is as anxious to meet us as you most probably are to meet him," she said. "And he would like to extend to you the hospitality of his lovely estate."

Lady Edwina had perused the letter while her sister had chattered on. She neatly refolded the paper, smoothing out the bends, creases, and similar indignities it had suffered in Lady Cecily's crowded reticule. She looked up at her brother.

"It is indeed a most cordial invitation to Haversham Hall. I know we shall be pleased to accept," she replied, inclining toward Lord Dynford as she answered for them both. "However, Cecily, Richard has been extremely ill and we shan't be able to visit for some time."

"Nonsense!" Lady Cecily declared forcefully. "A change of scene and some cheerful companionship will do Dickie a world of good."

"Indeed, a change is what Richard needs," Lady Portia spoke.

Lady Cecily turned her wistful gaze upon her brother. "I am so anxious for you all to meet!"

"I feel quite improved," Lord Dynford replied, smiling at her. "However, I cannot travel without my valet, and Pringle has broken his leg and surely cannot travel."

Lady Cecily began to pout. "Could you not have Nealy

serve you in that capacity for the short time we shall be away?"

"I harbor grave doubts regarding Richard's continuing recovery at the hands of Nealy," Lady Edwina remarked.

"Nealy is not so bad as we had thought," Lord Dynford said. "On the other hand, several weeks of the fellow's attentions . . ."

The expression on Lord Dynford's face suddenly brightened. "Trescott!" he exclaimed, turning to the man who was still picking up shards of pottery. "You may accompany me."

Trent looked up suddenly, his mouth gaping open. He dropped the few shards he had held carefully in his hand.

"I, my lord?" Trent managed to ask in a choking voice. He rose, shaking his head. "Oh, no, my lord."

"Of course. You are the perfect choice!" Lord Dynford assured him.

"La!" Lady Cecily jeered, pointing to the shattered remnants of Lord Dynford's pitcher. "Do you really consider this fellow an *improvement* over Nealy?"

"I really cannot, my lord," Trent repeated. "I . . . I have never served as a valet . . ."

"Nonsense, Trescott," Lord Dynford said. "You are far too modest. I have observed how well you discharge whatever duties are assigned to you. I am sure you will acquit yourself rather well as my valet."

"Quite honestly, my lord, I do not think that my accompanying you is a very good idea," Trent continued cautiously.

"Ah, I understand now," Lord Dynford said. "You fear that Pringle will lose his situation. Quite charitable of you, Trescott. But no. Nothing of the sort will happen, I assure you."

Trent continued to regard Lord Dynford with a frown.

"Oh, Trestle . . . or whatever your name is." Lady Cecily turned two large, pleading eyes to Trent. "My brother simply *must* meet Lord Haverslea soon. There is far too much for me to do to wait until Prinkle or Dringle—or whatever his name is—recovers."

"I have got to get Lady Cecily married," Lord Dynford exclaimed, laughing. "B'gads! You would not wish to be responsible for saddling me with *two* spinster sisters?"

228

"You leave me no choice, my lord," Trent answered quietly. He knelt and began to pick up broken pottery again.

The matter being settled, Lord Dynford turned to Lady Cecily. "How came Nigel to the barony, Cecily? As I recall, he was only a cousin."

Lady Cecily gasped. "Could it be that you have not heard of the scandal?"

Chapter Eighteen

"Scandal?" Lord Dynford and Lady Edwina echoed simultaneously. Lady Edwina felt rather like their repetitive Aunt Portia.

"Such a scandal," Lady Portia parrotted, then clucked her tongue.

"I cannot credit that you have not heard about . . ." Lady Cecily began incredulously. Then she pressed her pretty little lips tightly together and pronounced gravely, "You realize that it is entirely your own fault, of course. You should be in London, where you belong, instead of rusticating out here among the fields and flocks and herds."

"Richard!" Lady Edwina accused in highly offended tones. "Have you been rusticating out among the flocks and herds again?"

"Not I, Winnie, I assure you," he denied haughtily, clasping his hand to his breast. "Have *you?*"

"La, la!" Lady Cecily interrupted. "You may disport yourselves of me if you wish. However, the fact remains, if you two did not isolate yourselves from the *ton,* you would have heard of the scandal."

"We have no need of the entire *ton* to keep us abreast of the latest *on dits,* Cecily," Lady Edwina said. "We have you."

"Indeed, you have!" Lady Cecily affirmed, with a tiny little sniff. She paused just long enough for the loyal Lady Portia to echo her sentiments.

"Nigel has just come into the barony upon the most *horrid* scandal," Lady Cecily eagerly began to recount the lurid tale, which somehow seemed to improve with each retelling. "It seems his two cousins were arguing about money, which was nothing new, as according to Nigel, they never *ever* got along well and argued at the slightest provocation."

Her blue eyes grew wide. "Oh, Nigel tried his best to save Lord Haverslea's life, but his cousin had been seized by madness and had supernormal strength and agility! Before Nigel could act, the Mad Cousin stabbed and killed his brother!"

Her eyes grew wider still. "Then his Mad Cousin turned upon Nigel who, of course, was quick and clever enough to devise a plan to save himself!"

As her eyes could grow no wider without popping out of her head, she dramatically clutched her hands to her breast instead. "The Mad Cousin chased him into the woods, but just as he was upon the verge of stabbing Nigel, he slipped into the river and drowned!"

All attention snapped to Trent as he emitted a loud expletive of disgust. He looked up from the shattered mess he was still clearing away.

Overcome with shock, Lady Edwina ventured, "Did you say something, Trescott?"

"Nothing I should care to repeat. I do beg your pardon, my lord, my ladies," he excused himself. "A mere slip of the tongue. I fear I could not contain myself when I cut my hand upon a shard."

"I vow, Trestle . . . or whatever . . . you have certainly broken the spell of *my* narrative," Lady Cecily pouted, slipping her head to emphasize her injured dignity.

Lady Edwina rose rapidly and left her chair to stand by Trent's side. "Let us have a look, Trescott," she said. "Are you in much pain?"

"It is not serious, my lady." Trent said, clutching his hands together to his middle.

She took one of his hands in hers and turned the palm upward. Seeing no injury there, she reached for the other hand. Neither was this hand injured.

She shifted her puzzled glance from his hands into his eyes. His green eyes were clouded with pain, but he was not allowing any other emotion to show.

"Indeed," she remarked, still holding his hand. "I should say that was the least serious injury I have ever encountered."

He said nothing, but only continued to gaze into her eyes with that horrid, pained look. As he showed no outward

231

injuries, Lady Edwina could not help but suppose that the pain came from something which had hurt him deep inside.

She continued to hold his green eyes with her own, hoping somehow to understand.

But he merely answered, "With your permission, my lady, I shall take my leave."

"On the contrary, Trescott," she insisted. "I do believe that you are greatly in need of my assistance, although I am not quite sure how I may go about it."

"That is most kind, but I should not want to inconvenience you, my lady."

Lady Edwina was perfectly aware that her brother, sister and aunt were all listening most attentively to their conversation.

'Propriety by damned!' she thought. 'I have been found out by that odious Lord Scythe. Why dissemble before my own family?'

She looked directly into Trent's eyes and said, "You have become a very important member of my household, Trescott."

"La! Winnie, he is a *footman*," Lady Cecily said disparagingly. "Easily enough replaced. Send the fellow to Mrs. Haskell for a bandage, then come listen to my tale." She reached out and patted the seat which her sister had so recently vacated.

"With time, some things become irreplaceable," Lady Edwina said. Although she appeared to be responding to her sister's remark, she continued to gaze into Trent's eyes, hoping that he would somehow understand how important he had become to her and that she wished to help him.

"I would not see you hurt, Trescott," she whispered to him. "And it is quite obvious to me that you are."

"Indeed, my lady," Trent replied with a weak laugh. "It is nothing I cannot deal with on my own. Please, my lady. Let me go."

Trent stooped to gather the remaining pottery, then quickly left the room.

"At any rate, I was saying . . ." Lady Cecily was eager to resume her recounting of the Tale of the Horrible

Haversham Murder.

"Enough of your chatter, Cecily," Lady Edwina ordered. "Richard is now more in need of rest than of entertainment."

"Quite so," Lady Portia agreed.

Lady Cecily rose with great reluctance.

"La! I cannot see how anyone would want to sleep when they could listen to my quite exciting adventures!" she pouted.

Lady Edwina frowned at her sister and was upon the verge of scolding when Lady Cecily seized her arm.

"Oh, la!" she said, pulling Lady Edwina from the room. "We shall leave Dickie to his rest, then. We ladies have ever so much to talk about that would *never* interest a gentleman!"

The entire distance from Lord Dynford's bedchamber, down the corridors, into Lady Cecily's suite, Lady Edwina could not manage to unclasp her sister from her arm. Nor could she still her incessant chatter.

Lady Edwina recalled their old nanny recounting how Lady Cecily had begun talking at six months of age. She felt as if her sister had been at it continuously for the past nineteen years.

Lady Portia, while not physically attached to the two, trailed along behind, giving every impression that indeed she was attached.

"I met him at Almack's, of course," Lady Cecily continued her story.

Her sister was as shallow as the looking glass she so admired, Lady Edwina thought as she was literally dragged down the corridor. Certainly, she could choose her husband from the *haut ton* of London society. Sensible women like herself only fell in love with destitute vagabond footmen.

"I was a veritable *vision* that evening in my new primrose-colored gown! And he was so *taken* with me, even from across the room, that he *insisted* upon securing an introduction through the cousin of my dear friend Jane Sheftley—you met her—the girl with the bright red hair and all those freckles. Jane does so dote upon me."

Lady Edwina could just picture all the young gentlemen clamoring after her sister, just as they had followed after her during her first two seasons. But her sister lapped up their attentions like a cat with a bowl of cream. And this rich, handsome young baron had sought Lady Cecily, while she herself sat at home, enamored of a footman who could not decide from one moment to the next if he would kiss her or merely serve her luncheon.

"And even though I was already engaged for *every* dance, which of course I *always* am," Lady Cecily chattered on. "My poor Winnie, you have never been in a position to know how truly exhausting all that dancing can be as you always seem to be sitting out every dance."

Lady Edwina acknowledged silently that, several years ago, she had, indeed, been in a position to dance every dance. But as all her partners had seemed so foppish and lack-witted, she had found that she much preferred to sit alone. And the one man she had found interesting to sit and talk with was her footman, for pity's sake!

"At any rate, Nigel still managed to secure three dances away from other gentlemen just to dance with *me!*" Lady Cecily fairly beamed.

"Quite a charmingly persuasive fellow," Lady Portia commented.

So this was the gentleman of the letter, the gentleman who had been the cause of Lady Cecily's creating such a disturbance at Almack's. Lady Edwina was awakened from her own introspection to speculate on exactly how suitable a husband for her shatter-brained sister this gentleman would be after all.

"Although I do believe Gervaise DeLauney—you know Gervaise. Lord DeLauney's younger brother, the tall man with the extremely curly hair . . ."

When Lady Edwina gave no sign that she had the slightest idea of whom her sister was speaking, Lady Cecily waved her hand in the air and continued, "At any rate, I do believe he was about to call Nigel out."

Lady Cecily turned pitying eyes to Lady Edwina. "Poor dear Winnie. Not to know the thrill of excitement that two men are so *infatuated* with you that they are upon the verge of *dueling* over you!"

"I believe I shall manage to survive without such excitement in my life," Lady Edwina commented dryly.

Dueling! she thought with alarm. And she had thought that marrying Cecily off would alleviate her worries. Instead, the gentleman appeared to be one more fool she should have to deal with. Indeed, fools were abounding, popping up like daffodils in spring!

"But Nigel calmed him," Lady Cecily said with disappointment. "I vow, the man is *so authoritative!*"

Lady Edwina began to reconsider.

Lady Cecily had steered them into her bedchamber, where Mason was unpacking her mistress's numerous trunks and hatboxes. The lady's maid had withdrawn a pile of white silk drawers from the trunk and was now placing them on the scented paper in the top drawer of the chiffonier.

Across the bed, Mason had spread Lady Cecily's gowns. While Lady Edwina had never overly concerned herself with being modish, she had always attempted to maintain a certain stylish appearance in keeping with her position. Nevertheless, she could not help but marvel at the immensity of Lady Cecily's wardrobe.

There were muslin day gowns which ranged in color from the palest cream to a soft carnation pink to a deep cerulean blue. There was the infamous primrose-colored evening gown of Almack's fame, as well as a white silk evening gown ornamented with silken flowers of gold.

Spread across the floor were pairs of red and brown morocco walking and riding boots and pairs of tiny silk sandals and satin slippers of every hue to match the appropriate gowns. Cashmere shawls and lace fichus, reticules and ivory fans lay scattered across the top of the dresser and every table and chair in the bedchamber.

The turmoil which Lady Cecily had created in the Great Hall was as nothing compared to the utter chaos of her bedchamber! It appeared as if she had said to the milliner and modiste, "What have you?"; "I shall take it."

It would be just as well to allow her to enjoy herself now, purchasing what she will while she may, Lady Edwina decided. Upon her marriage, all of Lady Cecily's income would fall under the control of her husband. Knowing his younger daughter's propensity toward extravagance, their father had planned very wisely, if Lady Edwina did say so herself.

And she was silently very grateful for the fact that her father had also recognized that she was a young lady of some astute perspicacity and had left her fortune to her own control.

"Ah, there is so much to do! I intend to see that *my* wedding is the social event of the *season*," Lady Cecily insisted, carelessly tossing a peach sarcenet gown to one side to make room for her to sit upon the bed. "Indeed, for several seasons past and to come. And you shall assist me, Winnie. The wedding breakfast. The bridesmaids' gowns. The wedding gown. An entire new trousseau."

"Judging from the numerous trunks and boxes which your footmen carried in, I should think you had already bought your trousseau," Lady Edwina observed. "As well as your bridesmaids' gowns and an entire new wardrobe for Aunt Portia."

"I vow, Winnie, you are ever so droll," Lady Cecily said with a wave of her hand. "Whyever should Aunt Portia need a new wardrobe? *She* is not the one to be married."

Lady Cecily cast a critical glance over her sister's slightly rumpled lavender muslin. "Oh, and I *do* so hope you will deign to buy yourself a new gown, Winnie. I shan't permit you to look the dowd at *my* wedding."

Never in her life had she intentionally looked a dowd! And Lady Edwina was upon the verge of telling her sister just that, along with a few other choice remarks that sprang to her mind, but at the last second, she bit back the sharp retorts. Lately she was finding, much to her alarm, that everyone with whom she came into contact was causing her to show such various emotions as she had always before managed to keep hidden.

"I shall try not to disappoint you, Cecily," was all she replied.

But Lady Cecily's brain had already taken off on a flight in another direction entirely.

"There were some girls who asked me, 'La, Cecily, how

can *you*, an earl's daughter, consent to marry a mere baron?'" She screwed up her face and raised her voice to a mocking pitch.

"Jealousy, pure and simple, on their part," she maintained in a more normal manner. "Nigel is an extremely wealthy man and is possessed of vast, exceptionally productive estates. And while those who mock me are melting down the family silver to maintain their position at court, *I* shall be thoroughly and quite extravagantly enjoying myself!"

Lady Cecily turned pitying eyes to Lady Edwina. "And although you have never been in such a situation yourself, poor dear Winnie, you can imagine the thrill of having such a handsome gentleman *fête* you so lavishly!"

Lady Edwina's concern deepened. Not once had she heard her sister say that she loved this man, nor that he loved her. Did the silly chit fail to realize that it was the man and not the position or possessions which could bring happiness? She only hoped that, with time, her sister would realize this.

Lady Cecily gave a loud sigh. "Of course, we shan't be able to be married until Nigel is out of mourning. And it is all that miserable cousin's fault!" she said petulantly. She thumped her little feet angrily against the side of the bed.

"Well, perhaps not all the blame can be laid at the feet of the Mad Cousin," she said. Upon further reflection, she appeared to have taken a more charitable frame of mind. "There are rumors that a servant, whose identity is as yet unknown, assisted the Mad Cousin in drugging all the other servants so that he could perpetrate the dastardly deed unimpeded. To protect himself, Nigel has dismissed the old footmen and hired new—a very wise action on his part, I say. There," she added triumphantly, "I told you Nigel was ever so clever."

Lady Edwina usually paid no attention to such useless chatter from her sister, but the strange finish to the Tale of the Horrible Haversham Scandal sent a chill up her spine.

Chapter Nineteen

"So, Lord Elsington said that it was not his fault if Lady Beemish had been hanging out for younger sources of amusement, whereupon Lord Beemish took aim and fired upon Lord Elsington right in the middle of the dining room at Beemish House on Albemarle Street! And without even bothering to call him out first! Of course, they were both completely foxed at the time, just as they usually are, so of course Lord Beemish missed Lord Elsington and shot the top of old Lord Kingsley's cane out from under him and he fell over into the claret punch. Oh, I vow, this dust makes breathing positively *impossible!*" Lady Cecily interrupted her monologue to exclaim.

"If you would pause to take a breath from time to time you might not find it so difficult." Lady Edwina refrained from giving voice to the other, more unkind thoughts which ran through her head regarding her sister's incessant rambling.

Lady Cecily had removed one of her new, white kid gloves and waved it before her face. She looked across the carriage to her aunt for the lady's usual confirmation. But Lady Portia had spent the past two hours sleeping soundly while riding backward in the large, blue and gold Dynford berlin and had no comment to make whatsoever.

Lady Edwina also coughed from the dust which flew up from the carriage wheels.

"The dust is unpleasant, but not unbearable," she said.

"Perhaps the dust is not so miserable if one is riding backward. Exchange seats with me," Lady Cecily suggested.

"I assure you, either situation is equally uncomfortable," Lady Edwina said, reaching across the carriage to tuck in a rug which had come loose from about her brother's legs.

Lord Dynford had been dozing fitfully in his seat across from Lady Edwina. She had made certain that several lap rugs had been included in their baggage and had taken care to see that his lordship was warmly wrapped in at least one of them at all times.

"La! Winnie, you know perfectly well that you never allow anything to trouble you." Lady Cecily placed her hand to her bosom. "I, on the other hand, have always been of an *extremely* sensitive temperament. I vow, I suffer so from this dust. Exchange seats with me, dear Winnie," she pleaded.

"You know that you become nauseated when riding backward," Lady Edwina reminded her sister. "I was constantly being made aware of that fact whenever we traveled when we were children. I do believe that, until I made my coming out, I never once saw where we were going, but only where we were coming from."

"La! Winnie, what care I for a touch of nausea when I am upon the very brink of suffocation?" she exclaimed.

"Very well," Lady Edwina conceded. She knew she should receive no peace until she had conceded. "I shall exchange with you at the next posting inn."

"I vow, Winnie," Lady Cecily declared, fanning herself all the more furiously, "I believe I shall expire before then."

Lady Edwina sighed with exasperation. "Very well."

She rose from her seat. The carriage lurched and her bonnet struck the ceiling of the bouncing vehicle, crumpling the brim and disarranging her neat chignon beneath.

Lady Cecily managed to slip between her sister and the two other drowsing occupants and seat herself, but not before she had managed to tread upon Lady Edwina's toes.

Lady Cecily settled herself quite comfortably into the little indentation in the cushions which Lady Edwina had made.

"As I was saying," she continued with great enthusiasm, "old Lord Kingsley fell into the claret punch, upsetting it all over Lady Randall's white satin gown and turning it to a marvelous shade of crimson, which was a great favor to the lady on his part, if you ask me, as I believe — and mind you, I am not the only one I have heard remark upon this — Lady Randall is entirely too old and entirely too large to continue to deck herself out as a debutante."

Lady Cecily again waved her glove furiously about her face. "Oh, I vow, you were quite correct, Winnie! The dust in a moving carriage is *abominable* regardless of where one sits!"

Lady Cecily gracefully placed her hand over her mouth to hide a certain eructation which had suddenly begun to arise. "I also believe that I am becoming extremely nauseated from riding backward!"

"Then allow me to suggest that we again exchange seats, quickly," Lady Edwina offered with a benevolence which, at this point in their journey, she truly did not feel toward her most exacting sister.

They repeated the awkward process. Once again, another section of the brim of Lady Edwina's bonnet was crumpled. Once again, Lady Cecily did not fail to tread upon Lady Edwina's toes.

"There! That is ever so much better!" Lady Cecily exclaimed, settling herself against the soft blue squabs.

"Now, where was I?" she demanded, much restored in spirit. "Oh, yes. Lady Randall had had the audacity to wear a gown of white silk what was fit so tightly and cut to such an extreme decolletage that when the claret punch splashed her and she threw up her arms in alarm . . ."

Lady Edwina turned with disinterest to look out the carriage window, allowing her sister's continuous monologue to slip right by her. Once again, she found herself traveling somewhere, and yet viewing the place from where they had come.

She could not help but observe that while traveling might affect Lady Cecily's respiration and her digestion, she had never noted it to have any deleterious effects upon her vocalization.

Lady Edwina eagerly anticipated a quick arrival at their destination. She had never cared a fig who was expelled from which Club for being caught cheating at vingt-et-un. And she felt as if she knew far more about who had been discovered in dalliance with someone else's wife than she ever should!

Lady Edwina coughed again as the dust rose up around

240

her.

'What I do not suffer just to see Cecily properly married!' she lamented. She turned an ear briefly to her sister's continual chatter.

"Then old Lord Kingsley rapped Lord Beemish most soundly over the head with his quite ruined cane, but no one noticed because when Lady Randall had become 'exposed,' as it were, that priggish Miss Spalding—whom I cannot abide!—had fainted and, falling backward, flipped over the potted palms and out the window into the boxwood hedge beneath . . ."

Lady Edwina turned back to observing the countryside, feeling rather sorry for herself.

Lady Cecily's mind never ventured beyond this season's gossip and next season's fashions. They were traveling to meet her future husband who, if Lady Cecily were to be believed, was reasonably young, quite handsome, quite witty, and incredibly rich.

Lady Edwina considered herself an intelligent, perceptive, yet sensitive lady. After the few quite honorable proposals of marriage which she had rejected—not to mention the numerous dishonorable propositions which she had peremptorily dismissed—she now found herself nourishing a *tendre* for her footman, of all people! And, to make matters only worse, a footman who apparently could not make up his mind whether to pursue or reject her! Was there no justice in the world?

With these depressing thoughts dwelling upon her mind, and after an entire morning of caring for Lord Dynford and traveling with Lady Cecily, Lady Edwina was in no frame of mind whatsoever to be pleasant when the berlin began to bump severely even beyond its normal irrhythmic rumblings.

"Coachman!" Lady Edwina called and rapped on the roof. "What seems to be the problem?"

" 'Pears as if a wheel's come loose, m'lady," the coachman replied. "There's a village just up ahead, Little Oxlea, I think it is. We'll stop there and the baggage wagon'll go on ahead. Let's just hope the wheel holds out 'til we reach the smithy."

The wheel did indeed hold out. The carriage pulled to a stop before the large barn. The wide double doors at the front of the smithy were open. Inside the darkness, silhouetted by the fire, Lady Edwina glimpsed the big, beefy man rhythmically pounding iron upon iron. Another younger and much smaller man sat idly upon a barrel by the door, tossing a stick to a small, spotted dog that never failed to fetch and return it.

As the carriage came to a halt, the young man immediately perked up. Patting the dog behind the ears, he slipped from the barrel and hopped over to meet them. He walked with a limp and wore a black felt patch over one eye, but that did not seem to deter the proud set of his shoulders, nor the cocky set of his head, nor his cheerful greeting.

"No, no, Jimmy. I'll get it," exclaimed the big, burly smith who emerged from the glowing red darkness inside the smithy.

The big man reached up an arm almost as big as a ham and grasped the bridle of the lead horse.

Lady Edwina did not bother to listen to the conversation between the coachman and the smith concerning the necessary repairs to the carriage. She was too intent upon observing the smaller man limp slowly away to stand beside the two wide front doors of the smithy. His wiry shoulders appeared to droop and his head hung low as he watched the dust he could kick up with his one good leg.

The coachman tapped against the carriage door to gain Lord Dynford's attention.

"Begging your pardon, m'lord?" he said. "Your lordship's coach'll be repaired in no time at all. If it'd suit your lordship and the ladies, there's a bit of an inn across the way."

"Come here, Jimmy," the smith called, motioning with his large arms to the little man at the doorway.

Lady Edwina saw his face brighten again as he hobbled over to their carriage.

"Right, Tom," he answered brightly. "What needs doing?"

"Here's something you *can* do," Tom said.

The man called Jimmy was standing close enough to the window of her side of the carriage that Lady Edwina could quite plainly hear him mumble under his breath, "There's lots what I can do if you'd only let me."

Tom continued his instructions. "You can escort these fine folks to the inn while I repair their carriage."

"Oh, that wretched man!" Lady Cecily exclaimed when she saw Jimmy waiting for the footman to hand the ladies down from the carriage. She opened her parasol over her head and sidled as far away from the unfortunate Jimmy as possible, never daring to glance in his direction again.

For once, Lady Portia refrained from making any comment, but merely clucked her tongue as she followed Lady Cecily.

"Follow me, m'lord, m'ladies, if you will," Jimmy said with excruciating politeness.

Lady Edwina thanked him with a smile. "Were you wounded in the war?" she asked.

"That I was, m'lady," he answered with a proud lift of his head. "Waterloo."

"Oh, I am so sorry."

" 'Tweren't much," he replied with a shrug. "Compared to some. But I'd do it again for king and country."

He stopped and turned to her. His forehead was pushed down to a frown, but his one eye twinkled mischievously. "Only problem is, now, when I wants to flirt with a pretty girl, she can't tell if I'm winking at her or just nodding off for a moment."

He turned and headed toward the inn. With great difficulty, Lady Edwina refrained from smiling at the little man's indomitable cheerfulness.

She took her brother's arm. With his other hand, his lordship supported himself on the same cane he had used for his injured ankle.

"This is the beautiful town square," Jimmy said with a chuckle. He directed his remarks to Lady Edwina.

Lady Edwina found herself chuckling, too. The town square was a mere widening in the road which passed through the village. The carriage ruts were still filled with mud from yesterday evening's rain and the ladies were forced to step carefully between the puddles.

Several chickens scratched and pecked in the ridges between the ruts. A flock of geese suddenly appeared from around the side of the smithy, flapping their gray wings and honking a warning. They made straight for Lady Cecily, who began to wail.

"Shoo! Shoo!" Jimmy waved them away. Seeing the familiar Jimmy, the geese waddled off in the opposite direction.

"Oh, *why* did I ever leave the comforts of Dynford Manor?" Lady Cecily whined. "Oh, *why* did we have to stop here?"

Jimmy gestured toward the crudely painted wooden head of an ox which hung above the doorway and declared brightly, "Little Oxlea's pride and joy, the beautiful Oxhead Inn, established 1642 by Jack Thwaitesbury who was later murdered by his wife—she poisoned his meat pasty—after finding him in dalliance with the dairymaid."

Jimmy held the door open wide for them to enter. "The Oxhead Inn is here for the sole purpose of your pleasure and comfort at this brief pause in your long journey."

Jimmy remained outside. "Sorry to say, there's no private room, as there's not much traffic coming through this way, and certainly none as fine as yourselves, but I'm sure the innkeeper can make your lordship's party as comfortable as possible."

As he closed the door, he added, "By the bye, I highly recommend the meat pasties. It's an old family recipe." There was a merry twinkle in his remaining eye. Lady Edwina could not help but laugh aloud.

The common room of the Oxhead Inn was low-ceilinged and smoky from the poorly constructed stone fireplace at the far end. Fortunately, at this time of day, the inn was also empty.

"Oh, do you seriously expect *me* to stay *here?*" Lady Cecily demanded with a derisive little laugh.

"Are we staying here?" Lady Portia asked.

The plump innkeeper was still tying on a clean apron as he bustled up to Lord Dynford.

"Nothing fancy, m'lord," he said, bobbing up and down as far as his rotund middle would allow. "Meat pasties and ale."

Lord Dynford smiled and nodded. "Splendid. Thank you."

Lady Cecily was swishing at the seat of the wooden bench with her silken handkerchief. The wood had borne the weight of so many decades of bottoms that it was worn to a deep, gleaming patina. Deigning it clean enough, she sat.

"Oh," she sighed. "It is so *wonderful* to sit on something which is not moving!"

After the plain but quite satisfying meal, Lady Edwina rose. "I am weary of sitting and should like some exercise. Will you walk with me, Cecily?"

Lady Cecily shook her head most emphatically. "And dodge puddles? Or those horrid geese? I should say not! This room may be stifling, but it is infinitely safer than whatever lurks outside!"

"Oh, 'tis much safer inside," Lady Portia agreed.

"I should go with you, Winnie, but . . ." Lord Dynford smiled at her sheepishly and raised his cane.

"I shall be quite fine all by myself in this sleepy little village," she assured them.

Out of doors, Lady Edwina opened her parasol and crossed the street. The geese and chickens had taken themselves elsewhere. The puddles were evaporating in the warm sun of early autumn.

The Dynford carriage was tilted up to receive the repaired wheel.

"But I can do it!" she heard Jimmy's voice insisting from the other side of the carriage.

"Back off and let a man do his work," she heard Tom's voice snap his answer.

They were standing on the other side of the carriage such that she could not see them nor they her, yet she could hear every word across the quiet village road.

"There's chickens to be fed," a feminine voice offered.

"I didn't come through Waterloo to feed chickens, Pamela!" Jimmy declared angrily. "I'm still a man and I can do a man's work."

"You should just be thanking the Lord you're back at all," said a much older feminine voice. Then the same voice, in an extremely sad tone, added, "Such as you are."

"There's more to being a man than eyes and limbs, Mum,"

Jimmy said. "All you can see is what I've no longer got, not what I still can do!"

Lady Edwina saw the man named Jimmy dash away from the carriage as fast as his limp would permit. He disappeared around the back of the smithy.

The coachman was bringing the team around to hitch them again to the berlin. Not wanting the others to realize that she had been eavesdropping upon what had been a private, family conversation, Lady Edwina ducked quickly back into the inn.

"I vow, I am so relieved to be away from that place!" Lady Cecily declared as the berlin finally left Little Oxlea far behind. She shuddered. "I feel as if I should have a huge, scented, steaming hot bath."

"I should like a bath as well," Lady Portia said.

"And those abominable pasty things!" she wailed. "Do you suppose they were poisoned as well? They have given me a horrid case of dyspepsia."

"They were horrid," her aunt agreed.

"Strange," Lord Dynford remarked. "I found Little Oxlea rather picturesque, and the pasty . . ." his lordship chuckled, ". . . tasty."

Lady Edwina spent the remainder of the journey attempting to ignore Lady Cecily's ceaseless complaints, Lady Portia's constant echoes, and Lord Dynford's endless contradictions regarding the dirt, the food, the dust, and the bumps.

Even when she succeeded in closing out the incessant chatter of her family, she found little peace of mind. The grinning face and single, twinkling eye of the wiry little man named Jimmy continued to pop into her thoughts. He seemed such a cheery fellow, she could almost smile when she remembered him. But then his smiling face would dissolve into the unhappy cripple that those other people insisted upon making of him.

Why was she worrying herself about a man she did not know and would never see again? she demanded of herself.

Did she not have enough problems of her own already? All these thoughts were giving her an incredible ache in her head.

With these concerns running through her head and the carriage quite brutally shaking the rest of her body, by late afternoon Lady Edwina arrived at Haversham Hall in far more foul a mood than was customary with her.

She reached up to try to unbend the brim of her bonnet. She realized with dismay that there was nothing which could be done until she could take it off and tend to the damage. Even then, she feared, the bonnet would be quite ruined. Blast that Cecily and her airs and vapors!

The Dynford berlin slowed as it rounded the drive leading to the front of Haversham Hall. The gentleman standing at the top of the wide marble stairs flanked on either side by low bushes began to descend the steps as the carriage came to a halt at the base of the stairs.

"Cecily, my dearest! How I have missed you!" Lord Haverslea exclaimed when he saw her alight from the berlin. He hurried to Lady Cecily's side and bent forward to kiss her. She turned her head to offer him her cheek so that he would not disarrange her stylish bonnet.

"And how elegant you look, my dear," Lord Haverslea said, holding her out at arm's length to admire her in her yellow silk traveling suit. "One would never suspect you of having been traveling for hours, but of having just stepped from your very own drawing room."

Lord Haverslea turned and gently took Lady Portia's small, withered hand into his. "And it is so good to see you again, dear Aunt Portia," he said. "I may call you Aunt Portia, may I not? I must say, I have grown so fond of you, dear lady, that I feel we are connected by blood rather than by marriage."

Lady Portia's wrinkled face flushed and dimpled with a wide smile. "Dear boy, such a shameless flatterer!" She shook her crooked finger at him. "Sometimes I fear our Cecily will have to keep her eye on you around the ladies."

Lord Haverslea patted her hand reassuringly. "Have no fear. There is none but Cecily who would suit me so well."

Lord Haverslea excused himself from the ladies to greet Lord Dynford, who was just descending from the berlin after extricating himself from the tangle of lap rugs.

"Lord Dynford. It has been a long time. So good to see you again! I am ever at your disposal, sir," he said with a gracious bow.

"Lord Haverslea, how pleasant to see you again," Lord Dynford replied.

"Please, please. You must call me Nigel," he insisted. "I sincerely hope you will feel so inclined, sir, as I hope to enjoy a most cordial relationship with all the members of my Cecily's family."

Lord Haverslea turned to Lady Edwina.

Her face and her old, rose pink merino traveling suit were covered with dust. Her pink bonnet was quite ruined. Strands of hair had worked loose from her chignon and straggled out from under her bonnet no matter how many times she had attempted to push them back into place. Her curls now hung limp on her cheeks. Lady Edwina would have preferred not to look quite so old and dowdy when meeting her sister's future husband.

But Lord Haverslea made an elegant bow and said, "And this must be the charming Lady Edwina. It is a great pleasure to meet you at last. Permit me to suggest that you always wear that particular shade of rose as I do believe it enhances the blue of your eyes."

"How kind of you to notice," Lady Edwina replied with genuine surprise. She, too, had always felt that this particular color flattered her. How gracious of him to draw attention to that instead of to how bedraggled she looked.

She noted his mode of dress and thought, indeed, he would be the type of man to note even such a small aspect of a lady's toilette.

His jet black hair was fashionably styled. His intricately tied cravat was immaculate. His jacket of maroon sperfine was superbly cut. His pantaloons were the perfect shade of champagne. Upon the third finger of his right hand, he wore a single, large pigeon's blood ruby set in heavy gold.

Lord Haverslea smiled most engagingly. He bowed and

looked up at her with eyes every bit as green as James Trescott's.

Her surprise had rendered her unusually silent. Realizing that she bordered on rudeness, and for want of anything better to say, Lady Edwina found herself remarking, "Excuse me, sir. Are you quite certain we have never met before?"

Lord Haverslea chuckled. "I am certain we have not. Once having seen you, dear lady, a man could not help but lay his heart at your feet."

"There, Winnie," Lady Cecily said, slapping at Lady Edwina's arm with her loose glove. "Did I not tell you he was the most charming man in the world?"

Lady Edwina smiled politely. "Indeed, you did, Cecily."

"Your baggage carriage arrived earlier," Lord Haverslea said. "I trust you will find everything arranged to your satisfaction. My staff could not help but comment upon the speed with which your servants had everything off the carriage and into the house."

With Trescott in charge, Lady Edwina could credit Lord Haverslea's tale, but she could never imagine Stokes moving with anything remotely resembling speed.

Lord Haverslea extended his arm to Lady Portia. "But I am sure that you are exhausted from the journey. Permit me to extend to you all the comforts which Haversham Hall has to offer."

He began to conduct Lady Portia up the wide stone steps and into the Great Hall. Lady Cecily seized Lord Dynford's arm and followed Lord Haverslea into Haversham Hall.

Lady Edwina, quite alone, made her way up the marble steps. As she crossed each precisely cut stone, she noted that they had been scrubbed immaculately clean. The butler nodded to her as she entered the Hall. At least, she assumed he was the butler. He appeared rather young to her way of thinking to hold such a responsible position, but appearances could be deceiving, she reminded herself. And after all, she was used to Haskell. Compared to him, anyone would look young.

Lord Haverslea conducted them through the Main Hall with its polished marble floor and paneling of warm, burled oak. Even in the late afternoon, the Main Hall was dark with shadows.

In contrast, the drawing room they were conducted into was bright with the yellow-orange rays of the setting sun reflected off the freshly painted white walls and gilt pilasters.

"Mrs. Standish, my housekeeper, has arranged some orgeat and ratafia biscuits for the ladies," Lord Haverslea said, gesturing in the direction of the small table of refreshments which the sturdily built little woman had just finished arranging.

"Oh, Nigel you remembered my favorite!" Lady Cecily exclaimed. "Oh, you are a dear!"

Turning to Lord Dynford, Lord Haverslea added, "There is something a bit more bracing if your lordship should so choose."

"That sounds splendid," Lord Dynford replied.

He helped himself to a snifter of brandy, then proceeded to seat himself on the maroon and white striped sofa.

"I vow, I thought I should have died upon the journey!" Lady Cecily declared. She tugged at the yellow satin ribbons of her bonnet. She was about to toss the expensive bonnet at a nearby chair when Lord Haverslea took it from her and handed it carefully to Mrs. Standish.

Then Lady Cecily made her way to the table in the center of the room and eagerly partook of a glass of orgeat and several biscuits in rapid succession.

"In the unhappy event of your demise, I should be exceedingly distraught," Lord Haverslea declared. "Where else should I ever find another comparable to you?"

Taking several more biscuits in hand, Lady Cecily sat upon the sofa beside Lady Edwina, who had sat beside their brother. She leaned over Lady Edwina. Heedlessly, she nearly spilled the orgeat over her sister's traveling gown. She nudged her brother's arm to get his attention.

She whispered quite loudly, "Well, Dickie, now that you have seen him again, what do you think? Is he not simply wonderful?"

Lord Dynford nodded his head thoughtfully. "Seems to me to be a most hospitable fellow," he agreed.

Lady Cecily then turned to Lady Edwina and demanded, "Well, Winnie, and what do you think of him?"

"Cecily," Lady Edwina replied. "You should know by now that I never make hasty decisions."

Lady Edwina rose and strolled to the open window. Lady Cecily returned to the refreshment table. Before she could reach for another glass of orgeat and several more biscuits, Lord Haverslea took her hand.

"You would not wish to spoil your appetite for the superb dinner I have ordered," he told her and gently guided her to where Lady Edwina was standing by the window.

"Are you quite refreshed from your journey, Lady Edwina?" he asked her.

"Yes, thank you, Lord Haverslea," she replied.

"I see you take an interest in our gardens."

"They are quite admirable."

The lawn was well manicured. The bushes and hedges had all been pruned back quite closely. Several sections of walk appeared to have been recently repaired, and several sections of garden appeared to have been newly landscaped.

"The gardens nearest the house are passable, at the moment," Lord Haverslea said with a small shrug of his shoulders. "My late, lamented cousin considered matters other than the care of the estates to be of prime importance. However, one can scarcely entertain well with the house in poor condition. Therefore, I have begun work on repairing the house and expanding the gardens."

"An extensive undertaking," Lady Edwina ventured.

"To be sure," Lord Haverslea declared proudly. "If it pleases you, I have planned a tour of the house and gardens so that you may see my efforts more closely."

"That will be most pleasant, Lord Haverslea," Lady Edwina replied.

"And while you are visiting, I also hope you will begin to feel toward me those sentiments which one might feel toward a brother, and that you will begin to call me Nigel."

Lady Edwina merely bowed her head in response.

Chapter Twenty

Lady Edwina stood by the window in her bedchamber. Stokes had finished arranging her hair and helping her into her deep rose-colored silk evening gown quite awhile ago and had gone down to the servants' dining hall. She chuckled softly to herself. Undoubtedly, by now the perky little lady's maid would be enjoying herself immensely, steeped in below-stairs gossip up to the eyebrows.

Lady Edwina felt it was still just a bit earlier than was proper for her to go down to dinner. She drew the heavy, maroon velvet draperies aside to gaze out over the lawn.

The drapery fabric was not new. It had suffered from age and wear, yet it appeared to have been cleaned and well repaired recently. The furnishings appeared to have undergone equal refurbishing.

'Another of his lordship's renovations?' she wondered.

Lady Edwina actually was gratified to see that her sister would be marrying a man who took his duties, as owner of this lovely house and steward of the baronial fortunes, quite seriously.

'Gracious, handsome, clever, sensible.' Lady Edwina enumerated Lord Haverslea's apparent virtues. She recalled the way in which he had taken over the care of Lady Cecily's expensive bonnet and had also been able to curb, if only for the time being, Lady Cecily's tendency to overindulge in orgeat and ratafia biscuits.

'Perhaps he is, indeed, the ideal husband for Cecily,' she mused. She wished him a great deal of good luck with the lot in life he had chosen for himself.

Lady Edwina found that while she had been meditating, she had been fidgeting with the draperies. She pulled her hand away quickly. It was so unlike her to fidget! Why ever in the world should she need to fidget?

To distract her from the detested fidgeting, she glanced at the clock on the mantel. The little gilt hands pointed to seven, she noticed. She also noticed with dismay that while she had ceased fidgeting with the draperies, she was now fidgeting with the Cluny lace which bordered the neckline of her gown.

She decided that now was the proper time to make her way to the drawing room. Perhaps the walk would give herself something to do besides that annoying fidgeting.

As she entered the corridor, she saw Stokes tiptoeing into Lord Dynford's bedchamber. And she had been carrying a tray. What on earth was that girl up to now?

Lady Edwina tapped at the door of his lordship's bedchamber, then pushed it open, demanding, "Stokes, whatever are you doing?"

She came to an abrupt halt when she saw Trent taking the tray from Stokes and placing it upon the table which stood in a small alcove by the windows. He was just preparing to sit down. Stokes was just preparing to leave.

"He asked me to bring it, m'lady," Stokes began to whine as soon as she spied Lady Edwina. "He said he had so much to do . . ."

"Thank you, Stokes. That will be all," Lady Edwina told her.

As Stokes left, she continued to glance back over her shoulder until she had pulled the door firmly closed.

"Trescott, since when have you required the services of a lady's maid?" she asked, walking to stand directly before him in the alcove.

Trent backed away ever so slightly. "I must own, I had never before realized exactly how much work being a valet entailed."

"Even the busiest valet finds time to go down to dine."

"I would really rather not," he said coolly.

"I am sure that Lord Haverslea's staff would make you feel welcome," she tried to reassure him. "After all, you are the valet of an earl, even if it is temporary."

"I would really rather not," he repeated.

"I shall ring for someone to help you to find your way to the servants' dining hall this first time if you fear that you cannot find your way in an unfamiliar house," she offered.

Trent gave a little snort. "I think I should be able to manage to find my way, *if* I were going. But I really would rather not."

Lady Edwina shook her head and clucked her tongue. "Trescott, I would never have supposed you to be one to take on airs upon being elevated from footman to valet."

Trent bowed low. "It is not my recent elevation of situation, my lady. Since that first golden moment when I dined upon chicken broth and porridge with your ladyship, I have found all other company quite insipid."

"You are quite the flatterer, sir," she returned. "Nevertheless, this is extremely unusual behavior, Trescott."

Instead of remarking upon her comment, he merely said, "With your permission, my lady."

He reached out to smooth several strands of hair back into place.

"You must look your loveliest when you go down to dinner tonight, my lady," he told her. "It would not do to offend Lord Haverslea."

"Trescott, you know I never offend anyone who is not already asking to be offended," she informed him.

"I do not believe it wise to offend Lord Haverslea, regardless of how offensive he may be."

"Lord Haverslea is hardly offensive! Why, he has been hospitality itself to my family. Trescott, you are saying some of the strangest things I have ever heard."

"I should say I took a poor third place when compared to Lady Cecily and Lady Portia," Trent said with a grin.

"Aunt Portia does not count, as she only repeats."

"Quite so. I stand corrected."

"Perhaps I have kept you from your dinner too long and you are suffering from lack of nourishment and that is why you are saying these strange things. Lord Haverslea is a most pleasant man."

Lady Edwina was puzzled. Trent had a most unusually worried look upon his face.

"My lady, I know that you are, by nature, a most cautious and perceptive lady," Trent said very slowly as if trying to impress his words upon her. "May I be so bold as to urge you to use all your caution and perceptiveness to assess Lord Haverslea's suitability as a husband for your sister."

"I thank you for your advice, Trescott," she said. Then she gave a little laugh, trying to dismiss the dreadfully somber mood which Trent had generated. "Although I shall not be needing it."

"You may not believe you need my advice, but I hope you will take it anyway, my lady," Trent responded. "Now, you must leave."

Lady Edwina tilted her head to look up at him. "His lordship commented upon the speed with which you unpacked," she ventured, just to see what reaction she could evoke from him.

Trent backed up another pace. "Did his lordship see me?" he demanded.

Lady Edwina could not help but note the frown and the worried look that returned to his eyes.

"His servants merely remarked upon it to him," Lady Edwina said. "And what if he did see you? If a cat may look at a king, surely his lordship may lay eyes upon a valet."

She smiled at him. When he failed to respond to her jest, she frowned and said, "You appear to dislike Lord Haverslea. Did something happen here before our arrival?"

Trent nodded. "According to Lady Cecily's account, a great deal was happening here before our arrival."

Lady Edwina frowned harder. "You know perfectly well what I mean. What could have happened to cause you to feel such animosity toward his lordship? Why are you so worried that he will see you? Won't you confide in me? Don't you know I shall help you if I can?"

"What possible reason could I have to dislike his lordship?" he responded with a bitter laugh. "Why, I can tell you, my lady, I do not even know this man."

He took her arm and escorted her to the door. "Now you shall be late for dinner, and that simply will not do!"

As she stepped into the corridor, she heard Trent close

the door quickly behind her.

The dining room was large and brightly illuminated. Dozens of fragrant white candles burned in the gilt wall sconces hung in every other panel of the gold-colored walls and in the three silver candelabras upon the large rosewood table. The walls appeared newly painted, as did the white cornices and pilasters.

Three huskily built, dark-haired footmen in maroon and gold livery, supervised by the young butler, Kirby, began to serve them immediately.

"I greatly regret that we haven't more gentlemen at our table," Lord Haverslea apologized. He had changed into white silk dress breeches and a jacket of maroon velvet over a gold-colored brocade waistcoat.

"Gentlemen do seem to be rather scarce in the Haversham family at the moment," Lady Cecily added with a little giggle.

Lord Haverslea directed just the tiniest frown at Lady Cecily and shook his head.

"Oh, I do beg your pardon!" she called down to the quiet little lady who, earlier, had entered the drawing room almost undetected and now sat at the other end of the dining room table in much the same manner.

"She truly meant no offense, Charlotte," Lord Haverslea kindly apologized to the lady.

The lady said nothing, but merely bobbed her head quickly up and down.

Lady Edwina began to take more notice of the unobtrusive lady seated next to her. She was of middle years, short, rather plump and of a decidedly florid complexion. The lady was dressed entirely in black wool crepe.

In the drawing room, Lord Haverslea had introduced her only as the Dowager Baroness, Lady Haverslea. But he had called her Charlotte, Lady Edwina noted with alarm— the very name which Trescott, in his delirium, had cried out with such dismay.

'Do not start indulging in flights of fantasy, Edwina!' she scolded herself. 'You are becoming as mad as your sister! How many women do you think there are in England who bear the name of Charlotte?"

Nevertheless, Lady Edwina felt compelled to cultivate the acquaintance of the Dowager Baroness Haverslea.

"I am so pleased to have Charlotte with us here tonight," Lord Haverslea said, smiling at the dowager.

"If the old girl were not so curious to meet me, I vow, you should never have got her out of that dreadfully gloomy old Dower House," Lady Cecily said with a giggle.

"Cecily!" Lady Edwina exclaimed in horror.

"Cecily, dear, I fear your *potage de poissons à la russe* will turn cold before you can have eaten it if you continue conversing," Lord Haverslea told her quite calmly.

"Yes, of course, Nigel," Lady Cecily said, smiling up at him. Lady Cecily dipped her silver spoon into the gilt-edged china soup plate, lifting up a small piece of sturgeon with the clear broth.

After taking a small taste, she declared, "I vow, Nigel, it *is* delicious." She devoted her entire attention to finishing her portion.

Lady Edwina was surprised and, at the same time, greatly relieved to see that Lord Haverslea had the ability to stop her sister from uttering any more of her thoughtless remarks.

The soup was indeed excellent and quickly consumed, to be readily replaced by a *côte de boeuf aux oignons glacés*.

"I do believe that retaining my late and greatly lamented cousin's French chef was one of the wisest things I have ever done," Lord Haverslea said as he urged his guests to partake of the beef sirloin and glazed onions, and then he himself did the same.

"After all, it was one of the footmen who drugged the wine, not a case of the chef having poisoned the sauce," Lord Haverslea added with a slight chuckle. "I suppose I have nothing to fear from Antoine."

"There, I told you my Nigel was clever, as well as being possessed of superb taste," Lady Cecily said. "After all, he did choose to marry *me!*"

Lord Haverslea smiled pleasantly at Lady Cecily. Then, with a look of utmost concern upon his handsome face,

Lord Haverslea resumed the abandoned conversation with Lady Haverslea. "I do hope that you do not consider the Dower House gloomy, Charlotte. If there is anything which displeases you I myself shall come to inspect it and to order any repairs which you deem necessary."

In spite of Lord Haverslea's kindnesses to her, Lady Haverslea merely shook her head and answered quietly, "The Dower House is acceptable just the way it is, thank you."

As the Dowager Baroness seemed extremely reluctant to converse, Lord Haverslea explained to his other guests, "Charlotte removed to the Dower House immediately after that most unpleasant incident here. I tried my utmost to convince her that there was no need for her to leave with such haste, as I do not take up that much space here — yet," he added, throwing a smiling glance in Lady Cecily's direction. "But Charlotte insisted."

Lord Haverslea shook his head and clucked his tongue.

"Unfortunately, Charlotte has been a virtual recluse since then," Lord Haverslea continued. "I try to encourage her to receive visitors, or even to pay a few social calls. I have no idea why she always refuses."

"I prefer my solitude for the time being," Lady Haverslea replied quietly.

"Then it is, indeed, good of you to come to visit us now," Lady Edwina commented. "Did you have a pleasant journey?"

Lady Haverslea merely nodded.

Lady Cecily looked up from her beef long enough to comment, "La! Winnie, the Dower House is only located on the other side of the woodlands from Haversham Hall."

"Charlotte intends to return there at the end of this evening," Lord Haverslea said. "I have tried to convince her to stay, at least while you are visiting us. We certainly have room enough."

"It is most kind of you, Nigel," Lady Haverslea repeated, "but I prefer my privacy."

It seemed to Lady Edwina that no matter how many times Lord Haverslea tried to include the Dowager Baroness in the conversation, she gave only the briefest of answers and rarely ventured any comment on her own.

"We shall miss your company," Lady Edwina said. "Will you be returning for another visit, or have you other plans?"

"I am, as yet, uncertain of my plans," the Dowager answered, glancing at Lord Haverslea.

Undaunted by the lady's lack of enthusiasm, Lady Edwina continued, "I am sure you will be much more comfortable in your own home."

"This used to be my home," Lady Haverslea commented in a voice so low that Lady Edwina at first had difficulty realizing that the lady had said anything to her at all.

Lady Edwina found that she was quite at a loss as to what reply she ought to make to the lady's remark. She debated upon what course of conversation to pursue with the quiet lady.

The entrée was removed. Each guest was offered Genoese cakes and pineapple cream.

Lady Edwina had continued to observe the Dowager Baroness throughout the course of the meal. Her ladyship merely picked at the excellent food. She never made a comment unless called upon.

'I have never encountered anyone more shy. One could find oneself in a room with this lady and believe oneself to be alone,' Lady Edwina mused.

While the gentlemen lingered over their port, the ladies retired to the drawing room.

Lady Cecily and Lady Portia began a very careful study of exactly what the large drawing room contained. They perused each painting. They lifted and examined each vase, each candlestick, and each leather-bound volume which sat upon the rosewood side tables. They scrutinized every item, right down to the very last jeweled snuffbox on display.

While her sister and aunt were embarrassing her in such a manner, Lady Edwina deliberately sought out Lady Haverslea. She indicated the seat beside the lady on the small, maroon and white striped sofa. "May I?"

She took her ladyship's lack of a reply for assent and seated herself.

"Forgive me for not doing so earlier, Lady Haverslea. Please accept my condolences upon your recent bereavement," Lady Edwina said.

"You are most kind," she responded quietly. "Had you ever made the acquaintance of my husband?"

"I regret to say I had not," Lady Edwina answered.

Lady Haverslea sighed. "I thought not. Most people found it extremely difficult to offer sincere condolences upon his untimely demise."

Lady Edwina regarded the lady with surprise. 'What an extraordinarily strange thing to say about one's husband! Even if it were true!'

"But I always managed to get along with him well enough," Lady Haverslea continued.

"I suppose getting along with one's husband is greatly to be desired," Lady Edwina commented.

Lady Cecily and Lady Portia had made their way about the room and now seated themselves together upon the gold brocade-covered sofa across from Lady Edwina and Lady Haverslea.

"There now, Winnie," Lady Cecily interrupted. "You have had the opportunity to observe him better. I demand to know what you think of my Nigel!"

"I must own, Cecily, I am exceedingly surprised," Lady Edwina answered.

"Surprised? Why ever should you be surprised?" Lady Cecily demanded.

"You seem to have rather good taste in men after all."

"La! Winnie, I vow, you are so amusing!"

"Quite an amusing girl," Lady Portia echoed.

"Cecily, we were discussing how important it is to get along well with one's husband," Lady Edwina told her.

"Indeed, Winnie?" Lady Cecily asked with a derisive laugh. "You are *so* knowledgeable on that subject."

Lady Haverslea raised her dark eyes to Lady Cecily and told her, 'I am, my dear. And I do hope that *you* realize how important it is to get along well with one's husband."

"La! Lady Haverslea, *I* seem to have the wonderful ability to get along well with *everyone*," Lady Cecily exclaimed.

"She gets along well with everyone," Lady Portia confirmed.

"But a husband is someone special," Lady Haverslea insisted quietly. "It is important to know as much as possible about the man you marry."

"La! Ignorance is bliss," Lady Cecily declared with an airy wave of her hand.

"The late Baron and I were betrothed for over a year before our marriage. Even before our betrothal, we knew each other very well, as we had grown up together. His mother and my mother were first cousins on their mother's side, you know. When we were very small, we were taken for a few weeks every summer to our great-grandfather's estates in Sussex."

"I vow, personal reminiscences tend to turn dreadfully boring. Aunt Portia, I do believe we missed seeing those lovely little figurines by that window over there." She indicated a far corner of the room which Lady Edwina knew perfectly well that Lady Cecily and Lady Portia had seen before.

"Cecily! What a horrid thing to say!" Lady Edwina declared.

"I vow, Winnie, I thought it rather sensible, myself," Lady Cecily protested. "After all, I am to be Lady Haverslea. I should know precisely what the estate entails."

With a little flip of her head, Lady Cecily rose and proceeded to the far side of the room, with Lady Portia in tow.

Lady Edwina struggled to control her urge to give her sister a sound thrashing.

"I must apologize . . ." Lady Edwina began.

But Lady Haverslea had apparently taken no notice of Lady Cecily's exceedingly rude behavior and continued her tale.

"It was the summer I turned fifteen. I knew I should make my coming out the next season, and that this would most probably be my last summer to be just a simple child at Great-Grandpapa's. I thought Milton quite special at the time, silly young thing that I was."

Lady Edwina had sat listening to Lady Haverslea without making a comment.

"Am I boring you, too, my dear?" she asked.

"No!" Lady Edwina replied most emphatically, afraid that the Dowager Baroness should even remotely connect her behavior with that of her thoughtless sister. "To the contrary. I find your story to be quite interesting."

"You are a dear girl to say so," Lady Haverslea said, reaching out her plump, pink little hand to pat Lady Edwina's. "And to sit here listening to me rattle on."

"Your carriage is waiting, Charlotte," Lord Haverslea said as he approached her from the doorway. "Are you still quite sure I cannot induce you to accept our hospitality for the night?"

Lady Haverslea startled so when his lordship spoke to her that she dropped her handkerchief.

'My gracious, the poor lady is upon the verge of nervous prostration!' Lady Edwina remarked to herself.

"Poor Charlotte, your nerves are still frayed," Lord Haverslea said sympathetically. He bent to retrieve the dropped handkerchief for Lady Haverslea. "Perhaps it will be beneficial after all if you go home for a good night's rest."

"Yes, Nigel."

"But we would be so happy to have you join us again tomorrow when I conduct everyone on a tour of some of the more interesting rooms in Haversham Hall. You will come, Charlotte?"

"Perhaps I shall," she replied quietly.

Chapter Twenty-one

Lord Dynford and Lord Haverslea had just returned from a morning ride about the park and a tour of the stable. Their highly polished black top boots clicked across the marble floor of the Hall. Lord Haverslea brushed a twig of hay from his maroon riding jacket and, as he walked, he slapped his crop against his buckskin riding breeches.

"Lord Haverslea—"

"Please, call me Nigel," he insisted.

"Very well, Nigel," Lord Dynford conceded with little reluctance. "You undeniably have a superb eye for horse-flesh. But I must own, I have never seen a stable which consisted solely of black horses."

Lord Haverslea shrugged. "Call it a whim. I find I sit much better upon a black horse."

"How extraordinary! Do you suppose it is because of your black hair?" He pulled at his own fair hair and chuckled. "Do you suppose I should attempt to purchase a palomino?"

Lord Haverslea frowned. "I highly doubt that others would find similar advantages from such a match."

Lord Dynford pursed his lips and nodded.

As the two gentlemen passed the morning room, Lord Dynford spied Lady Edwina and Lady Portia.

"B'gads, Winnie! You never saw such prime horseflesh!" he exclaimed. "The ladies must join us some morning."

"Perhaps I shall," she replied. "However, I trust I will not be disclosing any family secrets when I say that Cecily rarely rises before ten o'clock, even when in the country."

"I believe my dear Cecily is possessed of a most delicate

constitution," Lord Haverslea said.

"Such a beauty must get her proper rest," Lady Portia stated.

"Aunt Portia, on the other hand, rises at daybreak," Lady Edwina continued.

"It is so difficult to sleep when one grows old," Lady Portia complained.

Lady Edwina continued, "I felt I should keep Aunt Portia company."

Lady Portia patted Lady Edwina's arm. "Such a dear."

"I trust your early hours will not render you too tired to enjoy the tour of the house which I hope to conduct for you all after luncheon," Lord Haverslea said.

"Nothing could keep me from enjoying such a tour, Lord Haverslea," Lady Edwina assured him.

But Lady Edwina had failed to consider the fact that Lady Cecily would be accompanying them.

"This is the State Bedchamber," Lord Haverslea later explained as he swung open the door.

The room was sparsely furnished, yet appeared filled with the large walnut bed. The walls were also paneled in austere planks of rich walnut. To one side of the bed stood a walnut highboy, its cabriole legs bending out in graceful curves. To the other side stood a small gilt gesso table flanked by the slender curves of a delicate walnut chair.

The draperies and bed curtains were of aged hand-loomed white wool. Swirls and whorls of fanciful embroidered fruits and birds, leaves and flowers covered the fabric. The blues, golds, and greens had retained their vibrant hue, but the reds had faded to a warm rose.

The room smelled of beeswax and musty old wool.

"It's lovely," Lady Edwina exclaimed breathlessly.

"On one of her processions, Queen Anne slept here. It is a family tradition to maintain the room ever in readiness for any monarch's visit. Unfortunately, my late cousin had no such taste for maintaining family traditions."

"A pity. You have an interesting heritage, Lord

Haverslea," Lady Edwina commented.

"Faugh! What a dreary old room!" Lady Cecily exclaimed, waving her hand before her nose. "I vow, it certainly looks as if no one has bothered with it in a hundred years. It needs to be aired, scrubbed, and completely refurnished!"

She fingered an edge of the aged bedcurtain, then gave it a disdainful little flip away from her. "Then it would be a proper room for a proper monarch!"

"Cecily, don't be a proper bore," Lady Edwina scolded, yet kept her voice to a whisper so as not to interrupt what Lord Haverslea was saying to the others. "It is a Haversham tradition. Now do be quiet, so we may all enjoy what his lordship has to tell us."

"I vow, *she* could tell us more," Lady Cecily said in a tone of voice much too loud to be mistaken for a whisper. She pointed rather conspicuously at Lady Haverslea, who had joined the party shortly after luncheon. "*If* she ever summoned the courage to utter more than two words at a time."

"Not everyone is blessed with your garrulous gift, Cecily," Lady Edwina said sarcastically.

"That is true," Lady Cecily agreed. "What a pity for them."

Lady Edwina decided that if everyone were possessed of such gifts as Lady Cecily, what a pity it would be for them all!

"Still and all, the lady should say *something* from time to time. Otherwise, why would she even bother to come? It is quite beyond me," Lady Cecily continued to complain. "She sits there like a plump little blackbird, watching everyone with those beady little black eyes of hers, casting such a pall over our festivities."

"Do try to be a bit more gracious, Cecily," Lady Edwina said with exasperation. "Some day, with any luck, you will be the Dowager Baroness Haverslea—if Nigel does not strangle you first because you have driven him quite to the point of madness with your incessant, mindless chatter."

"My Nigel? Murder someone?" Lady Cecily laughed derisively. "La! Winnie, that is positively ludicrous!"

"Come with me now," Lord Haverslea said, offering his arm to escort Lady Portia about. "This is the perfect time of day at which to view the Gallery."

Lady Cecily immediately clutched Lord Dynford's arm. This left Lady Edwina to walk with the silent Lady Haverslea.

One wall of the long, narrow gallery was composed almost entirely of windows which opened onto the extensive gardens. The sunlight poured through the large windows, completely illuminating the room. Yet the angle of the gallery to the angle of the sun was such that no direct rays of light fell upon a single painting, thus forestalling any damage.

Haversham ancestors lined up for review upon the walls. Lord Haverslea forged ahead, introducing them one by one. The Dowager Baroness began to hang back a bit from the others. Not wishing to be the odd man in the intimate little group walking ahead of her, Lady Edwina remained with Lady Haverslea.

Lady Edwina peered up at the canvas and oil faces peering coldly down at her. A gentleman with a pointed black beard and wearing a large millstone ruff about his neck seemed to watch her with his green eyes as she moved down the line to inspect a gentleman with shoulder-length black curls and a wide collar extending from shoulder to shoulder, a froth of lace tumbling down the front of his gold-trimmed red jacket. A lovely lady wearing a powdered white wig and headdress twice the size of her head stared at her with the same green eyes.

So as not to appear as rude as her sister had been, Lady Edwina commented, "What a striking resemblance between so many of the Havershams!"

"The green eyes? The black hair? Oh yes, she had black hair, too, as a young woman, or so she said." Lady Haverslea pointed to the bewigged woman in the portrait. "Milton's great-aunt, Minerva Haversham," she explained with a chuckle. "She was quite, quite old when she passed away a few years after Milton and I were married. She attributed it all to a Black Irish ancestor, who passed his

266

dark, handsome looks down the line."

Lady Edwina observed each portrait carefully. "There are worse things to pass on to one's children than such a handsome visage," she remarked.

She could not help but note that the black hair, fair complexion, and vivid green eyes were almost identical to James Trescott's.

Could James Trescott be the illegitimate child of the present Lord Haverslea's father? Such things were far from unusual. Of course, that long-ago Haversham ancestor was by no means the only Black Irish to have had children. On the other hand, that theory might explain Trescott's animosity toward the present Lord Haverslea.

It was much easier to suppose that than to connect Trescott with the footman who was the suspected accomplice of the Mad, and now dead, Cousin of Lady Cecily's tale.

Lady Haverslea tapped Lady Edwina on the shoulder, rousing her from her speculations. She crooked her plump little finger toward Lady Edwina. "Come with me," she said.

By now, Lord Haverslea and the others were far down the gallery and quite heedless of the missing members of their little party. Lady Edwina followed Lady Haverslea as she led her away from the group and slipped silently down the maze of corridors through which they had come.

As they entered the drawing room, Lady Haverslea raised her hand to point to the portrait over the mantelpiece. An enormous and very recently painted portrait of Nigel, Lord Haverslea, hung there. The portrait extended from the top of the mantel all the way up to the high ceiling of the drawing room and from one side of the mantel to the other. Lady Edwina certainly had to own that the present Lord Haverslea did not seem to be one to do things by halves.

A look of chagrin passed over Lady Haverslea's face.

"Oh, dear, I am becoming so forgetful in my old age," Lady Haverslea mumbled to herself. "Things have changed here so drastically and so quickly, it is sometimes difficult for me to take it all in."

She turned to Lady Edwina and said apologetically, "A portrait of Milton used to hang there. Nigel had it taken down and his own hung two weeks after the funeral."

Lady Edwina raised one eyebrow. "How quickly he managed to have his new portrait done," she observed.

Lady Haverslea grimaced. "Nigel never was one to waste time, especially once he has made up his mind to do a thing. I did manage to persuade him to give me Milton's portrait for the Dower House."

She turned to indicate the wall behind her. She pointed to a pleasant, but quite ordinary, watercolor landscape. "And there—there was a portrait of Milton's brother, Trent."

The Mad Cousin, undoubtedly. Small wonder the portrait had been taken down and replaced by something much more innocuous.

"Nigel was about to burn it." Lady Haverslea shook her head and made little clucking noises with her tongue. "And it was such a nice portrait, too."

"Such a waste," agreed Lady Edwina. On the other hand, she did understand why Lord Haverslea should not like to keep the portrait of the man who had attempted to murder him.

"Nigel was so eager to rid himself of both portraits that it was not too difficult for me to persuade him to give them to me for the Dower House."

Lady Edwina studied very carefully the little lady dressed in black standing by her side. 'Why should she want to keep the portrait of the man who had killed her husband? Unless she is using it for archery practice!'

"I should like to have you visit me at the Dower House, Lady Edwina," Lady Haverslea said. "Then you will be able to see the portrait of Milton."

"Yes, I should be most happy to," Lady Edwina responded. "And I am sure Lord Haverslea would be pleased to know you were making an effort to—"

"No, no!" The dowager baroness said, glancing about her with wide eyes. She twisted and tugged at her linen handkerchief. "I do not want him there. I would like you to

268

come alone—and to tell no one."

"We are a small party, Lady Haverslea," she reminded her. "Someone will surely notice my absence."

"Say you are unwell. Say you are tired from the journey. Then come to visit me. Please," Lady Haverslea said in a most pleading tone of voice. "It would be so lovely to have someone to talk to."

"Aha, I have found you! Have you two been alone, plotting against me?" Lord Haverslea demanded. He was laughing as if it were a capital joke, yet Lady Edwina noted with a growing uneasiness that the laughter did not extend to the searching look in his eyes.

She recalled Trescott's warning not to offend Lord Haverslea. How could Lord Haverslea construe her polite conversation with the quiet and quite harmless Lady Haverslea as offensive in any way?

Lady Haverslea had started so badly that she had to sit in a small chair, her hand clutched to her heaving breast.

"My dear Charlotte, are you quite well?" Lord Haverslea asked, rushing to her side. "I am so sorry to have startled you."

His lordship looked so abjectly penitent that Lady Edwina chided herself for such imaginings as she had been harboring regarding the gentleman.

"Winnie, we missed you," Lady Cecily declared. "Why did you leave us?"

Lady Haverslea looked up at her suddenly. "I am afraid I had become too tired to continue the tour. Lady Edwina was kind enough to accompany me back to the drawing room."

"La! Winnie, it must be so unsettling to find oneself growing old and tired," Lady Cecily said. "But whatever could you have found to do to occupy yourselves without us?"

"Lady Haverslea and I have been enjoying a perfectly marvelous talk just between the two of us," Lady Edwina responded.

"Lady Edwina, you disappoint me," Lord Haverslea chided her with a jovial grin which belied the narrowing of his eyes. "I have been told that you were a most singular lady in that you did not indulge in gossip."

"Indeed, you have been informed correctly," Lady Edwina told him. "There are a great many topics of discussion which would not be considered gossip."

"Please enlighten us as to what one of them might be," Lord Haverslea asked, the smile still frozen to his face.

"Why, my lord, now you disappoint me," Lady Edwina responded, returning his smile with an icy smile of her own. "I had thought a gentleman of your wit and intelligence could devise some topics of your own."

The smile began to fade from Lord Haverslea's lips.

Lady Haverslea's eyes grew wide. "We were discussing your new portrait, Nigel," she answered quickly. "And an exceptionally good likeness it is too. Is it not, Lady Edwina? Did I not just remark to you what a marvelous likeness it was to Nigel?"

Lady Edwina nodded and replied, "Most certainly." She was puzzled by the lady's exceptionally nervous state. Could it be that the strange occurrences here had deprived the lady of her wits?

Suddenly Lady Haverslea began to walk toward the door. "If you will all please excuse me, I shall take my leave. I find I am most unwell."

"Charlotte," Lord Haverslea came up to her, but the dowager backed away. "Shall I send for a maid to accompany you home?"

"Quite unnecessary, Nigel," she answered quickly. "It is still daylight and a short stroll through the woods will perhaps alleviate my . . . my headache. I thank you for your hospitality this afternoon."

"We would be exceedingly happy to have you join us again tomorrow," Lord Haverslea invited. "If the weather remains fair, we shall tour the gardens."

"The prospect sounds delightful," Lady Haverslea remarked with little enthusiasm. "Until tomorrow, then."

Lady Edwina was puzzled. It appeared that the dowager baroness was not quiet because she was still in mourning but because she was terrified of Lord Haverslea. After his strange accusations of their plotting against him, she was beginning to think that perhaps the lady had some reason.

After dinner, Lord Haverslea, Lord Dynford, Lady Portia, and Lady Cecily took their usual seats about the card table which one of the large, dark-haired footmen had set up in the drawing room.

Lady Edwina found it difficult to distinguish one footman from another. Like the identical black horses in his stables, Lord Haverslea seemed to collect the dark-haired footmen as ornaments to complement his own dark good looks. And my goodness, they were all so big!

Lord Dynford began to deal the first hand of a rubber of whist which each player had expressed the firm intention of pursuing until well into the night.

After only a few minutes of watching the others play, Lady Edwina stifled a yawn.

"I do believe the journey has overtaxed me far more than I had at first realized," she told them. "If you will excuse me, I believe I shall retire earlier than usual this evening."

The players were far too occupied with their hands to reply immediately. At length, Lady Cecily said, with exaggerated sympathy, and without looking up from the cards she held, "Poor Winnie. I vow, you have been spending too much time with that gloomy old Charlotte. Are you, too, growing old and tired?"

"I am sure I am not so decrepit that I cannot make my way up the stairs without assistance," Lady Edwina replied sourly.

"I suppose that being married helps a lady to retain her youth," Lady Cecily continued. "Spinsters seem to age so rapidly."

"Perhaps that is because some of them have younger sisters who drive them to distraction," Lady Edwina replied through tightly compressed lips.

"Shall I send a footman to light your way, Lady Edwina?" Lord Haverslea offered.

"Most kind of you," she told him in a more pleasant tone

271

of voice. "But neither am I becoming so blind that I cannot find my own bedchamber."

She bid the little party good night and made her way through the halls alone to her room. From under the doors, Lady Edwina could see the lights from the candles which burned in her own bedchamber and in her brother's bedchamber only a little distance down the hall.

She could hear Stokes moving about in her room. There was no movement from inside his lordship's room.

'Trescott must be sleeping,' she told herself. 'Surely a man who would not even go down for his meals would not be found wandering about this quite large house just for a lark.'

The sound of someone dragging something exceptionally heavy came from the bedchamber farther down the hall. Lady Edwina crept softly to the doorway. For some reason which she could not have explained if her very life depended upon it, she slowly turned the shining brass knob so that it made no sound. She pushed the door open just wide enough to peek inside, breathing a silent prayer of thanks for Lord Haverslea's fastidiousness, which made the servants so diligent that the well-oiled hinge did not creak.

It was a large bedchamber which had apparently not been in use for several years. In the center of the room stood a large, black trunk. It was obviously a trunk of expensive and expert craftsmanship, despite its present well-worn condition. The dilapidated trunk in no way corresponded to the rest of the rich gold-colored velvet bedcurtains and mahogany furnishings of the room.

Most surprising of all was the figure of Trent, bent over the open trunk.

From the trunk, Trent withdrew a blue wool jacket with cuffs of red and gold braid down the front—the uniform of the Royal Horse Artillery, and a major, no less.

He put it on and stood before the cheval glass, brushing the lint from the front and the sleeves.

She stared at him, speechless with shock. What audacity! What unmitigated brazenness!

Nevertheless, Lady Edwina had to own that the sight of

his broad shoulders and slender waist and hips under the superbly fitting jacket made her heart pound and her blood burn.

Then Trent bent down over the trunk again. Lady Edwina watched him as he began very carefully to sort through the remainder of the contents of the trunk. He ran his hand slowly over the silver-handled hairbrushes, but passed over them and continued on.

"Aha!" The sound which he made was barely louder than a breath.

Lady Edwina watched with disbelief as Trent pulled a small leather purse from the trunk. He opened the brass clasp and withdrew from the purse what appeared to be quite a large quantity of folding money, as well as a handful of coins—mostly farthings and large, brown halfpennies, from the look of it. He tucked the money into his waistcoat pocket.

Lady Edwina was sick at heart. Perhaps James Trescott had not pinched the Dynford silver, but he was not above stealing from their host!

She slipped through the doorway, closing the door behind her quickly and quietly so that no one else should see them.

"Trescott! How could you?" Her wail of distress was barely louder than a whisper.

"My lady!" Trent exclaimed, peeling off the jacket with great speed. "How long have you . . . ? I thought you were downstairs with the others."

"Obviously. And you may consider yourself exceedingly fortunate that the others are still downstairs," she told him angrily. "Have you any idea what would have happened should anyone else have discovered you?"

"No harm was done, my lady," Trent said. "You have merely stumbled upon my worst fault. I am insatiably curious."

"Curious?" she repeated. Several rapid little steps brought her directly before him. She poked angrily at the bulge in his waistcoat pocket. "*This* is more than curiosity, Trescott!"

Trent did not answer her, but folded the jacket he held

273

very neatly and replaced it in the trunk. He closed the trunk.

"What! Are you not going to take the silver-handled brushes, too?" she demanded.

"Of course not, my lady," Trent replied coolly. "They would not fit into my pocket. At any rate, they are engraved, which makes them deucedly difficult to pawn."

He pulled the trunk back to a space beside a large wardrobe, from where it had apparently come.

"I am a lady of reasonable intelligence, Trescott," she began.

"I should say of admirable intelligence, my lady," Trent interrupted her in a soft, gentle tone of voice.

She waved her finger at him. "Do not attempt to distract *me*, Trescott. You know perfectly well by now that I am a lady of singular purpose. I also am at liberty at the moment. Why do you not explain this to me?"

"Because I cannot explain it to you—not now, my lady," Trent said.

He was frowning. His green eyes were searching her face. Was he looking for approval of what he had done or was he looking for understanding?

"If you would forebear to mention this to anyone until I *can* explain . . . ," he requested, not in the pleading voice of one caught in a crime, but in a calm, low, and reasonable tone.

She could not allow him to perpetrate this crime without suffering the consequences. She *must* turn him over to the authorities, as was her duty. Yet she could not bear to think of James Trescott transported off to Botany Bay, all the way at the other end of the world, or worse, sent into the next world by way of a short drop at the Tyburn.

As much as she wanted simply to turn around and forget that she had witnessed any of Trent's indiscretions, she told him, "I cannot do that, Trescott. You know I cannot remain silent regarding a theft."

Trent smiled sadly at her. "Yes, my lady. I know you very well."

Lady Edwina frowned and pressed her lips together, reconsidering his request. At length, she said, "You realize, of course, that I must at least inform my brother of this. I do not think we shall be able to retain your services after you have comported yourself in this shameless manner."

Deep down inside, she knew that it was an empty threat. How could she ever bear to let him go?

Trent answered her quietly, "I doubt that I shall be remaining with your ladyship's household much longer, at any rate."

"What!" she could not hold back her surprise nor her dismay. In her utter bewilderment, she said the first thing which came to mind under the circumstances. "Well, do not expect us to write you a glowing reference after this matter!"

Then the man had the audacity actually to grin at her!

"My lady, after this, one way or another, I shall never be needing a reference again."

The man's actions and requests were becoming increasingly incomprehensible with each passing minute!

"If I cannot have your favorable reference, may I at least have your assurance that you will say nothing of this to your brother, or to anyone else, for just a little while longer?" he asked.

She shook her head. "Not without some sort of explanation. I *must* know why you have done this! Perhaps then I could help you sort this problem out properly."

"That is very kind, my lady, but I do not want you to become involved in my problems."

She reached out and clasped his hand tightly in hers. "Trescott," she said. Then she looked more intently into his eyes and said softly, "James. I . . . I care about what happens to you. I would help you out of this predicament, if you would only explain to me the reasons behind your most unusual behavior."

"I cannot explain this to you now," he said, taking his hand from her. He drew a deep breath. "If all goes well, I shall try to explain to you. Or someone else will tell you their version."

The man was becoming more incomprehensible by the

moment!

"No!" she insisted. "Now, Trescott! I *must* know why you took that money."

When he still refused to answer, she cried, "You *must* tell me! It was bad enough when you were only my footman, but I simply cannot allow myself to be in love with a *thief!*"

She clapped her hand over her mouth. She had actually said it—and he had heard her, quite clearly, too!

"So, you are in love with your footman, my lady," Trent said. The corners of his mouth were threatening to turn up into a definite grin. The manner in which he called her his lady told her that he was not making reference to her actual title.

Lady Edwina gave her head a defensive little flip.

"I daresay, I am not the first lady, nor shall I be the last, to nourish a *tendre* for her footman."

The grin burst forth upon his lips in full abandon. "On behalf of footmen everywhere, may I say, I certainly hope not."

Trent took a single step which brought him directly before her. He slowly reached out his hand and placed it upon her shoulder.

"Had you ever considered the possibility that your footman was also very much in love with you?"

His hand now moved slowly up her throat.

She swallowed hard. She was barely able to breathe. It was so difficult to say, "You are . . . ?"

Trent nodded. He wrapped his arm about her, drawing her gently and pressing her close to him.

"Oh, yes. Very much in love with you."

He smoothed his hand over her chin and lifted her face to his.

She looked up at him, offering her lips. She felt the sweet warmth of his breath on her cheek. He bent closer to her, brushing his lips gently against hers in a tentative kiss. She felt her heart pounding faster as she responded, pressing her mouth to his.

He kissed her firmly now, enveloping her in his arms and pulling her so close to him that she felt the buttons of his waistcoat indent the softness of her breasts and his own desire for her press insistently against her hip.

"This is most improper, James," she protested breathlessly, at the same time reaching her arms up to entwine about his neck.

His face remained close to hers. She could feel his soft, full lips moving against her cheek as he whispered, "Lady Edwina Danvers and her footman. Indeed, most improper."

He enfolded her in his arms, his hands moving slowly and firmly across her arms and shoulders, down her back to cup the soft roundness of her bottom, then up again to mold the soft swell of her breasts. He pressed kisses upon her lips and cheeks and throat.

Her own sensuous response to his impassioned caresses did not disconcert her in the least. She had been dreaming of doing just this for a long, long time.

"Oh, James, no!" She placed both hands upon his chest and, swallowing hard, pushed herself slowly from him.

She raised her hand to wipe away the tears which had begun to form. It mattered very much to her how long she had dreamed of his embrace, but the silences and secrets which stood between them mattered as well.

"I cannot . . . it is just not possible," she managed to choke out. "We must be sensible, James. Sensible! And you must tell me why you are so disturbed by Lord Haverslea and why you would steal from the man. And why do you bear such a striking resemblance to so many of the Havershams?"

"So you have remarked it?" he asked, breathless and swallowing just as hard as she. He backed away from her and began to pace the room in clear agitation. He reached up and ran his fingers through his disheveled black hair. "Are you asking me if I am the by-blow of a Haversham?"

"Are you?" she asked him quite directly.

"Would it make a difference to you?" he returned. "Can you love a thief but not a bastard?"

"You must know by now that I shall love you whoever you are," she told him, holding his eyes with hers so that he stopped his pacing for just a moment. Then he broke her

277

gaze and began to pace again. "But I must know *who* you are," she continued, "and why you are doing these strange things."

He did not answer her. Blast that stubbornly reticent man!

"Why did you take that money from a perfect stranger's trunk?" Lady Edwina persisted.

"No one is perfect, my lady," he told her with a grin.

"And why must you always be so damned clever at evading my questions?" she demanded in exasperation.

"Why must you be so damned persistent in asking questions which I cannot answer?" he countered angrily. Then just as suddenly, his deep voice sounded more contrite. "No, no, Edwina, my love. I did not mean it that way."

He advanced upon her quickly and caught her up in his arms again.

"Only trust me, Edwina. For a little while longer, trust me." His voice would have held a pleading quality had there not been such a strong element of command in his words.

"How can I trust you? I cannot even trust you with someone else's money!"

"Ah, but you can trust me with the silver," he said, grinning down at her.

"James! This is serious!" she cried.

The smile fell from his face and he released her from his embrace. "I *am* serious," he told her. "Deadly serious. And I would not have you involved in the danger I face."

"Danger? Now you tell me of danger? I must know what is happening," she demanded.

Trent said nothing but only moved toward the door. He turned back to her.

"Won't you keep my secret for just a little longer?" he asked.

Lady Edwina watched him as he left her standing alone in the strange room, her lips still quivering from his kiss and longing for more.

Chapter Twenty-two

"M'lord," Kirby announced from the doorway of the drawing room. "From Lady Haverslea." He offered Lord Haverslea the folded paper on a small silver tray.

"Whatever could it be, Nigel dear?" Lady Cecily asked, rising to go stand beside his chair. She peeked over his shoulder, resting her hand on the soft maroon velvet of his jacket.

Lord Haverslea broke the seal and quickly perused the short note. His expression remained impassive, but Lady Edwina saw the lobes of his ears turn crimson and his nostrils flare as he tried to keep his upper lip from curling.

"How unfortunate," he said coolly. He rose and began to pace up and down. "It is a note from Charlotte. It appears she is still unwell and has declined my gracious invitation to a tour of the newly planted gardens and to dinner afterward."

The knuckles of his fingers whitened as he crumpled the note into a tight little ball and threw it into the cold fireplace. It bounced and rolled behind the large arrangement of red and gold chrysanthemums.

"Blast! I despise having my plans disrupted."

Lady Cecily began to pace beside him. She patted his arm and said comfortingly, "There, there, Nigel, dear."

"They strive to defeat me at every turn," he murmured. "But I shall succeed by my superior wit. I always have. I always shall."

"Of course you have," Lady Cecily reassured him. "You have done everything humanly possible to make Lady Haverslea feel welcomed at our little gathering. By no stretch of the imagination can it be considered your fault if the morbid old biddy persists in her reclusive habits."

279

"Dear Cecily," Lord Haverslea said with a sigh as he threw himself languidly back into his chair. "Sometimes I believe that you are the only one who understands me."

"I do?" she asked, as if quite surprised by this newly discovered talent of hers. "Well, yes, of course I do, Nigel dear."

"Ah, well then!" Lord Haverslea declared, to all appearances recovering his good spirits. He slapped the arms of the chair as he rose quite rapidly. "We shall simply enjoy ourselves without her."

"Of course, Nigel," Lady Cecily concurred as she took his lordship's arm. "It serves her right for missing such a splendid excursion."

"I know I shall," Lord Dynford said with great enthusiasm. "I am greatly interested in seeing the modifications and improvements you have made to your gardens and landscapes, as I have recently begun to consider making certain alterations to our own estate."

Lady Edwina watched her brother with certain forebodings. Lord Dynford's eyes were gleaming with the same sparkle that the very mention of flight brought to them.

Lord Haverslea led the little party through one of the tall doors which opened from the drawing room onto the wide, flagstone, rear portico.

Lady Portia and Lord Dynford followed them. Lady Edwina came alone. She had a great many things to ponder. She preferred to walk alone.

Lady Cecily turned and called back over her shoulder, "Winnie dear, do you suppose widows as well as spinsters become increasingly eccentric as the years go by?"

"If you are extremely fortunate, Cecily, you will not find out what either of them do," Lady Edwina replied tartly.

The stone stairs, flanked by low-spreading yew, ended at the brick garden walk, which was bordered by closely cropped boxwood. The intricate patterns of bricks led them past feathery beds of purple Michaelmas daisies and pillows of rusty red chrysanthemums.

The path widened under an arbor of twining grapevines with two stone benches sheltered at either side. Then the path went past the entrance to a boxwood maze. Lord Haverslea pointed out each new addition with great pride.

The low hedges on either side of the path opened suddenly onto a recently planted rose garden. Several gardeners were still pruning the bushes in early preparation for the autumn. They stopped their work and pulled at their caps as his lordship passed.

Lady Edwina noted that the men were short and wiry, and had hair of a mousy brown color—quite different from the strapping, dark, house servants. Indeed, her sister had been correct. Lord Haverslea had replaced the butler and the footmen, but only those.

"How lovely this garden will be next summer, Lord Haverslea," Lady Edwina said.

"No. It is not!" came Lord Haverslea's unexpected shout. His pale face grew livid with rage.

He strode angrily toward one gardener and wrenched the shovel from the man's hand. He stabbed the blade of the shovel into the soil at the base of one rosebush. With uncanny strength, he lifted the entire load and flung bush and shovel across the flower bed. The bush landed with a dusty plop. The shovel went clattering across the bricks.

His lordship grabbed the hapless gardener by the front of his shirt. Lady Edwina feared that Lord Haverslea would toss the unfortunate little man in the same manner with which he had tossed the plant.

Trent's words of warning regarding displeasing Lord Haverslea again rang through her head. She also began to reconsider Trent's admonition regarding Lord Haverslea as a suitable husband for Lady Cecily.

"I was very specific regarding the placement of the roses!" Lord Haverslea growled directly in the man's face. "If you cannot follow my instructions *to the letter*, then perhaps you would do better in someone else's employ!"

"Yes, m'lord. I mean, no, m'lord," the man stammered.

Lord Haverslea released his grasp on the quaking man's shirt, leaving him to stumble backward over the as yet unplanted rosebushes which were scattered about.

His lordship lifted his chin and straightened his shoulders

as if shrugging off his irritation. He dusted his hands off one against the other and smoothed the front of his jacket. He returned quite calmly to Lady Cecily.

"Unfortunately, there are occasions when one must be exceedingly harsh with servants. Otherwise they will simply run rampant through the household," he explained, gently taking her hand in his arm.

Lady Cecily offered Lord Haverslea no resistance when he moved to take her hand.

"Quite true, Nigel," she agreed. Lady Edwina thought she detected a quaver in her voice.

For once Lady Portia made no effort whatsoever to voice her agreement with Lady Cecily or Lord Haverslea.

Upon returning to the drawing room, Lady Edwina glanced at the clock on the mantel. It was three o'clock.

Lady Edwina was quite undecided. She had promised Lady Haverslea that she would visit today. On one hand, if the lady were truly ill, she might not be receiving today after all. On the other hand, Lady Haverslea might appreciate a call to cheer her.

'There is one other possibility,' Lady Edwina thought. 'Perhaps Lady Haverslea is simply feigning ill health in order to avoid Lord Haverslea. She might be perfectly well and awaiting my visit.'

In any case, Lady Edwina decided that she would at least make the attempt to call upon the dowager. Perhaps she could discover why the lady dreaded Lord Haverslea so.

"In spite of the coolness of the breeze, the sun was exceptionally hot today," Lady Edwina said, raising her handkerchief to her damp forehead. "I fear I have contracted the most ferocious headache."

"Such a pity to grow old and infirm," Lady Cecily said.

"What a pity," Lady Portia said.

"If you will excuse me, I will retire to my bedchamber," Lady Edwina excused herself.

"By all means, my dear," Lady Portia said. "Is there anything we can do for you?"

"Thank you, no, Aunt Portia. Stokes and I can manage quite well on our own."

The others made no comment as they were all much too busy assuming their seats and preparing to play one more rubber in their continuing game of whist before it was time for tea.

Once in her room, Lady Edwina donned sensible walking shoes and took a light wrap with her. She crept quietly down the back stairs and was almost to the door which opened onto the side portico when a hand clapped down upon her arm.

She whirled quickly about.

"James!" she cried, clasping her hand to her bosom as if to quiet her pounding heart. "You nearly scared the life from me!"

"And where might you be going with such secrecy?" Trent asked.

She met his level gaze. If he could persist in keeping secrets, could she not have one of her own?

"It is just . . . I simply should like to have some privacy for a moment."

"Is privacy not available in your bedchamber?" he asked. "I shall have some brought up immediately!"

She laughed with him, then countered, "But what a surprise to find you here, James. You usually only travel between Lord Dynford's bedchamber and that empty room."

Trent grimaced. "I've been waiting to see you, Edwina. You are going out, and I should like to know where and why."

"You have been waiting for me? How could you know that I was intending to go anywhere?"

"You cannot fool me, Edwina. When Stokes informed me that you had taken to your bedchamber with the megrim, I became suspicious."

"Do you think me incapable of suffering from the megrim?" she asked.

Trent reached out to take both her slim shoulders in his hands. He drew her to him. Slipping the shawl from her shoulder, he stroked the soft skin of her arms.

"I have seen you continue to persevere after three days without sleep and with precious little food," Trent answered softly. "That is why I know you would not let such a trifling thing as a headache interfere with what you would consider social obligations. I supposed you were up to something and I have been waiting to ask you. Where are you going, Edwina?"

"Are you the only one who can have secrets?" she countered.

He held her tightly to him for a moment. Then he answered, "Do not plague me with my secret, Edwina. I only asked where you are going alone. Don't you know by now that I am concerned for you?"

Ashamed now of her stubbornness, she answered, "The dowager baroness has invited me to tea."

"I believe it is customary, when paying a social call, to leave by the front door," he observed.

Unwilling to delve into a lengthy explanation of Lady Haverslea's request for secrecy, Lady Edwina merely answered, "The lady is exceedingly shy."

"Is she so shy that in order to visit her, you must sneak up upon her like a rabbit?"

Lady Edwina responded to his remark with a halfhearted laugh.

Inexplicably, Trent suddenly turned serious. He held both of her arms in his hands. "Edwina, do not go. It may not be safe."

"Not safe?" Lady Edwina repeated incredulously. "Do you suspect that the poor old dear will put arsenic in my tea and wall me up in the cellar?"

"Something ill could befall you if you venture out alone," he said obscurely.

"Since you are so appalled by the thought of my making an excursion alone, then you may accompany me," she suggested.

Trent backed away, shaking his head. "I cannot. And I suggest that you do not go either."

"Nonsense, James," Lady Edwina said. "The dowager baroness is perfectly harmless."

"Perhaps *she* is . . ." Trent began. Then he frowned and stood firmly before her. "Edwina, I cannot permit you to go!"

Laughing, she nudged him aside and proceeded through the door. "*You* cannot permit *me?* Ha! Honestly, James. You *have* begun to take on airs."

The Dower House was understandably smaller than Haversham Hall. Lady Edwina acknowledged that it had not been used for many years. Still, the house held an air of dilapidation and decay which Lady Haverslea in no way merited.

Several bricks were missing from the front walk. The shrubbery surrounding the house had not been trimmed in many years. The curved pediment of the front door was badly in need of repainting.

The housemaid admitted Lady Edwina. The painted walls of the foyer were peeling in places which showed definite damage from rain leaking through the front windows.

The housemaid showed Lady Edwina into the small drawing room. The ceiling was low and coated with soot. The blue and white figured paper was peeling from the walls near the ceiling.

'Lord Haverslea has offered to have the place repaired,' Lady Edwina mused. 'Is this just another result of the Dowager Baroness's reluctance to have his lordship anywhere near her?'

"I am so glad to see you," Lady Haverslea said enthusiastically when she saw Lady Edwina. "I lay awake all night for fear that you would not be able to come."

She bustled to Lady Edwina's side and took her hand. She led her to the sofa and pulled her down to sit beside her. Lady Edwina noted that the cushions of the sofa were rather lumpy and that the green brocade covering was wearing thin about the piping.

The housemaid brought in the tea tray and set it on the low table before Lady Haverslea.

"It is so good to have visitors," Lady Haverslea said as she began to pour the strong, hot tea from the little china pot. "Milk? Sugar? I am so glad to have you here."

Lady Edwina was silently berating James Trescott. How could he suspect this lovely lady, deprived of her husband and her lovely home and forced into this genteel poverty, of committing any crime worse than sneaking an extra pastry before dinner?

Nevertheless, as inconspicuously as possible, she inspected the contents of the cup which Lady Haverslea handed her. Yes, it was the proper color. She lifted the cup to her lips, but before she drank, she sniffed. Yes, it smelled like proper tea. Still, she waited until Lady Haverslea had taken a sip of her own tea before she drank.

"Do try one of these little sandwiches," Lady Haverslea invited. "I only have a man of all work and the housemaid now, but I think she is rather a good cook, too. Do you not think so?"

Convinced of the safety of the food, Lady Edwina helped herself to a small sandwich from the blue china plate. She noticed a small chip in the plate which the sandwich had helped to conceal.

But the little bread and butter sandwich was tasty and Lady Edwina answered, "You are fortunate to have her."

"My housemaid is good company for me as I am all alone here," Lady Haverslea continued. "You know, your sister was quite correct. This Dower House is old and dreary and quite gloomy. I daresay, if I were a woman given to fancies and delusions, this house would be enough to give anyone forebodings of haunts in the night."

"It is quite charming during the day," Lady Edwina offered weakly.

"But so lonely," Lady Haverslea continued sadly. "I know it is improper to speak ill of the dead, but, quite honestly, Milton never could have been considered sparkling companionship. Nevertheless, he was someone to talk to. I know it sounds strange, but sometimes, somehow, I feel Milton's presence with me still. There he is now," she added with a sweep of her arm toward the side of the room which had heretofore been at Lady Edwina's back.

286

Lady Edwina turned with alarm, quite expecting, in this gloomy old house, to see the blood-soaked shade of the late Lord Haverslea standing before her, demanding justice for his foul murder.

But Lady Haverslea's outstretched arm merely indicated the portrait of his late lordship hanging above the mantelpiece.

"He was such a handsome young man," Lady Haverslea said. "Until he started to grow fat, and then I rather think he began to resemble a bullfrog, don't you?"

Lady Edwina took a deep breath and swallowed with relief. She nodded and took another bracing sip of tea.

She wondered if there were some strange element in her physical composition which attracted fools and madmen much as a magnet attracted iron filings.

Lady Haverslea extended the plate of small sandwiches to Lady Edwina. "Try another, my dear. It is so good to have a visitor again. Everyone came to see me after Milton's funeral, but I do not believe they came so much to offer condolences as to see if they could hear any additional gossip about Milton and his poor, unfortunate brother."

Lady Edwina was puzzled. "Poor" and "unfortunate" were hardly words that one would use to describe the murderer of one's husband, no matter how seriously one took one's obligation for Christian forgiveness.

Lady Haverslea sighed and added, "I was so glad when Milton's funeral was over!"

"Was there no funeral for your husband's brother?" Lady Edwina asked.

Lady Haverslea gave a derisive little laugh. "No. I mean, at least Nigel had enough sense of propriety to arrange a very short, private memorial service for Trent. But there was no funeral because they never recovered the body from the river. I suppose he's fish food now," Lady Haverslea said with a shrug, and popped another sandwich into her mouth.

Lady Haverslea rose and started to walk to the door. "Such morbid thoughts for such a lovely young lady. Come, my dear. While you are here, I might as well show you the other portrait as well."

"The portrait of Trent Haversham?" Lady Edwina asked.

Lady Haverslea nodded. "I only met the boy . . . oh, dear. Just listen to me calling him a boy. But he was just a boy when I first met him and that was how I always thought of him."

Lady Haverslea led Lady Edwina from the damp, dreary drawing room.

"Trent was usually away at school after his mother passed away," Lady Haverslea continued. "His father was always so preoccupied with the running of the estate. And the only dealings Milton ever had with him were, well, unpleasant, to say the least."

Lady Edwina followed Lady Haverslea down a darkly panelled corridor toward the rear of the Dower House. The thought briefly flashed through her mind that, while Lady Haverslea had not poisoned her tea, perhaps she was luring her to the basement for her imminent immurement.

"But he was quite a grown man the last time I saw him— quite handsome, too, if I may say so. I only did see him that one time again," Lady Haverslea added sadly. "The night Milton died."

Lady Edwina was surprised by the calm—no, almost flattering—way in which Lady Haverslea talked about the man who had murdered her husband.

Lady Haverslea opened the door into a small, dusty library. The threadbare draperies were drawn closed and, in spite of the bright sunlight of an early autumn afternoon, the room was deeply shadowed.

Lady Haverslea pulled at the drawing cord. The drapery slid back, illuminating the portrait on the far wall.

Lady Edwina's heart pounded in her ears and her breath stopped midway in her throat as the familiar green eyes set in the fair complexioned face capped with waving black hair stared out at her from the canvas.

She felt as if the floor beneath her, indeed, as if the very earth, were opening up to swallow her whole! She was so overwhelmed with shock that she did not even bother to try to find her way to a chair. Her knees buckled under her and she fell into a little heap on the floor.

"Edwina, my dear!" Lady Haverslea exclaimed. "Are you quite all right?"

"James!" she choked.

"James? No, no, my dear," Lady Haverslea corrected her with a laugh. "You have been extremely inattentive. How many times have I mentioned that my late brother-in-law's name was Trent?"

"No, no!" she managed to gasp. "That is James Trescott, my footman!" she repeated over and over.

"But, that means Trent is still alive!" Lady Haverslea declared.

Lady Edwina's entire body rocked back and forth in a motion she had no power to stop. "A highwayman! A footman! A thief! A murderer! Oh, was this his secret? Oh, why could he not have confided in me?"

"Oh, dear, I do hope madness does not run in the family if Nigel truly does intend to marry Lady Cecily," Lady Haverslea murmured, shaking her head from side to side with pity. Then she bent over Lady Edwina and patted her shoulder.

"Edwina, please! Calm yourself," she ordered. "You are beginning to make as much sense as your sister!"

This ultimate insult brought Lady Edwina back to her senses.

"You are quite right. I am acting the complete fool," she admitted, rising and straightening her skirts. Having left her reticule in the drawing room, she dabbed at her watery eyes with her bare fingers.

"Now that you appear to be quite yourself again, would you mind explaining to me please what that signified?" Lady Haverslea asked, gesturing to the place on the rug where Lady Edwina had collapsed.

"My footman," Lady Edwina mumbled, still sniffing.

Lady Haverslea offered her handkerchief. Lady Edwina wiped her eyes, then her nose.

"How can I explain?" she began. "We found him, feverish, bleeding. We took him in, as our footman. He . . . he said his name was James Trescott, that he was a soldier

289

from London, that he had no family, but . . ."

"Trent Haversham returned home by way of London after serving in His Majesty's army for four years on the Continent," Lady Haverslea told her. "And unless you consider only his insignificant little sister-in-law, and a cousin I doubt Trent would want to remember, he indeed has no remaining family."

"Well, I suppose then, technically, he did not lie to me after all," Lady Edwina said.

"And you are quite certain that they are one and the same?" Lady Haverslea asked.

"Yes!" she cried, slowly approaching the portrait. She reached out to touch the painted image on the cheek. "How many times have I studied his face as he went about his duties? How many times have I pictured his face before me? I would know my James anywhere."

Lady Edwina spun about to face Lady Haverslea. "But my James cannot possibly be Trent Haversham. My James is kind and clever, witty and intelligent."

"So is Trent."

"But Trent Haversham killed his brother," Lady Edwina insisted. "He attacked his cousin, ran mad through the woods, threw himself into the river and drowned. Lord Haverslea told us all so himself. As did Cecily, several times."

"And you believed him?" Lady Haverslea cried.

"Of course," Lady Edwina answered. "We have no reason not to."

Lady Haverslea gave a deep sigh of resignation. "I could tell you the truth, but what good would it do? It is Nigel's word against Trent's as to what happened. And no one will believe the words of a foolish old widow, addled with grief."

"You know who really killed Milton."

"As do you, Edwina," she said quietly, returning Lady Edwina's level gaze.

"And now you know that Trent Haversham is still alive. Then you *must* tell the truth," Lady Edwina insisted. "You cannot allow your husband's murderer to go unpunished."

Lady Haverslea backed rapidly away from Lady Edwina.

"I cannot do it. You see what horrors Nigel is capable of perpetrating. I am a widow, alone. What might happen to me?"

"Nothing will happen to you," Lady Edwina insisted. "I shan't allow it!"

When Lady Haverslea continued to stand, shaking her head in adamant refusal, Lady Edwina advanced upon her and seized her plump shoulders. She fixed Lady Haverslea with her gaze. "Charlotte, you must speak! Trent is an innocent man. You cannot allow him to live as a fugitive the rest of his life. And in spite of all her foolish ways, you cannot allow my sister to be hurt by marrying Nigel. And I cannot . . . James and I cannot live with this secret between us!"

A sad, sympathetic smile crossed Lady Haverslea's face. "You are in love with Trent."

"Trent. James. Whatever you call him, or he chooses to call himself—yes. I love him. And I will not allow him to be hurt any longer."

Lady Haverslea raised her chin bravely. "Then for Trent's sake, and yours, and even for the sake of your silly sister, I will—even though what I am about to do may put us all in great danger."

In spite of the chill that was shivering in her spine, Lady Edwina said, "Send your man for the constable. We must go to Haversham Hall."

Lady Edwina grasped Lady Haverslea's hand again and dragged her most insistently toward the door. She began to walk toward Haversham Hall with a quite deliberate stride.

Chapter Twenty-three

Trent watched Lady Edwina's slim figure receding into the woods until the door closed off his view.

Oh, what a stubborn one she was, he thought, shaking his head. He wished he could have gone with her, but how dare he venture out in broad daylight?

But he was being so foolish. What possible harm could come to Lady Edwina while paying a pleasant social call to a lonely widow?

He began to make his way up the servants' stairs, pondering the ironies of Fate. Who could have foreseen that this trip should have proved more beneficial to him than his own original plan? Left to his own devices, he would have still been waiting in the gamekeeper's cottage. As Lord Dynford's valet, he had access to the house and had been able to retrieve his money.

Trent patted his waistcoat pockets. The folding money in one pocket and the jingling coins in the other gave him a feeling of hope that he had not had in many months. At last he had what he needed to accomplish an important part of his plan. Whatever the scheming Nigel had paid that maid to help him, Trent would now be able to offer her more, if she would only tell the truth.

As he rounded a turn in the shadowy corridor, he almost collided with another servant. The young woman let out a shriek of terror.

She was so terrified that she could not even turn to run away from him, but pressed her back against the wall, then slipped to sit on the floor, her hands clasped before her face, screaming, "It's you! It's you!"

"Yes, it is I!" he responded. "But who am I that you

should be so terrified of me? For that matter, who are you?"

He grabbed her arms and pulled her hands from her face. "Ripley! Annie Ripley!" he said when he recognized her. "The scullery maid with the wine bottles."

"Yes! Oh, yes!" she cried, falling to the floor again.

"But this is perfect!" he exclaimed. "I have been looking for you."

"Oh, Mr. Haversham, you've been looking for *me?*" she wailed. "You've come back from the grave with the sole intent of avenging yourself upon me! Have mercy! Have mercy!"

"Don't be such a goose!" Trent told her sternly. "I most certainly have not."

"You've not come to avenge yourself?" she demanded. "What kind of a ghost are you?"

"I've not come from the grave, you silly girl."

She stopped her screaming and looked up at him, wide-eyed. She stretched out her hand and pinched his cheek. Suddenly, she scrambled to her feet and backed away from him.

"Oh, you *are* alive! That's worse!" she screamed. "Now you've *really* come to do me in!"

"No, no!" he protested.

"Very well, you have me in your clutches," Ripley proclaimed bravely, ignoring Trent's protests. She threw her arm up over her eyes and lifted her chin to bare her throat to his anticipated vengeance. "Do your worst!"

Trent chuckled in amused bewilderment. "Ripley, have you been going into Haverton on your day off to watch those dreadful gothic melodramas?" he accused.

She paid him no heed. She clasped her hands together and held them out in front of Trent in a pleading, and very melodramatic, gesture. "You must grant me one last request, Mr. Haversham," Ripley begged.

"Last request?" Trent repeated, still perplexed by the maid's strange behavior.

"Don't kill me yet," she begged. Then her eyes narrowed. She gasped hoarsely as she grasped his arms, "Not until I've killed Lord Haverslea!"

Trent stood staring at her, wide-eyed and slack-jawed.

"Kill Nigel?" was all he could repeat. "Why should you want to kill him when . . . I thought he paid you to help him." Trent pulled the money from his pocket and showed it to her. "See. I've come searching for you to see how much it would take for you to tell the truth—that I did not kill my own brother."

"Pay me! Lord Haverslea never paid me!" she cried with injured pride. Then she pouted, "What kind of girl do you think I am—taking money? He said he'd *marry* me!"

Before Trent could repeat her incredible claim, Ripley burst into tears. "Oh, Mr. Haversham, I have been cruelly received."

Trent placed his arm comfortingly about her shoulder. He tucked his money back into his waistcoat pocket and withdrew his handkerchief instead.

"Do you mean 'deceived'?" he corrected.

"That, too," she agreed, then exclaimed, "Lord Haverslea lied to me! He made love to me. He promised that he'd marry me if I'd help him with his plan to become the baron."

Ripley sniffed loudly and wiped at her red eyes with the handkerchief. "I know it was wrong of me. I know I never should have. But he was so sweet, so charming. He gave me pretty ribbons, and a card of pearl buttons, and even a lace fan! He said I'd be a baroness." She sniffed loudly. "Fancy me, a baroness."

Ripley sniffed again, then blew her nose loudly into the handkerchief.

"But then he brought this lady into the house!" Ripley wailed. "And I find out that *she's* the one he's going to marry, not me! And why? 'Cause *she's* a fine lady—an earl's daughter and very rich and *so* beautiful. And me? I'm still just a poor scullery maid—and now I always will be!" She wailed all the louder.

"Ripley, I believe that you and I have a great deal to discuss," Trent said attempting to guide the weeping girl toward the servants' quarters. "Perhaps you could calm yourself if you rested a bit."

"No, Mr. Haversham," she said, pulling sharply away from him. She blew her nose hard into the handkerchief one last time, then pressed it back into his hand. She lifted her head proudly. "I've nothing to discuss. I've been reduced and disbanded . . ."

"You've been what?"

"Reduced and disbanded," she repeated. "Honestly, Mr. Haversham, if you don't mind my saying so, sir, maybe you should go into town to watch a few of them melodramas yourself. Maybe you'd learn some new words."

"Seduced and abandoned!" Trent declared with sudden insight.

"That, too," she agreed. "And I won't rest until I've had my revenge!"

Revenge? Trent wondered. As he stood wondering what wild plans were formulating in the unhappy girl's mind, Ripley burst through the green door into the main section of the house.

Trent followed her, from curiosity and from his desire to try to stop her before she could do something in this irrational state which she might later come to regret even more than her past indiscretions.

Ripley marched boldly into Lord Haverslea's room and began rummaging through the drawers of his wardrobe.

"Ripley, I hardly think disarranging his lordship's room is what usually comes to mind when one contemplates revenge," Trent told her.

"No, no!" she said, tossing small clothes and cravats about the room. "I know they're somewhere about."

"What do you seek, Ripley?" Trent asked.

But Ripley did not answer him. She left the bedchamber and made her way to the library. Trent followed, too curious not to want to know what Ripley intended to do and still hopeful of being able to prevent her from doing anything stupid.

"Ah," she murmured with satisfaction. "There you are."

She lifted the small wooden case from the shelf and opened it, exposing a set of pearl-handled dueling pistols.

"Well, that certainly looks more like what one usually

thinks of as revenge," Trent observed. "But please, Ripley, put them down before you hurt someone."

"But that's exactly what I mean to do, Mr. Haversham," she said.

"These are dangerous weapons—not mere toys. Give them to me before you hurt yourself."

Ripley ignored his protests and began to load one pistol.

Trent was silent, watching her competence with surprise. "Ripley, where did you learn to handle . . . ?"

"Don't remember the name?" she asked, then shook her head. "No. You would've been too young. My father was the gamekeeper. You might be a bit older than me, Mr. Haversham, but I'd wager I was handling firearms such as this while you were still eating jam tarts at Eton."

"Ripley, this is still not a good idea. Put the pistols down," Trent told her. He tried to speak as soothingly as he could, knowing that shouting would only cause Ripley to become more agitated. "We shall go to the constable and give him all the particulars."

Ripley shook her head. "I'm a scullery maid. I'll end up swinging at Newgate. And his lordship? He'll take a nice tour of the Continent until the scandal blows over. No, sir, Mr. Haversham. If I go, I'm taking his bloody lordship with me!"

"Ripley, try to understand. *I* am the true Lord Haverslea now. Nigel has no power over you anymore." Trent cautiously approached her, his hand outstretched for the gun. "Put down the pistol and we shall talk about this."

"Back up then, 'Lord' Haverslea," she threatened, waving the loaded pistol in his direction.

Trent complied. In her agitation, Ripley might not care which lord she did in, so long as she got one of the Havershams.

Ripley tucked the pistol under her arm and began to load the second one.

"I *have* talked to Lord Haverslea. He just laughs at me and says he's changed his mind. I've done with talking." She took a pistol into each hand. "Now I want my revenge!"

* * *

Lord Haverslea, Lord Dynford, Lady Portia, and Lady Cecily sat about the card table which had once again been set up by the window in the drawing room.

"So," Lady Cecily pronounced, laying down her winning hand, "when he encountered Lady Beemish upon Lord Elsington's lap, Lord Beemish told him—"

"I've got you now, *Mr.* Haversham!" Ripley cried as she burst into the drawing room, brandishing a dueling pistol in each hand.

"I vow, I have never seen such ill-mannered servants!" Lady Cecily declared without even glancing up at the offending maid. "When *I* am Lady Haverslea, she will surely be dismissed."

Taking up the pack of cards, Lady Cecily began to shuffle the next hand. "Anyway, Lord Beemish drew his pistol and said—"

"Stand away from these people, Nigel, or I'll shoot them, as well!" Ripley demanded.

"No, no!" Lady Cecily protested. "Lord Elsington's given name is Gerald. And what Lord Beemish actually said was—"

"I've come for my revenge!" Ripley declared.

"I vow," Lady Cecily complained, slamming the pack of cards face down upon the table. "Shan't I ever be able to finish this tale without interruption?"

At last, Lady Cecily looked up from the card table to see that Lord Dynford and Lady Portia had both risen and were very slowly moving away from Nigel. Nigel had also risen and was staring down the barrel of the pistol which Ripley had pointed directly at his face. Very slowly, Lady Cecily rose to join her brother and her aunt at the far side of the room.

"Nigel, what is the meaning of this?" Lady Cecily demanded once she had moved out of the line of fire.

"Drop that pistol, Ripley!" he ordered imperiously. "You cannot shoot me. I am Lord Haverslea!"

"You're a lying grass in the snake! A reducer of the flower of young woman Englishhood!" she cried in her agitation. "You ain't the Baron. You never was. Trent Haversham is."

"Trent Haversham is dead!" Nigel declared.

Trent strode boldly into the drawing room. "Quite the contrary, Nigel. I am very much alive. And I *am* the rightful Lord Haverslea!"

"But, you are James Trescott, my footman!" Lord Dynford exclaimed.

"I am Trent Haversham."

If Nigel felt any shock upon seeing the cousin which he had believed was dead, Trent could not detect it upon his face. The man was as cool now as he was on the night in which he had murdered Milton.

"Trent Haversham is dead," Nigel insisted. "I saw him drown!"

"I washed ashore, Nigel. I was found by the Dynfords and nursed back to health," Trent explained. "And now I have come to clear my name—the name which you besmirched!"

"Trent Haversham sullied his own name when he murdered his brother and tried to murder me," Nigel continued to tell his tale with extraordinary sangfroid.

"*You* are the murderer, Nigel," Trent said. He turned to the bewildered group still huddled on the other side of the room. "Nigel stabbed my brother, then tried to kill me, in order to clear the way for his own succession to the barony."

"This is ludicrous!" Nigel exclaimed. "Who will believe this incredible tale?"

"But it's true!" Ripley cried, waving the pistol directly under Nigel's nose. "And now I'll shoot you for the rank murderer and vile reducer of young womanhood that you are!"

"The what?" Nigel asked, bewildered.

"She means seducer," Trent interpreted.

"You learn them new words fast, m'lord," was Ripley's comment to Trent.

"What has this to do with you, anyway, you impertinent chit?" Lady Cecily demanded.

" 'Tis my shame, m'lady," Ripley answered, never taking

298

her eyes from Nigel. "I helped him drug the old Baron and his brother and the footman," Ripley said.

"But they said it was a footman . . ." Lord Dynford began.

"The more fools they!" Ripley spat out. "Believing only a man could do it!"

"But why should you . . . ?" Lord Dynford asked.

"He promised he'd marry me," Ripley wailed. "He said he'd make me a lady!"

"You? A lady?" Lady Cecily scoffed. "You are an insolent, lying chit and will never be anything more!"

Turning to Nigel, Lady Cecily demanded, "Isn't she, Nigel?"

"Well, of course she is. I mean, I may have had a small dalliance with the girl, Cecily," Nigel admitted. Then he raised his chin and arrogantly declared, "It is not my fault that the girl misconstrued everything and now seeks vengeance for imagined wrongs."

Nigel turned to Trent. "And you, you mere footman, you came here and noted your resemblance to the Haversham line. Then you and this ungrateful maid concocted your preposterous tale, thinking to derive some monies from it. Well, let me tell you, you are all sadly mistaken! Kirby," he called loudly. "Send a footman for the constable so that he can take this most impertinent piece of baggage as well as this unscrupulous footman off to prison where they belong. Immediately!"

"If I go to prison, you go with me," Ripley threatened.

The front door bell clanged loudly. No one moved.

"Kirby," Nigel called to the recently arrived butler over the barrel of the pistol. "We are not receiving today."

"Very good sir," Kirby responded, and went to inform the caller accordingly.

The bell clanged again, most insistently.

"Kirby, we are still not receiving."

"Kirby, open this damned door!" Lady Haverslea's voice bellowed from the other side.

This time everyone started. Had the exceedingly quiet Charlotte been storing her volume all these years for this one moment?

"Her ladyship seems most insistent, m'lord," Kirby remarked. "Shall I admit her?"

Before the butler could deny her ladyship once again, Lady Haverslea had opened the door herself and marched through the hall and into the drawing room.

"Edwina!" Trent exclaimed when he saw her.

Lady Edwina did not approach him. She did not even completely enter the drawing room, but hung by the doorway, regarding him silently.

What was the matter? Soon his name would be cleared. Soon they could be together!

"Edwina?" he repeated.

"What a charming tableau you have created," she said to him sarcastically. "No, no, do not tell me. Let me guess what you are enacting. It is 'Vile Crime Exposed,' is it not? Shall I tell you how I was finally able to solve this puzzle? I did it with no help from you, *Lord* Haverslea," she said, stressing his newly acquired title.

Suddenly her haughty demeanor vanished. She wrapped both arms around herself tightly, as if she were very cold. Trent could see the pain so very evident in her large, blue eyes.

"You never told me," she whispered hoarsely, shaking her head from side to side. "Why did you not tell me? You could have confided in me."

Before he could reply, Lady Haverslea had rushed up to him and smothered him in an embrace. "Oh, Trent!"

"Charlotte," he returned her greeting.

"I am so glad to see that you are still alive!"

"But he murdered your husband!" Lady Cecily declared from across the room.

"He's a murderer," Lady Portia echoed. "Isn't he?"

Lady Haverslea was shaking her head. "No. The time has come, Nigel. You have hurt me enough. You cannot hurt me any more than you already have. And I cannot allow you the opportunity to hurt Lady Cecily." Lady Haverslea cast a jaundiced eye at her. "Regardless of my personal opinion of her."

Lady Cecily raised both brows and placed her hand to her bosom. She alternated glances between her brother and her aunt, asking, "Was it something which I said? I vow, she is the most extraordinarily strange person!"

"And I cannot allow your evil ways to stand between two people in love, Nigel," Lady Haverslea continued, gesturing to Lady Edwina and Trent.

"Oh, Winnie, you little minx!" Lady Cecily declared with a loud giggle. "And with the footman, of all people!"

"I have lived with this knowledge in silent fear for too long," Lady Haverslea said. "Now, regardless of what you may do to me, I can remain silent no longer."

"Charlotte, what are you saying?" Nigel asked coolly. "You cannot possibly believe that I would harm you, poor dear."

"People have said I am too quiet," Lady Haverslea began. "Of late, I have often wondered if that is good or bad. Quiet people have the opportunity of observing things unobserved, if you take my meaning."

"I am afraid that Milton's unexpected death has rendered you quite incoherent, Charlotte," Nigel said. "Why do you not return to the Dower House for a rest?"

"Am I incoherent? Then I shall speak quite plainly," she declared boldly. "And you shall not like what I have to say. Trent Haversham did not murder his brother. I saw what Nigel did to Milton that night—and with a fruit knife, of all things! My God, Nigel, could you not have allowed him at least a little dignity in death?" she demanded. "Then I saw Trent Haversham, pursued by you, run from the Hall in fear of his very life."

"There was a certain resemblance between Trent and myself, Charlotte," Nigel said. "In your agitation and in the darkness of the night, you mistook us."

"I was upset, but I am not blind. *You* do not wear a military jacket, Nigel," Lady Haverslea said. "When you returned without Trent, I knew in my heart that you had killed him just as you had killed Milton, but I had no proof. And I was afraid."

"I will own, there is a certain resemblance between Trent

and this footman, but who will believe the ravings of a widow, mad with grief?"

"I had no proof," Lady Haverslea repeated, "until Lady Edwina identified Trent's portrait as her footman, James Trescott. Then I knew he *had* survived!"

"The portrait!" Nigel exclaimed. "I knew I should have burned the damned thing! But Lady Edwina will admit to being in love with this footman!" Nigel argued. "To what extent would she prevaricate, with the hope of advancing him to a station in life more acceptable to her own position?"

Nigel looked about the room, wide-eyed. "You are all in this together, conspiring to deny me my barony!"

The front door bell clanged.

"*Now* who is it?" Nigel demanded.

Kirby appeared at the door to the drawing room. "M'lord, a person is asking most insistently for a Major Trent Haversham regarding a position on his household staff. Shall I send him away, m'lord?"

"There is no Trent Haversham here. Send him away," Nigel ordered.

"Show him in," Trent said.

"Send him away!"

"Show him in!"

"I shall receive him," Lady Haverslea cried with exasperation.

"Major Haversham!" Sergeant James Bosley exclaimed, limping directly over to Trent.

"Jimmy!" Lady Edwina exclaimed.

"Oh, the pretty lady. Fancy seeing you here," Bosley said. The twinkle returned to his eye. "How's the meat pasties here, m'lady?"

Bosley then noticed the elegantly garbed, but obviously terrified guests at the other side of the room, the two breathless, disheveled women in the doorway, and the maid with the pistol pointed at another gentleman. He observed them carefully for a moment, then turned to Trent and said, "Excuse me, sir. I appear to have come at an inconvenient time."

"Quite the contrary, Bosley," Trent reassured him. "Pray, what may I do for you?"

"My sister's husband offered me work, but well, I can't live on their charity. A man needs to be independent, sir," Sergeant Bosley explained, lifting his head proudly. "I remembered your kind offer of work, and I've come to take you up on it, sir."

Bosley then glanced from one person to the other. "On the other hand, perhaps I might not be suited to working here after all."

"I shall be happy to take you on, Bosley," Trent assured him.

"Who is this person?" Nigel demanded.

"Sergeant James Aubrey Bosley, sir, late of His Majesty's Royal Horse Artillery," he answered proudly. "I served with Major Haversham on the Continent."

"Ha! There you have it!" Lady Haverslea declared. "This man, who is unknown to any of us, has just verified Trent Haversham's identity, thus proving that none of us are attempting to perpetrate any fraud."

"Nonsense!" Nigel continued to protest. "He is a friend of this footman, and is obviously known to the lady, who has admitted her love for the footman. How do I know that this man is not also an accomplice in the crime?"

"Well, sir," Sergeant Bosley replied proudly with a cocky set to his head. "If I'm not good enough for you, perhaps an entire regiment would satisfy you."

The front door bell clanged loudly.

"*Now* who is it?" Nigel demanded.

Kirby appeared at the doorway. "M'lord? Are you in to Constable Willis?"

Nigel made a dash for the door which opened onto the garden. Trent sprinted after him.

"Out of the way!" Ripley shouted. She tried to draw a clear shot at Nigel, but Trent and Constable Willis would persist in getting in her line of fire!

As Trent and the constable succeeded in dragging a frantic Nigel to the floor, Ripley sighed, "Bloody hell!" with disappointment and placed the pistols on the card table.

Once the pistols were down, Lady Cecily left her brother's side to stand over the screaming, struggling Nigel. She kept her distance so that his flailing arms and legs would not damage her lovely gown.

"Can you hear me, Nigel?" she asked loudly, peering down at him. "I do hope you realize that, under the circumstances, I really must cry off our engagement."

Chapter Twenty-four

Trent and Constable Willis needed the assistance of two extremely bewildered footmen to subdue Nigel and place him in the rear of the constable's wagon.

For some reason no one seemed able to explain, Nigel kept screaming, "Trent lied! He lied! He promised that this time he would stay dead!"

Lady Edwina still stood at the doorway, silent and waiting. Everything had happened so quickly, she was still trying to comprehend the significance of it. If only she could receive an explanation from James, or Trent—she was so confused, she did not even know by what name she should call the man she loved.

If only he would take the time to explain. But the new Lord Haverslea only glanced briefly in her direction as he hurriedly excused himself from the others in the drawing room.

She caught a brief glimpse of him again as he strode through the hall and out the front door to accompany the constable. He had removed the blue and gold Dynford livery and now wore his full regimentals.

Her breath still caught in her dry throat at the sight of his broad shoulders disappearing through the front door.

So they had been his uniforms after all. How could she have been so stupid! she chided herself. They had fit him perfectly, had they not?

She made a little grimace. He certainly had wasted no time in shedding everything connected with his service to the Earl of Dynford, she bitterly noted. Then, very quietly and very slowly because the idea hurt so badly as it came into her mind, she thought, 'Apparently, he has even discarded me.'

Lady Cecily had managed to find her way to the comfortable maroon and white striped sofa and had collapsed upon it. She appeared to Lady Edwina to be greatly enjoying all the kind attention she was receiving from Lady Portia and Lady Haverslea, who both stood solicitously over her.

"You poor dear," Lady Haverslea murmured.

"Poor dear," Lady Portia agreed.

"Such a shock! I must say, it came as quite a shock to me to discover that Milton was an embezzler. Imagine how badly poor Cecily must feel to discover that the man she loves is a murderer and a madman." Lady Haverslea shook her head and clucked her tongue, but Lady Edwina had the distinct impression that her ladyship was having a fine time gloating over Lady Cecily's set down.

"Such a shock!" Lord Dynford stood above her, his face grave, and pronounced, "You must understand, I surely cannot give my consent to such a union now, Cecily. How exceedingly unsuitable to have a madman in the family!"

"Believe me, it is perfectly scandalous," Lady Haverslea said.

"Ah, how shall we ever survive the scandal?" Lady Portia wondered. "I daresay, all sorts of people will be accosting us at every social gathering, just to talk with us about the scandal."

Lady Cecily suddenly brightened and sat upright. "Do you really think so?" she asked enthusiastically.

The thought crossed Lady Edwina's mind that if Nigel could restrain himself from stabbing any more cousins with fruit knives, he might pass unnoticed among her family.

"How shall poor Cecily ever recover from such a blow to her constitution?" Lady Haverslea asked.

"Perhaps a few weeks at Bath?" Lady Portia suggested.

"An outstanding suggestion, Portia! Shall you be accompanying her?"

"By all means, Charlotte. The poor dear should never be left alone after such a disappointment."

"Perhaps I might accompany you both," Lady Haverslea offered. "After all that has occurred, I feel that I, too, could use a few weeks at Bath."

"How perfectly delightful that should be," Lady Portia agreed. "Then, while Cecily is resting, we can stroll about, see what the shops have to offer, see who is attending the assembly rooms."

"We shall hire a house and make quite a party of it, I daresay," Lord Dynford declared.

"Edwina," Lady Portia asked. "Shall you accompany us?"

Lady Edwina shrugged. "There is nothing to keep me here. I may as well go to Bath."

Having noted that the attention had turned from her to other subjects, Lady Cecily frowned. She threw her hand over her forehead and slumped back upon the sofa, moaning.

Lady Portia withdrew a vinaigrette from her reticule and waved it under Lady Cecily's nose.

Lady Cecily emitted a shriek of disgust and batted at the vinaigrette. "Faugh! Aunt Portia, get that vile concoction away from me!"

"But my dear, you are so pale," Lady Portia remarked. "Are you quite certain that there is nothing we can do for you?"

Quite unexpectedly, Lady Cecily sat bolt upright upon the sofa. "Yes, there is!" she declared enthusiastically. "If you would be so good as to supervise the packing, Aunt Portia, I believe I shall depart Haversham Hall this very instant."

"While leaving for Bath as soon as possible seems to be a very good idea," Lord Dynford said, "might I suggest that it will be so much easier to find the place in the daylight? I suggest that we wait until the morrow."

"But I am not going to Bath, that horrid old, stodgy old place," Lady Cecily declared.

"But Bath is quite a pleasant place," Lady Portia said.

"Nonsense! I am returning to London!" she announced.

"London?" they all echoed.

"But of course. The shops are ever so much better there, Aunt Portia. And there are more parties, more gossip. I daresay, once the news of Nigel gets out, we shall be invited to every ball!"

A mischievous little smile crossed Lady Cecily's pretty face. "And there are a great many more eligible young men in London than at Bath! I vow, if I do not find a husband that is richer, and more handsome, and more charming than Nigel . . ."

"Do try to find one that is more sane than Nigel, too," Lady Edwina advised.

"La! Winnie, I shall do just that or I shall . . . well, I shall eat my bonnet!"

"I daresay, there are a great many men who surpass Nigel," Lady Haverslea commented acidly.

"Oh, a great many, Cecily dear," Lady Portia reassured her niece.

"Then let us all see to our packing this instant so that we may depart at first light," Lady Cecily suggested, clapping her hands enthusiastically.

"Well, at best immediately after breakfast," Lord Dynford conceded.

"The sooner I am away from here, the better," Lady Cecily insisted.

"I quite understand, Cecily dear," Lady Haverslea said.

"Quite," Lady Portia agreed.

"Indeed," Lady Edwina added with a sad sigh.

"I have a great deal to attend to if I am to leave tomorrow morning," Lady Haverslea said. "I must bid you all good evening."

"Will you come to your bedchamber now, Cecily?" Lady Portia asked.

"No, Aunt Portia. I should just like to sit here for a moment," Lady Cecily answered with a wistful little sigh. "It is quite soothing to contemplate the lovely garden in the light of the setting sun."

Lady Portia and Lady Edwina accompanied Lady Haverslea to the front door while Lord Dynford retired to his bedchamber.

"Cecily has made a remarkable recovery of her customary good spirits," Lady Portia commented as they crossed the Main Hall.

"I believe the anticipation of a return to London may take the credit for reviving her spirits," Lady Haverslea said.

"She did seem most eager to be gone," Lady Portia commented.

"Indeed, to send us all off to supervise the packing . . ."

"She was *too* eager for us to be gone!" Lady Edwina declared with sudden alarm. "You know perfectly well that Cecily *despises* being alone. What is she up to?"

The report of a pistol reverberated through the Hall.

"Cecily!" Lady Portia cried.

"The pistols!" Lady Haverslea cried.

"We left them on the card table!" Lady Edwina said. "How could we have been so careless? My God, what has that girl done?"

Lady Edwina was the first to burst into the drawing room.

Lady Cecily lay flat on her back in the center of the drawing room, staring up at the ceiling. The pistol clutched in her hand still sent up acrid wisps of smoke.

"Oh, Cecily! Cecily!" Lady Edwina dashed to her sister's supine body and fell to her knees at her side. Gathering her sister up into her arms, she cradled her head close to her heart.

Lady Cecily blinked and shook her head as she recovered from her fall. "I vow, that pistol has quite a recoil," she said with not inconsiderable surprise. "Knocked me right over on my . . ."

"Oh, Cecily! You gave us such a shock!" Lady Edwina scolded.

"Oh, do let me go, Winnie," Lady Cecily protested, pulling away from her sister's embrace. "You are quite ruining my coiffure."

Lady Edwina grabbed her sister by the arms and pulled her upright. She gave her such a shake that Lady Cecily's cherished coiffure came quite undone.

"How *dare* you scare us so! Have you any idea . . . ? Why do you not stop to think before you do . . . ? I thought you were dead! Oh, Cecily!" Lady Edwina cried, seizing her

309

sister again in a tight embrace. "I am so glad you are alive!"

"I am quite happy with the fact myself, Winnie," Lady Cecily replied, attempting to pat her loose curls back into some semblance of order. "But if you will excuse me a moment, I am not quite finished yet."

Quite bewildered, Lady Edwina released her sister.

Lady Cecily dropped the smoking pistol which she held and picked up the other, which lay at her side. She looked up to the large portrait of Nigel which hung over the mantelpiece.

"That one was for Annie Ripley, Nigel, you wicked, miserable, vile, rotten, evil, wretched, despicable, degenerate excuse for a human being," she pronounced vehemently. "And this one is for *me!*"

She pointed the pistol at the portrait and fired. With surprisingly good aim, the second bullet struck the portrait only inches from the first, completing the wide hole in the canvas where Nigel's face had been.

They looked down at Lady Cecily, who once again lay face up on the carpet.

"Nice shot," Lady Haverslea commended.

"Quite nice," Lady Portia concurred.

"Thank you."

Lady Edwina stood at the window of the drawing room. Stokes was upstairs, packing for her. The girl had learned to sew, to serve a meal without spilling, to nurse the sick. She was also overjoyed to be leaving Haversham Hall and returning to her beloved Pringle. As Stokes was proving to be a quite competent lady's maid after all, there was no need for her ladyship to supervise. So Lady Edwina had come downstairs to the drawing room, alone, to watch the stars come out, one by one.

Except for the last few rays of sunset, the room was dark as, in the confusion, no servant had come in to light the candles. The room was still filled with the acrid scent of gunpowder.

She was glad for the darkness and the solitude. Alone in

310

the darkness, no one would see her tears.

She pursed her lips. She had always prided herself upon being so sensible, so astute. How could she have been such a fool? she berated herself. How could she not have seen that James Trescott was actually a gentleman from the very first moment? His manners and his speech, his ability to run the household in her absence, his acquaintance with Sir George Cayley.

And he had played her for a fool! she thought angrily. All the while he was making love to her, he had been laughing at her to himself. She was an amusing diversion while he was recuperating. As soon as he had been able to assume his rightful position, he had pointedly ignored her. Now that he was the baron, he would be seeking a young wife. He would not want her.

That obnoxious Lord Scythe had been right about one thing—after he was gone, there would be no other suitors for a lady of Edwina's age.

"Edwina?"

She heard the familiar voice. She quickly reached up with her handkerchief and wiped the tears from her eyes. She lifted her chin as high as she could manage. It was hard to do when her throat felt so dry and tight. Without much success, she willed her hands to stop shaking and her quivering knees to support her as she turned slowly to face him.

"Lord Haverslea," she said as coolly as she possibly could. She inclined her head slightly. "I do not believe we have ever been formally introduced."

"Then allow me to bid you welcome to my home, my lady," he said with a courtly bow. "I beg you to forgive all the confusion, but I have just recently come into the barony—again." There was a trace of a grin about his lips and a twinkle in his green eyes that even the growing darkness could not hide.

"So I understand. However, I believe it came as no surprise to you."

She loved his sharp wit almost as much as she loved the man himself, but she could not allow herself to lapse into humor now. In spite of everything, she *did* have a certain dignity to maintain.

The smile disappeared from his face and eyes. "Actually, the first time came as quite an enormously unpleasant shock," he told her. "The second was merely a matter of time and planning before I could assume my rightful position."

She stood watching him warily for several interminable moments. He was watching her in turn. Several times, she took a deep breath as if preparing to say something. But the words would not come to her mind, much less to her lips, and so she remained silent.

He, too, said nothing, but continued to watch her in the ever-darkening room.

At last, Lady Edwina forced herself to say, "We shall be leaving for London early tomorrow, so I suppose I shall thank you now, on behalf of my family and myself, for your hospitality."

Lady Edwina watched with surprise the look of dismay which spread over Lord Haverslea's face.

"Must you go?" he asked.

"My sister has cried off her engagement to Nigel Haversham," she told him. "There is little point in our remaining."

After what seemed an interminable pause, he replied, "I am sorry to hear you feel that way, my lady."

"I must say, it has been a brief, but most interesting visit," she remarked, unable to keep the sarcasm from her voice.

"I regret that I have been unable to spend more time with you lately," he said. "I had a few other things to attend."

"I should have liked to have spoken to you earlier this afternoon."

"I would have, too, my lady. But you, of all people, are aware that a man's, or a woman's, duties often take precedence over his or her desires."

Lady Edwina nodded and sighed. "I believe that may be one of the few things about this entire affair that I *can*

312

understand."

She hesitated again, then asked, "How is Lord . . . excuse me, I mean Mr. Haversham?"

"I am afraid Nigel is quite mad, and a danger to himself and to others. He will be making a rather protracted stay at the hospital of St. Mary of Bethlehem in London. I shall do all in my power to see that he is maintained in a comfortable state."

"And Annie Ripley, poor girl? Will she be making a protracted stay in Newgate?"

"No. Nigel is quite mad, so anything he may say against Ripley will not be taken seriously. I have managed to convince the good constable that Ripley was holding the pistol upon Nigel under my instructions and that, otherwise, she had no part in anything that transpired here."

"That was inordinately kind of you, all things considered," Lady Edwina said. "And I am glad to hear it. The girl was not truly bad, but only horribly misled."

"I have sent her off to some of her relations in Ireland with enough money to set up a nice little millinery shop. I also gave her a rather stiff warning to avoid would-be lords like the very pox."

Lady Edwina nodded. "Wise advice, indeed, for all ladies to follow," she agreed. She found she was unable to keep the bitterness from her voice.

She began to move away from the window toward the center of the room. Lord Haverslea moved to block her way.

"Excuse me, Lord Haverslea. It has been a most taxing day and we depart early tomorrow morning. I should like to retire," she told him, unable to look into his eyes.

He remained in her path.

"I get the distinct impression that you are angry with me," he said, bending over in an attempt to peer into her eyes in the fading light.

"I rarely allow myself to be angered by someone I barely know," she replied haughtily.

"How might we go about becoming better acquainted?"

Her blue eyes narrowed and she raised her face defiantly

to him. "Why? So you can hurt me again?"

"I never meant to hurt you, Edwina. Will you at least listen while I explain?"

She nodded. "An explanation would not be out of order," she conceded.

"I wanted to explain, Edwina. Oh God, I have wanted to explain to you for so long! But what was I to tell you?"

One hand tucked into his waistcoat, the other finger raised into the air, he struck a pose of official pronouncement and declared, "Lady Edwina, I am wanted for the murder of my brother and the attempted murder of my cousin, but let me assure you, I am innocent."

"Indeed, that would have started a most absorbing conversation," she observed, tilting her head to look up at him.

He looked down again at her, the sparkle returned to his green eyes. She fought down the responsive little smile which threatened totally to undo the cold exterior she was trying so hard to maintain.

"When I first came to Dynford Manor, I did not know if I could entrust you or your brother with my predicament, or if you two would immediately turn me over to the constabulary."

She looked at him, her eyes wide with surprise. "Did I present *that* stern and forbidding an appearance?"

"Positively chilling, my lady."

"Good," she replied with a sharp little nod. "That is precisely the impression I wish to convey."

He chuckled, then proceeded, "After I knew you better, after I had fallen quite hopelessly in love with you, I wanted to explain, but I had no idea how to broach the subject. And even if I had told you, I had no idea how I might go about proving my innocence."

"You could have trusted me, James," she chided him.

"My real name is Trent."

"Yes, of course. I beg your pardon. James would have trusted me."

"James would also have done everything in his power to protect you," he told her, slowly stepping closer to her in the deepening darkness of the drawing room. "I seem to recall

314

James warning you not to anger Nigel, indeed to reconsider having approved of his marriage to your sister."

"But you have made such a fool of me!" she cried angrily. "Lady Edwina, poor old spinster, so anxious for any man's affection that she throws herself at the feet of this handsome, young footman . . ."

"What! And now that I am a lord, I am no longer good enough for your ladyship?" he exclaimed with a laugh. He held out his arms as if to embrace her, but she backed away.

"Does it really matter to you what I am, Edwina?" he asked. "Can you not love me simply for who I am?"

"I have always loved you for who you are," she replied. "But now that you are a lord, well . . ." she hesitated and hung her head. "Now I am no longer good enough for you."

"You? Not good enough for me?" he repeated incredulously. "But you are the daughter of an earl—"

"And I am twenty-seven years old," she began.

"Why, I had no idea you were such an aged crone!" he said, reaching out to touch her shoulder. This time, she did not draw away.

"Well past my prime," she continued.

"I shall get you a Bath chair," he offered, wrapping his arm about her shoulder and slowly drawing her closer to him.

"As Lord Haverslea, it is your duty to produce an heir," she said. And she was exceedingly glad for the darkness of the drawing room as it quite completely hid the flush of embarrassment she felt coursing up her cheeks.

"I eagerly anticipate doing my duty." With his other hand, he reached out to stroke her burning cheek.

"But you will want a younger wife to provide that heir," she offered weakly. "You will not want me!"

Lord Haverslea held her chin in his hand, tilting her face up to his.

"I would venture to say that, even at the advanced age of twenty-seven, you still have a few good years left to you."

His hand caressed her back and shoulders, sliding up and down her smooth arm, stroking her slim neck.

"Don't you know none of that matters to me, Edwina," he

said, holding her tightly to him. "I love you. That is what matters. I love you."

He bent his head closer to hers, brushing his lips against her hair and across her forehead. His lips meandered down her cheek to find her mouth at last. He kissed her, his lips both soft in their caress, yet firm in their insistence.

She drew in a great gasp of air. He did love her!

"I love you, too, Trent."

She returned his kiss with passion of her own.

His kiss trailed off onto her cheek. He whispered in her ear, "I propose that we marry just as soon as I can procure the license. Then we can discover just how many years we shall spend together producing wonderful little Havershams."

"You do want me," she half stated, half questioned. She still was finding it too wonderful to believe.

Slowly, in the darkness, he bent his head to her, pressing the warm softness of his lips against her own. As her passion rose to meet his, he wrapped her in the protection of his arms.

"Oh, yes, Edwina," he answered. "I want you."

Author's Note

In 1857, Sir George Cayley's coachman did indeed fly from a hill in Brompton, the family estate in Yorkshire, in a gliding aircraft designed by Cayley. (Upon landing, the coachman promptly resigned.) But the ideas which culminated in this historic event date back to at least 1799, when Cayley, then aged twenty-six, began making notes of his experiments in flight.

Although most of his contemporaries regarded his experiments as unprofitable and lacking in popular support, he was convinced that "aerial navigation" would "form a most prominent feature in the progress of civilization."

Sir George Cayley's articles regarding aerial navigation were published in *Nicholson's Journal of Natural Philosophy, Chemistry and the Arts,* vols. XIV and XV, in 1809 and 1810. He also published articles on an engine powered by air expanded by heat (that is, internal combustion) to propel this aircraft.

But flight was not his only interest. He took an active part in agricultural reform, railway safety, the abolition of slavery, and Parliamentary reform. In later life, he became a member of Parliament.

During the War with Napoleon, he experimented with air resistance on shots and shells in order to increase their range by changing their form from the traditional round shape to what we would now consider bullet shaped. He experimented with designs for a mechanical artificial hand and with theatrical acoustics. He patented an invention that he called the "Universal Railway," which was the forerunner of the Caterpillar tractor. In 1839, he founded the Regent Street Polytechnic, of which he was the chairman until his death in 1857.

As befitting his inclusion in a romance, he also wrote very charming love poems to his wife, Sarah.

WIVES, LIES AND DOUBLE LIVES

MISTRESSES ($4.50, 17-109)
By Trevor Meldal-Johnsen
Kept women. Pampered females who have everything: designer clothes, jewels, furs, lavish homes. They are the beautiful mistresses of powerful, wealthy men. A mistress is a man's escape from the real world, always at his beck and call. There is only one cardinal rule: *do not fall in love*. Meet three mistresses who live in the fast lane of passion and money, and who know that one wrong move can cost them everything.

ROYAL POINCIANA ($4.50, 17-179)
By Thea Coy Douglass
By day she was Mrs. Madeline Memory, head housekeeper at the fabulous Royal Poinciana. Dressed in black, she was a respectable widow and the picture of virtue. By night she the French speaking "Madame Memphis", dressed in silks and sipping champagne with con man Harrison St. John Loring. She never intended the game to turn into true love . . .

WIVES AND MISTRESSES ($4.95, 17-120)
By Suzanne Morris
Four extraordinary women are locked within the bitterness of a century old rivalry between two prominent Texas families. These heroines struggle against lies and deceptions to unlock the mysteries of the past and free themselves from the dark secrets that threaten to destroy both families.

Available wherever paperbacks are sold, or order direct from the Publisher. Send cover price plus 50¢ per copy for mailing and handling to Pinnacle Books, Dept. 17-368, 475 Park Avenue South, New York, N.Y. 10016. Residents of New York, New Jersey and Pennsylvania must include sales tax. DO NOT SEND CASH.